NO TOMORROW

CARIAN COLE

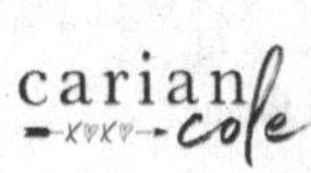

NOTE FROM THE AUTHOR

This book touches on some sensitive subjects such as depression, grief, mental illness, drug use, miscarriage, and more. Please read with caution.

This story builds slowly, and everything is not as it seems. I ask that you give the story and the characters time to develop.

Thank you for reading, and for your support!

Be kind to other readers!
Please leave spoiler-free reviews!

DEDICATION

For Sherry…

While reading this book, you sent me this message:
"I love you as a friend and worship you as a writer!"

I wish I could tell you, I love you as a friend, and I worship you as a reader.

You were so much more than a friend and beta reader to me. You were very much my lifeline in so many ways. I don't think you ever realized how much your friendship and your support meant to me.

I love you, my friend. I am lost without you.
I will think of you with every word I write, and I will never forget you.

CHAPTER ONE

1998 - PIPER

A menu sails across my desk and knocks over my paperclip holder.

"Earth to Piper Karel," my co-worker Melissa says, ignoring the destruction she just caused. "How interesting can reception work really be? I've said your name like three times! I'm calling in a lunch order soon and going to pick it up. Do you want anything?"

It's 10:30 a.m. and I'm still nursing the tea I made earlier this morning. I've been too buried sorting out my inbox to even touch my granola bar, let alone to think about what I want for lunch. I wonder what's going on in Melissa's inbox that lunch is her priority.

I hand the checkered menu back to her and return my paperclips back to their little rectangular magnetic house. "No, thank you. I'm good."

"Maybe if you ate lunch once in a while you wouldn't be such a stick, Piper."

"I *do* eat lunch, Melissa. I just like to eat at the park and get some fresh air instead of being in this office for nine hours straight every day."

"You miss all the fun leaving the office for lunch every day. All the good stuff happens in the lunch room in this place."

Ah, yes. The office gossip. Just last week I missed some drama. If

I'm ever up for a promotion, I can guarantee I wouldn't congratulate my competitor by dumping my salad into her lap.

"I just like some quiet time to myself sometimes," I reply.

"Right. Enjoy your quiet lunch then. All by yourself. As usual." She tosses her hair and flounces away with the menu tucked under her arm.

At twenty-one, I'm the youngest person in the office. I work for a small fashion design firm. Our activewear line is really popular nationwide and two seasons ago we partnered with a celebrity designer on a pair of yoga pants that put the company on the map. I started working here as a receptionist and general office assistant part-time my senior year of high school and was brought on full-time after I graduated. Answering phone calls and typing letters isn't exactly my idea of a career, but it pays the bills. The company is growing steadily and there are always openings for new positions. I'm just waiting for the right one to pique my interest, hopefully in marketing or product development. For now, I'm happy learning as much about the products and the company as I can.

When I took this job, I hoped it would be a new start for me across the board. I was looking forward to being around people who didn't know how awkward I had always been, and I thought I'd make new friends.

I was the girl who puked on the first day of first grade and who tripped wearing black pumps and a mini skirt on the first day of high school. I fell like a baby deer, legs sprawled, and flashed my panties with little kittens on them to half the school. They never forgot I was the puker, and they sure as hell didn't forget I was the one with the kitten panties. The boys purred and meowed at me for months, and the girls nicknamed me Pussypuker.

Fun times.

I had such high hopes for joining the working world—a real professional atmosphere. I didn't expect to be surrounded by married men who flirted with all the women. Or stressed-out coffee addicts who screamed about their spreadsheets. Or women who gossiped and stirred drama like they were paid to.

Welcome to adulthood.

And I certainly wasn't expecting Melissa, who graduated from high school the year before me, to start working here a few months ago. She was one of the elite popular girls in school. She had the nicest clothes, the nicest car, friends who hung on her every word, and all the most attractive guys panting after her. My awkwardness and random mishaps were a great source of amusement for her back then. She's much more subtle about mocking me now, but she's still just as annoying.

Just before noon, I take two steps into the courtyard of the office building when something smashes into the side of my head. Hard, soft, and...*flapping*? I reach up and touch a small sore spot above my temple. A small blue bird flutters haphazardly on the ground next to my feet before it flies off into a nearby tree.

What the heck? I scrunch my eyes against a dull pain in my temple, wondering what it says about me that a bird flew into my head.

Laughter erupts from my right. Melissa and a woman from accounting are smoking and shaking their heads at me. I'm pretty sure I heard the word *birdbrain* thrown in my direction.

Shaking off my embarrassment, I retrieve a compact mirror from my purse. The quiet park is just a few blocks away, but I want to make sure I don't have a gash on my head, which would only renew my humiliation. What I assume was the point of beak impact hurts, but after inspection, I see no blood—only faint redness... and a tiny blue feather stuck to my forehead.

"Crazy ass bird..." I mutter as I wipe the evidence away.

A horn blares and I jump, dropping my mirror, which shatters at my feet.

Shit.

"Pay attention, you idiot!" the driver yells. My heart jumps when I realize I've unknowingly walked into the busy crosswalk. The woman swerves her maroon sedan around me and the pieces of my broken mirror as I rush to the other side of the street, mouthing an apology.

Freakin' Mondays. If a black cat crosses my path, I'm calling it quits and going home to hide under the safety of my fluffy comforter.

As I near the park bench I've inhabited during my lunch hour for the past three months, there's something different in the breezy air that I can't quite put my finger on. The usual sounds of children laughing and leaves rustling seem muted, as if they've faded into the background. I am intrigued by something I haven't heard before—soft acoustic music.

The inviting melody grows louder with each step. The source is not far from what I consider *my* bench. I'm surprised to see it's not a radio playing, as I first thought, but a guy who appears to be in his early to mid-twenties, sitting on the ground with a guitar. He's leaning against a short decorative brick partition. A small, floppy-eared brown dog wearing a black bandana sits next to him.

As I walk past him to get to my bench, I notice that almost every visible inch of his body, with the exception of his face, is covered with tattoos. Black tribal designs peek from holes in his worn jeans. Faces, flowers, and clouds cover his arms, and the designs scatter over the tops of his hands and along his talented fingers. *Yikes.* I have one tattoo on my wrist—a tiny ladybug perched on a leaf—and it hurt like hell. Getting jabbed with a needle in the knees and elbows had to sting like crazy.

Maybe he's one of those people who enjoy pain.

I eye the musician with as much discreet curiosity as I can muster and busy myself with taking my chicken salad sandwich out of an insulated lunch bag. I fumble with the cling wrap, which is now stuck to itself and holding on as desperately as a crazy ex.

The guitarist gazes downward, long brown hair hanging across his face and past his shoulders. He's deeply immersed in the song. It's a dreamy, hypnotizing melody that almost sounds like several guitars, rather than just the one. I don't know the first thing about playing a musical instrument, but I can tell he's incredibly talented.

I chew my sandwich as a small crowd forms around him. He plays on, not looking up. The only indication he's aware of his audience comes when he gives a subtle nod to someone throwing money into the

Mason jar set in front of him. I guess he doesn't have to thank them because his dog is waving its onyx-padded paw at each donor.

Normally, I would expect people to pat the adorable dog on its furry head for being so talented, but they don't. The dog has the same untouchable air as his companion, as if there's an invisible stamp across both of them that says: *look, listen, enjoy, but don't touch.*

I'm intrigued and probably chewing with my mouth open as I peer between two women carrying huge black shopping bags. I'm inexplicably drawn to his voice and his look. He seems unique, hard to describe but attractive in a rugged way.

His melancholy smile carries a hint of sensuality. He's like an eclipse —simultaneously dark and light, and not safe to look at for too long without suffering a burn.

I frown when the women with the shopping bags throw change into his jar and walk toward the park exit. Throwing change into a water fountain is acceptable, but giving change to an actual *person?* That just seems wrong to me. I want them to give him fives, tens, or twenties— not quarters and dimes. Although he seems totally unfazed, I'm offended on his behalf.

Taking a sip from my water bottle, I slip off my three-inch black heels and tuck my feet beneath me. I pull a paperback out of my huge faux leather purse. This hour in the middle of the day is my time to relax and lose myself in the story I'm reading. To forget I still live at home with my parents and my teen sister who has more of a social life than I do.

At 12:50 p.m., I step back into my shoes, wishing I could stay here for the rest of the day, finish the romance novel I'm reading, and hear what the musician is going to play next. His music has swept away my annoyance over the head-crashing bird and the screaming driver.

Reluctantly, I grab my lunch bag and head back to the office, smiling at him as I pass. He taps his silver rings against the body of his guitar as he transitions to play the next song—a popular rock song. I can't remember the name of it, but I know it's going to be stuck in my head for the rest of the day.

On Tuesday afternoon the guitarist with his billboard of ink is in the park again. This time he's playing a different type of music with a Spanish vibe. It's fast and catchy—a burst of upbeat ambience under the dark clouds looming overhead.

I'm slightly unsettled as I sit on my bench. This is *my* place to come to relax every day, and now *he's* invaded it with his musical backdrop and his odd magnetic pull. I kinda wanted to give in to the gloom today, to be sad with the absence of the sun. But his music, along with the bobbing dance of his head and the obnoxiously bright tropical bandana around his dog's neck are making that impossible.

He looks up and meets my eyes as I chew my sandwich. The way he stares me down rivals the skill of my cat. Feeling slightly hypnotized and light-headed, I tear my eyes away from his and toss a small piece of bread to an impatient pigeon. A few seconds later I peek back and catch him grinning playfully at me as he shakes his hair out of his face, like he *knows* he made me feel spastic for a moment.

My stomach does a small flip, and I throw the last of my bread to the pigeon. I glance at the guitarist once more and my heart skips a few beats. He's still watching me.

He winks, smiles the most adorably sexy smile I've ever seen on a man, then returns his attention to his guitar.

Determined to hide my interest in what feels like subtle flirting, I pull my paperback from my bag. But even the weather won't let me distract myself from the guitarist. A light drizzle starts before I can open the book. The slightest amount of moisture is enough to make my hair look like I went and got a bad perm, which is not a good look on me.

As the rain comes down harder, I clutch my belongings against my body to keep them dry and sprint for the nearby gazebo. I curse myself for not bringing an umbrella today. I have them everywhere—about twenty of them at home, five in my desk, and two in my car. Not one of them with me when I need it.

Once under the shelter of the gazebo, I comb my fingers through my long hair, which is already damp and starting to curl at the ends. *Ugh.*

"Shit," I say under my breath. The outline of my bra and my nipples are clearly visible through my white silk blouse.

"It's just a little rain." The deep, smoky voice startles me, and I spin around to see none other than guitar guy and his dog standing behind me in the shelter of the gazebo. He drops his old beat-up guitar case and a tattered duffel bag on the wooden floor then runs his hands along the dog's coat, talking softly. I can't hear what he's saying, but I wish I could.

Shivering, I cross my arms over my breasts.

"If it's *only* rain, how come you're in here? You afraid your hair will frizz, too?" I say it playfully, but my heart is pounding as questions race through my mind. Did he follow me in here? Why? Is he just trying to get out of the rain, or have I made myself an easy target for who-knows-what by being alone in a gazebo?

He dries his hands on his dirty jeans and gestures to the dog. In a hushed voice, as if he's telling me a secret, he says, "He doesn't like to get wet."

My fight-or-flight instincts relax as I watch how much care he lavishes on his dog. The guy seems harmless, but I smile and move farther away from him anyway, glancing down at my watch as I do so. My lunch hour is nearly over.

My gazebo partner looks up at the sky. "It'll stop in a few minutes. It's just a quick shower."

I nod in response, my attention drawn to the earring he's wearing. The small blue feather dangles on a silver hook and nestles against his mane of long brown hair. The effect is very rocker-cool and reminds me of the bird that flew into my skull yesterday and left its little downy feather on my forehead. I wonder if it was some kind of premonition or a sign.

"You work nearby? Or go to the college?" he asks.

"I work in an office a few blocks that way." I point off to the right, even though my office is to the left. "And you?"

He tilts his head. "You're looking at it."

"So, you…?"

With a nod, he pulls a crushed pack of cigarettes from his shirt pocket and removes one with his lips. He replaces the pack and retrieves a black lighter from the front pocket of his jeans. "Yup. Work and live here." He curves his inked hand around the cigarette, protecting it from the wind as he lights it.

Oh. I've never talked to a homeless person. Seen them around, yes. Talked to one? No. Another shiver shoots up my spine. Crossing my arms tighter around my torso, I lean against the railing, squashing my purse so he can't grab it. He probably needs money to eat, or he could be a junkie needing a fix. Screw the rain and frizzy hair, I should make a run for it now before—

"This is one of the nicest towns I've been in." His voice interrupts my racing thoughts. "The people are friendly. They don't treat me like trash." He exhales a cloud of smoke and snuffs the half-smoked cigarette out on the bottom of his leather shoe. I wait for him to toss the butt onto the grass, but instead he shoves it in his pocket.

A lump of guilt forms in my throat. I relax my arms as I raise my gaze to meet his. There's no threat, no mania flickering in those eyes. I see blue—the color of the sky just before it turns to night, that subtle transition that marks one time of day to another. Perhaps his eyes are very telling, and he's also in a transition of sorts, moving from one phase of life into another.

We watch the rain fall, waiting for it to stop, but I don't really want it to. It's soft and lulling and brings stillness with it. The park is empty, except for this homeless guy with the amazing eyes, his dog, and me. By the time the rain stops, I'm fifteen minutes late returning to work, but I'm in no rush to get back. Something about being with the quiet stranger is surprisingly comforting. We leave the gazebo together, his dog trailing behind us down the walkway that leads back to my bench, his guitar-playing spot, and the rusty wrought-iron entrance.

"Nothing more hopeful and beautiful than gray skies and rainbows," he says as we walk.

I furrow my brow and wait in case he clarifies what he means. He takes his place against the brick wall, across from my bench. He sits on the wet ground and I wonder if rainwater seeping through his jeans will bother him or if he just deals with things like damp clothes. When he doesn't say anything else, I give him a last look and head back toward my office without saying goodbye.

As I pass through the gate and wait to cross the busy street I see it—a rainbow arching across the cloudy sky. And he's right. It's beautiful and hopeful.

CHAPTER TWO

PIPER

The guitarist is here again today, and he smiles a hello when he sees me. I shyly return the smile and sit on my bench, pretending to busy myself with my plastic container of tossed salad. My focus is truly on the incredibly beautiful rendition of "Für Elise" that fills the air. He plays with so much depth and emotion, I get goosebumps as he plucks each note on his guitar.

Pop, rock, classical…. Is there anything this guy can't play?

A man in a suit tosses a quarter into the Mason jar, and I want to shove his monogrammed black leather messenger bag up his ass. Does he not recognize beautiful music when he hears it? A quarter buys a piece of bubble gum or a ride on a rocking horse outside the grocery store. That won't buy live classical music. Huffing, I spend the next minute trying to find my pink wallet, which is lost in the file cabinet of crap I call my purse.

I have a five-dollar bill and a twenty-dollar bill. Chewing my lip, I look over at the musician. I like looking at him, though he's not my type. Not even a little bit. He looks like Jesus with his long hair and denim-blue eyes and that ethereal aura that bounces off him. I'm sure Jesus doesn't look like a homeless street musician, but if he were to come down and be all sorts of cool, I could see him looking like that.

People must flock to him in droves, especially women, because he's got a strange sexual magnetism about him. The guitar guy, not Jesus.

I've still got my hand stuffed in my purse, and I'm holding the five and the twenty. Five bucks doesn't seem like nearly enough to compensate for his talent. But giving him a twenty could be *too* much—I don't want to look like a desperate person buying his attention. Or he might think I'm some spoiled rich girl throwing money at the poor, dirty, sexy homeless guy.

I feel I should give him *something*, though, since I've been sitting here for the past week enjoying his music, even though I try to act as though I don't notice him and the fluid movement of his hands. And the way the feather blows against his cheek in the breeze. Or how his eyes track me when I enter the park. Or the way his eyelids close so very slowly when he's completely into the song he's playing. But just because I notice all those things doesn't mean I'm into him in *that* way. Homeless men with feather earrings are of no interest to me. I just want to show my appreciation of his craft. A simple gesture of thanks can turn a person's day around.

As I struggle between the five and the twenty, I notice a man with a food cart across the park. *Yes!* Food is much safer. I toss my salad container into my lunch bag and head across the park.

"What'll ya have?" the guy behind the cart asks when I approach.

Contemplating the plastic menu taped to the front of his silver cart, I wonder whether guitar guy is into hot dogs or hamburgers. What if he's a vegetarian? I finger the heart charm on my necklace nervously. Maybe cash would have been better, after all.

"Ma'am?" he urges, though there's no one in line behind me.

"I'll take a cheeseburger, a hot dog with no bun, a bottle of water, and a sweetened iced tea," I say quickly. "And can I have an empty cup or a bowl?"

He throws me an irritated glance as he flips a patty on his miniature grill. Minutes later, my stomach growls loudly as he wraps the burger and puts it into a plastic bag with the rest of my order. The tiny garden salad I packed for lunch can't compete with a juicy burger, but I'm determined to stick to my goal of healthy eating.

After I pay, the hunger pangs turn to nervous jitters as I walk down the paved pathway toward the musician. I wait off to the side until he finishes the song he's playing, not wanting to interrupt. The couple watching him smiles, praises him, and then walks away hand in hand. They don't tip him. I wonder what that feels like for him. Does it feel like rejection? Lack of appreciation? Or maybe it doesn't bother him at all and he just likes to play music for people.

He squints up at me as I awkwardly hold the bag out to him. Now that I'm standing closer to him than I was in the gazebo, I can see his perfect white teeth and the tiniest dimple in his left cheek. "I got you a hamburger and a bottle of iced tea. And a hot dog and water for your dog." I try not to get lost in the endless realm of his eyes as he studies mine. "You don't have to eat it if you don't want to," I continue, hoping I haven't offended him or gotten him something he doesn't even like. "I just kind of guessed."

A smile tips his lips. "You guessed right. I've been dying for a burger. Sitting here smelling the food coming off that cart every day has been driving me crazy." He stands, towering over me and making me feel even shorter than my four feet eleven inches. "I almost moved to the other side of the park, but I didn't want to give up the view of my favorite bench."

I follow his eyes, and my heart skips a beat or two or twenty when I realize he means *my* bench.

Is homeless guitar guy flirting with me?

"Sit with me while I eat?" he asks.

The invitation bounces my thoughts around like a ping-pong ball. Although he seems nice, I'm wary of sitting with a homeless person. I have no proof that he might not be a thief, a murderer, or any other brand of criminal. He may just hide it really well, as some do.

At least that's what they do in books and movies. Maybe I watch too many late-night movies… someone is always a victim or a suspect.

I scan the park surroundings, knowing I should politely decline, but I'm too intrigued by the tiny spark of excitement I felt when he asked me to sit with him. Other than a pizza with every topping imaginable or ice cream in a waffle cone, not much really gets me excited lately.

"C'mon," he urges. "I could use some real conversation." He rubs the dog's head affectionately. "He's a great listener, but he doesn't talk much."

His pleading smile convinces me to give in. I hold the bag of food while he packs up his guitar and shoves his Mason jar in his duffel bag. I follow him and his dog to a spot farther away, to a picnic table near an old stone bridge that arches over a road that hasn't been in use for years. My heart beats a little faster with apprehension as I glance behind us. There are about twenty people in various areas of the park, most of them still close enough to hear me if I let out a blood-curdling scream for help. I finally join him at the old wooden table.

The truth is, though, I think the slow realization that I might actually like this guy and *want* to spend time with him is making me far more skittish than the possibility that he might have plans to hurt me.

The beating of my heart calms to a normal pace when he fills the paper bowl with water and breaks the hot dog into bite-sized pieces for the dog. Then he unwraps the burger for himself. It's the second time I've seen him show special care for the dog, and I find it very endearing. It proves he's not an asshole and, in my naïve twenty-one-year-old mind, also that he's probably not someone who would hurt me. Serial killers torture animals. They don't worry about them getting wet, and they wouldn't feed a pet before feeding themselves.

He moans as he chews the burger, and the raw sensuality of the sound sends a heated shiver through my body. I cross my legs and focus on the dog lapping up his water.

"Mmm… this is so fuckin' good." He takes another bite with his eyes closed and moans again. "Thank you for this." He holds the burger out to me. "You want some? It's delicious."

"No, thank you." I lean away from him. Germs scare the heck out of me. I never share drinks with other people or use soap at people's houses unless it's in a liquid dispenser. I keep tissues in my purse in case I have to use a public restroom. Who knows who touched the toilet paper in there? Or if it rolled across the filthy floor before it was put in the dispenser?

"I already ate my lunch. I just wanted to give you something to say thank you for your music. I look forward to hearing it every day now."

"So you took the fast track to my heart by giving me food when I'm starving. Nice move, slayer."

My cheeks burn as he takes a sip of his iced tea, the rim of the bottle pressing against his full lips. *Damn.* He's way too good-looking and talented to be homeless and playing in a park in this small New England town.

After devouring the hot dog and water, his dog nudges my hand, wanting to be petted. Smiling, I stroke his soft, floppy ears, hoping he doesn't have fleas and that my hand doesn't end up smelling like dog. Archie the cat will probably bite me if he smells another animal on me. He's very possessive and territorial.

"What's his name?" I ask.

Guitar guy finishes off the hamburger and puts the wrapper in the plastic bag. "You want to know *his* name, but not mine?" he teases with a tone of mock offense.

"You can tell me your name, too."

"His name is Acorn. He's been my best friend and traveling buddy for two years."

I smile at the unique name. "It fits him. He's adorable."

He nods and places his hand on the dog's back. "He's loyal. And smart. Only took me a few hours to teach him how to wave when people give us money."

As I pet Acorn's ears, I catch his owner staring at me. He doesn't look away, but I do. "And your name?" I ask, focusing on the dog between us.

"Evan. But my friends call me Blue."

I summon the courage to look at him as I smile shyly. "It's nice to meet you, Evan."

He squints, almost as if he's wincing from a sharp pain, and the left side of his mouth pulls to the side into a frown. "You didn't call me Blue."

"Well… I'm not sure we're friends yet."

He nods slowly. "You're right. We could end up being much more.

Or less." He pushes strands of his long hair away from his face, revealing a five o'clock shadow of stubble on his cheeks. I haven't seen him with this much facial hair before, so he must shave pretty regularly. Or at least does sometimes. I'm envious of his defined cheekbones. "Time will tell."

I can't imagine us ever being anything other than a girl who eats lunch in the park and a homeless street musician, but I let him have his faith in time and what it might someday tell.

He leans back against the edge of the table top and stretches his long legs out. The soles of his black motorcycle boots are worn thin. "You're supposed to tell me your name now."

"Oh. It's Piper."

He repeats my name, and on his lips, it sounds different than I've ever heard the word sound before, as if I'm a special and mystical being.

I wish I was special and mystical, but I'm just... not.

"That's different. Does it mean something? To your parents?"

I shake my head. "No, my mother just liked how it sounded. Apparently, she bought a bunch of baby name books when she was pregnant, and Piper was her favorite. My father doesn't like it. He thinks it's a stripper name."

He lets out a deep laugh. "I've never met a stripper named Piper, and I've met my fair share."

I laugh along with him. "I've often wondered why my father was thinking of strippers, but that's probably something that's better left alone."

"Agreed."

A glance at my watch shows I'm five minutes late for work, but I don't want to leave the park to go back to the stuffy office and answer phones for the rest of the afternoon. Time drags there, as though the moment I walk through the door, the clock comes to a screeching halt, every minute an eternity. Yet somehow, my hour lunch flies by in the blink of an eye.

"Sucks to be on a schedule, huh?" Evan asks.

I sigh, but don't move. "Yeah, it really does."

"So don't go back to work. Spend the day how you want to. Go shopping. Go home and nap. Go for a long drive to nowhere. Sit here with me and people-watch."

How awesome any of that would be. "I can't do that."

"Why not?"

"Because I'll probably get fired. That's why."

"Would that really be so bad?"

I frown. "Of course it would. I can't *not* work. I'd be broke in a month. I'd lose my car. I wouldn't be able to buy clothes or pay rent...."

I want to eat my words immediately. I may have just insulted the only guy I've actually felt any sort of connection with or had any real conversation with in months. "I'm so sorry," I say quickly. "I didn't mean—"

He shrugs casually. "Don't apologize. I'm okay with what I am and what I do. I chose to live this way."

I narrow my eyes at him, thinking that I must have heard him incorrectly. "You chose to be homeless?"

"Yup. One day I grabbed my guitar and a bag of clothes and started walking. And I kept on walking." His eyes meet mine, all blue and serene with a splash of wild. "I still haven't stopped."

My imagination soars with visions of Evan walking non-stop, from one town to the next with Acorn. Sleeping under bushes and huddling under freeway bridges during downpours while cars race past them. I'm fascinated and also a little skeeved out over the concept of choosing to live on the streets. Just thinking about how he must live—not having a clean bed to sleep in—makes me feel itchy.

"Don't you worry about being able to eat... or where you're going to sleep...? Or—I don't know—where you're going to shower and all that?"

He shakes his head, the feather earring swinging against his mane of hair. "Nah. It all just works out. Like it did today. The girl I've had my eye on for days bought me and my dog the best lunch I've had in a long time, and now she's talking to me."

A blush heats my face, and now I wish I could blow off work and sit here and talk to him. But I really do have to get back to the office, so I stand and brush off the back of my pants.

Before I walk away, he grabs my hand and pulls it closer to inspect my tiny wrist tattoo.

"Ladybugs are supposed to mean good luck," he says.

"I know." That's why I got it, actually. Because ladybugs are cute and dainty and lucky. Everything I'd like to be. But instead, I'm awkward and clumsy and not very lucky.

"Did you also know in Norway, there's a myth that if a man and a woman see a ladybug at the same time, they'll fall in love and are destined to be together forever?"

The warmth of his rough fingertips gliding along mine is comforting, like slipping into a pair of favorite sweatpants on a chilly day. I slowly pull my hand away from his.

"No, I didn't know that." How does he even know about the myths of bugs in Norway? Is he some kind of guitar-playing bug studier?

"We just looked at yours at the same time."

"That doesn't count," I throw back with a smile. "It's a tattoo. It's not a *real* ladybug. And we're not in Norway."

"I guess we'll find out, won't we?" He grins as he picks up his belongings and walks away with his dog. After a few steps, he looks back and flashes me a smirk that's a jarring mix of boyishness and sex appeal. I shake my head as he heads back toward the park.

I tear my eyes away from the way his jeans hug his butt in the most perfect way and how his hair flows down his back, and walk in the opposite direction. I'll have to work an extra half hour tonight to make up for being late, but that's okay. I did my good deed for the day and bought a homeless guy lunch. Even if he claims he's homeless and jobless by choice, I don't really believe him. No sane person would do that to himself.

"Honey, if you're going to be late for dinner, you should call. I was starting to worry." My mother peers into the oven at whatever she's got baking in there.

"I'm sorry. I had to work late, and then I got stuck in some traffic." I wish for the millionth time the tiny apartment-like space I rent in my parents' basement had a kitchen, instead of the tiny refrigerator, single countertop burner, and microwave I have in a small nook down there. If I could cook real food in my own space, I'd decline having dinner with my parents and my sister every night so I could feel more independent.

Mom pushes her short black hair behind her ear. "Please don't let them take advantage of you in that office, Piper. First it's a half hour. Then it's an hour. I know how managers take advantage of their more submissive employees."

Cringing at the way she characterizes me, I drape my coat over a chair at the kitchen table, reach into the cabinet above the counter, and pull out four dinner plates.

"They're not taking advantage of me, Mom. I was late coming back from lunch, and I had to make up the time. That's all."

Donning oven mitts, she pulls a meatloaf out of the oven and then nudges the appliance closed with her knee. "I worked in an office for a long time. I know how some people get stepped on and taken advantage of, and I don't want you to be treated like that. Once you set a pattern, it will follow you forever. You need to have a firm backbone, okay?"

"Her? A backbone?" my younger sister Courtney repeats as she enters the kitchen. "She's the mushiest person I know."

"Is it pick on Piper day?" I ask as I place the dinner plates on the oak table. Meanwhile, our formal dining room—with a beautiful view of the flower garden in our backyard—sits unused, only to be occupied on holidays and rare special occasions. If I ever have a nice dining room, I'm going to eat in it every night, even if I'm noshing ramen noodles all alone.

The comments from my mother and sister bring back uncomfortable yet all-too-familiar memories of being the middle child, sandwiched between two sisters who are pretty damn close to perfect. They're both gorgeous, tall, confident, athletic, raven-haired beauties. They're graceful, popular, and excel at everything they set their minds to.

Then there's me, sticking out like a sore thumb with blond hair and light eyes. I'm so short the top of my head barely reaches their shoulders. I'm shy, socially awkward, and look like I am perpetually stalked by a dark cloud. The utter misfit in all our family photographs.

Years ago, I stopped trying to compete with them for attention and slipped into the background of our family. Nobody seemed to notice.

"No one's picking on you. I'm giving you some professional advice. That's all."

Just as the last serving dish is placed on the table, my father—tall, smiling, and handsome with just a touch of gray at his temples—joins us at the table. We each take the same chairs we've been sitting in since I was about five years old. The only difference in this family scene is the empty chair belonging to my older sister, Karissa, who's now in law school and happily engaged to a fellow law student. A man my mother describes as a *gorgeous hunk of perfect man* and *the kind of man she wishes I would find*.

I don't want to find a man at all. I'm open to meeting one, but the term *finding one* scares me. I'm lost enough on my own. I don't need to *find a man* equally as lost and disoriented with life as I currently am.

I think I need a man with his own compass.

After dinner, I make a quick exit to my space downstairs, a sigh of relief leaving my lungs as soon as I'm on the other side of the door that separates me from them. My plan is to get my own place next year, once I have enough money stashed in my savings account to give me a decent safety net.

Ditra, my best friend, has been after me for months to move in with her, but she's a major slob. She keeps food in her refrigerator until it can't be identified anymore. The stains on her carpet are oddly sticky and hard. And she's going through an experimental phase of fooling around with random men *and* women—sometimes at the same time— and that kind of oogs me out. I can't picture myself sleeping in the next room with my cat while she's just on the other side of the wall with her latest petri-dish date.

Living with my family for a while longer won't kill me.

Archie, my striped tiger cat, is staring at me with accusing green eyes from beside his food dish, which apparently has fewer morsels of food than he requires, even though I filled it this morning. Like the obedient human he's trained me to be, I add more food and give him fresh water before I change into cotton shorts and a T-shirt.

I do one hundred crunches.

I do fifty donkey kicks per leg.

I do fifty squats.

I wash my face, brush my teeth for two minutes, and comb the hairspray out of my hair so it's not a sticky mess when I shower in the morning.

I check Archie's dishes one more time and set the outfit I plan to wear tomorrow at the very front of my closet.

Nightly rituals complete, I grab Archie and carry him to the bedroom with me. I slip *Titanic* into the VCR and crawl under the comforter to watch it for the tenth time. I've seen it in the theater twice —once with Ditra, who was bored by it—most likely due to the lack of sex scenes—and once with Courtney, who cried but enjoyed it, even though she cursed out Rose for not letting Jack onto that floating door.

I love the movie and find some new special moment every time I watch it. I can't get enough of the romantic connection, the angst, and the unwavering fight for love and happiness. The hope and devotion, even in the face of heartache and tragedy, is fantastic.

I pull Archie against my body and pet his head, but he jumps off the bed and bolts out of the room, leaving me feeling rejected and lonely.

The soundtrack of the movie quickly pulls me back into the story, and the sad tune tugs at my soul, making me want to smile and sob uncontrollably at the same time. The park guitarist's music makes me feel exactly the same way.

CHAPTER THREE

PIPER

I never go to the park on Saturday. That's my workweek thing to help get me through the day. But I see no reason why I can't do my laundry tomorrow instead of today as I usually do. The sun is out, the sky is filled with fluffy white clouds, and I'm in the mood for some fresh air. And I have to admit—curiosity has me wondering if Evan plays guitar in the park on the weekends. I wouldn't mind hearing more of his music and seeing Acorn's paw waving around without having to rush to get back to work.

After a quick stop for a soy vanilla latte, I'm reminded it's the weekend by the fact that the park and surrounding area is filled with people who also aren't working today and all the parking spaces are taken. During the work week, I never have to find a place for my car because I walk from my office. After circling three times, I finally find an empty spot and shove a few coins in the meter to buy me some time.

There's a crazy number of adults and children in the park today, and I'm bummed to see my bench occupied by a woman and her two kids. Nervously, I peer around as I scout a quiet place to sit and finally settle on a mossy, shady spot under a big willow tree.

Leaning back against the thick tree trunk, I pull my book out of my bag and pick up where I left off, but my thoughts keep drifting away from the words on the page, as I hope to hear the beautiful sound of Evan's guitar. Perhaps he plays somewhere else on the weekends or does something entirely different. What does a homeless person do with his time? I can't picture him standing on the corner of a busy intersection, holding a "will work for food" sign, the dog waving frantically at traffic, but I guess anything is possible.

"You hiding from me way over here?"

I almost drop my book at the sound of his voice but quickly recover and squint up at him. His guitar case is slung casually over his shoulder, a black toothpick hangs from his lips, and the sun shines behind his head like a golden beacon. Acorn lies down in the grass next to me and leans his body against my leg. He's decided they're staying.

I try not to smile, but I think I already am. "Someone took my bench."

"I saw."

He sets down his guitar and sits on the ground a few feet from me.

"I wasn't sure if you came here on the weekends or only when you work."

"I usually don't. I was actually just wondering if you played here on the weekends."

"So you were thinking about me?" The teasing tone of his voice sends tingly zaps through my body like the static shock from rubbing on carpet. I wonder if we were to rub against each other if it would feel as electrifying as I think it would.

"No." The word comes out of my mouth too quickly. "I just like hearing your music." I wave my book in front of him. "While I'm reading. It's nice."

A mischievous glint flashes in his eyes. "I like watching you when you listen to my music. I can tell which songs you like the most."

"Really?" I ask, amused. "And how can you tell?"

"Your breathing changes. It's subtle, but I see it."

Knowing he watches me makes my heart and stomach feel like I'm in an elevator endlessly riding up and down because someone has pressed all the buttons and the lift has no idea where to stop.

"This is a different look for you," he says. I look down at my off-the-shoulder black shirt and my favorite pair of faded jeans and wonder if he thinks I look frumpy. "Not many women can pull off sexy secretary and adorable girl next door. I like both."

Compliments from good-looking men are rare for me, and I have no idea how to react. Do I thank him? Tell him even though he's wearing ripped-up clothes that probably haven't been washed in days or weeks that he still looks smoking hot? Comment on how the scent of sandalwood enveloping him is alluring?

None of those things come out of my mouth. I just sit there basking in the idea of being sexy and adorable with—knowing my luck—no doubt a super goofy smile on my face.

He touches my paperback and looks over the cover of the man and woman in a heated embrace. The man on the cover has long dark hair, just like his.

"You're reading romance?"

"Yes." I hope he doesn't think it's silly. "I read mysteries, too." I've literally never read a mystery, but it sounds good and diverse.

He pushes his hair out of his face and takes on that faraway, reflective look I've seen on his face before. "Romance is a bit of a mystery in itself, isn't it?"

I ponder that for a few moments. "In a lot of ways, yes, I think it is."

"I used to read a lot. It was a good escape from the bullshit of life when I needed it. But now music and people-watching do that for me."

"Reading books and watching movies are my escapes. You don't want to know how many times I've watched *Titanic*."

"Ahh." He smiles and nods. "Devastation masked in a love story. I see the appeal."

I laugh. "I know it's wrong, but it's so addicting."

"Trust me. I get it."

Acorn rolls onto his back. As we both reach to rub his belly at the same time, our hands accidentally touch. I pull mine away, startled by the weird shiver that travels up my arm and into my chest.

"Do you ever sing? Or do you just play guitar?" I ask.

I catch the briefest clench of his jaw muscles. "I sing sometimes. I just don't like to."

"How come?"

He stares at the dog, who has all his paws up in the air. "I guess I prefer to be in the background and not the center of attention. Less seen and more heard."

I know all about fading into the background of life. "I'd love to hear you sing someday."

He frowns, then smiles before he unlatches the guitar case and pulls out the scratched and scuffed-up instrument. "I'll make a deal with ya," he says. "I'll sing for you, just this once, if you let me buy you an ice cream after." He nods his head toward the ice cream cart across the park.

My leeriness of him is fading; all thoughts of him being some kind of big bad wolf fall to the wayside with the promise of singing and ice cream. I realize if all it would have taken to lure me in was ice cream and a song I probably could have been easily kidnapped as a child. But something about Evan isn't evoking that stranger-danger vibe I initially felt with him. I want to trust him, and even more, open up to him a little.

"Deal," I reply. "Ice cream is my weakness."

He sits cross-legged, the guitar in his lap and his tattooed knees shoving through the frayed holes in his jeans. Cocking his head to the side, he looks up to the sky.

"All right, Ladybug," he finally says, taking the toothpick out of his mouth and putting it in the pocket of his blue and gray flannel shirt. "I'll sing you a song I wrote a few days ago. It still needs some work, but it's a start."

Intrigued, I set my paperback aside as he plays a slow, faint melody that gradually grows deeper. When he begins to sing, the passion in his voice reaches straight into my soul and latches onto it. Possesses it. Despite the warmth of the sun, goosebumps scatter over my flesh in response to his unique, gravelly, but emotional tone. His eyes are hooded and downcast as he sings, and I realize when he performs his own music, he gets intimately involved—consumed by the melody. He pours his heart and soul into it, and the words and music carry traces of him along with them. And he was right when he said my breath changes when I listen to him play, because this song and his voice have made me breathless.

Now it makes sense—all the times I watched him lose himself in music. Those were *his* songs. The songs I recognized from the radio? He was different when he played those. Although he performed them perfectly, he didn't close his eyes to shut out the world or move his hands so passionately across the strings. The connection wasn't there.

But this, this private performance just for me, is like he's sharing his devotion to the art of words and sound. It's obvious he deeply loves what he creates. I'm honored and awed and quite enamored with him, his music, even his dog. The lyrics are dark, seductive, and sad:

And then there was you,
Slayer of my heart,
The one I would destroy,
Keeper of my heart.
You came like a dream, and I snuffed you out.
I'd love you if I could, but I don't know how.
I just don't know how, baby.
I'll make you cry, I'll make you sigh, and you'll beg for more.
Slayer of my heart,
Sweet as sugar,
Sexy as sin.
You're just my everything.
Then there was you,
Keeper of my heart,
Wish of my soul.
Don't ever leave, baby, and I'll never let you go.
Just like that, there was you.
Keeper of my heart… wish of my soul… Don't ever let go.
You're my everything.

After he sings the last word and strums the last note I take a deep breath. "Wow. That was just…" I grapple for words, but can't come up with any good enough. "Incredible. Amazing. Your voice gave me chills."

I want to hear more. Begging isn't beneath me. I can think of nothing I'd rather do than listen to him sing and watch his fingers drift over the guitar all day long, just for me, without the small crowd of people that usually surrounds him.

A hint of shyness reaches his crooked smile. "You're the first to hear that one." He strums his fingers across the strings.

"I feel special now."

"You should." He places the guitar back in the case and snaps it shut, causing Acorn's ears to perk up. "That's all for today," he announces, snuffing out my hopes to hear more. "Now you owe me an ice cream date."

My cheeks burn at his choice of words, and I feel a stab of unease as we walk toward the ice cream cart. Is this wrong? Having ice cream with a homeless guy who's sort of becoming a friend? I think his flirting is harmless. It's probably the way he acts with all women. It doesn't mean he likes me. And the strange fluttering of my stomach is just a side effect of listening to amazing music up close, like having front-row seats at a concert by my favorite band.

That's all.

"You're really talented, Evan," I say as we walk. "I don't understand why you're playing here in a park for dollars and change when you could be—"

"A famous musician?" He finishes my sentence as if he's heard this hundreds of times before.

"Yeah. I mean, I really think you could."

We stop at the ice cream stand and browse over the menu of flavors.

"I've had offers, been flown to L.A. and Seattle to meet with bands and producers and all that shit. That's not what I want. I don't care about money or being known. All I care about is playing music I love and being free. I don't give a shit about anything else."

His answer baffles me. Who walks away from the chance to make money? Why would he choose to stay on the streets?

He pushes my hand away when I take my wallet out of my bag.

"I can afford ice cream, Piper."

I hesitate, feeling bad. Not only for insulting him, but for allowing him to spend his money on me. I've seen what people throw in that tip jar of his. Reluctantly, I put my wallet back as he orders two cones for us and a scoop of vanilla in a cup for Acorn, who's waiting next to us with a wildly wagging tail and what could almost be a smile. My heart clenches at the dog's excitement, and all I want to do is take him home with me and give him a big bowl of food, a soft doggy bed, and some toys.

Where do Evan and his dog even sleep at night? On the ground? In a sleeping bag? In a tent? I wonder if the rest of his stuff is hidden under a bridge or in a shopping cart in the bushes, or who knows where?

"You okay?" he asks after he pays with a handful of folded dollar bills.

I force a smile. "Yeah, I was just thinking."

His tongue sweeps over his mint chip ice cream, and the glimpse of a silver bar pierced through it grabs my attention. I've heard that men get their tongues pierced to heighten the sensation when giving oral, and I wonder if that's why he has one.

"You know what I like, Piper?" He takes another lick. "People who say exactly what they're thinking."

Hint taken.

"I was wondering where you sleep." *And what you do with that tongue bar.* "I know it's rude, but I was just curious."

"It's not rude. We sleep under that bridge where we ate lunch yesterday. It's quiet and mostly dry, and the cops don't give me a hard time. Some nights, I can see the stars."

I swallow my ice cream too fast, and it spikes into my brain like an ice pick. "Oh."

"Do you like where you sleep, Piper?"

What a question that is. So simple to answer, really. But deep down, in the secret places of my thoughts, it's not so simple at all.

"Sometimes."

"Do you sleep alone?"

"No." I pause to gauge his reaction, wondering if he's fishing to see if I'm single. "I sleep with my cat."

He grabs the hand that's holding my cone and brings it to his lips. I watch in fascination as he licks my ice cream, without asking, without hesitation, and with his smoldering eyes locked right onto mine.

"I wanted to taste yours," he says, licking the pink raspberry from his lips.

I blink and swallow. "I-I don't mind," I reply, running my tongue over the spot he just had his mouth on. Our eyes meet as he licks his ice cream. It's a kiss that isn't a kiss.

An erotic shock jolts through me. My germ radar has gone dark.

Finished with the last bite of his cone, Evan picks up Acorn's empty dish and throws it in the trash, then walks me back to the tree where he found me.

"It's probably time for me to get going." I smile up at him. "Thanks for the ice cream. And for singing for me. I really loved it. If it was on a cassette, I'd probably play it over and over and over again."

Stepping closer, he pushes my hair behind my ear and holds his hand there with his thumb on my cheek. I can smell tobacco on his hand but it's not unpleasant. My breathing stills at the uninvited touch. My head screams at me to slap his hand away, but every other part of me savors the intimacy, the glimmer of desire in his eyes, and the sudden heat between my thighs.

"Tonight when you're sleeping with your cat in the place you only like sometimes, close your eyes and you'll hear the music. I promise."

He pulls away. Walks away. Every time I watch him walk away, I'm struck by a sudden fear that I'll never see him again. The feeling disappears just as quickly as it comes.

I'm still so buzzed by my unexpected reaction to his touch that I walk in a daze to my office building, only to realize my car isn't there and is parked about six blocks over in the other direction.

Damn!

His lyrics are still in my head as I trek toward my car, as I cook dinner with my mom that night, and later when I'm in my bed and close my eyes to drift off to sleep.

And then there was you,
Slayer of my heart,
The one I would destroy,
Keeper of my heart.

CHAPTER FOUR
PIPER

I've glanced at the digital clock sitting on my desk so many times this morning I've practically given myself a seizure. My heart pitter pats with every minute that brings me closer to noon.

What the hell is wrong with me? This isn't like me at all. I've never felt butterflies over a guy before—not even when I started dating Josh —my first, only, and now ex-boyfriend.

That was different, though. Josh and I were strictly friends with no feelings for each other whatsoever for two years, until one day we were having lunch and out of nowhere he suggested that we date. I stopped chewing my corned beef sandwich and stared at him for a few seconds, then agreed.

And that was it. We added kissing and groping to what we were already doing, and it worked. For almost a year. Then he went off to college a few hours away, and we slowly drifted apart. We never even slept together. We fooled around a lot, but every time things started to go further, we both froze. Not purposely… It just happened, like a reaction we couldn't control.

Josh is a sweet, easy-going guy. He never pushed or coaxed me. The crazy, giddy, I want-to-kiss-you-nonstop-and-rip-your-clothes-off passion wasn't there. I used to think those types of feelings weren't important as long as two people had trust and care for each other. And we had that. He made me laugh and he made me feel safe and comfortable. But now, after watching *Titanic* a bajillion times, I'm wondering why I didn't feel more with Josh. Did I unknowingly sacrifice chemistry and passion for comfort?

What am I feeling around Evan, anyway? It's not butterflies, exactly. It's more like fireflies. A spark of light and heat fading into the dark. A quick feeling of *ooh* that I can't wait to feel again.

It's unsettling, but even more than that, exhilarating.

When noon finally arrives, I head over to the park, and the absence of acoustic music hits me hard as I walk through the iron gates. I quicken my steps and strain to hear his guitar, but the air is populated with chirping birds and people talking as they walk by. Evan and Acorn aren't in their usual spot at the brick wall. As I sit on my bench, a pang twitches in my chest. I was hoping to see him today. I desperately wanted to feel that surge of strange excitement when he smiles at me. I wanted to hear what songs he would play today and guess which ones were his own.

As I eat my salad, I watch people walk by, everyone appearing to be in a rush to get somewhere. I fear I'm going to end up just like these people—rushing through the day and life in general to get to the next place, only to keep rushing more to get somewhere else. Maybe Evan has the right idea after all, being completely free.

I wonder if his quest for freedom has taken him away from here for good. Saddened by that possibility, I throw my salad container in my lunch bag and leave my bench to stroll around the park. Unlike the others, I walk slowly, shutting out the voices and rapid steps to enjoy the sound of the leaves blowing in the trees. Without conscious thought or plan, I find myself nearing the old stone bridge. The place Evan ate his burger. The same one he told me he slept under.

Biting my lip, I peer down the grassy slope leading to the old vacant road beneath the bridge. I take a deep breath and carefully walk the weed-ridden path.

I know I shouldn't be doing this, but I can't stop myself. I'm pulled by some type of magnetism I can't explain or resist.

As I round the stone wall of the bridge, I see him sitting on the ground. His legs are stretched out, his eyes are closed, and he's holding a rock the size of a baseball against his forehead. Acorn lies beside him with his head resting on Evan's leg—a perfect picture of man's best friend and guardian.

I waver a few feet away unsure whether to approach him or walk away and pretend I never saw him. He could be drunk or high. Why else would he be sitting so incredibly still, holding a rock?

I take a few hesitant steps closer, too overcome with worry and curiosity to leave without making sure he's okay.

"Evan," I say softly.

He lowers the rock, and his forehead creases when his bloodshot eyes focus on me.

"Piper?" Squinting, he shakes his head and peers around me to stare down the path I just came from, then levels his gaze on my face. "What are you doing down here?"

"I-I was worried about you." I'm a stalker now, seeking out homeless men under bridges. "Are you okay? You don't look so great."

He closes his eyes and leans the back of his head against the bridge. "I've had a migraine since last night," he mumbles. "I can't even stand up."

I take a few steps closer and kneel next to him, cursing myself for wearing a skirt and hoping I'm not flashing him. Thankfully, I'm wearing black silk panties and not silly kittens.

"Can I get you anything?"

"No, I just have to ride it out. The cold of the rock helps."

I swallow over the lump of sadness in my throat. He should have an ice pack and be sleeping in a clean bed in a quiet, dark room. I unzip my lunch bag, pull out my unopened water bottle, and set it on the ground next to him.

"You can have my water. It's cold," I say. "I could run over to the pharmacy down the street… get you an ice pack and some ibuprofen. Maybe something to eat?"

"Nah… I'll be okay if I rest." He grabs the water and untwists the cap. "You're sweet." After he gulps almost half the water, he presses the damp bottle against his forehead. "Been a long time since someone cared about me."

I touch Acorn's head and scratch between his ears, and his tail thumps happily. "He cares about you," I reply with a smile.

Evan flashes me a weak grin. "True... but having someone like you giving a shit about me is like winning the fucking lottery."

Every insecure molecule of me dances with sheer giddiness. Me? A lottery?

"I think your migraine has given you brain damage."

"My brain is fine."

Our eyes meet. The usual light in his blue eyes has been snuffed out, leaving them eerily vacant, as if he's no longer behind them. I miss the carefree man with the charming smile, puppy dog eyes, and beautiful music.

Cautiously, I reach out and touch his forehead, gently caressing his warm brow, and whisper to him, "My mom used to rub my head when I was little and didn't feel good."

When he closes his eyes, his long, dark lashes touch his cheeks. "Mine never did."

Taking a breath, I lean closer to him. The pavement digs into my knees, but I ignore it, focusing on balancing so I can use both hands to reach him. I rub his forehead and temples, surprised by the softness of his hair under my fingertips.

His pained expression gradually softens under my touch. He inches his hand across the pavement until he bumps against my bare knee. I don't move away and he stays there.

"You have magic fingers, Ladybug."

God, that voice... gritty and low with pain but so damn sinfully sexy. I massage his forehead for a few more minutes, then push his hair back away from his face before I lean back on my heels.

"I hope that helped you feel a little better."

With a nod, he lies down, using Acorn's furry body as a pillow, and I can tell by the way the dog curls around him that they sleep this way often.

Worry plagues me as I walk back to my office, and Evan's sad eyes haunt me for the rest of the day. I can't imagine how awful it must be to feel sick and not have a bed to sleep in, a bathroom to use, or medication and something to drink and eat.

Or someone to take care of you other than your dog.

Hours later I'm at home eating balsamic honey chicken over wild rice, feeling incredibly grateful for everything I have. I have a family who, annoying as they can be, loves and cares about me. A kitchen full of food. A queen-sized bed with a warm down comforter to snuggle under every night. A steady paycheck.

After dinner, I say good night to my parents and retreat to my space downstairs, debating between watching a movie, calling Ditra, or reading in the bathtub until I shrivel up like a prune.

Bathtub wins!

Until I open the mirrored door of the medicine cabinet to grab a hair clip and an opaque orange bottle of painkillers catches my eye— prescribed to me a few months ago when I had my wisdom teeth pulled. I never finished them because they made me throw up.

Fingering the bottle, my mind spins a web of good intentions.

I take the bottle into the kitchenette, grab a plastic bag from my junk drawer, and toss the pill bottle into the bag. Seconds later, I've added a can of cold ginger ale, an unopened bag of pretzel sticks, and an apple. Before I know it, I'm in my car, driving toward the park with my care package of pills and goodies on the passenger seat next to me.

He's sick. He has no one. I'm a caring person. I often put food and water out for stray cats and toss peanut butter cookies to our neighborhood squirrels. This is the same thing. I'm not trying to shift into any kind of caretaker mode with him. I only want to be a nice person and stay on the good side of karma.

Finding a spot for my car is much easier at night since most of the stores are closed. The park is vacant and eerily quiet. Clutching the tiny canister of mace that's attached to my key ring in one hand and the plastic bag in the other, I make my way down the dark walkway that leads to the decaying bridge. Thankfully, there are scattered pole lights in the park, illuminating the main walking path, but they are fewer and farther between as I near the old bridge.

As I carefully descend the small hill, my heart races with trepidation. In my rush to leave the house, I didn't even think to change out of my skirt and heels into jeans and sneakers.

Stupid, stupid, stupid.

My breath catches when I find Evan in the same exact place, sitting on the ground with Acorn, a small solar lantern glowing next to them.

I look around nervously as I approach, afraid there might be other homeless men nearby. I almost expect a bunch of them to be down here, drinking and standing around in front of a garbage can bonfire like they do on television. But there aren't any other people here. There's just Evan and Acorn.

And me.

The clicking of my heels announces my arrival, and his head snaps in my direction. After giving Acorn a quick pet on the head, he stands and takes a few unsure steps toward me.

"Piper... what are you doing here?" He glances behind me. "It's not safe at night—"

Holding the bag up, I interrupt him by talking in warp speed. "I brought you a few things. A soda and pretzels and an apple and Vicodin."

Before accepting the bag from me, he takes a deep breath, his cheeks puffing out as he exhales. "You really didn't have to do that."

"I know. I was worried about you. You looked so sick earlier."

"I appreciate it. But I can't take these." He pulls the bottle of pills out of the bag and hands them to me.

I close my fingers around the bottle. "I thought they would help your headache."

"They would." He lets out a clipped laugh. "They really fuckin' would."

I narrow my eyes, and he nervously pushes his hair behind his ear.

"I'm an addict, Piper."

My stomach sinks. I was right—he's a junkie. I knew it.

He licks his lips, the metal piercing catching a sliver of moonlight reflection. "I've been clean for two years, but I can't take any chances and go down that road again. I'd rather suffer through the pain and everything else."

His eyes shift to the bottle in my hand as if it's a treasure. The line of his jaw clenches, his lust for the drugs invading the space between us. I've never been remotely addicted to anything but chocolate and ice cream, but I can guess how hard it is to stay away from something he craves badly.

I'm obviously failing at it myself.

"I'm so sorry, Evan. I totally understand." Flustered, I shove the bottle into my purse and quickly zip it shut. "I had no idea. I apologize." Leave it to me to wave drugs in front of a recovering addict.

"Don't worry about it. I feel better now, just tired."

"I'm glad." Pinned by his intense stare, my pulse quickens, unsure if he now sees me as a source of pills or something else.

I smile nervously. "You must think I'm nuts, coming down here twice. I'm not a stalker. I promise."

"No… I think you're just a really good person." He sets the bag of snacks down next to the lantern. "Way too good to be here with me."

"That's not tr—"

Without warning, his mouth is on mine, open and hot. Stumbling backward from the shock, I clutch the soft fabric of his flannel shirt as he grabs the back of my head and pulls my mouth harder against his. There's not one hint of gentleness in his kiss. It's raw, rough, and unapologetically demanding. When my lips part in an attempt to either moan or protest—I'm not sure which—his tongue invades my mouth, annihilating my words while he slowly slides his hand from the nape of my neck down to my waist. Those long fingers that move over the guitar strings so perfectly grip me so hard I'm sure I'll have bruises tomorrow.

He backs me up until my spine hits the cold stone wall, then pulls away, just far enough to stare down into my eyes but close enough that I can feel his breath against my face.

He edges his other hand up and closes it around my neck, the span of his huge palm covering my throat. My pulse thumps wildly against his grasp. I'm paralyzed, not just because he's got my throat in a chokehold, but because the undeniable flash of lust I see in his eyes is sending an army of white-hot electrifying tingles throughout my entire body. Warmth floods between my thighs despite the chill in the air. Closing his eyes, he lowers his head and slowly drags his nose across my cheek. He inhales deeply.

His voice is deep and husky when his mouth touches the corner of mine. "You should get out of here."

My heartbeat thunders in my ears. "I don't want to."

Exhaling with a low rumble, he releases my throat. He clenches the back of my neck, threading his fingers through my hair. Using the tension of my hair in his grasp, he pulls my face toward his. My scalp stings with the tightening of his fingers, and he silences my gasp by filling my mouth with his tongue. The metal bar dings against my teeth on the way in. Trembling from head to toe with a dizzying mix of fear and desire, I grip his shoulders for stability—or maybe just to get my hands on him.

Leaning closer, he moves his leg between mine, his jeans chafing against the flesh of my thighs as he coaxes them apart. The cool night breeze travels up my skirt and sends a shiver through my limbs. I move my hand to his chest, but he quickly snatches it and pins it against the wall above our heads, locking his fingers into mine. He slides his leg up against my crotch, lifting me about a foot off the ground, bringing my lips level with his.

My entire being spins into a euphoric haze as he kisses me deeper. I lose the ability to think or breathe. I surrender to his touch and become mindless, boneless, thoughtless.

And in that moment, utterly regretless.

I don't push this stranger away. I don't say no. The sighs and whimpers that drift from my lips while his mouth devours me beg for more. My body and mind consent. I have no choice but to straddle his leg, and the pressure against my clit makes me want to rub all over him like a cat. Drowning in him, I gulp his breath into my lungs. He's tobacco and mint-infused oxygen, resuscitating me.

Slowly lowering me to my feet, he moves his free hand to the hem of my skirt and lightly traces the edge of the material. The silver rings on his fingers are smooth and cold against my skin. He inches his hand beneath my skirt and squeezes my inner thigh posessively. I slip further down the rabbit hole when his finger languidly glides back and forth over the damp spot at the front of my panties, coaxing me, teasing me, luring me.

Blood flows back to my hand when he releases it from its prison against the stone above our heads. I flex my fingers and stare into his darkening eyes, wondering what the hell I've gotten myself into.

He presses his thumb to the thin material against my clit and traces a lazy circle. He watches me, his lips hovering over mine, and it's perfectly tantalizing the way his finger moves so unrushed, making me powerless to resist rocking into his touch for more. He's savoring my every fluttering breath, my every response. I can see it in the flash and burn of his eyes and in his ragged breathing—which is unexpected and provocative. Nobody has ever looked at me like he is.

And I'm sure no one ever will.

This man could rape me or kill me down here at the dark edge of the park. No one would know. He could easily walk away with his guitar and his dog, on to the next town. Free. Not a soul would ever know I came here on my own, allowed him to put his hands and his mouth on my body and conjure desire out of me.

Piper would never do such a thing, they'd say.

But I like this. For once, I'm not boring, safe, and predictable little Piper. I've walked willingly into the depths of the unknown, which comes under the guise of inked arms and a beautiful voice. He's my first taste of wild, and he's nothing short of delicious.

His husky whisper pulls me in. "Turn around."

Blinking, I suffer a brief hesitation. Common sense and morals almost reel me in from the edge I'm teetering on.

Almost, but not quite.

Slowly, I turn, and my hair is tugged to the side, forcing my head to whip to the left. He brings his mouth down on the back of my neck, with the graze of sharp teeth. He caresses my shoulders, then slowly trails his touch down my arms. Lacing our fingers together, he drags his lips from my neck to my shoulder while placing my palms flat against the wall.

My heart pounds so hard I'm surprised it's not cracking my ribcage. My fingertips grip the wall as the world spins like a top around me, and I fear I may pass out from—what? Fear? Excitement?

Anticipation. Exquisite anticipation.

With my head turned to the side, he's a large, looming shadow behind me. A few feet away, the lantern gradually grows dimmer and dimmer, running out of the energy that fuels it. Soon it will fade out completely, and we'll be in pitch darkness.

Encircling my waist with his hands, he leans down until his lips meet the outer curve of my ear.

"Do you think I'm dirty?" he whispers as he tugs my skirt up to my waist. Just as the glow of the lantern dies out, he tears my panties off and throws them to the ground.

Gulping, I answer without even thinking. "Yes."

"Good. I'm going to make you dirty, too," he growls against my ear. "And it's never going to wash off."

I silently agree with his prediction as his hands move down my hips to cup my ass cheeks, squeezing hard. He bites into the flesh of my neck, and his wet tongue follows, soothing and then sucking savagely, causing me to cry out as he slips a hand between my thighs. Long, talented fingers slide between my wet lips. My cry morphs into a gasp, and his lips curve into a grin against the side of my throat.

An owl hoots somewhere in the trees above us.

Acorn rustles on the ground beside us.

And behind me, the distinct sound of a zipper.

A light, misty rain blows on us in the breeze. We were born in the rain, I realize, as he plunges his rock-hard length into me, lifting me off my feet. Pain seers through my body, radiating from my pelvis to my limbs. With every thrust of his hips, my cheek presses against the stone, but I can't move. It hurts. *It feels so good.* I want it to stop. *I want more.*

He snakes his arm around my front, skims his hand down my stomach, and zeroes in on my throbbing clit, fingering it in perfect time with his deep strokes. I can feel my walls tearing and stretching to take his width. The primal eroticism makes me quiver and clench around him despite the sharp pain.

Leaning his forehead against the top of my head, his damp hair hangs down over me, tickling my cheeks and bare shoulder, bringing with it the scent of sandalwood, coconut, and tobacco. My clit pulses and spasms in his fingers as he brings me to orgasm, my moans and short yelps pervading the silence of the night.

I yelp when he abruptly pulls out, spins me around, and covers my mouth with his before I have a chance to catch my breath. Wobbling on my high heels, I grip his arms, lost in the whirlwind of feelings assaulting my body and mind.

Did we—? What did we just do?

Tangled around his ring-clad fingers, my hair is pulled, guiding my head down. Slowly directing me to kneel on the ground.

"Suck me," he rasps, dragging his knuckles across my cheek as he gazes down at me. "Let me watch you."

Grasping his stiff, damp cock in my hand, I take him into my mouth and lick and suck him like I've done this a hundred times before—which I haven't. He tastes salty and metallic, a cocktail of us. If memories had a flavor, ours would be salt and blood. It's disgusting and beautiful, and I lose my mind. This man is a drug and I'm an addict. I'm high on him and us, lost in the twirling world around me, every smell, sight, and touch heightened and vivid and so incredibly disconnected and hazy.

Maybe he slipped me a roofie when he kissed me. Maybe he had something on his tongue and now I'm high as a kite. Or maybe this is all just a crazy-ass sex dream and I'm going to wake up next to Archie the cat any moment with *Titanic* playing in the background.

I gag on the cock slamming into my tonsils.

Nope. This isn't a dream. I'm choking on a stranger's dick.

This isn't me. This isn't me. This isn't me.

"Piper...." Grabbing the back of my head, he breathes out my name as hot cum propels down my throat. I swallow him and he slowly pulls out, skimming over my lips. I wipe my wet mouth with the back of one hand while my other clenches the side of his leg.

He helps me to my feet before zipping himself back into his jeans, and I avoid any eye contact, attempting to straighten my skirt over my bare ass. My panties, my favorite pair with the pretty lace trim, are lost somewhere on the ground.

As I try to focus in the dark, Evan leans down to capture my mouth with his, but I quickly turn my face away, escaping the kiss. My mouth no longer feels like my own. My lips are numb, my tongue tingly, my throat burning.

"I have to go." My voice shakes as I shiver uncontrollably and step away from him, tripping over my purse as I do so. I don't even remember dropping it. Nor do I remember the misty rain stopping. I quickly snatch up my purse and throw the strap over my shoulder.

"I-I have to go," I repeat and sprint through the foggy darkness in the direction I came from, running my hand along the damp stone until I find the end of the bridge, ignoring his voice calling after me.

On my hands and knees I crawl up the hill and let out a sob of relief when I finally reach the asphalt path. My heels clack as I practically run toward the safety of the wrought-iron gates. The shape of my bench appears under one of the lamps, and I'm suddenly overcome with nausea.

Clutching my stomach, I run to the garbage can I've thrown my lunch into every day for months and vomit into it, my horrible retching echoing around me. Using the garbage can for balance, I fish in my purse for a mint and suck wildly on it before I continue to walk toward my car. The taste of vomit and sex in my mouth is overpowering, an acrid poison I will never forget.

I drive home like a certified lunatic. An endless stream of tears flow down my cheeks and I'm shocked I don't crash into something or get pulled over for speeding and driving erratically. When I reach my driveway, I'm relieved to see all the lights in the house are off except for the front porch, signaling they've all gone to bed.

Thank God.

Even with the heat in my car blasting, I shivered all the way home, and I'm still shaking when I let myself in the house and quietly go down to my room. Ignoring Archie's stare from beside his half-empty food dish, I toss my purse onto the couch, kick off my shoes, and make a beeline for the bathroom. I lock the door behind me.

The reflection in the mirror above the sink nearly makes me puke again.

I blink at the girl there as she stares back at me. I have no idea who she is. She's a mess, breathing heavy with her mouth partially open. Her hair is damp and looks as if she was recently electrocuted or is channeling Cher. The charcoal eyeliner and mascara she spent fifteen minutes perfecting this morning are now smeared under her puffy eyes and across her pale cheeks. Her lips are abnormally red and swollen, the corners of her mouth slightly cracked.

From sucking dick.

Trembling, I take a deep breath and try to get my shit together.

Half an hour ago, two of the most intimate parts of my body were stretched around a huge cock, and now there's dried cum on my chin and in my hair. My gaze drifts down to the blotchy red marks on my neck as memories of his lips, teeth, and hands biting, sucking, and gripping me sends another wave of odd euphoria through me.

I shouldn't be turned on by this… *should I?*

Pulling my clothes off, I decide I'll worry about that later. Right now, I need a hot shower and a gallon of soothing aloe and lavender body wash. I turn on the hot water and look at my naked body in the full-length mirror on the back of the door while the small room fills with steam. I zero in on the faint black and blue bruises in the shapes of his fingertips marking my waist, thighs, and throat. I lightly run my fingers over them in fascination, until a small stain of dried blood smeared on my inner thigh catches my eye. Frantically, I grab a tissue from the box on the vanity and wipe it across my vagina, and there's a few spots of bright-red blood. I toss it in the toilet and quickly flush it. I don't need *Exhibit A: Loss of Virginity* sitting in my wastebasket for Archie to pull out and drag around my room like a prize.

My heart jumps into my throat when I realize I don't know if Evan wore a condom. Gripping the edge of the porcelain sink, I play the moments over and over in my head while my pulse races, but I can't dredge up the sound of the wrapper being ripped open or a lapse when he might have been putting it on. Or taking it off. His stiff cock went directly from my pussy to my mouth in a matter of seconds.

There was no condom.

A swarm of anxiety sucks the air out of my lungs. How could I be so stupid and irresponsible to let a stranger screw my brains out under a bridge without protection? Me... who won't even use a public restroom unless it's a last resort. Me... who's been waiting for my first time to be some kind of off-the-charts romantic experience with a man I'd want to marry. Did I suffer temporary insanity tonight? It's like someone else just took over my body and my brain, and now I could have just lost my virginity, acquired five STDs, and gotten pregnant all at once.

With a homeless man.

My body sways with a dizzying freak-out, and I suck in another grounding, deep breath as I step into the shower stall, still trembling despite the scalding water. The tears don't stop. They mingle with the water dripping down my face as I scrub my flesh with a washcloth soaked in soap.

I'm going to make you dirty, too. And it's never going to wash off.

He's right. I can't scrub away the memories of how he kissed, rammed, and tasted. And I already know I'll lust over the bruises long after they've faded.

God help me, I don't want to wash any of it away.

I stay in the shower until the hot water turns icy cold, then wrap a thick towel around myself and go straight to bed, crawling naked under my blankets and falling instantly into a mentally and physically exhausted sleep.

I wake up groggy the next morning with a dull pain between my legs, an immediate reminder of what happened last night with Evan.

What exactly *did* happen last night?

I don't even know how to describe any of it. Was that a one-night stand? A quick down-and-dirty screw? I can only imagine what he must think of me now. Not that his opinion should matter, really. I mean, he's the homeless one. Not me. I have a job and a car and a bank account and a cat.

I also have blue, purple, and red bruises scattered all over my body from sex with him because the gift of speech completely took a hike out of my life last night when I should have been saying no.

He told you to leave, Piper. Remember? You said you didn't want to. Your ability to speak was working just fine when you said that. And speaking of your mouth, it was also functioning perfectly fine when you sucked and swallowed him as though he were your last meal.

Shit.

I'm lying to myself. His opinion matters to me very much.

The digital alarm clock on my night table beeps me out of my daydream, and I slam the rectangular button until it turns off. There's no way I'm going to work today with all the madness shuffling through my brain. I'll never be able to focus on documents or deal with the endless ringing of the phone, and lunch hour is a stressy dilemma I'm not ready to face. I'm too unsettled and embarrassed to go to the park today. What if Evan's not there? Or what if he is and he ignores me? What if he comes over to my bench to talk? What would we say to each other now? What if he kisses me, there in the park, on my bench, out in the daylight in public and not hidden away under a bridge in the dark?

My heartbeats quicken at the thought of his lips on mine again, warm and possessive, and the throaty rasp of his voice.

As petrified as I am about my actions and the possible ramifications, it doesn't diminish the other emotions fighting like hell to come to the surface. I like Evan. A lot. I'm undeniably attracted to him in ways I've never felt before. Whether I want it or not, he's ignited a spark of intrigue in me, and I don't think it's going to extinguish anytime soon.

If anything, I feel it's going to turn into a raging inferno that will burn 'til the day I die.

I crawl out of bed, use the bathroom, and pull on my robe before I call the human resources manager at my office and leave a message that I have the flu and won't be coming in to work.

With that out of the way, I heat water for tea in a mug in the microwave and pull out the yellow pages to search for a gynecologist in town. I then embark on the most awkward conversation of my life with a nurse about my "unexpected high-risk sexual experience." Fifteen minutes later I end the call with shaking hands and an appointment two weeks from today for a full examination and testing.

The next two weeks are going to be torturous.

How does Ditra do this with multiple people and not go insane?

I'm never having sex again.

Not until I'm married, at least.

Never did I think my first time would be like this. But when I peel back the layers of fear, I'm left with a pretty wild experience with an amazingly talented and sexy man who tore through my shyness like a dagger slicing silk. I'm just not sure how I feel about myself or him or any of it and continue to see-saw between being completely appalled one minute and daydreaming about him the next.

There's a knock on my door, and my mother enters my space before I can answer, which she has promised a hundred times she won't do anymore to respect my privacy. Someday I'll remember to lock the door that separates my living space from theirs.

"Why aren't you at work?" She glances around my tiny living room as if something illegal might be happening. "It's after nine."

"I'm not feeling well," I reply, not meeting her eyes and pulling my hair over to the front of my shoulder to hopefully cover the hickies and bite marks on my neck. "I called in sick."

"Sweetheart, your boss will never take you seriously if you call in sick for every little thing. They'll think you're lazy and irresponsible."

This is where I get my chronic worrying from. I love my mom, but she worries about everything under the sun.

"Mom, I have about a hundred sick days. This is only the second one I've taken since I started working there. I haven't even used any of my vacation time."

"Just be careful it doesn't become a habit." She eyes my teacup. "Do you need anything? Soup or tea? Toast? I can make you a tea with honey. That always makes you feel better."

"I have tea, but I had to make a phone call first. After I drink it, I'm going back to bed for a little while. I didn't sleep well last night. There's a bug going around the office that I probably caught. That's all." I bounce the tea bag up and down in my mug by its paper tag.

She nods and reaches for the doorknob. "Okay. I'll be home all day so let me know if you need anything."

"Okay. I'm sure I'll feel better once I get some sleep."

She closes the door behind her before Archie can make a run for the upstairs, where he likes to climb the drapes in the dining room and make bizarre chirping noises at the squirrels in the backyard.

Too bad I can't sleep for the next two weeks and just skip the fourteen days of worrying.

I've heard people can change suddenly, and maybe I have. My escapade with Evan under the bridge seems to have tilted me off my steady, boring axis, and I can't stop thinking about it.

I lie on my bed longer than I care to admit, staring at the ceiling fan going round and round, and replay all the moments of last night in my head. My body quivers and heats with the memories. I loved every minute of it. The second his lips touched mine and we shared the same breath, I changed. I felt it.

I want more.

For the next two days, I call in, faking the flu. It's not a total lie. I feel sicker than I've ever felt in my life. Sick with worry and sick with wondering if Evan is thinking about me, too. Because if he's not, I think I'll die of this sickness.

I'm tempted to call Ditra and spill it all to her, but I know if I do, she'll tell me I'm being dramatic, congratulate me for finally breaking out of my shell, and then want to hear every detail from the length of his dick to how long my orgasm lasted to when I'm going to see him again. She'll also want to meet him.

Ditra and I have been best friends forever. Literally. Our mothers grew up next door to each other and have always been best friends.

They got pregnant at the same time, and they had Ditra and me a week apart. Back then, they did practically everything together, so we were together all the time and just naturally became best friends, too. But I still can't bring myself to pick up the phone and tell her about Evan.

It's not because I'm ashamed of him. I want to covet him. Savor him. Keep him my own little secret. If no one knows, then he's just mine.

CHAPTER FIVE

PIPER

Thursday, I return to work to find the inbox on my desk piled a foot high with work. I immerse myself in it, grateful for the distraction. I eat lunch at my desk while I work, skipping my usual lunch break.

That doesn't stop me from wondering if Evan and Acorn are at the park and if he's looking for me or missing me, but I'm not ready to find out if I was just a quickie for him. I want to stay in my safe bubble of not knowing for a while longer.

On Friday, I do the same 'I'm going to work non-stop for eight hours' routine, and by the time five o'clock rolls around, I'm ready to head home, shower, and meet Ditra for dinner. We're meeting two guys she's friends with. I suspect one is supposed to be a potential set-up for me, even though I told her I have no interest in being set up with any guys right now. Ignoring my protests, she insisted I meet up with them tonight anyway. I finally agreed because I've been feeling stir crazy for the past week and getting out of the house will probably be good for me.

All this is running through my mind as I cross the office parking lot. As I get closer to my car I spot a white note tucked under the windshield wiper. I know it's from Evan before I pluck it off the windshield and read it.

· · ·

Ladybug,
It's too late to run away.
Come back.
I miss you. A lot.
~ Blue

Well, damn. He knows where I work. He knows which car is mine. Which means he's been watching me.

My body quivers with fear and delicious anticipation.

He wants me to come back.

I don't even have to think about it. Tucking the note into my purse, I already know I'll be going back to the bridge tonight after dinner. Because I want more. Of what, I'm not sure. Just *him*.

Three hours later, I'm walking into the small but popular pub downtown. Scanning the smoke-filled, noisy room, I spot Ditra and her friends at a high table a few feet from the bar. At the other end of the room, a band is setting up, and I breathe a sigh of relief that we're not sitting near the small stage. Last time we were here, the music was so loud we couldn't even hear ourselves talk.

I feel self-conscious wearing tight jeans, high-heeled black boots, and a V-neck sweater as I approach the table because Ditra's friend, who I'm naming Guy Number Two, has his eyes glued to my chest, and trust me, there's not much to look at. Smiling, I climb on the empty stool across from Ditra and Guy Number One, who she's obviously claimed because she's practically sitting in his lap.

I hope Guy Number Two is just a boob-ogler in general and I'm not giving off any overly sexual vibes. If I see Evan later, I don't want him to think my push-up bra is an invitation for another bang against the bridge.

"Piper, this is Phil and Mitch. Guys, this is Piper. Be nice to her. She's shy, but she's my best friend in the whole wide world, and I'll kick your balls if you misbehave."

"Duly noted," Phil the Ogler says.

"I'm so glad you came out with us tonight." Ditra leans across the table toward me. "You've been mopey all week. Every time I called you, you sounded like a zombie."

I pretend to be engrossed in the menu. "I told you I was just tired. I've had the flu."

"What do you do for work?" Phil asks.

"I'm an administrative assistant."

He sips his beer, and I try not to look at his receding hairline, which can't be a good sign if he's only in his early twenties. I think of Evan and his long, wavy hair and how erotic it felt tickling my skin when he was feasting on my neck. Closing my menu, I have no idea what I want to eat, but I decide all men should have long hair.

"That's cool," Phil says.

"And you?" I ask to be polite. I don't mind Phil and his receding hairline, but I'm currently in a hopeful something with Evan and therefore, unavailable.

"I'm a landscaper."

"We both are," Mitch jumps in. "We're partners and started the business last year."

"That's great."

I'm bored.

Ditra runs her hand up and down Mitch's muscular arm like it's a genie's lamp. "That's why they're so tan and muscular."

Instead of getting dinners, we order one of every appetizer to share. I debate getting a fruity alcoholic drink like Ditra ordered, but I don't want alcohol on my breath if I see Evan later. I have no idea if drinking is part of his substance abuse problem, but after the pill debacle, I want to be careful.

"I was thinking we could all go back to my place after dinner, have some drinks, and hang out," Ditra suggests after the waitress brings the food to our table.

"I'm down for that," Phil answers with his eyes on me.

I spoon small glops of ranch dressing and honey mustard sauce onto my plate from the large cups that came with the appetizers. I don't want to dip my food into the same condiment everyone else is dipping theirs. That's a germ farm I don't want to be part of.

"I wish I could, but I have plans after this," I reply.

"Plans?" Ditra repeats. "What plans? Sitting with your cat in bed and reading isn't a plan."

The guys laugh.

"Very funny, but no, not with my cat."

She nudges my leg with her foot under the table. "Well, now you have to tell me. "

"No, I don't." I flash her a teasing smile, knowing it's making her crazy I'm doing something she doesn't know about, but I'm not about to get into my personal life here in a bar with two men I don't even know at the table.

The guys divert the conversation to discussing a recent hockey game, leaving Ditra and me to chat about clothes and makeup while we share mozzarella sticks and crispy chicken fingers, but something in the back of my mind keeps distracting me. Then I realize it's not something in the back of my mind at all, but something in the back of the *room*.

The band has started to play, and a woman's sultry voice fills the bar. But that's not it, either. It's the very distinct sound of guitar echoing after her voice that's pulling me in, making my heart race. Turning my head toward the stage, I think my eyes must be playing tricks on me at first, but there's no denying the guy sitting on that stool, playing guitar on the left side of the stage under a blue light, is Evan. He looks different here, out of the park and surrounded by people. He looks sexier. More real. Somehow less of a fantasy.

True to form, he's not looking at the people around him at all, leaving me wide open to gawk at him from our table here in the corner.

The female singer has mile-long legs in skin-tight leather pants and an equally tight red T-shirt stretched across her chest, cut to show off her pierced belly button. She's gorgeous, strutting around on the tiny stage like a born rock star and shaking her waist-length white-blond hair. Skimming her hand up and down his arms and gyrating her hips against him as she belts out a popular Concrete Blonde song, she's making a show of flirting with Evan, and it's got me all in a jealous tizzy.

There's a lot of arm touching going on in this room, and I wonder if that's the universal *I'm totally into you* gesture.

"Piper? Are you listening to me?" Ditra grabs my hand, and I drop the French fry I was holding.

"Huh?" I tear my eyes away from the stage.

"You just completely spaced out on me."

Phil leans into my shoulder and almost spills his beer in my lap. "She was overcome by how awesome I am. It happens a lot," he jokes.

"Yeah, I'm sure that was it," Ditra says, rolling her eyes.

"I was just checking out the band," I say nonchalantly. "They're really good."

"They play here a lot," Mitch informs us. "I'm friends with one of the bartenders who works weekends. He says that singer brings in a lot of customers. She's hot as hell."

Ditra glares daggers at him. "Not exactly the best thing to say right in front of me if you're trying to get some of this."

Shaking my head, I take a potato skin from the platter and place it on my plate. I can't believe my best friend just referred to herself as *some of this.*

Mitch laughs and drapes his arm around her. "I can check her out and still have you, babe."

She plays coy. "Maybe. Maybe not."

It takes every ounce of will power I have, but I refuse to let myself look back at the stage for the next two hours. I had no idea Evan also played in local bars with a band. It's quite possible he plays at a different bar every night of the week and in the park during the day. I'm ashamed of myself for knowing nothing about a man who had several inches of his body buried in mine and who also has been consuming my thoughts for weeks.

When the music stops Evan's deep voice and laugh drift from the stage, audible even in the crowded room. I finally give in and look over to see the singer standing close to him, talking and laughing with him. A niggle of jealousy gnaws at me, and I wonder if he's had his hands and his tongue piercing all over her, too. I wouldn't blame him if he did because she's beautiful and talented. And tall. She's like a skyscraper compared to me.

As if he can feel me watching him, he suddenly looks away from her and searches the room until his eyes lock with mine. There's a flash of surprise on his face, then a quick glance to Phil sitting next to me, before that sexy smirk of his makes an appearance. I quickly turn back to the table and take a gulp of my iced tea, smiling randomly at Mitch, Phil, and Ditra, who's frowning at me with suspicion.

Within seconds, he's standing next to me, wedging himself between Phil and me, and I'm afraid I suddenly have the words *I totally screwed this guy* stamped across my forehead. My mouth opens, but no words come out because, suddenly, his lips are on mine.

"Hey, babe," he says casually after the kiss. "I didn't know you'd be here tonight."

Even a quick kiss from him brings on the dizzy and giddy feelings. "Same here."

The amusement in his eyes makes it all too obvious he's enjoying my surprise and awkwardness. "I'm just here with some friends," I say.

He turns his attention to the rest of the table, giving them a friendly nod. "Hey. I'm Blue, Piper's boyfriend."

Ditra's eyes bug out. "Her *boyfriend*?" she repeats. "Since when?"

"It's new," I answer before he can spout anything else. "I didn't really get a chance to tell you yet. It happened kind of fast."

Fast and hard. Under a bridge.

"Apparently so. And you're in the band?"

"No, I just play guitar with them if their usual guy can't make it."

I grab a chicken finger off the platter and offer it to him. "Have some chicken."

Ditra can't take her eyes off of him, which I'm starting to see is an effect he routinely has on women. "Do you want to join us?" she asks. "We can drag over a chair."

He chews the piece of chicken I gave him and swallows before shaking his head. "I'd love to, but my dog is out back, so I need to get going."

"Do you need a ride?" I ask. "Or did you come with friends?" I'm pretty sure he and Acorn walked here, but I don't want my friends to know that.

"Yeah, I came with the drummer."

Lies.

"I can give you a ride home," I offer. "If you want."

He reaches for my hand under the table and pulls it into his. "That'd be cool, if your friends don't mind letting you go."

"They don't mind," I reply, not giving Ditra a chance to say otherwise. I'm sure I'll get an earful from her tomorrow, but for now, I'm much more interested in spending time with Evan than I am in sitting here next to a guy I have absolutely no interest in while Ditra and Mitch get drunk enough to have sex with each other.

Evan leans closer to me. "I just have to grab my stuff off the stage. I'll meet you in the parking lot?"

I nod and place my linen napkin on the table. "Sounds good."

Ditra pounces on me as soon as Evan is out of earshot. "Piper? What the hell? Why didn't you tell me you were dating someone? Especially someone as smokin' as him?"

"We only just started seeing each other." I can't believe Evan came over here and proclaimed himself my boyfriend without any thought of how it would make me look in front of my friends. What if I was on an actual date with Phil?

Ditra is still all over me from across the table, twirling her straw violently in her drink. "Is this why you've been so out of touch lately? Because you've got some majorly hot guy?"

"He looks like a dirt bag," Mitch comments, tipping his stool back on two legs.

"Excuse me?" I practically snarl. "You don't even fucking know him."

Ditra's jaw drops. "Ooh, wow. I don't think I've ever heard Piper tell someone off before," she says, smacking Mitch's shoulder before she turns back to me. "You must really like this guy if he's making you all savage over him."

I jump down from the stool and grab my purse. "I'm not savage. I just don't like judgmental people." I pull twenty-five dollars out of my wallet and place it between the salt and pepper shakers on the table to cover my portion of the bill, then walk around the table to give Ditra a quick hug goodbye. "You're not mad I'm leaving, are you?"

"Of course not. I'd leave with him in a heartbeat. But you better call me tomorrow and tell me all about this guy. And no holding anything back. I'll be waiting."

I pull from her embrace to smile at her. "I will. Have fun tonight, but be careful."

Unlike me, who now makes it a habit of going off with random strangers.

"It was nice meeting you both," I say to Mitch and Phil, and then I'm heading for the door, my heart beating erratically with nerves and excitement.

Once again, I'm stepping into the unknown with zero idea of what or whom I'm getting involved in. I don't know what Evan wants with me or how he feels about me. He could just be looking for another quickie, and look how fast I just ditched my best friend and a potential date to be with him without any effort on his part other than a simple kiss. He didn't even have to ask me to drive him. I offered all on my own. I'm clueless as to how this all works, but maybe I should be playing hard to get or acting mildly disinterested in him instead of being so easy.

I've never been one for games, though. I like to be real. Authentic. I don't know how to flirt or tease or play the games other girls might know how to play to make a man chase her and to keep him interested. That seems like a lot of work, and knowing me, I would probably make a mess out of it anyway. It seems easier to follow his lead and hope he doesn't take me to a place I don't want to be.

When I get out to the parking lot, he's standing next to my car with Acorn, his bag, and his guitar case at his feet, and I get the feeling, while physically this is all this man is and has, there's a lot more going on inside him. Taking a deep breath, I walk up to him instead of getting into the car.

"I got your note."

He nods. "And you came here instead of coming to see me."

"I was planning on trying to find you afterward."

"Were you?"

"Yes."

He leans against my car fender and reaches out to move my long hair behind my shoulder. "You look pretty. Is that for me or that guy you were sitting with?"

I attempt to play it cool. "Definitely not for him. I just met him tonight. I only came to be polite because my friend is interested in his friend."

His mouth clicks as he taps his piercing against his teeth. "Were you coming to see me to be polite?"

"No."

"You've been avoiding me."

He says it with such sadness I almost burst into tears. I look at my feet and swallow the lump in my throat. "I'm sorry."

He tilts my face with a finger so I'm forced to look into his eyes. "You want to tell me why?" he asks softly.

"I was scared. I *am* scared."

"Of me?"

"Of you," I admit. "And other things."

His brow creases, his tongue moves across his lips. "You should've told me you were a virgin."

Ugh. I'm grateful for the dark hiding my blushing cheeks. "I didn't really get a chance to."

"True. I never would've done that if I'd known. I thought you wanted me."

I breathe in a shallow breath. "I did."

Grabbing my waist, he pulls me against his body and leans down, pressing his lips against my forehead and holding them there for a few moments.

"I like you, Piper."

"I like you, too," I whisper.

"I think I might need you in my life."

My stomach flip-flops.

"Let's drive back to the park," he suggests. "We can sit in the car and talk for a while."

"Okay." I slowly pull away from him.

"Do you mind if Acorn sits in your back seat? His paws are clean."

"Of course he can."

I let myself into the driver's side while he puts Acorn and his stuff in the back and then gets in the passenger seat next to me.

"How did you know this was my car?" I ask as I put the key in the ignition. "Have you been watching me?"

"I actually saw you getting into it one night before you first saw me playing in the park. Me and Acorn were walking around, and I saw you in the parking lot where you work. You dropped your keys, and when you reached down to pick them up, your sunglasses fell off your head and were all tangled up in your hair."

I nod, remembering that crappy day when everything under the sun seemed to go wrong.

"I thought you looked way too young to be driving, and I wondered if you could even see over the dashboard."

"Really?" I ask, offended and humiliated. "You're going to be one of those people who make fun of my height now?"

I've heard it all over the years. Pipsqueak, Shorty, Tinkerbell. And let's not forget Pussypuker, which has nothing to do with my height and everything to do with my supreme awkwardness.

"Go easy, baby. I think you're fucking cute and sexy."

Ignoring my frown, he reaches across the car and holds my hand as I drive. It makes me feel so excited inside that I have to force myself to focus extra hard on actually driving the car, especially when I'm so lost in my thoughts I almost run a red light.

"Do you want me to drive?" he asks when I slam on the brakes at the last minute. "You seem a little distracted."

"I'm fine. I'm just not used to someone holding my hand while I'm driving."

"Do you want me to let go so you don't kill us?" he teases.

I tighten my fingers around his before the light turns green. "No," I answer with a smile.

When we get near the park, he directs me to a dead-end side road, and I stop the car and turn off the lights and engine when we reach the end of the street near the woods.

"I don't think anyone will bother us here," he says. "You mind if I smoke?"

"Not at all."

He lets go of my hand to light up a cigarette, and I turn the key to lower his window for him.

"You said you were scared."

"Yeah…"

He exhales smoke out the window and waits for me to continue without prompting me.

Running my finger over the leather steering wheel, I search for the right words and come up short.

"I'm afraid I might be pregnant. Or that maybe you have something."

"Something?"

"Yeah. Like something I could get."

"Oh." He flicks ashes out the window. "*That* kind of something."

"Yeah."

"I didn't come in you, so the chances of you getting pregnant are slim. And you can't get pregnant from swallowing."

"I know that," I say defensively.

"Just making sure."

Does he think I'm stupid? It might have been my first time, but I'm not a total moron about sex.

"I haven't been with anyone in a long time. Two years, maybe. Maybe more."

A wave of relief washes through me hearing that. I was afraid he's been wandering around sleeping with all sorts of women in different states from coast to coast.

"Okay."

"I don't blame you for thinking I'm scum, Piper. I know how I look, being homeless, having long hair and tattoos, not being able to take you on a date. You deserve better."

"I don't think you're scum at all. And I like the way you look. I didn't think you had a disease because you're homeless, Evan. You're just really good-looking, and I figured you probably sleep with tons of women."

That makes him laugh. "A few. But definitely not a ton. And I usually use protection. I just couldn't fuckin' wait to get inside you. You scrambled my fucking brain."

"I know the feeling," I mutter.

"And just so you know, I shower several times a week. There's a kid that works at the truck stop on the highway. I give him guitar lessons, and he lets me use the shower early in the morning. He even gives me soap and shampoo. I'm squeaky clean," he says with a grin.

I shake my head and smile at him. "I wondered how you always smell so nice."

He takes one more drag off his cigarette, throws it out the window, and then grabs my hand again.

"Next time, I'll be prepared. Okay? And I'll try to go a little slower."

Next time? There's going to be a next time?

"And if it'll make you feel better, I'll go to the clinic downtown and get tested."

The idea is tempting, but I think it's safe to assume Evan doesn't have health insurance like I do, and he'll end up with a huge bill to pay. That makes me wonder how he even gets his bills in the mail. Does he have a PO box? Or does he have to pay for everything immediately and in full with cash? How does anyone even get in contact with him? This homelessness situation is very confusing to me.

"Um, I think that might be expensive," I say.

"I have some extra cash for emergencies."

Oh no. I can't let him do that. What if he gets sick and needs the money? Or what if Acorn gets sick or hurt? What if they need food?

"You don't have to do that." I face him. "Do you promise me you're telling the truth?"

"I give you my word." His eyes hold nothing but sincerity, and it soothes my nerves somewhat. I've heard liars have shifty eyes, but his are calm. I decide to keep my appointment to get tested to myself and only bring it up if a scary result comes back. Otherwise, there's really no point insulting him by telling him I ran to a doctor after having sex with him. No guy wants to hear that.

We hold hands across the inside of my car and listen to the radio in the dark. He tells me he started playing guitar and writing songs when he was about eight or nine years old and how his older brother introduced him to weed right around the same time. He explains how the words came easier when he was high, and it took him almost ten years to realize he couldn't keep smoking weed every day. He admits he dropped out of high school during his junior year.

I listen intently as he tells me about the other drugs he then started to use—most I don't even recognize the names of. While rubbing his thumb along the inside of my palm, he tells me how it took him another four years, a stay in rehab, and threats from his family and friends for him to get off the harder drugs. I've only smoked pot a few times and didn't like how it made me feel or all the coughing it made me do, so I can't truly understand his addictions. But it's clear from the emotion in his voice that he had a very strong love/hate experience with drugs and alcohol.

"Living straight and sober made me feel restless. That's when I left and started living like this. Being free became a new high." He lifts my hand to his lips, and my breath hitches when he kisses the tiny ladybug tattoo on my wrist.

"Now you're my addiction." His low, gravelly tone sends ripples through my stomach.

Letting go of my hand, he leans across the small car and kisses me. I open my mouth for his tongue, welcoming the familiar minty-smoky taste of him. As he kisses me, he reaches across my body, finds the seat lever, and pulls it while pushing the headrest with his other hand until I'm leaning all the way back. Acorn quickly scooches over to the other side of the back seat to make room for the sudden invasion.

He leans over me in the front seat, still kissing me hungrily. When I reach up to put my arms around him, he slowly moves his lips down the side of my throat, sucking and biting a tantalizing path to the V-neck of my sweater, pulling the fabric down to expose the pink silk push-up bra cradling my breasts. I send up a silent thank you to Victoria's Secret for designing a bra that makes even my small breasts look good.

He drags his tongue into my cleavage, stopping at the front clasp and undoing it with his teeth. God, there really is something to be said about a man who knows what he's doing. Bracing one arm on the seat next to my head, he moves his lips slowly up the slight curve of my breast, pushing the fabric to the side until I'm completely uncovered. He lets out a deep sigh that makes my heart pound even harder as he circles my nipple with his tongue, sucking it between his lips until it aches for more. I moan softly and arch my body up into him with my fingers gripping his shoulders. The metal of his tongue piercing flicks over my taut nipple, sending hot tingles down my thighs and deep into the center of my core.

He moves his hand down my body and he unbuttons and unzips my jeans in a flash. I wiggle beneath the steering wheel, helping him push my pants down. Breathlessly, I tug his shirt up, needing to feel his warm flesh beneath my fingertips. He slides his hand under my saturated panties, cupping all of me in his hand, his palm pressing against my already-throbbing clit. His mouth comes back down on mine, hard and desperate as he touches my wet lips, spreading me open with two fingers and entering me with a third. Gasping, I dig my nails into his shoulders and kiss him back just as wildly, unable to stop myself from moving my hips in rhythm with his finger-fucking.

I want to cry and beg when he pulls his lips from mine. I'm convinced I can't survive a moment without his mouth, his breath, and his taste. But he proves me wrong when he slides another finger into my tight, wet depths, and the metal of his silver skull ring rims my entrance, heightening the pleasure. Eyes closed in ecstasy, I try to tug him back to my lips, but instead, he bows his head to my breasts again, licking one, then the other, sucking and nibbling my aching nipples until my entire body is in a frenzy.

I want all of him, everywhere. There's not a part of me that I don't want him to own. I tangle my fingers in his long hair, holding him to me as I arch up into his mouth and thrusting fingers. My gasps and cries fill the car as I come, but I can't hold back or hush myself. He's taken away all my self-control with his lips, fingers, and scent.

Still stroking me slowly, he lifts his head to finally kiss my lips as I try to catch my breath. "You're such a sweet, sexy little thing," he whispers. "I've been losing my fucking mind thinking about you."

"I've been thinking about you, too," I reply breathlessly.

"Good." He slowly pulls his fingers from my quivering body and presses his palm against my sex again, cupping my heat as my body recovers from orgasm. "I want you to keep coming back for more."

"Okay," I agree dreamily.

He smiles, and we kiss again—another long, deep, and consuming kiss that blurs the lines of where I end and he begins. *This*... this is everything I've been hoping for in a man.

After a few minutes, he pulls away, and his eyes are dark and lust-filled. "You should probably go home. It's almost two o'clock."

Reluctantly, I put my seat back up and fix my clothes, wondering how the night flew by so incredibly fast.

"Should I drive you to the park entrance?" I ask hesitantly. "Is that the best way for you to get to the bridge?"

He nods. "Yeah, but I can walk from here. It's not far."

Shaking my head, I start up the car. "I'm not going to let you walk."

"I walk everywhere, Piper."

I turn the car around and head toward the main road. "I know, but I'm not going to let you walk in the middle of the night when you're in my car already. That's silly."

He doesn't say another word until I pull up in front of the park entrance. The street is empty and spooky quiet. Farther down the road, I can see the traffic light near my office change from red to green, and it seems out of place with no cars to stop and go.

"I'm glad we ran into each other," he says, breaking the silence.

"Me, too."

He cocks his head at me, his hand on the door handle. "Were you really going to come see me after your date? Or were you just trying to be nice?"

"It wasn't a date. And yes, that was honestly my plan after I found your note. All I wanted to do was see you again."

"Just checking." He climbs out of the car, opens the door to the back seat, and pulls out his stuff. Acorn hops out, yawns, and shakes his body; waiting patiently while Evan leans back into the car.

"Come see me tomorrow."

My stomach and heart jump with a burst of unexpected excitement. "Here?"

"Yeah. At the picnic table."

I nod and smile. "Okay."

He winks and closes the car door.

Even though my space at my parents' house is supposed to be my own, I know they will freak out if I take Evan and Acorn home with me, but that doesn't stop me from wishing I could do just that as I watch them walk off into the dark to go sleep on the cold, hard ground.

CHAPTER SIX

PIPER

It looks like a bomb went off in here. The words my mother used to say to me on a daily basis echo through my head as I stand in the middle of my bedroom, surrounded by clothes scattered all over the floor and on the bed.

I can't find anything to wear. Well actually, I found a lot to wear. I'm just not sure *what* to wear.

Something easy for him to slip his hands into.

No! my mind screams. *Stop thinking that way.* Geez, a guy gives me a few orgasms, and all I can think about is his hands on me. My stomach does its all-too-familiar thud. What if that's all he's thinking about and that's all he's interested in? Maybe I'm a booty call.

No. I refuse to believe that. Not after he spent hours talking to me last night and telling me all the good and bad parts of his past. He held my hand almost the entire time. And he called himself my boyfriend in the pub. Holding up a thin sweater to see how wrinkled it is, I wonder if he meant that or if was he just kidding in front of my friends.

God. Men are difficult.

Sighing, I pull on a pair of jeans and a black T-shirt and tie a long-sleeved flannel shirt around my waist in case I get chilly. He already knows how short I am, so I slip into black combat boots instead of something with a high heel.

My phone rings as I'm heading out the door, and I know it must be Ditra because no one else calls me. I hesitate at the door, debating whether I should answer it or not, and then let my answering machine pick it up.

"Piper..." Her voice comes over the speaker. "I know what you're doing, and it's not going to work. You can't avoid me, and you know it. You have to call me and tell me all about your mystery man. Oh, and I had sex with Mitch last night. He had the smallest dick I've ever seen in my life. I'm not even sure it classified as sex; it was *that* small. So—"

Beep. The answering machine clicks and cuts her off. Immediately, the phone starts to ring, and I laugh when the machine picks up again.

Her voice fills my room again. "Your stupid machine cut me off. Anyway, you better call me. Love ya."

I make a promise to call her later when I'm back home. I'm hoping after spending some time with Evan today, I'll have an idea of what we actually are to each other. Then I won't have to answer Ditra's cross-examination with vague answers.

He smiles when he sees me approaching the picnic table, and I think it should be illegal for another person to be able to flip my insides all upside down the way he does.

His smile falters to a slight frown when I hand him one of the lattes I'm holding.

"I got us bagels, too," I say, sitting next to him at the table. "And I stopped at the pet place and picked up some dog biscuits for Acorn." At the mention of his name, the dog's ears perk up and he looks at me expectantly.

"Do you want a cookie?" I ask him, taking one of the bone-shaped biscuits out of the bag. He takes it gently from my hand and crawls under the table to eat it in private.

"What?" I ask, noticing the odd look on Evan's face.

His voice is flat. "Don't try to take care of us, Piper."

"I'm not… I'm just being nice."

"I know. And I appreciate it. But we're fine."

"Okay." The happiness I felt a moment ago fades and morphs into embarrassment. I push the bag with our bagels in it away from us and take a sip of my coffee.

"Piper… hey." He moves closer to me until his leg presses against mine. "I didn't want to make you feel bad."

"I'm fine." I smile and push my hair out of my face. "Really."

I can tell by his raised eyebrow he doesn't believe me. "I just don't want you thinking you have to feed me. We're not starving." He takes the bagels out of the bag and lays them on a napkin. "I want your friendship, not a handout."

"It's not a handout," I protest. "I get a coffee and bagel every morning, and I thought you might want one, too."

"It's sweet. I just don't want you to be one of those chicks who takes on a 'let's take care of the loser guy' project."

His words sting, even though I'm sure he didn't mean them to. "It's just a bagel and coffee, Evan. That hardly constitutes a project."

"I wish you'd call me Blue. Nobody calls me Evan."

Using the plastic knife that was in the bag, I scrape some of the mound of cream cheese off my bagel and smile shyly. "Are we friends now?" I ask.

"We are." He straddles the bench so he's facing me. "The ladybug is hard at work making us soul mates," he says with dazzling eyes and a crooked smile full of cockiness. I laugh but my insides are doing acrobatics.

"Is that right?"

He bites into his bagel and nods as he chews. "Yup."

Our eyes linger on each other, the air between us full of hope and desire mixed with wisps of caution and defiance. If this keeps up, I may just start believing in his bug myths.

"Do you play in bars often?" I ask, needing to break the silence that looms over us.

"Maybe two or three times a month. I could probably get more gigs, but I have to bring Acorn with me, and not all the managers let him inside. I'm not just gonna tie him up outside and leave him."

"I'll watch him for you if you ever need me to. I could take him for a walk, and he could sit in my car with me while he waits for you."

He leans closer and kisses the spot just below my ear, then pauses there with his nose in my hair, breathing me in. I savor the tickling sensation of his breath against my neck and flutter my eyes closed.

"Will you wait for me, too?" He moves his lips to my neck.

I lean my head against his. "If you want me to," I murmur.

"I want." He closes his mouth over my collarbone, and pulls me closer, between his legs. A turn of my head brings our lips together, and we kiss slow and soft, unlike the fiery, impatient kisses we shared before. Does the tenderness hint at emotion and care, or is this his well-orchestrated strategy to make me even more inebriated with him?

He pulls away and stares into my eyes, keeping his arm tight around me.

"I felt you wander," he says.

"I'm sorry."

"I can back off if you're not into this."

I grab his hand. "No," I reply, shaking my head back and forth. "I-I don't want you to." I lace my fingers with his to solidify my words. "I'm just a little... thrown, I guess. By all of this. And what we're doing."

"We're enjoying the moment. Right?"

"Right." I picture myself introducing him to my parents. *This is Blue, who I enjoy long moments with...*

He gazes across the park, his eyes a shade darker than they were when we were kissing. I wish I hadn't questioned his motives.

"Piper, right now I can only live moment to moment. I don't mean to sound like a dick, but you can either take it or leave it. Don't analyze it. I like you. I want to spend time with you. But that's all I got right now."

I let his words sink in, wondering where the ladybug myth is now. Regardless, I have to appreciate his honesty, even if it makes my heart ache.

Here, in my own moment, I'm a girl who's crazy about a guy. Of course I want the dates and the title and the commitment and the hope of endless tomorrows together. But I still wouldn't trade these random moments with him for anything.

Pressing my lips to his cheek, I whisper, "I'll take it."

He grabs the back of my neck and pulls me to him. The deep, demanding kiss is back, this time with a vengeance. The tightness of his grip beneath my hair and the rapture of his mouth on mine feels as if he wants to inhale me, swallow me, consume and own me. I don't fight it because I feel the same way.

I want this man to be mine. His lips, his touch, his lust, his smile, his love. I want it all, and I'll wait a lifetime for him if that's what it takes. Call it lust or love. Call it whatever you want. I'm in deep. I'm drowning in him, and no lifeboat is coming to save me.

The longer we kiss, the more my body and heart want. His tongue rolling around mine stirs up a surge of desire that travels through my veins like liquid fire. My breasts ache to be touched and sucked by his amazing lips, and my thighs burn to be wrapped around his waist.

He groans into my mouth when I touch his cheek and run my hand through his hair, and then he pulls away with a heavy breath. "We better stop, or I'm going to drag you under this table like the dog did that cookie."

I laugh, but I'm not sure I'd be able to stop him if he did just that.

"Keep laughin', Ladybug," he warns with a naughty, sexy grin as he lights up a cigarette. "I'll show you I ain't kidding."

Smiling, I reach for my latte and finish it off, inwardly composing myself before I lose all control and pull him under the table myself. His lethal combination of hot and cute has managed to steal my virginity and sexual shyness in a matter of days, and it's got my head spinning and my heart pounding and my panties melting.

"So… did you live around here… before?" I ask, hoping to get our minds off under-the-table shenanigans.

"I lived in New Jersey."

"Is that where your family is?"

"Most of them."

"Do you think you'll go back there?"

He shrugs. "I'll wander through, but I won't live there again."

"What made you come to New Hampshire?"

"I wanted to see the leaves in the fall."

Ah, a man after my own heart. I look up at the trees surrounding us, gauging their color. "They'll start to change soon. Probably in about three weeks." As I talk, he moves his hand under the back of my shirt and stays there, warm against my spine. "Did you really just walk to New England when you left Jersey two years ago?"

"No. I traveled all the way to California, hung out in some cool places, then moved to the next place."

"You walked all the way to the West Coast?" I ask in disbelief.

"No." He laughs. "Sometimes I hopped a bus or a train, or I hitchhiked."

"Oh. Don't you ever miss your family?"

"Sure, sometimes. If I pass a payphone, I drop them a line. Let them know I'm still alive."

"They must worry about you, no?"

"I think they're used to it by now. They're not the worrying types."

"My mom would never get used to that. She's ready to call a search party if I'm half an hour late from work."

"Yeah, well, mine has had years of practice."

I wonder when he plans to move on from here. The question sits on the tip of my tongue, but I don't let it out. I swallow it down, and the words scurry to that place inside me where insecurity, doubt, and denial all huddle together, afraid to come out.

"How 'bout you?" he asks. "Have you always lived here?"

"Yes. My grandparents and parents were all born here. It's home."

"You ever think about leaving?"

"No, not really. I wouldn't mind going somewhere else for a vacation, but I've never had the urge to move away."

"Do you think that's true contentment or just staying where you're comfortable?"

He's echoed the question I've posed to myself many times in many different scenarios.

"I really don't know. Is there a difference?"

"I think there is. Either is okay as long as you're happy. Me? I never feel content. There's always that feeling that there's more out there I need to see. More people I need to meet. More things I need to do. It haunts me."

"You're restless."

"Yeah. I want it, though." The grip of his hand on my waist brings a dull pain, and I realize his fingers are directly over the fading bruises from the night under the bridge. A wave of heat warms my inner thighs. "I want contentment," he says.

"I'm sure you'll find it." I hope he finds it right here in this tiny town, with me.

"Hope so. Otherwise, I'll be wandering forever."

"Maybe you can wander yourself back here every fall," I say with a shy smile I hope is slightly flirty.

"Maybe I can."

We finish our bagels, and then he takes his guitar out and plays every song I request. I laugh and try to pick songs I think he won't know or can't play, but he plays every one, even a childhood favorite—the theme song from a cartoon. Then he switches it up and asks me to guess the band and title of a piece of a melody he plays, and I fail miserably.

"C'mon. Don't you listen to music at all?" he asks, laughing.

"I do, but I never know what band I'm listening to."

He shakes his head as he puts his guitar back in the case. "In your defense, those were songs that never got a lot of air play, but they're some of my favorites."

I hope he's not disappointed in my lack of song knowledge. I'm sure the beautiful singer of that band he played with knows every title to every song and I wonder if that's a trait he's interested in. Music seems to be his life, so it wouldn't surprise me.

By now the sun is starting to set, the sky turning a blazing orange and pink, but I don't want to go home yet.

"Do you want to go for a drive?" I suggest.

There's no hesitation. He just nods yes, and I hope that means he's enjoying our time together as much as I am. He grabs his things, and we head toward my car. That's when I truly understand he doesn't have anything other than his guitar, his duffel bag and all it contains, and his dog. Naively, I had thought he had more belongings stashed away somewhere.

"Why don't you drive?" I offer when we reach my car. "I'm kind of a crappy driver."

He catches the keys I toss to him. "You don't mind?" He raises his eyebrow at me.

"No. I'd rather you drove." Not just because I'm sure he's a better driver than I am, but also because having a guy drive feels more date-like to me. That feeling amplifies when he opens the passenger-side door, waits for me to climb in, then closes it behind me.

"Where to?" he asks after he's run around the front of the car and climbed behind the wheel. I laugh as he moves the seat back to give his long legs room.

"Anywhere."

He smiles as he adjusts the rearview mirror. "Anywhere is my favorite place."

Anywhere turns out to be a random drive around town, past the street I live on without him even knowing it, and to a drive-in burger place. This time I let him pay without making a move for my wallet. We sit in the parking lot, eating burgers and fries and drinking thick vanilla malts. We take turns feeding Acorn a plain burger that the guy at the window was nice enough to make for us without the usual slathering of condiments and pickles.

"Do you need to be anywhere?" he asks as he pulls the car out of the parking lot.

"Nope. Nowhere."

It's odd having nowhere to go to be together. When Josh and I dated, we mostly hung out in his parents' finished basement or in his bedroom if they weren't home. He'd make us popcorn, and we'd watch the movies we'd rented, always laughing about how we wouldn't bring them back a week late this time. But they were always late and not rewound to the beginning, and we'd have to pay extra in fees. That was the extent of our worries as a young couple.

Evan drives as if he knows his way around very well, and I don't question it. Maybe he's walked every inch of this town, or maybe he's just so good at wandering aimlessly he can make it look natural. I don't care where we're going. My hand is in his, and he's singing along with the radio, turning to sing to me when there's a lyric about love or wanting someone, and it makes my heart almost beat out of my chest. He looks happy, free, and incredibly hot with the open window blowing his hair. For the first time, I wish I had a sports car because he would look so damn good driving a fast muscle car with his tattooed arm hanging out the window.

A quick shot of panic hits me when he turns down a dark road I've never driven before. To be honest, I'm not sure what town we're in. I've been so engrossed listening to his voice and just being with him that I stopped paying attention to our surroundings over an hour ago. Up ahead, I see nothing but total darkness, but as we drive farther, a few streetlamps appear. He stops the car just as the headlights reflect over the dark, shimmering water of a lake.

"Have you been here before?" I ask when he turns off the engine.

Nodding, he checks on Acorn in the back seat. "We're not far from the park. We just made a really big circle."

"Oh." I'm alarmed at my total lack of sense of direction.

He leans back against the headrest. "Thanks for letting me drive. It's been a long time."

"You're welcome. If you sing every time you drive, I may just let you chauffeur me everywhere," I tease.

"You like my singing that much?"

"I do, Blue. Your voice is like… chocolate."

He turns in his seat and looks at me like I'm crazy. "Chocolate?" he repeats with a laugh.

"Yes. It's all smooth and yummy."

He reaches across the car, grabs me, and pulls me playfully onto his lap.

"You finally called me Blue."

He takes my face in his hands and brings my mouth to his, kissing me until the shy smile fades from my lips. I fall into a euphoric daze again as his hands roam over my body, and he maneuvers me until I'm straddling him in the seat.

"I want you to drive now," he whispers against the soft sensitive spot of my throat.

"Oh… okay." I move to get off him, but his hands slide forward to cup my breasts.

"No." The metal of his tongue piercing is cold against my flesh as his mouth travels back up to my lips. "Drive *me*." He pulls me down harder against him as he whispers the words, and the hardness of his cock pressing against me through our jeans sparks an instant flash of heat between our bodies.

He stares up at me with his dark, brooding eyes as if he's daring me to stop him from unbuttoning my jeans, but I don't. Instead, I reach between us to unfasten his, and a sexy grin crosses his lips. His sensuality is contagious. With him, I feel sexy and beautiful rather than small and awkward. I let him push my jeans and panties down to my ankles, and I lift myself just enough for him to pull off one of my boots and slip one of my legs out of my clothes. Eyes still on mine, he leans the seat back and quickly pushes his pants down, pulling a single condom out of his pocket as he does so.

"For you," he says softly, holding the silver foil package between us.

I nod, watching him tear it open and then slip it over his shaft, and it seems like a shame to cover such a beautiful part of his body.

Taking my hand in his, he guides it to his cock, coaxing me to wrap my fingers around him. I grip him through the thin latex as he slips his hand between my thighs.

"You're so tight and juicy." His voice is ragged with deep breaths as his fingers caress and explore. "Come here." He grasps my waist with urgency, and he watches with hooded, possessive eyes as I slowly descend onto him.

Sudden, sharp pain accompanies the first few inches as his cock stretches me, but I bite my lip and take more, leaning my palms against his wide chest for leverage while he lifts and lowers me. My naked ass bumps against the leather steering wheel as I slowly ride him. Groaning, he wraps his arms around me and kisses me ferociously, our long hair in our faces and getting caught in our mouths.

We don't care.

Our bodies find a slow, deep, entrancing rhythm. We lose ourselves in every kiss and touch and find each other again. For the first time in my life, I don't feel out of place or disconnected. I feel beautiful and wanted. I feel—and I believe—that I belong right here with Evan and nowhere else in the world.

Maybe I'm crazy and this is just a crush that will fizzle and fade.

But the way my heart flutters in my chest and the way he holds my face and stares into my eyes like there's nothing else in the world to look at makes me believe we're going to be so much more.

I gasp when he moans and thrusts himself deeper and harder into me, and he moves his hand between us to stroke my clit. Within seconds, he's got my entire body quivering at his touch and completely under his control despite me being on top. I start to come just moments before he does, but we ride the height of the surge and shudder together, breathing heavy as our lips clash against each other, seeking and claiming more.

He smooths my hair back from my face and plants soft, warm kisses on my lips, down my throat, and over my chest until my breathing calms. I stay in his arms with absolutely no thoughts of running away from him—unlike the last time.

"You're so fuckin' perfect," he whispers between kisses, and I feel like I could soar to the moon.

"I'm not," I reply. "But you make me feel like I am."

"You are, baby. You are. And you better not disappear for a week again," he warns.

"I won't. I promise."

We separate and quietly pull our clothes back on. The inside of the car is steamy and smells of sex and smoke. I want to bottle the scent and sprinkle it on my pillows and bed sheets to linger in all night. My legs are still wobbly, and my sore insides sting when we walk Acorn in the grass around the lake, but I don't mind the lingering effects of being with him. Every movement is a reminder of him inside me, as close as close can be, and I want to emboss it all in my flesh.

After Acorn does his business, Evan drives us back to the park, which does turn out to be only fifteen minutes from the lake.

"How is it that you know this town better than I do, and I grew up here?" I joke as he turns off the headlights but leaves the car running.

"Because I wander, and you don't."

Hmm. I've never quite thought about it before, but he's right. I'm a creature of comfort and habit.

Usually. But not lately.

"I had fun today," I say, saving my non-wandering habits to analyze later.

"Yeah?" He gives my lips a quick kiss. "Me too. I'll see ya soon."

He's out of the car with his belongings and Acorn before I have a chance to say anything, and now I'm driving home all sorts of confused and unsettled. I feel like I was reading a book that ended abruptly, with the remainder of the pages missing.

I was hoping he'd want to see me tomorrow and at least let me know that, but he left without any solid indication that he ever wanted to see me again, other than as some girl who sits on a park bench and listens to his music.

My fingers grip the steering wheel my bare ass crack was shoved against just an hour or so ago. "See ya soon," is pretty general and vague and not a real plan in any way after having sex in a car. Especially if he enjoyed it.

This sucks.

Later, when I'm lying in bed with Archie, who is attempting to suffocate me by sitting on my chest, I use my mental microscope to analyze every word and every touch we shared today. I grab onto anything I can perceive as a sign he wants to see me again, and I form a little pile in my mind. On the very top of that pile are the words, *Don't disappear again.* Surely he wouldn't have said that if he planned on ditching me.

My boring life has unexpectedly become filled with an onslaught of excitement, sex in any place but a bed, and emotional stress. I'm overwhelmed, petrified, anxious, and falling head over heels in love.

CHAPTER SEVEN

PIPER

Monday morning, I'm half an hour late to work. I took a melatonin to help me sleep the night before, and even though Ditra suggested it, telling me it's all natural with no side effects, I struggled to wake up enough to make it to work on time. I guess having vivid dreams about things floating across my room and waking up with brain fog aren't considered side effects.

Two coffees, a nasty side-eye from my boss, ten phone calls, and a few hours of research later, it's lunchtime and I'm walking nervously to the park. How did what used to be my daily hour of peace and calm become a mishmash of anxiety?

An irresistible guy with a guitar and an adorable dog showed up; that's how.

Bluesy rock music in the air tells me he's there before he comes into view, and I can't help but smile as I walk through the iron gates and see him sitting on a stool in his usual place. I'm sure the stool is much more comfortable than sitting on the ground, and I wonder where it came from. His eyes are closed and his body is swaying slowly and seductively as he plays. Watching him transports me to a private visual cinema of flashbacks of how his body moves and sways sans guitar.

I shake my head to clear those visions, which I shouldn't be having in the middle of the day, surrounded by strangers, just by merely looking at him. Minutes later, I almost choke on my spoonful of yogurt when the unusually long song ends, and he raises his head to look directly at me with a fierce hunger in his eyes like that of a wolf staring down its prey. He nods to the small crowd around him and then quickly packs up his things to come take a seat next to me.

"I liked that song," I say. I'm surprised he walked away from the small crowd. People were throwing more cash into his jar than I've ever seen them give. "I could tell it's one of yours."

He shoves up the sleeves of his sweatshirt and stretches his arms. "It's new. It's called 'Butterflies and Madness.'"

"I like it a lot. It was like a mix of everything you've ever played all at once. It sounded amazing."

His eyes light up at the compliments, and I'm enthralled with how the color of his eyes can change so quickly. "That's what I was going for. You've inspired me."

"Me?"

"You." He clicks his tongue piercing against his teeth, a habit I've noticed a few times, usually when he seems to be wrestling with a thought. "You didn't come see me yesterday."

My mental pile was right after all. "I didn't know if you wanted to see me. You didn't say anything—"

"Yeah, I'm not good with plans. I just kind of assume things will happen."

I laugh at his honesty. "That can make things a little confusing."

He grins and nods. "I know, babe."

I'm sure thousands of women are called babe on a daily basis, but to have it said to me in such a deep, sensual, caressing voice that makes my insides turn to mush is nothing short of amazing.

"I can't call you, Piper. I don't have a phone or even a fucking calendar. Most of the time, I'm not even sure what day it is. I can't take you to nice dinners or to movies or any of that fun shit. I'm working with limited options here."

My heart constricts, and emotion clogs up in a lump in my throat. "None of that matters to me."

He touches my cheek and turns my face toward him. "You sure about that?" A veil of sadness shrouds his blue eyes again, and I'm struck with the need to do anything to take it away.

"I'm positive."

He leans closer to me, and I think he's going to kiss me, but instead, he brushes his stubbly cheek against mine and nudges his lips against my ear. "Then bring your sweet ass here after work." His hoarse tone drips with raw sexual power, and I submit. A burst of sheer excitement courses through me, and I feel like, if someone were to cut me open right now, my veins would drip glitter and rainbows.

"Okay," I reply with a soft exhale. "I'll be here."

Here. There. Anywhere. None of it matters as long as I get to hear his voice, stare into those cobalt eyes, and feel his lips on mine.

For once, the afternoon at work goes by quickly. I call my mother from my desk to tell her I won't be home for dinner and then move my car from the office parking lot to a safe spot on the street. Leaving it at the office after hours would raise questions, and I don't want anyone poking around in my personal business.

I'm surprised to see Evan and Acorn waiting at the gates for me, one with a smile and one with a wagging tail. Blue takes my hand in his and looks up and down the street at the five o'clock traffic before talking.

"You mind if we go for a walk?" he asks.

I shake my head, and he puts his stuff in my car before he leads me down the street in the opposite direction from my office. We walk about four blocks until we reach a dead-end street with very few houses and zero traffic. As we approach the woodsy end of the road, I realize we're in the same spot where we had sex in the car the other night. He stops walking and gestures to the last house on the left, which is set back from the road, surrounded by trees.

"I love this house." He stares across the lawn affectionately. "There's just something about it."

The Tudor-style house he loves has clearly been abandoned for a long time. The stone and stucco are dirty with age and lack of care. The dark wood trim that probably once gave the home a very distinguished storybook feel is now hidden behind decaying leaves. The focal point of the house is definitely the arched wooden front door with its huge iron knocker and handle which is less than inviting given its surroundings. The grass is overgrown and riddled with weeds and twigs, and the windows have been boarded up with sheets of plywood. I try to see the house through Blue's eyes. Perhaps he sees beyond the ruin. I see that in Blue in so many ways. His unusual perspective isn't distracted by the dirt and decay that might turn others away. I feel like he sees beauty where others refuse to look.

"Let's take a look around back," he says, tugging my hand.

"Isn't this trespassing?" I ask in a hushed tone.

He laughs. "I'm a professional trespasser, Piper. It's what I do. Don't worry about it. No one is around."

True enough.

We follow the cracked driveway to a stone walkway that takes us to the backyard, which is surrounded by woods. There're no other houses for as far as I can see, except for the house to the left, which is almost a quarter mile away. A four-season porch is off the back of the house, with long-forgotten plants and a hopefully empty birdcage visible hanging in the window. In its time, I'm sure the porch must have been a beautiful place to sip tea and read.

"How sad such a beautiful house has been let go like this," I say.

"It happens a lot. Once a home, now a bunch of empty rooms with nothing but memories."

"I wish we could go inside. I'd love to see all the rooms and the decor and what they left behind."

"We can't go inside. But we *can* go in there."

Puzzled, I follow his gaze to a small toolshed in the far corner of the yard.

I blink at the dilapidated building. "In there?"

"Yeah. Come on." He whistles for Acorn, who has wandered off into the weeds. The dog perks up his ears and trots over to follow us.

I worry about ticks and snakes as we walk through the high grass, but Evan seems oblivious to those concerns. When we reach the shed, he lifts the rusted metal latch and swings the wooden door open with a creak. I hold his hand and stay behind him. As he goes inside, he pulls me in with him.

Even though the sun is starting to set, there's still enough light for us to see our surroundings, although there's not much to see. A few old yard tools hang on one wall, and some old buckets and paint cans are piled in the corner. The wooden floor is dusty beneath our feet, and cobwebs lace random places over the walls and in the corners of the small window. I'm pretty sure we're standing in bug central, and I'm petrified of spiders or any other creepy crawly.

I grip his hand tighter and wonder why on earth he wanted to come in here. There's nothing of value or use at all.

"It's starting to get dark outside," I hint, but he continues to look around, clicking his piercing as he does so.

"I have a lantern," he says absently, obviously forgetting his bag is back in my car.

"Are you looking for something?"

"No. I'm looking for some*where*."

I scrunch my eyebrows together. "What do you mean?"

"I think I'm going to stay here."

His answer only heightens the state of confusion I'm already in.

"Stay here?" I repeat. "As in live here?"

"I don't live anywhere, Piper. But I could sleep here instead of under the bridge. It'll keep me out of the rain and wind."

I blink, overwhelmed with the wave of facts that keep getting buried under the feelings I have for him. He's homeless. And he's honestly serious about moving into an old toolshed in the yard of an abandoned house. There's no apartment hunting with this guy. Nope. He's going to live in this dirty shed. Whether he considers it living here or not, that's what this boils down to.

"And we'd have a place to hang out together and be alone," he adds, squeezing my hand so tight his metal rings dig into my fingers.

I sway a bit as my gut lurches with a new realization. This place, this shed, will ultimately become a love nest if I want to continue to see him.

There will be no couch or bed.

No TV and VCR to watch movies.

No kitchen to keep snacks in.

No bathroom.

"It'll be nice," he continues. "I bet there's lots of crickets chirping at night and the sound of the leaves blowing in the trees. This thing has a tin roof. Do you know how fuckin' cool that'll sound when it rains?"

The organic excitement in his voice is like that of a child's—so pure and honest that I'm carried along to that place with him.

"It's perfect," I say softly.

He kisses the top of my head and puts his arm around me. "It is."

As we walk back to my car, he asks questions about my job, showing genuine interest in my life, and I hope he's forgotten about his idea of staying in the shed. When we finally reach my car, he takes his things, and when he kisses me on the street, I wish I had one of those minivans with a fold-out bed in the back and curtains over the windows. I would let him and Acorn live in it, and he wouldn't have to look for a *somewhere* anymore. Maybe he'd finally want to stop wandering and walking.

"I have something for you," he says with his hands still on my waist. "It's just something I made when I couldn't sleep and was thinking about you."

"You were thinking about me?"

He kneels and opens his duffel bag. "I think about you a lot. Why does that surprise you?"

"I don't know. No one has ever told me they were thinking about me before. I thought I was just… un-think-about-able."

He studies my face as he stands. "That's fucked up."

He grabs my hand, and I watch as he wraps a bracelet around my wrist and clasps it. I inspect the bracelet under the streetlight, running my finger lightly over the colored beads strung on a thin, black leather cord. I marvel at one tiny bead shaped and painted like a ladybug.

"You made this? For me?" My voice cracks, and I bite my lower lip to keep it from quivering.

"Yeah. I know it's not much. I just wanted to give you something."

"I love it. The ladybug is adorable."

"I wanted you to have a reminder. You can't piss off the ladybug and defy the love myth."

I stand on my tiptoes and throw my arms around his neck, hugging him tight. "I'm never going to take it off."

"Someday you will." He pulls away and rakes his hand through his hair. "Or someday I'll fuck up and you'll throw it at me."

He's wrong. I could never be mad at him, and I'm never taking the bracelet off.

Two days later, I'm invited over to the shed by way of another note I find on my car seat when I'm leaving the office. I guess it's a good thing I always forget to lock my car, and I probably never will again now that I know he'll leave me notes.

Due to the nonstop rain, I haven't seen him since the night he gave me the bracelet. Not being able to see him or talk to him was definitely starting to upset me. But the rain has stopped, and now I have a note telling me he misses me and wants to see me. It makes me happy enough to overlook the shed part.

Before going to see him, I drive across town to my house to change into comfy stretchy jeans and a sweatshirt, unsure of what else to wear on a shed date. While I'm there, I eat a peanut butter and jelly sandwich, then fill Archie's dishes and grab two cans of soda and an unopened bag of chips to bring with me. I know he doesn't like me bringing him things, but I can't change who I am, and I'm a person who likes to give to others. I'm also a person who likes snacks. If we're going to be sitting around talking, then we should have cold drinks and munchy food. Or maybe this is just my attempt to try to sprinkle some kind of normalcy into this unconventional situation.

When I pull up in front of the abandoned house at the end of the dark street, I can't get out of my car. The invisible hands of common sense and logic grip me, trying to force me to spin the car around and go back home.

I almost do.

But then I see him walking down the driveway toward me, a lit cigarette hanging out of his mouth, untied boots thudding on the asphalt with that sexy, confident walk.

And then that smile. It's that magical smile that's sexy as hell one minute and adorable the next that's going to be my undoing.

He opens my car door and leans his arm on the roof as he peers in at me. "You coming out of there?"

I take my keys out of the ignition, grab the bag of snacks, and climb out of the car. He steps back just far enough to pull me forward to close the door behind me. Then he backs me up against the side of the car. He takes the cigarette out of his mouth with his thumb and forefinger and turns his head to the side to blow out a cloud of smoke.

"Thought you forgot about me." Today, his voice is deeper and scratchier. I wonder if he's getting sick or if he's been singing in a smoky bar downtown instead of just playing guitar.

"How could I forget you? It's been raining, that's all."

He moves forward until his body touches mine. "Maybe that's when I want to see you the most."

"When it's raining?"

He moves his hand hesitantly down my arm. "As much as I love the sound of the rain, the moody gray clouds and the rainbows, the storms trap me. I can't stand the thunder and lightning and all the wind. That's when I need you the most. You're like my own little sunbeam." A weak smile touches his lips. "You chase the storm away."

I stare up into his eyes and see my first glimpse of the other side of Blue. But I'm so entranced with his lyrical words and being considered a sunbeam that I don't hear what he's saying.

"Then I guess I better find my umbrella," I say with a smile. "And next time it rains, I'll come find you."

His response is a sizzling kiss that nearly melts me into the car door. "C'mon. Let's go inside."

The way he says it makes me think he's somehow gotten into the abandoned house, but as I follow him up the driveway, he passes the walkway leading to the front door and leads me to the backyard. He holds my hand as we walk through the wet weeds toward the shed. A dim orange glow illuminates the small window, and I assume he must have his lantern on inside. The door of the shed is open a crack, and Acorn pokes his nose out when he hears us approaching.

"Hi, little guy," I say as we step inside, and he immediately starts wagging his tail and bouncing on his front paws.

"I think he likes it here," Evan says.

I stand near the door and peer around the small, dim space. I'm afraid if I move, I'll walk right into a spider web. A sleeping bag is on the floor under the window, and Acorn's dishes are on the other side of the room, next to Evan's guitar case.

"We can sit on the sleeping bag." He moves the lantern from the middle of the floor to one of the corners. "Or we can sit on these old lawn chairs I found. I just have to clean them off."

"Um...." I gnaw my lower lip and try to fight off all the phobias that are engulfing me.

"What's wrong?"

The breath I've been holding whooshes from my lungs. "It's just a little scary in here."

"Scary how? What are you scared of?"

"Spiders, mostly. And bats."

"The only thing in here that can hurt you is me."

A shiver creeps down my spine. "Would you?" I whisper. "Hurt me?"

He backs me up against the cobweb-strewn wall and leans his arms on either side of my head, trapping me.

"I don't want to, but I will. And you'll keep letting me." He brushes his lips across mine. "You falling in love with me will destroy us both."

My heart pounds so hard I'm certain he can feel it against his own chest.

I force out my next question. "You think I'm falling in love with you?"

"Why else would you be here?"

I tremble as he grabs my waist and presses his hard body against mine. I want to deny his accusation, but his lips on mine stop the lies from spilling from my mouth. I'm pinned like a butterfly specimen, splayed open with no way to hide, vulnerable to his physical and emotional scrutiny.

"I know you want me, Piper." He slides a gentle hand along the curve of my hip, then down over the back pocket of my jeans. He cups my ass cheek in his hand and squeezes hard—like he's claiming ownership. "And I know you're falling in love with me."

"Blue…." I say his name like what he's saying can't possibly be true.

"Don't worry, baby. I think I'm falling in love with you too."

He lifts me off the floor in a single motion that seems effortless. I wrap my legs around his waist and my arms around his neck and hold on tight while he carries me to the other side of the room, releasing my hold on him only when he lowers me onto the thin sleeping bag.

"And…." His eyes darken for a moment and it fills me with that flash of worry that he's got one foot ready to run if I get too close. He's scared. Maybe as much as I am. "… it's scaring the fucking hell out of me."

He climbs between my parted legs and lowers his mouth onto mine, kissing me in that crazy, desperate way he does, like there's something inside me he needs and can't find.

When I can't breathe anymore, I pull away. His long hair falls into my face as I stare up into his eyes. The thin sleeping bag offers no protection from the wooden floor, and I shift slightly beneath his weight while I gather my thoughts.

"We can be scared together," I whisper reassuringly, trying to convince both of us that it'll be okay. Although honestly, I'm not sure anything can extinguish the fear his eyes convey.

He nods, his eyes locked onto mine, and slowly rubs his thumb across my bottom lip. The shaking of his hand is like a vise around my heart, and it clenches and explodes into millions of little pieces aching with love and protectiveness over him.

"Have you been in love before?" I ask softly. Did she hurt him? Was she the reason he left his home? Did she kick him out?

It takes him a few moments to answer, and he uses those moments to slowly remove my clothes while I use those moments to hope his answer is no.

He trails a finger from my stomach all the way up between my breasts, and my nipples harden into peaks from the feather-light, tickling touch.

"I have," he finally answers, gently cupping my breasts and pressing his palm against the sensitive tips. "Been hopelessly in love."

Jealousy creeps in like a monster, distracting me from the exquisite sensation of his warm hands on my body. "What happened with her?"

He bends down and circles my breast with his tongue, flicking his piercing over my aching nipple. The cool silkiness of his hair fans out over my skin.

"It wasn't a woman. I was in love with drugs."

The truth is unexpected but equally devastating.

He kisses a trail along my throat, his tongue teasing me while he palms my breast. "And now I'm in love with music and freedom. And a little sweet, sexy chick with a funky name."

He flashes me his irresistible, crooked grin. I feel immediately grateful that his shaky hands have stilled and in place of the sadness in his eyes, I now see playfulness. Smiling, I reach up and touch the feather hanging from his ear.

"Tell me about this. Something as unique as this must have a story, right?"

"It does."

He sits up and leans against the wall, and I rest my head on his lap as he lights up a cigarette. Acorn curls up on the sleeping bag next to us and rests his chin on an old, ratty stuffed penguin. I wish I knew what Acorn's backstory is and if he sleeps on the toy because he's afraid someone will take it away or if it gives him comfort. Probably both.

"I have this aunt who rescues birds," Evan explains. "She must have at least a hundred birds of all different species. She has three that are over fifty years old."

"Wow. I didn't know a bird could live that long."

He nods and exhales. "Some do. They often outlive their owners. That's how she got them. The relatives of the deceased didn't want them."

"That's so sad."

"It is. My aunt lives in an old house with a massive screened porch, and the birds are everywhere. It's noisy as fuck, too. Some talk, some chirp and sing, some just squawk, but she loves them. When I was younger, I used to visit her and help her take care of them. Every night, I'd climb out the bedroom window and onto her roof and smoke to try to chill out from the bird noise in my head. Sometimes she'd come out there with me, and we'd look at the stars and wait for the birds to sleep."

"Were you two very close?"

"Yeah. She's my mom's sister, and I was closer to her than I ever was with my mom. When she was around." He runs his hand through his hair, pushing it off his face. "She had this one cool little blue bird. I'm not sure what kind of bird it was, but it was much smaller than a blue jay. It used to sit on my shoulder and chew on my hair, and it would fly right to me as soon as he saw me. He was my favorite for years, and when he passed away, she made me the earring out of a few of his feathers. She told me it would protect me and bring me peace." He smashes out his cigarette. "I'm still waiting for the peace part."

"It sounds like the bird really liked you."

He shrugs. "I think he just liked my hair and wanted to make some kind of epic nest."

I laugh. "You want to know what's funny? The first day I saw you, a little blue bird flew into my head right outside my office. It scared the heck out of me."

"Are you kidding? A bird flew into your head?"

"Yeah. Awkward stuff always happens to me. It's embarrassing. I'm like a weird loser."

"Hey." He kisses my temple. "You're not a loser. You're cute. And you're real."

"Real?" I repeat.

"Yeah. You're… you. You follow your heart, even though it's taken you to a fucked-up person like me. You don't pretend to be someone you're not. Even though you're kinda awkward, you're still the most beautiful chick I've ever met. Inside and out."

"Me?"

He lets out a deep laugh. "You repeat everything I say."

"Sorry. You just say things no one else has ever said to me."

"I might be the first to say them, but I won't be the last. Trust me."

I don't want to trust him on this. I want him to be the only guy to ever say words to me that make my heart and stomach jump around with excitement.

He turns and slowly crawls over me like a large jungle cat, pushing me down on my back as he moves. He studies me with an odd frown on his face and runs his hand down the length of my body, then up again to rest on my hip.

"Don't think about tomorrow, Piper. I can see it in your eyes, and it'll only drive you crazy."

I'm already crazy, though. I'm crazy about him, and I'm crazy for letting him fuck me here on an old, musty sleeping bag next to his dog and a stuffed penguin missing an eye, in a toolshed that smells like gasoline and fertilizer.

The thing about being crazy is that it can slowly become normal before you even realize it.

CHAPTER EIGHT

PIPER

Last night, there was a message from Dr. Green on my answering machine, asking me to call her back at my earliest convenience. She left the message three days ago, but I had no idea that little red, flashing four on my machine indicated an important message. I assumed the four messages were all from Ditra, and I refused to listen to them because I knew she was beyond the joking stage about me not telling her all the details about my current life, and she had moved into the worried and demanding phase.

In a few days I'll call Ditra and share everything with her. But first I need to call Dr. Green and find out what my test results are.

Even though I don't have a coworker immediately within listening distance of my desk, I wait until they all leave for lunch before I call the doctor's office back.

"Hi, this is Piper Karel. I'm returning Dr. Green's call," I tell the receptionist.

"One moment, please. I'll connect you."

My palm is sweaty against the plastic phone as I listen to hold music that should be soothing but isn't. The only music that soothes me now is Blue's.

I'm sure the doctor is going to give me the worst news of my life once this moment of hold ends. We all know if she had good news, she would have left a simple message on my answering machine at home. She wouldn't be torturing me by making me call her back.

Finally, the hold music is cut off.

"Piper, it's Dr. Green. How are you?"

"I'm fine," I reply, wondering if she expected me to be feeling sick, itchy, and feverish by now. Or maybe suffering with morning sickness.

"Great. I wanted to tell you that all your test results came back negative."

My mouth falls open in surprise and I tap the volume button on the base of the desk phone to make sure I'm hearing her properly. "Are you sure?"

"Yes. Is anything going on to make you question the results?"

"No… not at all. I've just been worried."

"I know, and that's why I wanted to talk to you personally to put your mind at ease."

"Thank you. I appreciate that."

"As we discussed during your appointment, if you are going to be sexually active with a partner you're not feeling overly safe with, then I suggest you use condoms in conjunction with the birth control pill. I'd like to see you in another three months for a checkup and to run the tests again."

More tests. That means something could still be dormant inside me, waiting to sprout up at the most inopportune time.

Gulping, I twist around to make sure I'm still alone. "Do you think that's necessary?"

"Given the information you revealed during your appointment, yes, I really do. It's your choice, of course."

Her words paint a much prettier picture than the reality of what happened during my appointment. The reveal of information was me having a sobbing, hysterical meltdown with my feet in stirrups and my ass at the edge of a paper-lined exam table. Dr. Green and her nurse were both incredibly sweet and comforting during the exam as I rambled on tearfully about Evan and the bridge and the bending over and the dick sucking. They listened to me with empathetic, nonjudgmental smiles. The nurse held my hand as I was spread, scraped, and poked, then gave me a paper cup of ice water and a box of tissues. When I had finally calmed down enough to get dressed, I was given a small plastic bag filled with condom samples and pamphlets about safe sex.

"Well, yeah, but I've talked to my boyfriend since then, and he hasn't had as many partners as I originally thought."

The word boyfriend feels foreign on my tongue, as if I'm speaking another language or perhaps telling a lie.

"That's good to hear. I still highly recommend practicing safe sex at all times and a checkup in three months. You can call back to schedule. And if you have any questions in the meantime, please don't hesitate to call me or make an appointment to come see me, all right?"

"I definitely will."

Relief overpowers me when I hang up the phone, and it's so overwhelming I actually feel dizzy and sick to my stomach. I grab my water bottle and take a few sips between deep breaths.

"What's wrong?" Melissa asks, appearing suddenly and dumping a pile of file folders onto my desk. "These are from Anne in accounting."

"I'm fine."

"You look weird."

Ignoring her, I slide the files closer so I can begin to organize them by priority. Melissa can't take a hint, though, and continues to stare at me until I look back up at her questioningly.

"You know what's odd, Piper? I could have sworn I saw you the other night, making out with that hippy homeless guy that's always hanging around downtown, begging for money."

My jaw clenches as I narrow my eyes at this girl who loves to antagonize me. I knew someday this was bound to happen. Evan and I haven't exactly always been discrete about public displays of affection.

"Don't you have work to do, Melissa?"

"Aren't you even going to deny it?"

That's when it truly hits me like a brick wall. I'm in love with Evan, and I don't want to hide or deny it. I refuse to live a lie or cover up my feelings for him just to satisfy other people or to avoid being judged by them.

Love isn't dictated by what a person does for work or where they live.

"Why should I deny it? He's sweet, incredibly talented, and hot as hell."

"He's *homeless*, Piper. Are you fucking serious?"

"I am," I admit casually. "By the way, how's your fiancé? Is he still unemployed?"

Melissa makes a disgusted face, and I fear she's going to come right over the top of my desk and murder me here on the spot.

"You're a bitch," she seethes. "No wonder you can only get a homeless guy to date you. Nobody else would ever want you."

I feel guilty as she stomps away in the direction of her cubicle with tears in her eyes, but she instigated me. Saying hurtful words to someone isn't something I enjoy at all, but as my mom is always telling me, I have to fight back sometimes so people don't walk all over me. It's not my fault Melissa is a rude, judgmental bitch who constantly goes out of her way to make me feel bad, so maybe she deserves a jobless fiancé.

❧

Blue usually hears my car pull up in front of the abandoned house every night and waits for me at the shed door, but today when I get there, he's not standing at the door. Instead, he's sitting on the floor with his guitar, surrounded by a notebook and scraps of paper. He's so immersed in scribbling madly with a black crayon that he doesn't even look up at me.

"Blue?" I say softly.

Without acknowledging me, he rubs his hand across his forehead and plays a few notes, then shakes his head, starts over, shakes his head again, plays a few notes, then bangs his hand on the body of the guitar.

"Fuck!" he yells, reaching for the pack of cigarettes lying next to him. I glance over at Acorn, who's curled up in the fleece dog bed I bought for him earlier in the week. He was so happy when I gave it to him he wagged his tail and spun around in circles for about fifteen minutes before snuggling into the bed with his cherished penguin.

"Evan." I take a few steps closer to him. "Are you okay?"

He takes a deep drag on the cigarette and blows smoke up over his head. His eyes are wild, bloodshot with exhaustion, his expression tortured. The handsome smile I love is nowhere to be seen.

"Do I look fucking okay?" He grabs a bottle of vodka from beside him that I somehow didn't see until now and takes a gulp of it before slamming it back down and picking up the crayon to write more on the tattered notepaper.

My heart sinks like a two-ton rock into my gut. "You're drinking?"

I kneel in front of him and touch his hand, but he yanks it away as if I burned him.

"I'm trying to write, and I can't fucking get it. It's all a mess." Eyes darting across the page, he shakes his head in frustration and crumples the paper into a ball and tosses it a few feet away with the others.

"It's okay," I say softly. "Maybe you just need to take a break for a few minutes."

His lip curls up in anger. "I don't need a break. I need to fucking get this song right."

"It sounds good, from what I heard," I say, and that's the truth. I didn't hear anything wrong at all with the piece he was playing. It sounded just as awesome as all his other songs.

The face he makes is one of complete disbelief and repulsion. "Don't pacify me. Are you deaf? It's pure shit. It's making my fucking ears bleed."

I want to tell him how wrong he is, but it's obvious he's too far down into the tunnel of his own head to listen to any sort of logic, reason, or honest feedback from me. I don't understand why this particular song has him so stressed out. I don't think anyone expects it to sound a specific way.

My worry for him heightens as he presses his fingers into his temples, screws his beautiful eyes shut, then strums a myriad of beautiful notes in tune to the nodding of his head, then mumbles something I can't understand to himself. Sighing, he scribbles some more onto his paper and repeats the process all over again.

It slowly sinks in as I watch him. *He* expects it to be a certain way. He must be suffering from a self-imposed artist vision of perfection that's got him all wound up.

When he goes for the vodka again, I reach out and grab the bottle from his hand just before it reaches his lips.

"Evan… I don't think you should be drinking this. You told me you had problems with alcohol in the past."

He glares at me, eyes flickering with flames of anger and defiance. "I told you a lot of things." He yanks the bottle from my hand, and the liquid sloshes around inside. "Don't get all AA with me, Piper. Leave me alone or just get the hell out of here. Please."

The venomous tone and nasty words slice through the comforting smile I had forced onto my face, and I slowly rise to my feet, hoping with all hope an apology will quickly chase away the hurt.

"Fine." My voice shakes with the start of tears when I'm met with deafening silence. "I'll leave."

Chewing my thumbnail, I wait for him to look up at me, to ask me not to leave, to pull me down onto the sleeping bag and kiss me senseless, but he's completely submerged in the song and whatever notes or lyrics he's fighting a battle with.

"Are you doing drugs?"

The muscles of his narrow jaw tighten, and his tongue sweeps across his lips as he lifts his head to look at me. "No, I'm not. But thanks for the vote of confidence."

"Evan, that's not wha—"

"Thought you were leaving." He turns his attention back to the notepaper, making his feelings very clear.

I grab my purse that's hanging from one of the hooks that once held a rake, leaving the bag of snacks for him and Acorn on top of the wooden crate we use as a table. I'm still expecting him to stop me when I walk through the door, and I'm sobbing big wet tears and gulping breaths by the time I get into my car and drive away. I swipe my hand across my eyes and peer into the rearview mirror, but the street is still dark and vacant.

Just like Evan's eyes were tonight.

I toss and turn all night, mad at myself for not trying harder to talk to Evan. In hindsight, I should have handled his bad mood better, been more supportive and less judgy. And now I can't call him and he can't call me to talk it over, and I can't just drive back over there in the middle of the night.

Staring up at my ceiling fan spinning round and round, similar to the carousel of my mind, I wonder if he's still agonizing over the song. I wonder if he's drunk. I wonder if he wishes he was on drugs.

I wonder if he regrets not stopping me from leaving as much as I wish I hadn't left.

The awkwardness of that night and the unconventional inability to call him to find out if he's okay and to figure out if *we're* okay keeps me from going back to see him for days. I have no idea what kind of state he could be in or if he even wants to see me again.

On the third day, I'd possibly give a kidney to find a note in my car, but I find something even better—him. At first, I think I must be hallucinating as I walk across the office parking lot toward my car. I blink at the vision of him leaning against the hood, wearing a black sweater and leather jacket I've never seen on him before. His long hair blowing away from his face in the autumn breeze makes him look like an edgy model on the cover of a rock magazine, exuding confidence and dripping sensuality. When his face lights up with a smile, all my doubts fade away, and I know we're okay. I know *he's* okay.

"Sorry about the other night," he says when I'm close enough for him to pull me into his arms. "I was having a bad day."

"I'm sorry, too."

"Do you have any plans?" he asks.

"Nope."

"I do." He flashes me a cocky grin and takes my car keys from my hand.

"I guess you're driving?" I tease, going up on my toes to kiss his cheek.

He slaps my ass playfully. "Get in."

I'm excited when he drives down Main Street, away from town, and turns onto a favorite road of mine that's home to old farmhouses that still raise horses, cows, and chickens. Many of them have farm stands set up on the side of the road.

"Come over here and kiss me." With just a few words, he's got my heart racing and my mood soaring.

Smiling, I lean across the seat and quickly press my lips to his. Before I can lean back, he touches my leg just below the hem of my skirt.

"You're wearing new lipstick."

I love that he notices little things like this. "It's called Raspberry Razzle Dazzle. I mostly bought it for the name, but now I kinda like the color."

The callus on his finger snags on my black stockings as he inches his hand farther under my skirt.

"I want your lips on me." He glances at me, then back to the road. "I want you to suck me."

"Now?"

I watch in shock as he unbuttons his jeans then pulls the zipper down, using his knee to keep the car straight on the road. My eyes take in the thick bulge straining against his faded black boxers.

"Isn't this dangerous?" I ask as I turn my body toward him.

"Unless a cow jumps in front of us or you bite me, we're fine, babe." He grasps my thigh and pulls me closer. "C'mon, beautiful."

Throwing caution out the window, I push his jeans and boxers down just far enough for me to grab his hard cock and bow my head between him and the steering wheel. The moment I take him into my mouth, he moans and slides his free hand all the way up my skirt. After he rips through my thin nylon stockings, the burst of cool air between my legs is quickly followed by the warmth of his hand as he moves his fingers between my lips.

I suck him harder as he thrusts a finger inside me, and I hope he doesn't get distracted enough to crash the car. I don't want to be found dead in a mangled mess with my head wedged into the steering wheel and a cock in my mouth. My parents would be horrified. Ditra would be impressed, though.

His cock grows harder and hotter, pulsing against my tongue, and the thrust of his hips toward my face sends waves of erotic excitement through me. Nothing turns me on more than his moans and sighs, his dirty talk, and the way his body reacts to my touch. As I wrap my lips tighter around his shaft, he pushes two fingers into me and rubs his thumb against my clit, touching it with just the perfect amount of pressure. I drag my lips and tongue up to the tip of his cock. He lets go of the steering wheel to fist my hair and pushes me back down, holding me there with his cock rammed against the back of my throat, followed by spurts of hot cum.

Still holding my hair, he pulls my head up and kisses me before letting me fall back onto the passenger seat. I'm still trying to catch my breath as I kick off my shoes and wiggle out of my ruined stockings. Then I pull my skirt back down and try to compose myself.

"I don't know how to love you, Piper," he says roughly. "But I know I love you a little more every day."

I turn to look at him with tears brimming in my eyes because his words are masked with so much sadness and regret, my heart hurts.

"Love doesn't have rules, Blue. The way you love me is perfect. And I love you. That's all that matters."

The click of his tongue piercing against his teeth is his only response, and that's okay. Our love may be unexpected and flawed, but it's ours. That's all that matters.

What I see before me sucks the breath right out of my lungs. We hardly spoke on the way back into town, other than deciding on what to get at the drive-thru burger place.

He insisted I enter the shed first, and he came in slowly and nervously behind me.

Flameless electric candles in assorted sizes are placed around the sleeping bag and a few on the small wooden shelf nailed into the wall. There's even two small ones placed by Acorn's bed. A glass vase in the corner sprouts six red silk roses. The tiny space glows warm amber, and if I let my eyes blur, the space resembles a cozy rustic cabin bedroom in the mountains. Speechless, I look over at him. He watches me, drinking in my reaction.

"It's beautiful," I say wistfully.

He steps toward me and takes my hands in his, leaning down to kiss the top of my head. "I wanted to give you the first time you didn't get. Something romantic you can remember."

I ignore the fact that he preceded this romantic gesture by asking me to blow him while he was driving my car, a cigarette dangling from his mouth, and a dog in the back seat. It's the thought that counts, right?

"This is so sweet," I say. "Where did you get all this?"

"At the dollar store. I didn't want to leave real candles burning in here. I don't want to burn the fuckin' place down."

I laugh and nod. "I like them. We can keep them."

"I thought maybe you could take one home with you and put it by your bed. So you know I'm thinking about you."

I tighten my hands around his. "I'd love that."

He slips his fingers from mine and slowly pulls my blouse over my head, laying it on the floor before circling my waist with his hands. "You…" he says, leaning down to kiss my neck. "You don't know how you wreck me."

My eyes close and my head falls back in bliss as he sucks the flesh of my neck between his lips and gently bites.

"My head is fucked with you. Every note, every word I write is haunted by you…" He unclasps my bra and whisks it off to cup my breasts in his palms. "All I can hear is your voice. All I see is your eyes. All I can feel is your body…"

His lips leave my neck and come down on my mouth, hard at first, then gradually softer. I can tell he's struggling to be slow and gentle as his breathing grows ragged and deep.

"I'm sorry," I whisper against his lips.

"Don't be. I need it. I need *you*."

Fueled by his words, I push his leather jacket from his shoulders. It falls with a thud to the floor when he shrugs it off. The new black cable-knit sweater comes off him next, and I run my hands up his toned, inked torso, reveling in how beautiful every inch of him is. He helps me step out of my high heels and skirt, and I briefly recall my torn stockings on the floor of my car.

He backs us up to the sleeping bag as we kiss. He kneels in front of me and my body trembles when he kisses a path from an amazingly sensitive spot behind my knee all the way up to my inner thigh. I grab his head in surprise when he lifts my leg over his shoulder and starts to devour my pussy with his lips and tongue. I clench at his long hair as he fucks me with his mouth and flicks the metal piercing over my clit. Just as I'm on the verge of climaxing, he pulls his mouth away and looks up at me with a lusty grin.

"You don't get to come yet," he scolds in a raspy voice. "I want this little pussy to come all over my cock."

I almost have an orgasm just hearing him talk dirty to me, and those burning eyes of his aren't helping. I run my fingers through his hair and tighten my leg around him.

"Tell me what you want, Piper."

"Just you," I reply, pulling him closer. "Any way I can have you."

Kisses all over my stomach and breasts lull and excite me, my body humming with desire and love and feelings I have no way to describe.

He gently pushes me down on my back and then kneels between my legs, riveting his eyes onto mine as he takes his jeans and boots off. He moves slowly, deliberately teasing—and I love every second of it. Tattoos illustrate almost every inch of his rock-hard body like a map of dreams and visions coming to life. Jet-black hair falls in silky waves down his chest, and I ache to run my fingers through it and feel it brush against my skin. I reach for him eagerly as he leans his arms on the sleeping bag on either side of my head, and I run my hands up the length of his spine to clasp my hands behind his neck.

"Always feels like I'm crushing you." He strokes his finger across my cheek.

"You're not going to crush me. I like you on top of me."

Taking a deep breath, he brings his face closer and kisses the tip of my nose. "I like being on top of you. And in you. I just don't want to hurt you."

Smiling, I wrap one of my legs around his and rub my foot languidly up and down his leg.

"You're not hurting me."

"I don't just mean like this."

A feeling of doom creeps into my gut, giving me emotional whiplash with the feelings of love and desire I was lost in just mere seconds ago.

I swallow hard before answering. "Then don't." That seems easy to me. If you don't want to hurt someone, then just don't let it happen.

"Things with you are so easy but so fuckin' hard, Piper."

"I don't really know what that means."

"Shh… Let's not talk."

"You scare me sometimes. I'm always afraid I'm going to wake up tomorrow and you'll be gone."

"I promise to give you as many tomorrows as I possibly can."

"You promise?" I need to hear him say it again because I want all the tomorrows forever.

"Promise." His lips touch mine and then he kisses his way down my torso. "Spread your legs, baby," he says when he reaches my belly button.

I open my legs as wide as I can, and he bows his head between my thighs. Warm breath and full lips tease mine in the most erotic kiss imaginable. Sighing with pure content, my back arches as his tongue glides slowly through my slit, from ass to clit then back again. He grasps my outer thighs in his hands to spread me even wider for him, making me moan and grab fistfuls of his hair as he fucks me wildly with his tongue. I nearly lose my mind when he inches up to suck on my pulsing clit, and the hard metal of his tongue piercing heightens the sensation. Shudders quake through my body, and he holds my legs apart, not allowing me to squeeze my thighs around his head to quell the need building in me.

"Blue...."

With lightning-fast speed, he moves up and thrusts his cock balls-deep into my pussy right as I'm mid-orgasm. A cry escapes me, and I wrap my arms and legs tight around his sweaty body, grinding my hips against his as I continue to shudder uncontrollably. Suffocating me with his wet, musky mouth and tongue, he ignores all my gasps and whimpers as he pummels me slow and deep.

I gulp his breath into me and rake my nails down the flesh of his back, enraptured with his giving and taking control over my body. When my breathing has calmed, he turns us onto our sides with his cock still buried inside me and lifts my leg over his hip. He caresses the back of my thigh and squeezes my ass, pulling me against him as he rocks into me. He cups my neck and brings my lips to his again, and we kiss hungrily as the ecstasy starts to build all over again. The angle of his cock in this position feels amazing and has me dripping over him. As our bodies slam into each other, he moves his hand down between my ass cheeks to finger my hole alongside his dick, then slides it back up to press his slick finger into my ass. I squirm in surprise, but he holds me firmly in place.

"Don't move," his deep voice whispers, and he slowly slides his finger into me, stretching the tight flesh.

Hushing and soothing me with his lips, he begins to thrust his finger and cock into me simultaneously. The mix of sensations is erotically intoxicating and has my entire body in a frenzy, aching for more despite the slight invasive pain. When I moan with a mix of frustration and pleasure, he growls in response and sinks deeper and faster into me, catapulting us both into orgasm. I watch him as he comes, and I'm caught up in the way his eyes close and his full lips part as he groans and how his wild hair sticks to his forehead. He's hot as hell, and I've never met a man more breathtaking.

Or heartbreaking.

I used to be in bed every weekend night by eleven. Sometimes midnight if Courtney and I watched a movie together or if I was reading a really good book and kept reading just one more chapter. Since I've started seeing Blue, I stay with him until I can barely stay awake, and then I drive home, sometimes at two or three in the morning.

It's 2:45 when I quietly creep down to my apartment after spending the night with Blue and having our romantic first-time sex do-over. I highly doubt most first-time sex experiences include having a finger in one hole and a cock in the other, but everything with Blue is unique and out of the ordinary, and that's one of the things I really love about him.

"Where have you been?" I jump and do an insane ninja-style flailing of arms, dropping my purse and my flameless candle in the process. I reach for the light switch in the dark and see Ditra sprawled out on my bed.

"What are you doing here?" I demand. "You scared the shit out of me. And how did you get in here?"

"Courtney let me in. Hours ago, I might add." She sits up and scrutinizes me. "You look like you just got your brains fucked out."

Sitting on the edge of the bed, I make a face at her and kick off my shoes. "How can you tell? And I'm not saying I did. I just want to know what kind of visual evidence a good fuck leaves?"

"Well, smeared lipstick for one. Red and puffy lips. Messy hair. Dazed orgasm eyes."

"Dazed orgasm eyes?" I repeat, laughing. "What the hell is that?"

"It's kind of how people look when they're stoned, only it's an orgasm high. Or low."

I toss a throw pillow at her. "You're insane, you know that?"

"Maybe. But I'm right, aren't I?"

With a sigh, I stand and quickly change into yoga pants and a faded T-shirt.

"Fine. Yes. We had sex. Are you happy now?"

"I already knew you did. I know you, Piper."

I pile some pillows against the headboard and settle myself next to her. I'd like to say I'm surprised she's cornered me like this, but I'm not.

This is the type of friend Ditra is. Sometimes that's good, and sometimes it's annoying as hell.

"You've been avoiding me for weeks. Remember our weekly dinner? When's the last time that happened?"

"I'm sorry… I've just been really distracted."

"No shit. I understand how exciting it is to fall in love, but I'm worried about you. You've never just cut me off from your life before."

"I haven't cut you off," I protest, hating she feels that way. "I just needed to get my head together about things before I wanted to talk about it; that's all."

"I left you about a hundred messages."

"I know."

"I'm not leaving until you tell me what's going on. I'll sleep here if I have to. I fed your cat and cleaned his litter box, so don't think you can use that as an excuse to go off and avoid talking to me."

Shaking my head at her, I realize I don't even know what to say. I know she wants giddy girl talk like we used to have when we were sixteen. She wants me to reveal every detail about Evan and what we do together. In a lot of ways, I want to because I'm happy and excited and I want to tell her how amazing he is. But I can't do that without also telling her about some of my worries and fears, and those are the things she will hone in on and analyze the hell out of and want me to analyze right along with her. I'm not ready to analyze. And then, of course, there's Evan's living situation.

"Piper? Talk to me. You're gnawing on your lip like a rabid dog. That means you're confused."

"I'm not confused… Okay, maybe I am a little bit."

"Would you just talk to me? I'm your best friend. I know I'm a pain in the ass, but I love you. You know that, right?"

I smile at her. "Of course I do. And I love you, too."

She climbs off the bed. "I'm going to go make us some tea. When I get back, let's talk, okay? You're just going to spit it all out."

"All right. While you're doing that, I'm going to use the bathroom and wash up a little."

Thankfully, she doesn't make any comments about me wanting to clean myself up, and ten minutes later, we're back in my bedroom. Archie prances around the bed and puts his butt in our faces.

"Is it that guy who was at the bar that night? What was his name? Red? Blue?"

I grin at her as I sip some of the warm, sweet tea. "Blue. His real name is Evan."

"I was surprised. He's not the type of guy you usually go for. Don't get me wrong, he's wicked hot. I mean… those eyes and the hair and the tats. Holy shit."

"Trust me. I know."

"Where'd you two meet?"

"At the park by my office. I go there every day during my lunch break to read."

"Oh. Does he work near there, too?"

"You could say that…."

"Is he a full-time musician?"

"Yes, in a way."

Her eyebrows rise. "Why are you being so vague? Is he some kind of porn star? If he is, I'm down with that. They make a shit ton of money."

"Ditra! He's not a porn star. Jesus! He plays guitar in the park."

"Like a concert?"

"Yeah, sort of like that."

She frowns with confusion. "Every day?"

I finally give in. "He's a street musician."

She looks at me expectantly, waiting for more of an explanation, and when I don't give it to her, I see the gradual realization cross her face.

"He plays in the park for money," she says.

I nod.

"So people give him tips as they listen and walk by. He's not getting a paycheck."

"Right."

"So he doesn't quite have a real job."

I shake my head and place my empty teacup on my nightstand. "No. Not really."

"Are you giving him money?"

"God, no. Nothing like that."

"He's not living out of his car, is he?"

She must notice me wince, because her face and shoulders fall as she stares at me.

"Tell me he's not, Piper," she begs.

"He doesn't even have a car," I finally say. "He's homeless." There. I said it. Now she knows. "I know what you're going to say. But I love him. I honestly, truly love him. He makes me happy and he makes me feel beautiful, and he's smart and funny and so talented. I don't care about where he does or doesn't live. It doesn't matter to me."

For a moment, she looks as if she's gone into shock. She's just sitting there staring at me, unblinking, with her mouth partially open. Eventually, she shakes her head a little and runs her hand through her hair. "Fuck. I seriously don't even know what to say."

"Then don't say anything. I don't want you to."

"Do you parents know?"

"Are you kidding? Of course not. You know how they are. They'd lock me down here and never let me back out."

"True. It's just... you're so beautiful. You're smart and sweet, and you have a good job. You don't have to settle for someone like that—"

"Settle?" Anger rises in me. "I'm not settling. I want to be with him."

"I'm not trying to make you mad. I'm just trying to understand. Cut me a little slack, okay? This wasn't what I was expecting."

"I don't want to talk about this anymore. I'm tired."

"You're not getting rid of me. We're talking about this whether you like it or not."

"You'll never understand."

"Maybe not, but I'm trying to. Where exactly does he live?"

Letting out a deep, frustrated breath, I pull my knees up to my chest and wrap my arms round my legs. "When I first met him, he was sleeping under an old bridge in the park. He walks around and plays guitar during the day, and on some nights, he plays in bars for money, like the night we ran into him. But now he's sleeping in a shed in the backyard of an old abandoned house. It's on a dead-end street. No one is ever down there. It's safe."

"A shed? So where do you guys hang out? Where are you having sex? Are you paying for sleazy hotel rooms? You could get fleas, Piper. Or bedbugs. You have massive OCD and germ issues, and you're fucking in cheap hotels?"

"No. We hang out in the shed. He has a sleeping bag. It's not really dirty at all. He cleaned it."

"You're fucking in a shed?" she practically yells.

"Stop it!" I hiss. "First of all, we're not *fucking*. We love each other. You're making it sound dirty, and it's not."

"Well, it sounds sleazy. Can't you at least bring him here?"

"No. My parents would be all over it and ask a thousand questions. Plus, he has a dog. I can't bring a dog in here. Archie would be petrified."

"Does the dog sleep in the shed, too?"

"Yes. He's a really nice dog. He's calm and well behaved, and he's always clean. They both are."

"Piper, I seriously don't even know what to say at this point. This is way worse than what I was thinking."

"Why? Why is it worse? He's a nice guy. Isn't that all that matters?"

"No, it isn't! You're only twenty-one! You should be going on dates and having sex in a real bed in some guy's apartment. Not in a fucking shed on a dead-end street! I care about you, you idiot. And this is all sorts of fucked up. Even I wouldn't do something like this, and I'm the crazy one here!"

"You're not crazy. You're just experimental."

Leaning back against the pillows next to me, she covers her face with her hands. "You're going to make me cry. See what you do? You see the good in everyone."

"Why is that bad?"

"It's not. It's wonderful. It's why you're the best friend in the whole world, and it's probably why this homeless Blue guy loves the shit out of you." She leans on her side to study me. "He does love you, right?"

"I'm pretty sure he does."

"I just don't want you to be used. You're not supporting him, right?"

"No. Not at all. Sometimes I pay for things, but he does, too. It bothers him when I try to pay."

"Good. Let him pay if he can."

"Don't tell anyone about me and him, Dee. I'll tell my family when I'm ready."

"I won't tell anyone, I promise. Who would believe me, anyway? Are you going to keep seeing him? Do you think this is serious?"

"Yes, I'm going to keep seeing him." I pet Archie, who's decided to plant himself between us. "I just don't really know what the future holds, and that's what scares me."

"What do you mean?"

"He doesn't stay anywhere very long. He goes from place to place and only stays a few months before he goes on to the next place he wants to see."

"You don't think he'll stay here now that he's involved with you?"

"I don't know. I've hinted at wanting him to stay, but he gets really skittish and vague. I think he's afraid of commitment. Not sexual commitment, but commitment to plans and future."

"Like a job and a house and being an adult?"

"Exactly. He seems to just want to wander around and play guitar."

"Oh my God. This has heartbreak and years of emotional trauma and therapy written all over it. Are you okay with that? Falling in love with him and then being dumped so he can trek around?"

"No... I'll miss him like crazy if he leaves. I'll be devastated."

"Okay, so if he loves you, then why can't he get a job? Then you guys can get an apartment and not be shacking up in a shed." She lets out a laugh. "Shacked up in a shed!" she repeats, giggling.

I glare at her and fight back the tears of frustration burning my eyes. "It's not funny. I'm going to talk to him about an apartment and see if I can ease him into it. I almost have enough money saved up for a deposit and furniture, and I have a few thousand saved for emergencies. I need another month or two."

"And what if he says no? What are you going to do then?"

"I don't know. I can't think that far ahead." If I let my brain wander that far, I get bombarded with a thousand what-if scenarios that I just can't handle right now.

"Well, you might have to. I guess he could stay with me for a while, until you guys get it all figured out. I have that empty room in my apartment that I'm using for a closet, but it will seem like the Ritz to him after sleeping in a shed. If you say he's trustworthy, I don't mind if he stays there so you have a safe place to hang out. You can move in, too, if you want. I don't mind at all."

"That's really sweet, but I doubt he'd go for it. I could ask him, though."

"I would definitely try to talk to him. I'm not too keen on a homeless stranger living in my apartment, but I don't like this fucking in a shed business at all. You are way better than that. Actually, I don't like any of this, to be honest, but I'm trying to deal with it because I can see how into this guy you are."

"I love him, Dee. I think he's my soul mate," I say softly. "I just felt this… connection to him the moment I saw him. And I'm pretty sure he felt it, too."

"I don't really believe in that shit. I believe in chemistry and things in common and great sex."

"That's because you've never felt it."

She shrugs. "Maybe. What I'm feeling is that you better stop blowing me off to hide. You can't just immerse yourself in him and let him take over your life. I'm going to expect us to go back to our Wednesday night dinners. He's not going to die without you for a night." She pulls back the comforter and fluffs up one of the pillows she's lying on. "Now, I don't know about you, but I'm freakin' exhausted. I'm sleeping here with you."

I fall asleep wondering how Evan will react to the suggestion of living with me, either at Ditra's or in an apartment of our own, and I dream of us living in a cute yellow house with white shutters and a white picket fence with Acorn sitting on the porch with his penguin.

CHAPTER NINE

PIPER

I'm not at all prepared for this meeting today. Actually, it's not really a meeting; it's my annual performance review. Every year near the end of the fourth quarter, I have to endure this awkward analysis of my skills, progress, attitude, team player-ness, growth, and goal completion status. The hardest part is having to fill out the self-analysis section of the paperwork that has to be turned into my manager and human resources. Doesn't everyone rave about themselves and their accomplishments in hopes of getting a raise? Nobody is going to fill out that form detailing how much they've sucked for the past twelve months.

I would have been honest and admitted my less-than-stellar performance, though. That is if I had remembered to fill out the form. I probably would have outlined my decline in performance over the past few weeks.

But instead, I'm hearing it from my boss.

"You've completed all your yearly goals, and up until recently, your performance has been excellent. I have noticed, however, that for the past few weeks, you seem very distracted. You've come back late from lunch many times, you've suddenly had several sick days in a very short time, and at times, I've caught you staring off into space. The quality of your work isn't suffering, but I'm concerned nonetheless. If you're going through something and need to change your hours, or need to arrange for time off, I am more than happy to discuss it with HR."

"Oh no, that's not necessary. I apologize for all of that. I promise to do better. I've just had some personal things going on lately, and I'm so sorry I've let it affect me."

"I'm wondering if perhaps you're bored? You've been in the same position for several years, and I feel you've outgrown it. I believe your potential isn't being fully explored in your current position."

I hope Ditra never has to sit through one of these meetings because the words *performance* and *position* would have her all giggly with innuendos.

"I wouldn't say I'm bored." I am, though, now that I think about it. Answering phones, doing data entry, and filing are not exactly exciting.

"In the beginning of the year, we're going to have some marketing assistant positions opening up. I think you'd be great in that department, if you're interested?"

My attention is instantly piqued. "Yes. I'm very interested in that."

She pushes the self-assessment form across the conference room table to me. "Excellent. We'll meet again at the end of January to discuss. In the meantime, I'd like you to fill out this form and submit it to me by the end of the week, just so I have it in your file. It's required by HR."

"I definitely will. Thank you for being so understanding. I'm looking forward to hearing about the new positions."

She shuffles through my paperwork in her manila folder. "For now, you'll be receiving a ten percent increase and a two thousand-dollar year-end bonus."

Two thousand dollars!

"That's very generous. I can't thank you enough."

Nodding, she takes her glasses off her face and perches them on her head. "There is one other thing I'd like to talk to you about, off the record, so to speak."

"Okay...."

"I have a daughter your age, and you remind me a lot of her. You've worked for me since you were in high school. I've watched you grow into a beautiful, intelligent woman. Recently, I've heard through the grapevine here at the office that you're involved with a man of... very limited means with an unfavorable lifestyle. I have to admit I'm concerned. It's very easy to get sucked into a situation or an unhealthy relationship that's not the best for us. I apologize if I'm overstepping. I just want you to be careful, and I hope it's not the reason for your recent attendance and focus issues."

I'm slightly taken aback. Not offended, because I know Olivia means well. I just don't quite know how to respond. I'm not going to deny that I'm seeing Blue. And I'm furious because I know the "grapevine" is Melissa and her big-ass gossip-mongering mouth.

"I appreciate your concern, Olivia. And yes, I am seeing a guy who chooses to live differently than most of us, but he's a very good, caring person. I'm not in any danger."

"Very good. I'm not going to pry any further, but know that my door is always open if you need an ear."

"Thank you." I grab my form and walk back to my desk, then go to the ladies' room to touch up my makeup and have a moment to gather my thoughts. And who do I run into in front of the sinks and mirrors? None other than Melissa. Without any thought or plan or self-control, I push her, and she stumbles back into the electric hand dryer.

"What the hell is wrong with you?" she demands.

"Keep your nose out of my personal life."

"I don't know what you're talking about."

"Save your lies. I know you told Olivia about who I'm dating."

"If I have to cover for you every time you're late because you're adopting the local strays, then it *is* my business. And I'm worried about how sanitary you are. We don't need you spreading crabs on the toilets."

"Mind your own fucking business."

She scoffs down at my four-foot-eleven, petite frame. "What are you going to do about it, Piper?"

I apply my lip gloss slowly and glance at her reflection in the mirror.

"Oh, I don't know," I say casually. "But it would be a shame if something happened to your BMW out in the parking lot. Especially with degenerate homeless men milling around. I hear they like to key paint jobs, cut break lines, and slash tires just for fun. I'd be careful if I were you."

She glares at me, eyes burning with anger and hatred. "You're a crazy bitch."

I shrug carelessly and wash my hands as she practically runs out of the room, and I smile at myself in the mirror with satisfaction. I'm done with allowing her to bully me, and it feels good to finally fight back and give her a taste of her own medicine.

I'm trying not to shiver as I huddle in the corner, sitting on an old throw pillow. Acorn is curled up on my lap in a ball, and I stroke his soft ears and muzzle as I watch Blue write on notepaper and play verses on his guitar, then repeat the process over and over again. He's in one of his moods today, but thankfully, he's just chain-smoking this time and not drinking. I've been watching him for hours, being quietly supportive from over here in the corner. Hours ago, we drank hot cocoa that I brought with me from Dunkin' Donuts, but it only warmed me up for a few minutes.

"Blue? I'm getting tired. I think I should go."

He raises his head and looks at me with a blank expression, as if he had no idea I was still there.

"Are you okay?" I ask.

"Yes, I'm okay. I'm just tired. There's so many words in my head, and they go up and down and all around, and I can't rest until I've gotten them in order. Can't you see that?"

Gently moving Acorn off my lap, I crawl over to Blue. "You don't have to do it all tonight," I say with a soft smile. "If you get some rest, your head will probably be clearer. Then you can sort the words and the notes better."

His eyes dart back and forth between me and the scattered pieces of paper around him. "I don't know…." He rakes a hand through his long, tangled hair. "I really should do it now."

Carefully, I take his guitar from him and lay it off to the side. A flash of panic sparks in his eyes, and I lean in and kiss him, hoping to distract his mind.

"You really should do *me* now," I whisper seductively, palming his cheek.

Sucking in a breath, he grabs the back of my neck and pulls me to him for a hungry, demanding kiss. His tongue sweeps over mine, and his breathing grows heavier as I stroke his cock through his jeans with my free hand.

"Take your coat off," he commands as he quickly pulls his thick sweatshirt up over his head.

It worked. I flipped the switch.

Forcing myself to ignore the cold, I take off all my clothes and kneel in front of him, goosebumps pebbling my flesh. His eyes drink me in, and he cups my breasts in his hands, chafing his palms against my nipples that are already peaked from the assault of cold air.

"You're so fucking beautiful, Ladybug," he whispers, burying his face in my cleavage and running his tongue along the curve of my breast. I wrap my arms around his head and hug him to me as he lavishes kisses and love bites across my chest and neck. "Lie down and tell me to fuck you." His hoarse voice oozes sexual power, and makes my insides quiver.

Pulling the comforter aside, I crawl onto the mattress and lie on my back, bending one arm under my head and moving my other hand slowly down between my parted legs as he watches me, mesmerized by the private show, the song and the words rambling through his brain forgotten.

For now.

"I want you to fuck me," I whisper.

Standing, his eyes stay riveted on my hand fingering myself as he kicks off his boots and slips out of the rest of his clothes.

"Lick your fingers," he says, kneeling between my legs. His eyes flash royal blue-black as I raise my hand to my lips to lick the length of my index finger before sucking it into my mouth.

A sexy-as-hell grin curves his lips as he watches me, his cock extending from his body, and he grabs my ankles, raising my legs until my calves are pressed against his solid chest. My pulse races when he reaches for my waist and pulls my body against his, sinking his cock into me with targeted finesse. The sudden thrust makes me cry out, which only fuels him to drive harder and faster into me. He's a wild man, fucking me deep and furious with my ankles on his shoulders.

A light sheen of sweat glistens his body, and his hair flails around his head like a thrashing metal head in concert. He's lost again, only this time in the depths of my body rather than strings and pages and notes and words. He leans over me, bending my legs with him until my thighs are pressed against my breasts, and claims my mouth with his. Digging my nails into his back as he drills into me, I let myself spin out of control with him, not caring about the cold or my growling stomach or the wind howling outside. Nothing matters more to me than making him happy and giving him what he needs to ease his self-torture and bring him peace. I can be drug, lover, and best friend for him. I'm convinced I can be the peace he's missing, just as he is mine.

He's asleep within minutes after we collapse onto the mattress together, both of us exhausted, sweaty, and breathless. After gently pulling the blanket up over his shoulders, I carefully untangle my body from his and sit up, scanning the dim room for my clothes. Pieces of notepaper are everywhere, and I pick up the ones that are closest to me and arrange them in a neat stack in case he wants to look them over tomorrow. As I put the stack of paper off to the side, I can't help but notice that the top sheet is filled with nothing but random scribbles. The words and musical notes I assumed he was writing don't exist.

His arm instantly snakes around me, distracting me from the paper, and I drop it as he pulls me back down next to him, molding his body against mine.

"Stay," he murmurs. "I hate when you leave in the middle of the night."

I hate it, too, but I've never been able to bring myself to stay overnight in the shed. I'm afraid of getting caught by the police and arrested for trespassing. I'm even more afraid of the spiders that might be waiting for me to fall asleep so they can come out and do whatever scary shit spiders do. I'm afraid I'll have to pee in the middle of the night. And then again in the morning when I wake. Traipsing out into the edge of the yard and squatting amongst the weeds and trees sucks.

This is the first time he's ever asked me to stay, though, and I hope it's a sign he's becoming more attached to me and doesn't want to let me go. Technically, there's no reason I can't stay overnight. I don't have to be at work tomorrow, and I know Archie has enough food and water to hold him over until I get home. For sure, my mother will worry if she realizes I never came home, but I'm an adult and can stay out all night if I want to, whether she likes it or not. It was part of the agreement when I moved downstairs that they would allow me to be independent and not pry too much.

Settling back into Blue's arms, I pull the blanket back over us before all the heat of sex escapes.

"I love you like there's no tomorrow. Don't ever forget that," he says with his chin against my shoulder. My heart swells in my chest as it does every time he says those special words. Hugging his arm tighter to my chest, I say it back, even though I'm sure he's already sound asleep. Unfortunately, sleep doesn't come as easy for me as it does for him. The fear of looming bugs hinders me from relaxing enough to close my eyes.

"Acorn," I whisper, and he lifts his head from his fleece dog bed in the corner to look at me questioningly. "Come here, puppy." I pat the bed next to me, and when he happily trots over, I lift the edge of the blanket for him to crawl in beside me. He licks my hand before making himself cozy next to me under the covers. Sighing, I feel warm and protected, snuggled between Blue and the fuzzy dog I've also fallen in love with.

CHAPTER TEN

PIPER

For the first time since we met, we're having dinner in a local diner while Acorn waits in the back seat of my car on a blanket with a special bone I bought for him. I can't even describe how good it feels to be out in public on a real date with the guy I'm in love with.

Christmas music is playing in the background, and I feel festive in my fuzzy white sweater and matching mittens and hat that I've put on the chair next to me. I keep glancing at Blue while I read the menu because he looks incredibly handsome tonight. His hair is freshly washed, all fluffy and wavy. The subtle scent of the cologne I gave him a few weeks ago fills my lungs with hints of sandalwood and vanilla. And don't even ask me how a man can look so hot in a black sweater, but he sure as hell does. The knit fabric accentuates his wide shoulders and chest and makes him look positively cuddly and sexy.

I worried that Blue might appear out of place somehow or act awkward being in a restaurant, but I was wrong. He's completely relaxed and natural, exuding his usual magnetic confidence. I catch several of the waitresses gawking at him as they walk by, but I curb my jealousy. He never flirts back, and I've never caught him checking out other women. Not once. His eyes are always on me, and they truly are a window to his thoughts, revealing his good and bad moods as well as his deepest emotions. There's no way I could ever question his love for me because it's so undeniable in the way he looks at me. That can't be faked or forced. And neither can the flashes of need and desire I often see when I catch him staring at me.

Dinner was his idea, prompted by him making extra money this week after playing in a few bars. I feel bad letting him spend money on me, but I also know I need to let him pay and take care of me once in a while so he doesn't feel like he's taking advantage of me.

"What's good here?" he asks.

"Hmm... They make a wicked good burger. And the chili cheese fries are amazing."

His face lights up. "Fuck yeah. We're getting those."

"And they have Cherry Cokes with real cherry syrup."

"Let's get that, too."

After the waitress takes our order, he reaches across the table and holds my hand in his. "I'm glad we did this. I'm sorry it's not to a nicer place. Someday, I'll take you to a five-star restaurant, baby."

"Don't be silly. This is perfect. We'll never get Cherry Coke and chili cheese fries in a fancy restaurant."

He flashes his boyish grin. "You're probably right. I have a few more gigs lined up this month. The guy who usually plays guitar in that band is getting married and going on a two-week honeymoon, so I'll be filling in for him."

I nod as the waitress puts our drinks in front of us, and I immediately reach for mine, being the sugar addict I am. "That's great."

"At least I'll have some extra cash for once. They talked me into singing at a few of the upcoming gigs. I know how much that turns you on, so you could come. If you want to."

"Are you kidding? I'd love to. Acorn should be okay in the car for a few hours while I'm inside. I could check on him a few times."

This is actually the third time we've left Acorn in my car. Twice so we could go inside a store and another time when I practically dragged Blue to urgent care when he had a terrible cough. Acorn was well behaved and didn't try to dig his way out of the car or bark his head off.

"I like when you come listen to me."

"I'd love to be there every time you play. You know I can't get enough of you," I tease.

"Trust me, babe. I know."

The waitress returns and places our food on the table, and when she's gone, I take a deep breath to prepare myself for what I'm about to ask Blue.

"Christmas is next week, and every year, I use that week for my vacation time since I never take a real vacation."

"You should go somewhere. Like Disney or Aruba. I'm sure Ditra would love to go with you."

I spear a fry with my fork and shake my head in frustration that the conversation has already gone in the wrong direction.

"I really don't want to travel right now, especially over the holiday. But I wanted to ask you if maybe you want to come over for Christmas Eve?" I keep talking so he can't say no yet, even though his face has taken on the liking of a deer caught in the headlights. "It's just going to be my family… my parents, my younger sister, my older sister and her fiancé, and probably my grandparents. It's casual. My mom makes homemade soup and chili and a bunch of desserts, and we open a few presents."

He shifts in his chair and clicks his tongue piercing. "I don't think that's a good idea."

I keep the smile plastered on my face. "It'll be nice. You can't spend Christmas all alone."

"I always do. I don't mind. I have Acorn."

"I know… but I'd really like it if you came. I want you to meet my family, and I want them to meet you."

Taking a bite out of his burger, he shakes his head. "It's not a good idea," he repeats. "What the fuck would I tell them when they ask me what I do? That's what parents do. You want your parents to know how I live? Have you told them?"

"Well… no. Not yet. I thought if they got to know you first, I could eventually tell them. By then they'd already like you, so it probably won't bother them as much." I don't entirely believe that, to be honest, but we have to start somewhere.

"No."

"We can just avoid the questions for now and give vague answers. Or I can tell them just not to ask you stuff... I can tell them you're a very private person. There's nothing wrong with that."

"No," he says again.

"Stop saying no."

"No."

"Blue... please. It would really mean a lot to me if you came. I want you be a real part of my life."

His jaw clenches, and he lets out a sigh of clear irritation. "Do I look like I want to be a part of someone's life, Piper?" he asks in a low voice. "I don't even want to be part of my own fucking life right now. If I wanted to sit around with family and rock around the Christmas tree and open presents, don't you think I'd go back home? I can't do it. Not with them or with you."

Leaning back against the stiff fake-leather chair, I stare down at my plate, afraid if I look at him, I'll burst into tears right here in the middle of the diner. I never expected him to jump up and down with excitement, but I definitely wasn't expecting his reaction to be so cold and mean.

He reaches for my hand again, but I pull it away, which gets me a head shake in return when I peek at him. "Piper, come on. Tonight was supposed to be nice. Don't ruin it with all this."

"I didn't realize I was ruining it," I reply, pushing my plate away from me. The smell of the chili suddenly makes me feel nauseous.

"That came out wrong. I'm just not ready to be meeting your parents. If you want to come over after your thing with your family, or on Christmas Day, that'd be great."

I'm starting to worry about the way he says *come over*. Like the shed is a permanent home. None of this is making me feel very confident about suggesting we stay at Ditra's or get a place of our own, but I'm still hoping I can eventually talk him into that.

Sometimes, though, too much hope leads headfirst into the unexpected brick wall of reality.

I wait until we're back at the shed to approach Blue with the idea of getting off the streets. Or out of the backyard, as the case currently is. He immediately lights up a cigarette and starts to pace around the tiny area, as if I just asked him to do something so outlandishly impossible that he can't even comprehend it.

"You need to just chill," he says between hand-shaking inhales.

"It was just a suggestion...." My voice sounds much calmer than I feel inside. "I just got a big year-end bonus from work. I was saving for an apartment before I even met you. What's the big deal if you move in with me? I'm not asking you for anything else—"

He whips around to face me. "Aren't you, though? Look around, Piper." He swoops his arm around in a grand gesture. "Look what you're sitting on. An air mattress and a down comforter. Look at the dog." He points to Acorn in the corner. "Sleeping on a dog bed with ceramic dishes next to him. There's a curtain on the goddamn window. I'm standing on a wool throw rug from Bed, Bath, and fucking Beyond. There's a tiny cabinet of snacks over there with a plant on top of it. There's a battery-powered space heater keeping us warm. What next?" he practically yells. "A mini fridge and a microwave?"

Okay. So maybe I slowly started to make this space a little more comfortable for us. But could anyone blame me? "I-I just wanted you to have some nice things. And Acorn loves all his new stuff. Look how happy he is." The dog wagged his tail so hard when I bought him dishes and toys that his butt wiggled for almost an hour.

"I don't want nice things. Or any things. Why can't you understand that?"

I bow my head from his yelling and manic expression. "I don't know. Why should we sit here and freeze and have nothing? I guess I don't understand any of this."

"No. You don't. Stop trying to. Stop trying to fix me or change me or save me or whatever crazy needs you have in your head. Those are things *you* want, not me. I told you weeks ago. Take what you see or leave it. But don't try to dress it up in curtains and blankets."

"Okay. I'm sorry."

"I don't want you to be sorry, Ladybug. I want you to just *accept*. I'm not going to live in an apartment with you and get a job and have a bank account and meet your family and build dreams together. It's not happening."

My heart jackknifes at his words. "But why?"

He stops pacing abruptly and stares at me with a look of sheer torment on his face. "I don't know."

When my sisters and I were young, my father would never allow us to "I don't know" as an answer to anything. He told us it was unacceptable. Lazy. A ploy to hide the truth from others and, sometimes, from ourselves. My initial instinct is to tell Blue he *has* to know, but the remorseful tone of his voice tells me he truly, honestly, and genuinely doesn't know. And the little voice in my gut tells me I should be very worried about that, but I ignore it because ignorance is the path to delusional happiness.

"So when I get my own apartment, are you and Acorn going to at least come over? Not move in, but come over at night and on weekends and hang out and watch TV with me and let me cook us dinner? Instead of us being here?"

"I don't know," he says again. "I guess. Maybe."

My father would be having fits over these answers, and I'm on the verge of it myself, but I summon up all my inner strength and stop myself from throwing a sobbing tantrum or demanding real answers because I'm pretty sure he doesn't have anything remotely resembling answers or reasons. Forcing both of us to face that fact doesn't seem like a very good idea right now. Not when he's back to pacing and biting the inside of his cheek and acting all twitchy.

I switch gears like an Indy race car driver. "Evan, come sit down with me. We don't have to talk about this now. We can play cards… or we can cuddle and talk about music and books." None of my suggestions seem to be appealing to him, even though those are his favorite things to do. "We can fool around," I add as a bonus, in a flirty voice, because that's something he always wants to do.

"I need to walk."

"Walk?" I repeat, glancing at my watch. "It's eleven o'clock."

"Don't care. I just want to go for a walk."

My nerves ignite with panic. This can't be good. He's turning down sex to walk aimlessly around town. What if he keeps walking?

"Do you want me to come with you?"

"No. I think I just need a few minutes alone."

My heart and my hope pitches like a pile of rocks straight into my stomach.

"Oh. Okay."

He reaches for the latch on the door but turns, his eyes softer. "You could stay here with Acorn. He'd like that. And I can see you when I get back."

"Are you sure? Will I be safe here alone?"

"Hell yeah. Nobody ever comes down here. And there's a hunting knife under the mattress."

A knife?

I suppose the knife is hidden in the event he ever needs it for self-defense, but I wish I had known it was there. Random hidden weapons make me feel a little nervous.

He leaves for his walk without kissing me goodbye, which is unusual for him. Blue's very physically affectionate with me. Whether it be sensual, erotic, or sweet, he's usually touching me in some way, and he always kisses me hello and goodbye.

I take off my shoes, sit on the bed with my back against a pile of pillows—yes, I brought them all over here—and pull the thick comforter over me. Acorn immediately lies on my feet with his penguin. I'm tempted to just go home where it's warm and take the dog with me, but I'm worried Blue will be even more upset than he already is if he comes back to find both of us gone. I'm not sure if upset is an accurate word to describe his current mood. Disturbed and anxious might be better descriptors. Cornered, even.

In hindsight, I wish I hadn't brought up Christmas and the apartment because it completely wrecked our first real date night. If I had kept my mouth shut, we'd probably either be having wild sex right now or he'd be playing some new songs on his guitar for me, and I wouldn't be sitting here freezing while he's walking off a mood.

I wait.

And wait.

I move the space heater closer to the bed and get up and do jumping jacks to warm myself up, and then I crawl back under the blanket and coax Acorn to crawl under with me. We huddle together, keeping each other warm. I'm hyper aware of every noise outside—tree branches, the wind, an owl, the creaking of the old wooden shed walls. I'm petrified, but I'm even more scared to walk across the dark yard to get to my car in the street, so I hug Acorn and try to shut it all out.

I love Blue. I'm trying my best to accept him for who he is. I understand his wandering spirit. But I'm cold and confused and scared, and as much as I try to convince myself that I can love Blue *for now* and give him the freedom he seems to desperately need, I can't deny that my heart has been hoping for more. The sad reality of us is that I'm hurting him by wanting more just as much as he's hurting me by not being able to give more.

We're stuck... and I have no idea where we're supposed to go from here.

CHAPTER ELEVEN

PIPER

I have a love-hate relationship with the holidays. Especially Christmas. I love the music, the movies, and the decorations. I love the sense of spirit, the coming together of friends and family. I love buying and wrapping gifts. What I hate is the stress and the greed and the rushing.

This year, I also particularly hate my older sister sitting on her fiancé's lap next to the fireplace with her big-ass beacon of an engagement ring on her finger and a pile of presents next to her that's taller than I am. All presents from him, wrapped up in telltale paper clearly from upscale stores like Tiffany and Nordstrom.

Yes, I'm a jealous, immature bitch for feeling this way, but that's just where I am in my life right now—hating people who have what I want. And I don't mean material things. I mean having that special person involved in every part of your life.

I finger the beaded bracelet Blue gave me a few weeks ago, which I haven't taken off once and which has more value to me than any diamond tennis bracelet ever could. But *he's* not here, and I wish he was.

As I sip my crystal glass of eggnog, I try to picture Blue here with me, sitting on the loveseat beside me and opening presents. I can easily imagine him laughing and joking with my family, even playing holiday songs on his guitar. Once upon a time, my grandfather played the banjo, and I can imagine him and Blue talking in great depth about music. My grandmother would touch his hair and tell him how unfair it is for a man to have such beautiful, wavy hair.

That illusion quickly fades, and in its place, I can see my father drilling Blue with questions about what he does for work, what his five-year plan is, and why he's wasting time playing music when that's a dead-end dream for hippies. I can hear my sisters giggling about how good-looking he would be if he would cut his hair. I can understand why Blue wouldn't want to deal with any of that.

My mother approaches me where I sit in the dining room. "Honey, why are you hiding way over here? Come sit with the rest of us. Grandma can't even see you sitting this far away."

"I'm not hiding, Mom. There wasn't any place to sit."

"There's always room. Don't be so shy, sweetie. I thought your boyfriend was going to join us. Your father and I were looking forward to meeting him. You've practically moved in with him, and we haven't even met him yet."

My fingers tighten around my glass. "I haven't moved in with him."

"Piper, you're hardly ever home anymore. That poor cat cries all night for you."

My head snaps to face her. I'm sure she must be exaggerating. "What? He does not."

"Yes, he does. We can hear him from up here. I've gone down to check on him, and he's just sitting at the door, meowing. The poor thing misses you."

God, now I feel terrible. I had no idea Archie missed me when I wasn't home. He usually ignores me or only comes near me when he wants food or to have his head petted for five minutes exactly. Not a moment less or longer or he'll bite or scratch me.

"My boyfriend couldn't make it. I'm going to go see him later, after we open the presents."

"I don't think you'll be going anywhere tonight. It's snowing, and I don't want to be worrying about you driving around on Christmas Eve in ice and snow. Your grandmother will be worried sick, too."

"Mom—"

"I know you're an adult, Piper, but that's no reason to be unsafe or cause your family to worry about you on a holiday. And what kind of man lets a woman drive around at all hours of the night anyway? Especially in the snow."

I am not at all in the mood to go down this road with her tonight. I've heard it all many times in the past few weeks. "Mom, can we not do this tonight?"

Her bright red lips part, then close to a thin smile. "You're right. It's Christmas. But promise me you won't go out tonight. The roads are so bad that your grandparents are staying here. Haven't you looked outside?"

I've been too busy daydreaming to think about the weather. When I told Blue yesterday that I'd be coming to see him tonight, I had no idea it was supposed to snow today. *Dammit*. My sucky driving sucks even worse in bad weather. Even if my mother wasn't trying to ground me like a teenager, I wouldn't be keen on driving across town tonight.

"Okay." I give in. "I'll stay home. But tomorrow I'm going to see him."

"If that's what you want to do. I'd much prefer he come here for dinner, but I'm not going to argue with you. Now come sit in the living room with the rest of the family."

I try to enjoy the rest of the night and be happily joyous, but I'm just not feeling it this year. I miss Blue and Acorn, and my heart aches to be with them. I'm worried about Blue being alone, especially if it's snowing and he can't walk anywhere to get what he needs or clear his mind.

Ever since the night at the diner, his dark mood has clung to him like a shroud. There have been a few fleeting moments when he's laughed and smiled, but it seemed forced. He's been dark and cloudy, much like the storms he both loves and hates, and I wonder when the rainbow of light and color will return.

CHAPTER TWELVE

PIPER

Eight inches is no joke. It's much deeper than it sounds. Especially when it's an unplowed dead-end street. Luckily, I don't have to stop until the very end of the street, so when my car starts to slide and fishtail down the slight hill, I'm grateful there's nothing I can crash into.

Once the car stops sliding, I park crookedly in front of the old, forgotten house, wondering how I'm going to get to the backyard because the driveway hasn't been plowed and the walkway hasn't been shoveled. Because it's an abandoned house and it has to keep looking abandoned, even though Blue is basically living on the property. I understand that he can't be shoveling a path for me, and as I schlep through the snow toward the house, I'm worried about leaving all these boot prints on the property. Just as I'm walking around the side of the house, Blue appears.

"I thought I saw car lights," he says, leaning down for a kiss. "I didn't know if you were coming today since you didn't show up yesterday."

"It was snowing, and my mom was freaking out about me driving and upsetting my grandmother—"

His warm lips are on mine again. "Don't worry about it," he says with a smile. "I missed ya."

"I missed you, too."

"Jump on my back and I'll carry you the rest of the way. The snow is almost up to your waist, shorty."

Laughing, I smack his arm. "It is not."

"Jump on anyway." He turns, and I jump on his back, hanging on to his shoulders and giggling as he trudges through while Acorn frolics around beside us. At the shed door, we stomp our feet to get rid of the snow and then quickly scoot inside.

"Wow," I exclaim instantly. Blue's been busy... rearranging. Everything's in a different place, as if he moved all the stuff in the room clockwise. The best part, the part that makes my heart jump into my throat and gives me such a burst of happiness that I almost cry, is the tiny fake Christmas tree in the corner decorated with a few strands of glistening silver tinsel. One wrapped present is placed nearby. Blue's standing in the middle of the room, smiling from ear to ear.

"I cleaned up a little, and I fixed the door so it shuts better. And I got this tree."

"It's beautiful." His smile and bright, excited eyes are drastic changes from the last time I saw him when he was still sad, depressed, scribbling, and walking around all night. That mood lasted for days, and I was starting to worry he would never come out of it. Seeing him relaxed and happy again is the best present in the world, and I have to throw my arms around him and hug him because I missed this version of him so much. His embrace is tight and fierce enough to make my ribs hurt, and I wonder if he misses himself when he gets that way.

"I know I've been fucked up," he whispers into my hair.

"It's okay. We all have bad days."

We slowly let go of each other, and he crosses the room to get the present from under the tree. "This is for you."

I bite my tongue to keep myself from saying, *"You didn't have to get me anything,"* because I know how much it bothers him when I say things like that. Instead, I take off my coat and sit on the bed to open his gift. I unwrap it slowly, wanting to relish and remember this moment with my first Christmas present from him. Inside the cardboard box, under crumpled white tissue paper, is a tiny wooden trinket box with a blue bird painted on the front. A few small scratches mar the surface of the wood, but I'm not bothered by them at all. My breathing stalls for a moment as a wave of total adoration for this man washes over me.

"It's so beautiful."

"Open it," he urges.

I do, and it begins to play a melody. It takes me a few seconds to realize it's not just any melody—it's the first song he ever sang for me that day in the park. It sounds very different coming out of this itty-bitty box, but it's definitely "Slayer of My Heart."

I gape at him. "Oh my God… is this your song?"

"It is."

I'm almost speechless with the shock of such an unexpected special gift. "It's amazing," I finally say, still holding it delicately in my hand. "How did you do this?"

He sits next to me, and the air mattress sinks considerably under his weight. "There's this old guy downtown who owns an antique shop. Sometimes I play in front of his store. Mostly for him, though, 'cause he likes music. I bought it from him, and he knew a guy who could make it play my song."

Tears are in my eyes when I turn to put my arms around him again. "Thank you. I love it, and I love you."

"I wrote that song about you, so I felt like you should have it."

Wow. A song about me. And those lyrics… How did they go again? My mind races back in time to grasp them, but he yanks me back with a touch of his hand on my thigh and his lips burning across my cheek.

His voice is low and husky, filled with pent-up desire. "Take your clothes off."

"Wait… You have to open your presents first." I grab the bag I brought in with me and pull out three gifts—two for him and one for Acorn, who starts to rip his open as soon as I give it to him. Within seconds, he's got the peanut butter-stuffed bone in his mouth. Blue and I laugh as Acorn carries it over to his bed and gets into serious chewing mode.

"You just made his year."

"Good. Now open yours."

He tears his first gift open almost as fast the dog tore into his and slowly pulls the journal out of its dust bag.

"Piper…" He runs his fingertips over the pebbly black leather. "This is fuckin' awesome." He raises it to his nose and inhales. "I so dig the smell of leather."

I smile at him sniffing his gift. "Me, too. And it's so buttery soft."

"It's wicked soft. And you got me a pen." He twirls the pen around in his fingers the way a seasoned drum player spins their sticks. "This is really cool."

"Open the next one."

"You shouldn't have gotten me so much, babe," he says as he unwraps his second gift. "I feel bad I only got you one."

"Stop. It's not a competition. What you gave me is priceless. It's your song. And the bird… I know how much it means to you. It makes it even more special to me."

He nods solemnly and carefully pulls the beaded necklace out of the thin black velvet box.

"These are onyx and hematite," I say quickly, hoping the way he's staring at it isn't a sign that he doesn't like it. "It's for healing, luck, and protection."

"Man… I don't know what to say. This is so thoughtful. And special. Like you." He clasps the necklace around his neck and touches it at the front of his chest. "I don't deserve you."

"Of course you do. Don't be silly."

"I should've been with you yesterday. I know that, Piper. I'm a dick, but I'm not a stupid dick."

"Blue, you're not any kind of dick."

"I am. And you let me be one. You're the first person to ever make me wish I wasn't like this."

"Isn't that part of love? Loving someone no matter what? Inspiring them? Wanting to be better together?"

"For some. You sure as shit make my life better."

"You make mine better, too. Of course I wish you were there yesterday, but it's okay. We're together now, and I'm happy."

He puts his journal off to the side and then pushes me down on the bed, slowly crawling on top of me. "I'm gonna show you how happy you make me," he says hoarsely and grinds his hard cock against my thigh. Capturing my mouth with his, he kisses me so deep I lose my breath and my mind, and I tumble into a sensual, woozy, dreamlike state. Blue has a way of making me feel entirely euphoric, floating, and disconnected from the rest of the world.

Standing, he towers above me and pulls his shirt off, then unbuttons his jeans and tugs the zipper down. Grabbing his cock, he pulls it out while shoving his clothes out of the way. I lie back and stare up at him, admiring his lean, muscular body and the ink that decorates it. He's like a walking coloring book, all lines and images and shades of gray and muted color. Even in the chilly room, my body instantly heats when he strokes his hand up and down the length of his shaft. Reaching for me, he grabs a handful of the front of my sweater and yanks me up into a sitting position, bringing me eye level with his cock.

"Open your mouth."

I obey, opening my mouth like a starving bird as I stare up the length of his body to meet his smoldering gaze.

"Put your hands behind your back," he commands. "I don't want you to touch me."

His deep voice on those words burns through me like a shot of bourbon.

I cross my arms behind my back, and he slowly slides the crown of his cock across my waiting lips, moistening them with his salty pre-cum before filling my mouth with his throbbing erection. I open wider to take him in and let him slide in and out of my mouth. As he moves faster and deeper, I close my lips over his hot flesh. I know what he wants. I know what he craves. He doesn't want me to blow him; he wants to fuck my mouth like he fucks my pussy.

Holding my head in his hands with his fingers buried in my hair, he rams to the back of my throat until his balls slam against my lips and chin.

Breathing air into my nose, I press my tongue up against him and tighten my lips around him. The muscles in his stomach and thighs tighten and flex, and his breathing grows deeper and ragged. He's almost there. Every part of him is focused on my lips, my mouth, my eyes. His control over me is an illusion because the true control is all mine. Moaning softly, I suck my cheeks in around him, swirl my tongue over his cock, and then lean my head back, almost letting him slip from my mouth.

"Fuck...." His hands tighten in my hair and he yanks my skull back to him, sinking deep into my mouth as he comes with thrusting hips and deep, growling groans that make my insides quiver. Sucking him harder, I milk every bit out of him until his hands are limp on my head and he pulls away to drop to his knees in front of me.

"You destroy me, babe. Come here." He pulls me into his arms, kissing me even though I just had a mouthful of his cock and cum.

"Merry Christmas."

"That was beyond fuckin' merry." Pulling my sweater up with one hand, he rips off my bra with the other and scatters kisses and random bite marks over my upper body as he takes off the rest of my clothes.

Breathless, we fall onto the bed together, pulling the blanket over us, and he moves between my open legs to lick me until I'm in a multiple-orgasmic daze, barely able to form coherent thoughts. Kissing me softly, he wraps me up in his arms and sings to me as I fall asleep, and just when I didn't think I could fall any harder for him, I do.

❧

For my week stay-cation from work, I've been spending my time checking out apartments and hanging out with Blue as much as possible. If it's not too cold for his fingers, he still plays at the park on most afternoons. Twice this week, he played at the bar, and I loved listening to him actually sing and play guitar live and watching him move around so confidently on the stage. Judging from the reaction from the other people in the bar, they loved him, too.

Despite my mother's mounting disapproval, I've stayed with Evan overnight several times this week—only going home to shower, change, and take care of Archie. Blue's been in a great mood, and I feel as though we're in a good place together. We're moving forward slowly but surely. He didn't take me up on my invitation to accompany me to look at apartments, so I left it alone to avoid pushing him into a bad mood again. My hope is once I move into my own place, I can slowly coax him into short visits, which will hopefully lead to him agreeing to move in. Surely he'd much rather live in a nice apartment with me than in the shed.

Today, after much inner debate, I took the leap and put down a deposit on the apartment I like most. It's half a duplex, which is like two small houses stuck together. I like that better than an apartment building because it feels more like a home to me. It's perfect, with two bedrooms, lots of windows, a small galley kitchen, large living room, and bathroom. As a bonus, it's pet friendly and has a small fenced-in yard. I'd be lying if I said I didn't envision Acorn running around that yard, chasing a ball someday.

To celebrate, I meet Ditra for dinner, and we talk about guys and work and decorating ideas for my new place. Ditra loves to paint and she knows how to do faux painting for accent walls, so I'm excited to really make the place my own. We make plans to meet up next week for our dinner ritual and shopping. I'm glad we're back on track and she's forgiven me for becoming a temporary hermit while I got my head together. I'm thankful she's not the type of friend to hold a grudge.

After dinner with Ditra, I drive across town to see Blue, and I tell him excitedly about the apartment as we sit on the bed together. I take Ditra's advice to not push him to help me move, or to come over or to stay the night or move in. She thinks he has a fear of commitment and needs things to go at his own pace and be "his" idea. I agree.

"You look happy," he says when I finally stop babbling on about my new closet space and the quiet street I'll live on.

"I am. I've wanted my own place for such a long time."

"You deserve it. I loved my first place. It was kind of a shit hole, but it was cool."

"Was that in Jersey?"

"Yeah. I lived with my buddy, Reece. He's probably still there."

This is the first he's ever mentioned any of his friends and I make a mental note to remember his name in case he brings him up again. "What did you like most about it? Having your own place…"

Head cocked to the side, he thinks about his answer. "I guess being able to just chill and be me. Living in a space that's a reflection of me instead of trying to be comfortable in someone else's space."

"I know what you mean. My parents have lived in our house since they got married. You want to hear what drives me crazy?"

He grins. "Tell me."

"They have this big dining room filled with all kinds of fancy stuff, and they never use it. It sits empty. I think we've eaten in there twice since I was born. And I hate it. It's such a waste. If that was my house, I'd eat every meal in there, on the expensive plates, and stare out the window at the flowers and bushes they pay a landscaper to take care of. Even if I was just eating freakin' ice cream, I'd sit there. I wouldn't be waiting for a special day."

Laughing, he leans closer and kisses the top of my head. "You're adorable. I'd make every day special for you if I could."

"You do," I reply softly. "I wish you could see that."

"Me, too, Piper. Me, too." He stands and takes my hands, pulling me up off the bed to stand in front of him. "You mind if I lay down? I'm getting a bad headache."

"Of course not. Do you want me to get you anything?"

"No, babe, I'm okay. I just want to lay down in the dark."

"Do you want me to stay? I can rub your head."

"Nah. I'll be okay. Why don't you meet me at the park tomorrow? I heard it's not going to be too cold."

"Okay." I squeeze his hands. "Are you sure you're okay?"

"Yeah. Tomorrow will be better. I want you to go home and eat ice cream in the dining room after your parents go to bed."

I laugh. "I just might do that."

Cupping his face in my hands, I pull him down so I can kiss his lips. "I hope you feel better. I'll bring coffee and bagels in the morning."

"Don't do that. We'll go together."

"Okay." I pull on my coat and bend down to give Acorn a kiss on his head. "You be a good boy and we'll get you a doughnut." He thumps his tail on the edge of his bed and licks my cheek.

As I pull the door shut behind me, Blue is already lying on the bed with his arm over his forehead, and I have to force myself to leave him alone and not run back to try to help him feel better. I get it, though. Sometimes it's easier to rest alone.

CHAPTER THIRTEEN

PIPER

For the fifth time, I push up the sleeve of my jacket so I can check my watch. I glance around the park, expecting to see Blue and Acorn walking toward me.

But I don't see them anywhere. And it's now an hour past our usual Saturday morning meeting time at the picnic table near the bridge. *Our place.*

A weight of worry sinks into my stomach and explodes like a bomb, striking up shards of panic. What if something happened to them? Maybe he got arrested for living in the shed and Acorn has been taken to a pet shelter. Maybe he got run over by a car while he was walking here. Maybe he's still not feeling well, and he's all alone, sick, and in pain.

All the maybes and what-ifs come at me like bullets from a machine gun, each one pelting my heart until I can't take anymore. Closing my book, I stand to leave and embark on my own search party, and that's when I see them walking toward me in the distance. Every molecule in my body relaxes with instant relief, and it's so overpowering that I almost need to sit down again to recover.

Acorn has a tennis ball in his mouth, and he bounds to me when he recognizes me, as if he can't wait to show me his new treasure. Laughing, I take the fluorescent green ball from him.

"Where did you get this?" I ask the dog playfully. "You're very excited about it!" I toss it a few feet away, and he runs to retrieve it and immediately brings it back to me. We do it three times.

"He'll do that all day," Blue warns after kissing me hello.

"I love seeing him so happy with things."

"I do, too. I get the feeling he didn't have toys when he was a pup. Sorry I'm late. I stopped to talk to a girl. She's the one who gave him the ball."

"Oh. What girl?" I say the words before I realize how nosy and jealous they sound.

He shakes his hair out of his face, and the blue feather earring swings across his cheek.

"Just a girl I talk to sometimes. I usually see her when I play over near the antique store, but I ran into her on the way into the park."

"And she had a tennis ball with her?"

He laughs. "She brought her dog here, and she had a whole pack of tennis balls. She asked me if I wanted to hang out with her and let the dogs play together."

"Oh." I wonder if I'm not the only girl he has a relationship with. There could be a whole tribe of women who also noticed the hot, talented, magnetic homeless musician and his cute dog. Perhaps, like me, they threw caution to the wind to befriend him.

And more.

"Babe…" He leans down to meet my eyes. "Are you jealous?"

I glance over at Acorn playing with his ball. "No…."

He grins cockily at me. "You are."

"I am not," I say defensively.

"You're the only one I'm involved with. I didn't hang out with her. I came here to be with you. I don't hook up with other women."

"I hope not."

"The ladybugs would get mad at me if I even thought about another chick. You think I want them to swarm on me and eat me?" He pulls me into his arms and kisses me as I laugh.

"That would be a horrible way to die," I tease.

"Fuck yeah."

As we leave the park to drive to the bagel place, a woman with her black lab waves at Blue. She's not at all how I envisioned her. The woman in my mind was a sexy, young girl with dark hair, perfect makeup, tight jeans, and an unbuttoned coat revealing alluring cleavage. In reality, the woman is in her upper thirties and attractive in a very natural, no-makeup-needed way. Her hair is up in a messy ponytail. She's wearing gray sweatpants, sneakers, and a big, puffy white jacket. A wedding band is clearly visible on her waving hand. When she smiles and waves hesitantly at me, I feel like an idiot for being jealous, insecure, and hallucinatory.

"Do you feel better today?" I ask in the car on the way to the café. When he doesn't answer me, I glance away from the road to look him over. His hair is messier than usual, as if he forgot to brush it or run his fingers through it this morning. And when he walked up to me earlier in the park, I thought he had dark circles under his eyes.

"Yeah. Why?"

"Last night you said you felt sick. I think you had a migraine?"

He lights up a cigarette and lowers the car window a few inches, saying nothing further.

"Blue? Were you lying to me about not feeling well?"

"Why the hell would I lie to you?"

"I don't know," I reply, as a feeling of unease creeps over me. "You're acting kinda weird. Like either you don't remember it or you lied about it."

"I'm acting weird? First, you think I'm fucking other women with tennis balls. Now you're accusing me of lying to you."

"I'm not accusing you. I also suggested maybe you don't remember."

"Why wouldn't I remember last night?"

I pull into a parking spot outside the café and put the car in park with a frustrated and equally nervous sigh.

"Why are you getting so defensive?"

"I'm not. I just don't get where this convo is going."

Me either.

"Did something happen last night? Were you sick? Did you go somewhere? Was something wrong?" I reach for his hand and entwine our fingers. "Just talk to me."

"I am talking to you. What the fuck is this interrogation for? I thought we were getting breakfast."

"We are. I'm just confused."

"About what?"

I blink at him, trying to sort my thoughts. He somehow turned us in a circle, and now I'm completely confused to the point where I feel like I've done something wrong.

"Let's just forget it." I force a smile. "I'm starving, and I'm sure you are, too. Let's just get our bagels and coffee."

Instead, he turns in the seat to face me. "Do you trust me, Piper?"

"Yes. As much as I can. I'll admit it's a little difficult sometimes because I don't know where you are all day, or at night for that matter. We can't call each other. You won't meet my family. You don't want to move in with me. You won't commit to any sort of long-term relationship. You keep us in limbo. Always vague. So I guess it depends on what kind of trust. Do I think you'd purposely hurt me? No, I don't."

"I mean it when I say I love you. I don't ever want to hurt you."

"I know that. And I believe it."

A small finch eating crumbs off the parking lot asphalt has caught his attention. Barely blinking, he watches the tiny bird with keen interest, and I wonder if it reminds him of his time with his aunt and her birds. Or maybe for him, it's just a welcome distraction from this conversation.

"I get lost in my own head sometimes. The music, the words, sometimes they take over. Sometimes I can't sleep for days, and I don't eat. Then I get fucked up 'cause I'm exhausted and hungry. I get headaches and I feel moody as shit, and it all fuckin' dominos until I find a way to reset." He tightens his fingers into mine. "I do better alone so I don't drag people down with me. But now I'm kinda crazy about you, so I'm trying to make it work. I would've left as soon as it got cold out if I didn't love being with you so much."

Finally, he's opening up, but the vagueness is still there like a thin blanket thrown over us. "I know you're trying. We're in this together, whether you're in a good mood or a bad mood. I don't need or want or expect perfect. I just want you."

The bird has flown away, and his gaze shifts down to our hands. He nods slowly and then talks in a very low, almost whispered tone. "I guess I really don't remember having a headache."

This is one of those moments in life when I can dig deep for answers and force him to face his problems or I can sweep it under the rug, kiss it better, and hope it never creeps out again.

I choose to kiss it better.

"Sometimes I can't remember what I did yesterday, either. Let's go get something to eat. I promised our fuzzy boy a doughnut, and he's been very patient."

The smile on his face washes away all my earlier doubts and unease, and I silently vow to stop analyzing him. Lots of people forget things and go through moods, myself included.

We spend the day driving around listening to music and talk about an article Blue once read about paint colors that are supposed to evoke certain moods. I jot down the colors in a pocket notebook I keep in my purse so I can try to find them when Ditra and I buy paint for my new apartment, because the first thing I'm doing is painting over all the stark-white walls.

By the end of the day, I have swept away and forgotten the confusion and the elephant in the room.

CHAPTER FOURTEEN

PIPER

The past two weeks have been some of the best of my life. I'm floating on a cloud, wearing a perpetual smile. Nothing can break through my wall of happy.

I've been in my apartment for three days, and it's seriously an indescribable feeling. *My very own place.* Ditra and I hung scattered wooden shelves on one wall of my living room and then filled them with books that have been stored in my closet for years. We surrounded the books with cool bookends and heavy candles we found at the flea market. I painted the entire apartment in earth tones, mixed in cool blues and grays, and added a few random bright red throw pillows to add a splash of color. As silly as it sounds, when I come home from work at night I just wander around the small apartment, squealing over how cute it is. How *mine* it is. Even Archie seems happier, because he finally has lots of windows to sit in and gaze out of. What really won him over is the new carpeted cat tree I put in front of the window in the living room. Now he can stare at the birds and squirrels in the backyard all day long. In between naps, of course.

Tonight I'm silently squealing in my new apartment for an entirely new reason.

Blue is here. In my apartment. I almost fainted with shock and excitement earlier today at the park when he asked if he could meet me here tonight. I was sure he'd bail at the last minute, but he's here right now with Acorn—and penguin—in tow, slowly walking around, reading the spines of my books and studying the photographs on my wall. He looks so ethereal here in my space, I feel like an angel came down from heaven to grace me with his presence. And Acorn seems to be having the same effect on Archie, who hasn't hissed or run away once.

I'm filled with butterflies, and I'm hoping this could be the start of something really good. I guess Ditra was right, after all. Blue just needed to do this on his own terms.

"So this is you." His deep voice is like thunder rumbling in the distance. Warning, yet seductive.

"This is me. Do you like it?"

Nodding, he crosses the room to sit with me on the couch. "I do. It's cozy. Safe."

"I picked the colors you told me about."

"I noticed. The red is sexy." His hand rests on my upper thigh, his fingers lightly squeezing. "Do you have a little red dress? Or a black one?"

My mind reels from the sudden shift in the conversation. "Yes, one of each, actually." There was a time last year when Ditra was buying me 'hook up' clothes and dragging me to clubs in an attempt to pick up guys. She picked up many, I picked up none, and three of those dresses are currently in the back of my new closet.

"High heels?" he asks.

"I have a pair of four-inch heels I can barely walk in. Ditra picked them out and I wore them once and ended up taking them off and going barefoot all night bec—"

He interrupts my babbling, and moves his hand farther up my thigh until his fingers are brushing against my lips through my slacks. "Go put it on. The red dress and the shoes."

"Okay... are we playing dress up?" I ask playfully.

His lips curve into a sexy, devilish grin. "I'll wait here."

I stand and smile suspiciously at him, my interest piqued. "Do you want something to drink or eat before I disappear for a few minutes?"

"Nope. Just you."

My blood warms in my veins. "Okay. Just help yourself if you want anything."

I disappear down the hallway to my bedroom to search for the shockingly short and sexy, low-cut red dress. I slip it on with nothing but a black silk thong underneath, and the material clings to my curves like a second skin. I breathe a sigh of relief when I find the four-inch stilettos in the back of my closet. Not sure why I didn't toss these when I moved, but now I'm glad I didn't. I finish the look off with red lipstick, a smudge of black eyeliner, mascara, and fluff up my hair with my hands as I walk back to join Blue. I'm doing my best to walk as sexily as I can in these ridiculous stilt-like shoes, but I almost skid and face plant when I turn into the living room.

The lights are off, and all the candles in the room are lit. I never actually light candles because I'm afraid Archie will catch his big fluffy tail on fire, but the room looks like a scene out of a movie with the flickering of flames and shadows. He stands when I enter the room, and he takes my hands in his and spreads our arms out.

"Oof," he groans, dragging his gaze up and down my body. "You're so fuckin' beautiful, Ladybug. I wish I could take your picture. I don't trust my fucked-up brain to remember you like this forever."

"You don't have to remember me. I'll always be here for you to look at."

He moves his hands to my waist and he lowers his head to kiss my lips. "Time will tell," he says, using one of his notorious cryptic replies. Still kissing me, he sways us back and forth in a sensual dance as he slides his hands from my waist to the backs of my thighs, then slowly inching the material of the dress up until his hands are cupping my ass.

"I'm proud of you," he whispers. "You're so... together. You don't give up on what you want."

"I try not to." I tilt my head up to look at him and lift my hand to caress the back of his neck. "Do you, Evan? Do you give up?"

"Why you callin' me Evan again?" he asks, brushing his lips across my cheek as he continues to sway us back and forth.

"Because it's your name. And I think sometimes you need to hear your real name."

His jaw muscles twitch. "You might be right."

"So do you?" I urge gently. "Give up on what you want?"

"Maybe what I want gives up on me."

Our lips meet again, and I pull away to give him a frustrated expression. "You love to talk in riddles, don't you?"

"I prefer to think of it as lyrical."

Before I can muster up a good comeback, he sweeps me up into his arms and carries me over to the couch, placing me down on my feet in front of it. When he sits, his face is level with the hem of my skirt. His smoldering eyes caress and undress me before his hands even touch me. Reaching between my legs, he hooks his finger under the thin strap of my thong and pulls it all the way down to my ankles. When I step out of it, he bunches my panties up in a small ball and shoves them into the front pocket of his jeans.

"I'm keeping these," he says.

"Okay. As long as you don't wear them..."

He smacks my ass and I let out a yelp. "Hey." I rub my hand over my stinging flesh.

"Did that hurt?"

"Yes."

"Turn around."

Turning away from him, I hope he doesn't slap me again, but instead he pushes my dress up to my waist. I feel the warmth of his lips on my ass, right where he slapped me, kissing away the sting. He moves his hands down my thighs, over my calves to my feet, grasping the stiletto heels and spreading my legs with a faint screech across the wood floor. My heart gallops with the hooves of a thousand tiny horses when he squeezes my ass cheeks, using his thumbs to spread my lips apart. I moan and whimper, arching my back to him as he licks me from behind. His tongue and his mouth are pure ecstasy, bringing my body to sinful heights of desire as his tongue laps my pussy to my ass and back again. Quivering and shaking, I reach back to grasp his shoulders for balance. He shatters my inhibitions, making me want everything and anything. The need to have more of him, deeper, harder, longer is completely overpowering. When I've finally stopped shuddering against his mouth, he spins me around and guides me into a kneeling position on the couch and slides his cock into my drenched core. Leaning over my body from behind, he tugs my hair to the side and he ravishes my neck, sucking and biting, leaving branding marks I'll love seeing tomorrow. I grip the couch cushions as he rips the deep neckline of my dress even farther and squeezes my breasts, making me come again as he pounds into me from behind.

At some point during the hours-long sexathon, he carries me into the bedroom and we christen my brand-new bed until the wee hours of the morning. Exhausted, sweaty, and giddy, we eat ice cream out of the carton in bed and watch a ridiculous horror movie. Something so simple as watching a movie together makes my heart leap with the hope of more normalcy.

When I wake up, Blue's not in bed next to me but the shower water is running in the bathroom, and it makes me smile that he's not using a truck stop shower standing in a puddle of germs. And he's singing. God, is he singing. His deep, growly voice resonates through my small house, giving me goosebumps. Sitting up, I stretch, and my muscles ache in protest from last night's physical workout. As I'm yawning with my arms stretched over my head, he comes into the bedroom in nothing but one of my mauve towels wrapped around his thin waist. Up until now, I haven't had the pleasure of seeing him undressed in any kind of decent light, and he is a sight to behold—all glistening lean muscle and ink. Wordlessly, I watch him pull on his jeans and sweatshirt. I fight the intense urge to offer to wash his clothes for him while he's here. I don't want to do or say anything to ruin the perfection of last night and today.

He leans down to kiss me before he sits on the edge of the bed to put his socks and boots on.

"Red is your color, babe. It brings out your fire."

"*You* bring out my fire," I reply, leaning my head on his shoulder.

"I'm going to walk down to the café and get us some donuts and sandwiches."

"If you give me a few minutes, we can go together, or you can take my car if you want."

He pushes his damp hair back and clicks his piercing against his teeth. "Nah. I like to walk every morning. And it'll give you some privacy."

Privacy went out the window a long time ago. He's seen me naked and spread. His cock, his fingers, and his tongue have been on me and inside me in one way or another more times than I can count.

"You can stay, Blue. As long as you want," I say tentatively. "You could still walk and wander. I won't hold you down. But this could be your home. It could be *our* home. If you want."

He strokes the back of his hand across my cheek, and his blue eyes lock onto mine for a few moments, thinking, contemplating, wandering. Half his mouth curves into a slight smile.

Only Blue could smile half-way.

"I know, Piper. Your heart is my home. The way you look at me, the way you make me feel, is my home."

"I meant—"

He touches his finger to my lips. "I know what you meant."

I don't push it. Things are too good to push. "Okay. The offer stands. Always."

"Always?"

"Always. Anytime. Forever. Without a doubt. Okay?"

Cupping my chin, he brings my lips to his and kisses me softer than he ever has. "I love you, Ladybug."

"I love you too."

Rising from the bed, he looks around the room slowly before turning back to me. "I'm leaving Acorn here instead of bringing him with me. Last I checked he was all cozy on the couch with your cat. He looked happy."

I laugh. "Finally, Archie has a friend."

From the doorway, he winks at me, and I don't get off the bed until his boots thud all the way down my hallway and out my front door. Sighing with happiness, I crawl out of bed and grab my robe to head for the bathroom, stopping to check Acorn and Archie first. Blue was right, they're both curled up on my new couch, napping away like they've been best friends forever. Smiling to myself, I glance out the large bay window to see Blue walking down the road with his guitar and his duffel bag slung over his shoulder, and I wish he didn't feel the need to have to carry everything he owns around with him constantly. Perhaps, in time, he'll feel secure enough to leave his belongings here. And maybe, if I'm patient enough, he'll finally agree to move in.

I take a shower, clean up the house a little while my hair dries, then I take Acorn into the backyard and play fetch with him, just like I envisioned when I first looked at this apartment. Maybe the theory of manifestation is true—that if you picture what you want in your mind, and focus positively on getting it, it will happen. Closing my eyes, I picture Blue living here... us making dinner together and eating on my small patio. Making love every night. Waking up in his arms every morning. Listening to him sing in the shower.

I want it to happen.

It *can* happen.

After playing with Acorn, I put a little makeup on and fix my hair. I make the bed and spritz it with some lavender bed spray I bought that's supposed to be calming.

I picture Blue in my bed tonight.

I envision us watching *Titanic* together, with Archie and Acorn at our feet.

I believe it can happen.

Acorn barks, and I run to the door, ready to throw my arms around him, but it's not Blue, it's just the mailman. I wait for him to move to the adjoining house and then I retrieve my mail, which is nothing but junk that I toss into the trash.

An odd sensation comes over me as I stand in my kitchen, like a cold breeze that wasn't there at all. The clock on the wall suddenly seems to be ticking exceptionally loud, forcing me to look at it.

My heart jumps when I realize three hours have passed since Blue left. Breakfast time has long passed, and even though I'm up for eating doughnuts and bagels any time of day, I know it wouldn't take him this long to walk to the café on the main road and then back here. Even walking slowly, it's not that far. I look out the front window, thinking maybe he'll just materialize since I'm looking, but there's no one on the tree-lined street at all.

Anxiety festers up, twisting my insides, but I try to squash it as I get my sneakers and jacket. People stop and talk to Blue all the time because they recognize him as the *guy who plays guitar* all over town. He probably ran into someone he knows at the café and is sitting outside playing his guitar and has lost track of time. It's happened before.

I drive to the café with Acorn sitting shotgun, and run inside.

"Have you seen a guy with long hair and a guitar in here, in the last few hours?" I ask the young guy behind the counter.

He shakes his head. "I've been here since six a.m., haven't seen anyone like that."

I thank him and go back to my car with a racing heart and mind, wondering where he could possibly be.

"Where's Blue?" I ask Acorn as we drive through town, and he perks his ears up. Blue doesn't refer to himself as Daddy as most pet owners do. Maybe he's too cool for that. Or maybe he can't deal with the underlying responsibility of the title. We drive to the park, and I take Acorn with me to walk up and down the paths, past my bench, and our picnic table, and down to the old bridge. The only things greeting us are memories.

Fear and frustration send tears to my eyes, and I brush them away as I drive over to the shed. Maybe he got a bad headache and went there to rest, knowing I would go there to look for him. I should have looked there first, instead of wasting time rambling through the park. Acorn's tail starts to wag as I pull in front of the old house, and I assume he thinks he's home or he knows Blue is here.

"Come on, pup," I say, letting him out of the car. He immediately jumps out and trots to the backyard with me not far behind. I fully expect to find Blue sleeping in the shed, but when I pull the rusty latch and open the door, he's not there.

And neither is anything else.

Acorn stands beside me, not wagging his tail, blinking up at me with a blank expression on his face that I'm sure looks just like my own.

The silence is thick as mud. I can almost feel the emptiness, take hold of it in my hand and squeeze it through my fingers. My breathing becomes unnatural and forced in my lungs, and a deep pain throbs in my chest and down into my gut. Acorn nudges my hand with his wet nose and I pat his head absently as I stare around in disbelief at the empty space.

Maybe he got robbed. Maybe someone came here and took everything. Or maybe the cops came, arrested him, and cleaned the place out.

Yes. That's exactly what happened. One of the neighbors must have caught on and reported us and now he's probably sitting in a jail cell waiting for me to come bail him ou—

As I spin to leave, I notice the white piece of notepaper stuck to the back of the door with an old nail. With a trembling hand I tear it off the door.

> *Ladybug,*
> *It was time for me to keep walking.*
> *Take care of Acorn for me.*
> *If you can, try to leave a space for me in your heart.*
> *I'm sorry.*
> *I love you like no tomorrow, little slayer. Don't ever forget that.*
> *~ Blue*

Tremors rock through my body so hard my teeth are gnashing against each other. Fury and heartache rages inside me like a tsunami, and I want to scream and tear the shed apart, to somehow destroy this scene around me and bring it all back to how it was yesterday. But I'm unable to move or cry or blink or even breathe because the man who meant everything in the world to me has just shattered every little piece of my heart and soul.

Why? How could he do this to me?

He just walked away. From me, and his dog, and our little life, and our love. I stare at his uniquely perfect writing, wishing it to morph into words I want to read like the notes he's left in the past. Words like *I miss you* and *come back*. Big wet, hot tears fall from my eyes like the beginnings of a rainstorm. At the thought of the rain, my fragile heart cracks and disintegrates, and I wail and shriek like a wild animal caught in a trap, mentally unhinged from the pain with no way to escape and on the verge of chewing out my own heart to get away from it all.

Falling to the dirty floor, I sob uncontrollably, digging my nails into my palms until the soft flesh breaks open and bleeds.

It hurts. Everything hurts more than I ever thought possible. The stabbing pain is so deep, burning in my heart and in my soul, searing into every part of my physical and emotional being. I'm sure it will kill me. Nobody can live through a pain like this.

Acorn whimpers and lies next to me with his head on my leg, always the caretaker, and I bow down and hug him to me like he's a lifeline. I cry into his fur until it's soaked and curly, until I have no more tears left.

Hours must pass, and it's brutally clear Blue isn't going to come back, no matter how long I sit here and picture him walking through that door, it's not happening. I don't have special manifestation powers at all. What I have is a terribly broken heart and lost faith in love and trust. When I can't sit there for a moment longer, I fold the note up and put it into my back pocket, and Acorn and I close the door of the shed behind us for the last time.

In a daze I walk past the house, and I almost don't even notice that the door of the four-season porch is ajar. I honestly can't remember if it's always been that way, but curiosity draws me like a magnet to pull the door open and cautiously step inside and take a look around. The air inside is stale and musty, penetrating through my stuffy nose. Whoever lived here at one time obviously loved birds, because several old bird cages hang from the ceiling, and quite a few rest on the floor. At the other end of the porch are two huge cages, the kind a big parrot would live in. Even though they all appear to have been cleaned, there are still random feathers of different sizes and colors scattered on the floor. Stepping farther inside, my eyes are drawn to three piles of sketchbooks, each pile approximately three feet high. I grab one of the books and flip through it, but its pages are empty. My brow creases as I pull one from the bottom of the pile, letting the rest tumble to the floor. This one is also empty. I check another from a different pile—and it's also void of any writing.

A shiver sprinkles up my spine as I realize these are the same notebooks Blue was always scribbling in when he was having a bad day. There must be two hundred of them here.

Why?

Putting the notebooks back on the disheveled stack, I slowly walk over to the corner, where a sheet is thrown over a pile of...something. My heart races as I lift the sheet, and I'm not at all prepared to uncover all the objects that were in the shed. Everything—the air mattress, the candles, the curtain, the throw rug, Acorn's bed. Next to this pile are two large garbage bins filled with empty bottles of assorted alcohol, matchbooks, and empty cigarette boxes.

Confusion mixed with nausea waves over me. Did he break in here to hide all this stuff? Or was he able to get in here all along? There's no way he had all those notebooks in the tiny shed, so they must have been hidden in here. But why? And for God's sake, why so many?

With careful, quiet steps, I walk over to the door that leads to the main house and attempt to turn the brass knob, but it doesn't turn. Peering through the dirty pane window of the door, there are no signs of life in the large kitchen; nothing left on the table or counter tops.

I bang on the door. "Blue? Are you in there?" My voice cracks with hope and despair. "Evan? It's me. If you're here, please come out and talk to me." I press my ear to the glass. "Please?"

There's no sound, no creepy feeling of being watched or listened to. I'm alone standing on a dirty porch, becoming more heartbroken and confused with each passing second. With the last tiny glimmer of hope snuffed out, I reluctantly give up and leave, grabbing Acorn's bed from the pile on my way out. I don't want any of that other stuff, but this poor dog deserves to have his own bed.

"Come on, Acorn." I head toward the car but the dog keeps stopping and looking back at the house, hesitating. "Come on, sweetie. I'm going to take you home."

It takes me twenty minutes to persuade Acorn to leave the property, even though he's left with me several times in the past weeks with no problem. Somehow, he knows Blue has abandoned him, and, like me, he seems to be in shocked disbelief, waiting for him to come swaggering down the walkway.

As I drive home, completely numb and emotionally catatonic, I replay last night and this morning in my mind, trying to pinpoint what went wrong, or at what exact moment a goodbye was said that I didn't catch. Looking back, there were none, and there were many, depending on how I interpret each moment.

I can't help but wonder if nothing was wrong at all, and he chose to leave when everything was perfect, to suspend us forever like snapshots in a photo album.

When I get home, I realize I don't have anything I need to care for a dog properly, and I'm not going to continue feeding him part of my meals as Blue did for who knows how long. A dog needs real food, a leash, a brush, and dishes. I drive to the nearest pet store to get everything I need and leave Acorn at my apartment. As I'm browsing through the aisles, I remember the ceramic dishes I bought for Acorn just a few weeks ago, which must be in the pile of stuff on the porch. I can buy new dishes, but those were expensive, and they were special because they have the words 'my dog rocks' printed on the side.

Next thing I know, I'm driving over to the abandoned house to retrieve the dishes even though I swore to myself I'd never set foot on that property again. The sun is setting in the distance when I arrive, and I try to fight off the tears and ache in my gut knowing Blue won't be coming around the corner of the house to greet me. Just as I assumed, the dog dishes are under the tarp with the other items. Shaking my head with a myriad of sadness and frustration, I pull them out and turn to leave, but stop in my tracks when something very odd catches my eye. All the notebooks are neatly stacked again, and I know damn well they weren't like that when I left earlier.

Am I losing my mind? Or has someone been here?

My heart pumps hard in my chest. For all the time I spent on this property hiding in that shed, I never once saw another person here except for Blue. So either someone's been in this house the entire time—which seems very unlikely—or Blue has been coming and going in here today, and could possibly still be here.

I race to the door to the kitchen and rattle the locked doorknob, then bang loudly on the door.

"Blue! Are you in there? I swear to God you better come out here and talk to me if you are!" I peer into the window, but I don't see anyone. "What the hell is wrong with you?" I scream. "I thought you loved me!"

The creaking of the empty birdcages swinging is the only sound.

Mumbling under my breath and with tears falling down my face, I walk to my car and drive away. But I don't go home, like I should—like a normal person would. Because right now I'm emotionally crushed with a broken heart and I can't think rationally at all. I drive my car to the next street over, park it in front of someone's house, and then walk back to the abandoned house in the dark. As quietly as I can, I creep back onto the porch, and hide myself under the tarp, against the side of the house. I pull the down comforter over me to keep myself warm, and the hysterical sobs start all over again because it smells of smoke and sex and us. Memories assault me like a swarm of stinging bees, and there's absolutely nothing I can do to escape them or not see them, to not feel their pain penetrating deep into my very soul. Closing my eyes does nothing to shield me from visions that are forever burned in my mind.

His smile. Him playing guitar. The way his eyes would sparkle or darken with emotion. Him hugging Acorn. His body on top of mine. The feather against his hair.

How could he take all my favorite things in life away from me? Everything I looked forward to each and every day—just stripped away from me. I know that he must know what this feels like. In fact, I believe that he knows exactly how it feels to have everything I need and want and love so much stripped away without the slightest warning. He's forced me to quit cold turkey and live without the high that being with him gave me.

I huddle under the tarp for hours, hoping and waiting for Blue to show up, but he never does. Exhausted with defeat and chilled to the bone, I walk back to my car, not even having the sense of mind to care that I'm walking around after midnight, in the middle of a dark road like a zombie. Numbness overtook logic hours ago.

I'm dragged out of my stupor the moment I open my apartment door to a horribly putrid smell. I gasp when I see the mess before me— dog poop and garbage strewn all over the living room and kitchen. Acorn is cowering in the corner and Archie is perched high on his cat tree with an expression of severe judgment and disapproval.

Oh my God.

I kneel next to Acorn, who's trembling with what I can only guess is a mix of guilt and fear.

"It's okay," I soothe, stroking the soft fur between his eyes. "It's not your fault." I coax him into the backyard so he can get some air while I clean up the mess. I can't even be mad at him because it's my fault for leaving him alone for so long. I don't know if Acorn's ever lived in a house before, and now that I'm forced to think about it, he's probably not used to being alone, either. Blue took him everywhere. Having a dog in my life is going to take some getting used to, but I'm not going to abandon Acorn like Blue did. I have no idea why he left his dog—his best friend—with me. Hopefully because he thought we needed each other, which is a lot easier to accept than the possibility that he's a selfish bastard who didn't care about either of us.

It takes me a while to scrub the stains out of the carpet, and I surpassed exhaustion hours ago. The new sheets on my bed are covered with the scent of Blue and the memories of our night together, so I crash on the couch to escape. I'm jolted awake by the doorbell. With a leaping heart, I run for the front door and swing it open to see my parents and sister with balloons and a flowering plant. Blinking at them, I wonder what kind of sick joke this is that they came here to celebrate my broken heart with colored balloons.

"Happy housewarming!" Courtney exclaims, throwing her arms around me. "I miss you already."

Oh shit. How is it Sunday already?

Forcing a smile, I run my fingers through my knotty hair. "Come on in."

"Honey, you look terrible," my mother comments, placing the plant on a small table next to the front door. "Are you sick?"

"You have a dog now? When did you get a dog?" my father asks, prompting Courtney to run to Acorn and fall to the floor next to him.

"Oh my God he's so cute! What's his name?"

My brain is in a fog from lack of sleep. "Um, he belongs to a friend of mine who asked me to take care of him. His name is Acorn."

My mom is still looking at me with growing motherly concern, and reaches out to touch my forehead. "Piper, what's wrong? You're pale and blotchy."

"I just have a bad cold, and I haven't been sleeping well." I hate lying to people. Especially my parents. "I'm fine, though. To be honest, I forgot you were coming and I overslept."

Her smile wavers. "We don't have to stay, we just—"

"No, Mom, it's fine. I want you guys to stay. Really. Just give me a minute to go wash my face."

From the safety of my bathroom, I can hear them whispering about me, and I cringe when my father suggests I might be hung over. Does he honestly think after just a few nights of living alone I'd start drinking?

"You should have a deadbolt on this door," my father says when I return to the living room. "I'll bring one over and install it one night during the week."

"Okay. This is a nice neighborhood, though."

"You can't be too careful. The dog is probably a good idea. Does he bark if he hears a noise outside?"

I can't recall ever hearing Acorn bark, not even when the doorbell rang, but I'm sure he must, because dogs bark at all sorts of things. "I think he does."

My sister flops on the floor on her back and smiles upside down at me. "This apartment is amazing. I can't wait to get my own place. Can I stay overnight tonight? We can make popcorn, and watch movies and—"

Oh no. I can't have an audience all day and night when I'm in the middle of a meltdown. I need way more time alone to get my head together. "I wish you could but I have to be up early for work tomorrow. How about Friday night?" Maybe by Friday, Blue will be back, we can put all this behind us, and everything will be good again. He might even be open to stopping by to meet my sister.

"You promise?" Courtney asks.

I smile, more at my daydream than at her. "Yes. I promise."

My mom starts to talk about how cute the apartment is, how she loves the colors and how bright and airy it is with all the windows, and Courtney announces how she wants to move into my old space in the basement. I'm barely listening when my parents tell her that isn't happening any time soon. My mind keeps wandering back to Blue. Why did he leave? Where did he go? What did I do wrong? Why wasn't love enough to get him to stay?

"Piper, did you hear me?"

Shaking my head, I turn to face my mother's questioning gaze. "No, I'm sorry, I didn't."

"We were hoping we'd get to meet your boyfriend today."

"Oh." I grind my teeth. "We kinda broke up."

"Who dumped who?" Courtney sits up, instantly interested, because she's at that phase in teen life when she loves any kind of drama and gossip.

I twist my hands together in my lap and force the words over the lump in my throat. "Um, it was mostly mutual. He had to move."

That's one way of putting it.

My mother smiles sympathetically. "I'm sorry to hear that. But it's probably for the best. You haven't been yourself while you've been dating that boy. You've been withdrawn and anxious. You're a beautiful young woman, you'll forget about him in no time and find the right one to sweep you off your feet."

I've already been swept, and I'll never forget Blue. He's always going to be the one who has my heart. I know that without a doubt. He might be complicated, but he's the right one and the only one.

"You can't trust a man who won't meet your family or come pick you up and take you out. He's obviously got something to hide, or he's just a user and doesn't know how to treat a woman. You're too good for someone like that. You're a good girl. Don't lower yourself," my father lectures. "Remember this, he's not going to buy the cow if he's getting the milk for free. You have to make him work for it and respect it."

Courtney goes into a fit of giggles while I look at my father like he's insane. "Dad, really? That's a horrible thing to say. I'm not a slut or a cow and I wasn't getting used. We really care about each other."

Glaring at my father, my mother jumps in to try to lessen the blow. "That's not what your father meant. You have a good heart, you're very giving and you trust everyone. People will take advantage of you."

I can't believe my father just referred to me as a cow and insinuated I've been handing out the goods. Even though I just got dumped in the worst way possible, I know Blue wasn't using me. I know he loves me as much as I love him. I just don't have the mental strength to explain any of it to my parents right now when my heart is still bleeding from the aftermath of Blue's sudden disappearance.

Hours later, I'm relieved when my parents go back home. Wearing a fake smile and holding back tears is exhausting. This should have been a happy day for me to show off my new place and make my parents proud of me. Instead, I'm a mess and my father thinks I'm a cow who took up drinking and allows men to use me.

Ditra would love that visual.

No matter what, I always end up being some kind of awkward outcast.

CHAPTER FIFTEEN

PIPER

I'm hardly ever late for anything. In fact, I'm usually a few minutes early for appointments and meetings. When my sisters and I were young, my mother was constantly rushing us around. She instilled in us that not being on time was bad manners. She definitely did not believe in being fashionably late.

But I never considered being late terrifying.

Until today.

"You're pregnant."

The room spins so fast I grip the edges of the exam table to keep myself from tumbling off onto the floor.

"Piper?" Dr. Green touches my shoulder and motions for the nurse to get me a cup of water.

My head reels, my vision blurs, and the doctor's voice echoes around me. "That can't be...." I shake my head slowly. "It must be a mistake. I'm on the pill. You gave it to me."

"It's not one hundred percent guaranteed, unfortunately. Have you been taking it every day?"

"Yes," I reply, but that's not exactly true. There were those nights when Blue asked me to stay in the shed with him, and we snuggled, and talked, and made love all night. When I finally went home the next day, I either forgot to take the pill or skipped it because I didn't know what else to do.

I take the cup from the nurse and gulp the cold water, flooding my throat and stomach, hoping to wash this all away. There must be a way to undo this and make it not so.

I'm smart. I'm responsible. I'm not the kind of girl who gets pregnant. That happens to other girls who aren't careful.

That's you now, Piper. A cow who got used and thrown away with a dog and a baby.

I stare into my empty paper cup. "Actually... I think there may have been a few times I forgot to take it."

"It has to be taken every day to be effective." Dr. Green flips through her notes in my folder and then glances back to me. "I'm going to assume you weren't using condoms at the time?"

I shake my head, humiliation thrumming through my veins like acid.

"H-how far along am I?" I ask.

"Looks like just about ten weeks. We'll schedule an ultrasound in two weeks and you can see your baby. You're welcome to bring the father."

"We're not together anymore." I tremble uncontrollably and burst into choking tears. The nurse hands me a box of tissues and I balance it on my lap. "He left...."

"Piper, I'm very sorry to hear that."

Ten weeks. It's been eight weeks since Blue left. During that time, I've prowled every park and train station in a hundred-mile radius trying to find him, to no avail. He could be anywhere by now.

"I don't know what I'm going to do...." I sob, blotting my eyes with the scratchy tissue. "I don't even know where he is."

Dr. Green hands me a business card and several pamphlets with photos of pregnant teens and babies on them. "We have a counselor on staff. I think it would be good for you to talk with her about your decisions and choices."

The words ricochet between my ears. *Decisions and choices.*

Somehow, just like that, my quiet, boring, little life is gone forever.

CHAPTER SIXTEEN

PIPER

"It's nice to have you home for dinner. We've only seen you twice since you moved out," my mom says from behind the platter of ziti and meatballs in the center of the table.

"I've been really busy with work, I told you I started my new position as marketing assistant last week."

"That's terrific. Do you like it?"

I nod and swallow my food. "Yes, it's been great. I even have a small office now."

"Did you get a raise?" Courtney asks. She's changed in the past month, and appears older to me, and less innocent. Her black hair is much shorter now, and she's started to wear more make-up. I wonder if she's dating someone, but I don't want to ask about that when I'm about to drop a bomb on my parents.

"Yes." I wipe my mouth with my napkin. "I was given a small raise."

I take a sip of my iced tea and breathe in a deep breath. "I need to tell you all something… just please don't freak out."

My father puts his fork down in preparation. I probably shouldn't have started this conversation in those words, but I just want to get this over with and go back to my apartment.

"Use the Band-Aid approach," Ditra had advised. *"Don't do it slow and easy. Just rip it off and come right out with it."*

"I'm pregnant. A little over three months."

My mother's face pales to a porcelain white, and next to her, my father's jaw clenches and he shoves his plate away, knocking it into his glass of water, which tips and spills. Courtney's eyes bug out and she looks from me, to our mother, to our father, and back to me again. Waiting for a response. Just like I am.

I lick my lips nervously. "I'm going to keep it," I throw into the silence. "I've talked to a counselor already and that's what I've decided is best."

"Piper." My mother's eyes are glistening with tears. "How could you let this happen?"

"I knew it," my father says gruffly. "I knew something like this was going to happen."

"It was an accident. I was on the pill but I forgot to take it a few times. I didn't realize I could get pregnant so fast."

My father slams his fist down hard on the table and we all jump. "You forgot?" he yells. "You forgot you were ruining your entire Goddamn life?"

Yes. I forgot because I was caught up in love and whispers and music and the sound of raindrops…

"A baby is a huge decision," my mother says. "You're only twenty-one. And what about the father? Are you back together? Does he want to be part of this baby's life?"

My father shakes his head. "I don't give a damn what he wants. You can bet your ass he'll be paying child support."

The counselor warned me my parents would react this way. That it's a natural reaction to a surprise pregnancy. I absorb their emotions for a moment, let them expel their anger and shock, before I force myself to continue. "No. He doesn't know."

"You have to tell him. He's just as responsible as you are."

"I know, Mom. But I don't know where he is."

"Well then we'll find him. We can hire a lawyer if we have to and garnish his paycheck for support. It happens all the time."

If only life were that easy. If only *Blue* could be that easy. "I have no idea how to find him. I don't even know his last name."

"What?" my father roars. "How do you not know his last name? Is this the same guy you dated for months? The one we never even met?"

"Yes, Dad. I've never been with anyone else."

"And you never thought to ask him his last name?" he asks incredulously. "Doesn't that usually happen during a first conversation?"

The urge to cry and defend myself, to throw myself on the sword to defend Blue is strong, but I keep myself in check. "It's complicated. Can we just forget about him? I'm going to have this baby on my own, without him."

"Piper, this is very serious. You have to tell him, and we're not going to just let him sail off into the sunset and leave you a single mother struggling with a baby."

I play with my fork, my brain spinning for the right words.

"He's homeless," I finally reveal. "I don't know his last name, or even if his first name is real. He doesn't have a phone, or a job, or an address. Believe me, I tried to find him months ago. He's just…gone. I didn't know I was pregnant when he was still here. I'm sure if he knew, he would have stayed."

"Tell me this is some kind of sick joke you and your sister made up," my father says, glancing over at Courtney, who shakes her head vehemently.

"Dad, it's not a joke. It's all true."

My mother leans her elbows on the table and buries her face in her hands. "This is completely crazy," she mutters. "I don't understand any of this. How did this happen?"

"I met him in the park. He's a street musician."

"So he's a fucking derelict, probably running from the law. I'll bet he's a burn-out, too. That baby's going to be born addicted to crack."

"Daddy, that only happens if the mother is on crack. Sperm can't be on drugs," Courtney interjects.

"Go to your room!" he bellows.

"Dad—"

He points to the hallway and glares at her. "Go. Now."

My sister gets up and makes a dramatic exit, slamming her door when she reaches her bedroom upstairs. I rub my hand across my throbbing forehead. "Can we please just calm down?" I beg softly. "This is already hard enough for me to deal with."

My father is now pacing the room with a glass of scotch in his hand.

"You think *this* is hard?" he asks. "This is nothing. Wait until you have a little meth baby. Or AIDS. And how exactly are you planning on supporting a baby? Have you thought about any of this?" He downs the remainder of his scotch and goes to the cabinet to refill his glass. "I don't understand you, Piper. You've always been different than your sisters. But having sex with homeless men? Your mother and I didn't raise you to behave like this. What the hell is wrong with you?"

"There's nothing *wrong with me*. You'll never understand. He's not a bad person just because he lives differently. And people can't help who they fall in love with."

"Yes they can, Piper. Respectable young women don't let dirty homeless men put their hands on them. You throw them a dollar and you walk the other way. You don't spread your Goddamn legs."

"Bill, that's enough. This is our daughter, and that's our grandchild."

My father puts his hand up, his face twisted with disgust. "No. This isn't my daughter. *My* daughter—the little girl I raised—wouldn't lower herself to such filthy behavior. I don't know who the hell this person is." He slams his glass down on the dinner table. "I'm going out. I can't even be under the same roof with her."

I knew this conversation wouldn't go well, but I never expected my father to be so sickened by me and my unborn baby that he would actually leave the house to get away from the sight of me.

He and Blue have that in common—walking away without communicating.

My heart aches as I slowly lift my head to meet my mother's eyes across the table. Her lips are pursed in a thin line, her chestnut eyes pooled with emotion. Without a word, she places her napkin on her plate and when she stands, I'm sure she's going to follow my father's lead and leave. Instead, she falls into the chair next to mine and pulls me into her arms.

"We'll get through this," she whispers. "I promise."

I cling to her, my body racking with sobs, afraid to let go for fear of losing another person when I need them the most.

"I'm so sorry, Mom. I never wanted this to happen."

She strokes my hair, like she did when I was young. "I know, Piper. It's going to be okay. I'm here, and I'm not going anywhere."

I wipe my eyes with my napkin. "I'm so scared. Now Dad hates me, I don't know where Blue is, and I have no idea how I'm going to raise a baby by myself. I don't know how to be a mother."

"Shhh... one day at a time. That's how you do it, just like everyone else." She smiles softly. "And your father doesn't hate you. He's going to need some time to accept this, but he will. Trust me."

"I'm just so confused...when I talked to the counselor she made me believe I could do this but now, I just don't know, Mom. One minute I think I'm okay and the next I'm falling apart."

"You *can* do this, Piper, if it's really what you want. Do you want to keep the baby? Are you sure?"

Still sniffling, I level my eyes at her and nod. "It's all I've been thinking about. And I'm positive I want to keep the baby. I can't imagine giving her up and never knowing what happened to her. I couldn't live with myself. I know I'd regret it."

"Her?"

I can't help but smile through my tears. "Yeah. I just know I'm going to have a little girl. I can feel it."

My mother takes a deep breath, but she's still smiling. "It's a lot sooner than I was expecting, but I guess I'm going to be a grandmother."

"It all feels surreal to me. I don't think I'm really going to believe any of this until she's here."

"I think all mothers feel that way." She hesitates for a second. "Is it true? About the father? You honestly don't know where he is, or what his full name is?"

I lean back in my chair and reach for my water. "It's all true. But he's not a bad person. I know it seems like he is, but that's only because you don't know him. He's caring, and talented, and smart. He isn't some dirty, scruffy guy with a shopping cart like you're thinking. He's good-looking, clean, and polite. It wasn't just a fling. We really love each other."

Her brow creases. "I don't understand why he would be homeless, or why you don't know his name or his whereabouts. That's not normal, Piper. It worries me a great deal. All of this is so unlike you."

How can I possibly explain Blue? I'm still trying to understand him myself, and I've come up with more questions than answers. "It's hard to explain. He's just different. I know Dad thinks he must be a loser and on drugs. When he was younger he did have a drug problem."

Her eyes widen and I continue before she starts to panic.

"But he was in rehab and he's clean now. He's just one of those wandering, antsy, creative artist types. He can't sit still." My voice hitches with emotion and I pause to compose myself. Talking about him makes me miss him so much more. I'd do anything just to see his smile and hear his voice again. "He's special, Mom. He's difficult, and he lives in his own world, but he's a good person. I don't regret being with him at all."

"I'm trying to understand, Piper. I never imagined any of my girls would be in a situation like this. Can you see him ever being a part of your life again? Or this baby's?"

"I don't know. In the immediate future? No. But maybe, someday. I think he'll come back eventually. At least, I hope he does." I do more than just hope. I wish, I pray, I envision, and I may have even briefly considered contacting a witch to put a spell on him.

Over the past few weeks I've asked myself a hundred times how I think Blue would react to the news of being a father, and every scenario brings me to a different conclusion. Sometimes I think he'd be happy, but other times, I think he'd be scared out of his damn mind and run, not walk, as far away as he could and never come back.

My mother starts to clean up the table. "I think you should move back home," she suggests. "It would be best for you and the baby to be here with us."

"What?" I straighten in my chair. "No. I can't do that. I love my apartment. I can't raise a baby in the basement, Mom. Even the cat hated it down there." Moving back home has to be an absolute, last resort when no other choices are available. I refuse to lose everything I've worked so hard for and let my life fall apart just because I'm pregnant. The counselor told me lots of single mothers go to college, have careers, and live happy, normal lives even though most of them thought they couldn't do it all in the beginning. I just have to stay focused on my goals, be a good mother, and make decisions that are best for me and the baby.

"Before you say no, will you please think about this? How are you going to take care of a baby living alone? You work full time. Daycare costs a fortune and will take up most of your paycheck. If you live here, I can take care of the baby all day while you're at work. It will be much easier for everyone involved."

I can't deny that most of what she's saying is true. I've already started researching local daycare centers and the weekly fees are a shock.

"Do you really want to be a babysitter all day? You just retired last year. I thought you wanted to do crafts. Learn to golf with Dad. Enjoy life while you're still young."

She waves her hand at me. "I can still work on my craft projects, and golf on weekends, if I want to, which I really don't, but don't tell your father that."

I hold my ground. "I can't move back in here. I need my space, and independence. If you're serious about wanting to help me, what if I just bring the baby over here every day on my way to work, and pick her up after? Then the baby won't have to be with strangers all day, and I can keep my apartment. I'll even pay you."

She gives me the side-eye as she wipes down the kitchen table. "Absolutely not. You are not paying me to watch my own grandchild."

"Okay, but do you think that's really something you want to do? After my maternity leave?"

"Maternity leave," she repeats, closing her eyes as if she's trying to absorb the words. "I never thought we'd be talking about this. Not for a long, long time."

Neither did I.

"The answer is yes, Piper. Of course I'd love to take care of my grandchild every day. We'll do this together. I'm not going to let anything happen to you and this baby. Do you have a good doctor? I'd like to go to your next visit with you. Or I could take you to my doctor, the one who delivered you and your sisters…"

"Mom," I warn. "Slow down. You're making my head spin. I have a doctor, but you're welcome to come with me and supervise if you want to."

"I just want to be sure you're getting the best care." She puts her hands on her hips and lets out a deep sigh. "All right. We have lots of time to plan and get all the things you're going to need. Don't worry about your father, I'll talk to him and he'll calm down. Everything will be okay, I promise."

I want to believe her, but deep inside, little voices are whispering otherwise, and they're hard to ignore.

CHAPTER SEVENTEEN

2002 - PIPER

"Come on, Lyric. We're going to get lunch." I reach out to her, but she doesn't take my hand. She's way too engrossed with an orange and black caterpillar that's creeping along the edge of the sidewalk. "I'm sure Mr. Caterpillar has somewhere to be, too." She stares up at me, her big blue eyes full of curiosity and... contemplation. Always thinking, debating, and wondering, this little one.

I wave my outstretched fingers. "Come on, sweetie. You can have a smoothie when we get there."

"Storeberry?"

"Yes, strawberry."

Bribery is usually my last tactic to motivate her, but my stomach is growling and I have a pile of work waiting for me at home that I need to review for a meeting scheduled on Monday. Lyric hums happily to herself for the remainder of the walk from the parking lot to the café. A breeze blows our hair across our faces and I breathe in the warm air, welcoming the first signs of spring. I enjoy all the seasons, but I've had enough of winter. I can only handle so much snow, sweater-weather, and slush.

The bell hanging on the café door chimes as we enter and I wave to Robbie, who's worked here for as long as I can remember.

"How are you two doing today?" he asks.

"We're good. Busy today?" Almost all the tables are occupied this afternoon.

"Yeah. The nice weather brings everyone out. You having the usual?"

"Yes, please."

He leans over the counter and smiles at Lyric. "Strawberry or orange today?"

Gripping my hand tighter, she leans against my leg and answers him with a shy smile "Storeberry."

He winks at her. "That's my favorite, too."

We step to the side to wait while he makes our lunch, and I bump into someone with his nose in a magazine.

"I'm sorry, I didn't see you," I say, maneuvering around him to wait near the candy display.

"Piper?"

I pull the candy bar out of Lyric's hand and put it back before looking up into a vaguely familiar handsome face.

It takes a few seconds for my mouth to move. "Josh. Hi... I didn't even recognize you."

How is it possible for someone to change so much? The last time I saw Josh he was wiry thin, his brown hair trimmed in a military cut, and he wore silver-rimmed glasses that always had fingerprints on the lenses. He was sort of a nerd. A cute one, but still a nerd. Not anymore. He must have taken up working out because his arms and shoulders are double the size they used to be. His hair, longer and lighter, hangs just past his eyebrows in a messy but sexy way. The glasses are gone, along with the oversized sweatshirts, jeans, and old sneakers he used to live in. Now, he looks incredibly trendy and put together in black pants, a gray sweater, and black leather loafers.

"It's been a long time," he says. The unsure smile I remember is now relaxed and confident.

"Yeah, it has."

"You look great, Piper."

I wish I did, but I don't. In fact, I'm pretty sure I'm still wearing yesterday's makeup. The only thing different about me is the toddler hanging on to my hand trying to steal candy.

"Thanks...this is my daughter, Lyric."

A brief flash of shock widens his eyes. "Wow. She's adorable. How old is she?"

"She's three."

"Damn. She has your smile."

Everyone says that, but I don't see it. All I see are Blue's eyes and smile. I quickly shove him out of my mind and focus on Josh.

"So, what are you doing here?" I ask. "Are you visiting your parents?"

He shakes his head. "No. I meant to call you but time kept slipping away. I moved back here last year. Landed a great career, bought a house, went through a bad breakup, spent all my time fixing up said house, and here I am. What about you?"

"Similar. Got a great job, got an apartment, got my heart broken, got pregnant, and spend my time chasing her around." I glance toward the register when Robbie calls my name. "That's my order."

"I gotta run, too. But hey, you want to grab dinner tomorrow night? We can catch up and shoot the shit."

I haven't had dinner with a man in years. Everyone said being a single mom wouldn't prevent me from dating, but it has. Meeting guys is hard. And when I do meet one, either I don't think they're good enough to bring into our lives, or they don't want anything to do with a woman with a child. Or they just want sex. On rare occasion, I've met one who's actually looking for love, which is just as much a hard no for me as sex is. So, guess I can't put all the blame on the men, because I come with my own set of dysfunctions.

But this is Josh, and he doesn't come with any strings or expectations.

"Okay. I'd like that."

If Josh senses my slight hesitation, he doesn't show it. "Give me your number and I'll call you tomorrow to get your address."

We exchange numbers. After we go our separate ways, I head home to immerse myself in work while Lyric plays with her dolls on the floor.

She's placed a toy teacup and saucer in front of Acorn and is chattering on endlessly. Lyric is an incredibly sweet, undemanding child who keeps herself occupied for hours. She doesn't throw tantrums, and while she sometimes debates with me, she doesn't argue or defy. Acorn is a wonderful fur-sibling, always patient and attentive with Lyric and her imaginary adventures. Although we had a rocky start, I feel very blessed to have such a happy, content little family.

Content. The word—the thing—that took away the only missing piece in our life. I turned fear, unexpected hurdles, and chaos into contentment. Into *my* form of contentment. Would Blue have been able to do the same? Would he have found what he wanted and needed in me and in our child if he had stayed and given us a chance?

I'll probably never know. And sadly, neither will he.

"I can't believe you're going out with Josh. We haven't seen him in forever."

I glare at her reflection in my bedroom mirror as I put my earrings on. "Don't get crazy, Dee. It's only dinner as friends."

"That's what it is today, but that doesn't mean in the future you won't be getting it on. Maybe now that he's hot he's got some alpha vibes."

"Alpha vibes? Maybe you two should hook up, then."

"Do you really think I came over here just to babysit? It's the perfect excuse for me to check him out," she teases.

The doorbell rings and I face her. "Well, he's here, so you can. You still have to babysit, though. Do I look okay?"

She stands and looks me up and down. "You look gorgeous as always. Why can't we be the same size so I can borrow your clothes?"

"Trust me, I'd much rather be the same size as you." Nobody understands how hard it is for me to find pants that aren't a mile too long or shoes that actually stay on my feet.

She follows me to the living room and sits on the couch with Lyric while I answer the door.

"Sorry, I'm early," he says.

"That's okay, come on in. Someone wants to gawk at you."

His eyebrow tweaks up and he steps inside. "Holy shit, Ditra!" He laughs when he sees her and she jumps up to hug him. "How the hell have you been? I thought you'd be married to some rich guy by now and living in Paris."

"I'm working on it. Did you bring your W-2?"

He grins. "I see you haven't changed."

"Never. But *you* on the other hand...." She eyes him like lunch. "If I'd known you'd end up looking like this I would have snagged you in high school myself."

I wish I could flirt as effortlessly as Ditra does. I'm not good at it and always end up saying something awkward or realize after the fact that I had something stuck in my teeth the entire time.

"Ditra is babysitting for me." I open the hall closet door and take out my coat. "But she's admitted she only agreed to so she could check you out."

"That's flattering and disturbing. You sure it's safe to leave your daughter with her?" He smiles playfully at Ditra. "You have any experience taking care of kids?"

"Yes, lots. I've been dating them for years."

"That was a good one," I say, leaning down to kiss Lyric's forehead. "Mommy's going out for a little while and Aunt Dee is going to stay and play with you, okay?"

She nods without looking up from her favorite picture book that's open on her lap. I'm not sure if I should be grateful or disappointed that she's not a little bit upset. I never go out at night, so this is new for her. I expected questions or brief pouting, but she's unconcerned.

"Piper, she'll be fine. Go out and have fun for once." She glances over at Josh. "All this girl does is work. I'm surprised you're getting her out of the house."

"We're leaving." I grab Josh's arm before Ditra can reveal more embarrassing facts about me. "Don't eat too much junk and don't forget to take Acorn out."

"Yes, Mom."

I've never been to the steakhouse Josh is taking me to, and I'm relieved he made a reservation because there's a line of people out the door when we pull into the parking lot. I'm not one of those people who love food enough to wait forty minutes or longer for it with a pager in my hand. I'd rather hit a drive-thru and grab a burger and fries and just be done with it.

From the moment we get in the car we fall into easy, relaxed conversation. We've run into each other and talked on the phone sporadically since we officially broke up, but that stopped years ago when I met Blue, and I have a hunch that's the same time Josh got involved, too. Being friends first and foremost has prevented time or distance from affecting us. Josh and I could probably go ten years without seeing each other and still be just as comfortable with each other as we were when we last saw each other. Right now, that's stability I could use in my life.

"Are you still working for the same company?" Josh asks as we open our menus.

The menu has a brown leather cover and is printed on parchment paper. It feels heavy and foreign in my hands and I long for the plastic laminated menus that my favorite diner has. I feel out of place sitting in this dim room with white tablecloth-covered tables and flickering candles. The piano music drifting from hidden speakers is probably meant to be romantic but I find it annoying, almost mocking.

I don't want to be in this fancy restaurant with Josh. I want to be in the diner with Blue eating hamburgers and drinking cherry soda.

"I am," I reply. "But now I'm in marketing and ad campaigns. I love it, I'm never bored."

"That's better than answering phones, huh?" Years ago, he used to call the office and ask me strange questions in a fake accent just to break up the boredom of my day.

"Definitely. So, what about you? Are you still in accounting?"

He puts his menu off to the side. "Yeah, but only part time."

I glance at him with budding curiosity. "Oh? What are you doing with the other part of your time?"

"Modeling and acting," he says with a big smile.

I stare at him, waiting for him to say he's just kidding. But he's serious. "Modeling and acting?" I repeat. "Really?"

He grabs a roll from the basket on the center of the table and takes a bite out of it. He chews and swallows before he answers. "Yeah."

"Josh! That's so freakin' amazing! What kind of work have you done?"

"Nothing memorable or overly exciting yet. Fashion shoots, and a couple walk-on parts for television and a cable movie. It's a lot of fun. I never thought in a million years I'd be doing anything like this."

"I'm blown away. And so proud of you. I never even knew you wanted to model or act."

"Me either. I just kind of fell into it. I met a photographer at the gym who asked if I'd be interested in modeling and he hooked me up from there."

"That's incredible. Can you show me any of it? Do you have pictures or the movies you were in? I'd love to see."

"Yeah, I have some of the pictures and magazines at home. You should come by and I'll show you."

"Of course I will."

Ditra will lose her mind when I tell her about this, and I wonder if Josh might be interested in taking her out as more than just friends. She could use a good, normal man in her life now that she's put her sexual escapades behind her.

I could use a normal man, too, but I don't want one. There's only one man for me.

"Your daughter is adorable," Josh says after the waiter comes to take our order. "Are you involved with her father?"

The mere mention of Blue gives me a small twitch in my chest. I sip my ice water, then shake my head. "No. We broke up before I knew I was pregnant. He doesn't even know she exists."

"Damn, that's harsh."

"I'm not keeping her from him, Josh. I would never do that. I have no way to get in touch with him. I wish I did."

"Was it serious? You and him?"

If the definition of serious is feeling like my heart was ripped out of my chest and abducted, then yes, it was serious.

"For me it was, and I felt like it was for him, too." I meet his hazel eyes. "It's a really complicated situation."

He nods with acceptance. "Enough said. I'll make a deal with you. I won't ask about your ex if you don't ask about mine. If you want to talk about him, go for it. If not, no big deal. None of my business."

Relief ebbs through me, dissipating the anxiety and heartache that always comes when I think about Blue. "Deal. And same for you, if you want to talk, I'm here."

If I can hide my heartache and savor my memories in peace, then I'm fine with Josh doing the same.

We share stories about our jobs and families over dinner, filling each other in on what we missed over the past few years. It's odd how so much is the same, but so much has changed, too.

"You should take Ditra out," I suggest when dessert arrives. "She hasn't had much luck dating. She's a little crazy, but I think she's ready for something serious."

An odd smile touches his lips and he scoops up a spoonful of crème brûlée. "I think she's a little more than I can handle," he admits. "And I gotta be honest, I'm not ready to get involved with someone. My last relationship messed me up."

I'm all too familiar with the flash of pain in his eyes and the invisible wall his words build between us. Honestly, it's all a welcome relief. Not because I want him to be hurt, but because he understands exactly how I feel.

We're on the same page.

CHAPTER EIGHTEEN

PIPER

I lock my office and wave goodbye to the co-workers who are working late. Digging out my keys as I exit the building and head toward my car, I run a mental list of everything I need to do on the way home. Put gas in my car. Stop at the grocery store for milk and bread. Pick up Lyric at my Mom's house, and ignore her when she points out that Courtney is on a date on a Friday night and I'm not.

My heart jumps into my throat when I throw my messenger bag and my purse onto the passenger seat. I pull my door closed and lock it. Taking a deep breath, I finally reach for the white piece of paper that's folded and sticking out of my cup holder.

I look out the windshield. Then the side windows. I glance in the rearview mirror, searching frantically for him.

No one is in the parking lot except for me.

An ache grows in my chest as I look down at the note in my trembling hand. I rub my thumb along the familiar texture of the paper. My teeth dig into my quivering lower lip as my heart and my brain battle.

My brain says tear the note up into tiny pieces and throw it away. Forget him and his ever-frustrating elusiveness. I have no room in my life for games. Besides, nothing written in this note can change anything. It will only rip open barely healed wounds and infect them all over again.

My heart says open it. Open it *right now*. Don't wait another second! I've been hoping and waiting for this for years. A sign. An explanation. A *something*. Maybe the words inside could change everything.

The heart always wins.

I slowly unfold the note, and I swear I can smell his scent on the paper. Smokey, minty, Bluesy.

> *Piper,*
>
> *I've walked a million steps and none of them have taken me from you. I've written thousands of words and none of them capture you. I'm haunted by you, driven by you, madly in love and lust with you. I want to be good for you. I want to give you everything. Someday I will. Please believe that. I don't want to hurt you. I'm trying to be better. Things are getting better. I'm so tired of the bad. I'm trying. Every day I'm fighting the voices and the words. I miss you. I miss Acorn. You don't know how much. Don't forget me, baby. Hate me if you have to, but don't stop loving me. I want you to be happy. I want it to be me so fucking bad.*
> *I'm sorry this is a mess. I'm sorry I'm a mess.*
> *I love you like no tomorrow. Always.*
> *~ Blue*

My hand shakes uncontrollably by the time I reach the last word. I read it again.

And again.

I read it over and over until I can hear his raspy voice say the words, and they cut like a knife, slicing through the center of my chest, tearing out my heart and soul. He was here—when? Hours ago? Minutes ago? Did he watch me go into the office this morning? Is he watching me now? Once again, I stare out the windshield into the parking lot, then turn to look out the side windows, then the rearview mirror.

He's not here. I'm still alone.

Sniffling and choking on the emotions wrenching up inside me, I fold the note and shove it into my purse.

Why would he come back here and not want to see me? I can't even comprehend it. I'd do anything to see him, to feel his arms and the warmth of his body around me again. If he loves me, why would he hide from me? After all this time, why wouldn't he want to see me face to face?

I wipe away the tears tracking down my cheeks and throw the car into drive. Maybe it's not too late—he could still be here, walking around nearby.

Five o'clock commuter traffic doesn't let me get very far, though, and I bang my hand against the steering wheel in frustration when I have to sit at the traffic light at the intersection near my office through three intervals. I scour the surrounding sidewalks, searching for his hair blowing in the wind, his backpack and guitar slung over his shoulder. The baby seat in the back seat catches my eye in the rearview mirror and my heart skips a beat. Did he see it when he put the note in my car? Did it scare him away? *Oh, God.* What if he thinks I had a baby with someone else? Now, more than ever, I have to find him and tell him about Lyric before he disappears again.

When the traffic lets up, I drive up and down the main street, past the park and all the places Blue used to play, but I don't see him anywhere. I know I should give up on this craziness—run my errands, pick up my little girl, and go home. But I don't. Like a magnet I'm pulled to the only other place I think Blue might be.

The house with the shed.

Years ago I made a promise to myself to never come back here and torture myself with the memories and the questions that haunt this place. I almost broke that promise several times over the years when I was missing Blue so damn much I wanted to do anything to feel close to him again. Every time I fought the urge and forced myself to stay home, playing the music box and staring at the flameless candle he gave me.

"I thought maybe you could take one home with you and put it by your bed. So you know I'm thinking about you."

That little flickering light left a lot to be desired.

I've been strong. I stopped searching for him, and I stayed away from our special places. But tonight is different, because he might actually *be* here.

I'm not surprised to see the old house hasn't changed at all; still a lonely reflection of what I'm sure it once was when people lived there. I check out the shed first, and I'm disappointed to see it's still empty. I have to question my own morals that I actually *want* to see the man I love sleeping in this old musty building. Next I check the porch, nearly jumping out of my skin when the wind slams the screen door shut behind me with a bang. If Blue is here, he definitely heard that. Disappointment grows when I see everything is exactly the same—the pile of notebooks, the tarp in the corner, completely untouched. Just to ease my mind, I try the door to the kitchen, and it's still locked.

I don't bother calling out his name as I've done in the past because I know if he's here somewhere, he had to have heard that door slam, and if he did, then he's purposely avoiding me. I can understand him not wanting to confront me in the parking lot of my office, but I'm here now, on his playing ground, and if he doesn't care about me enough to come out of the shadows, then there's nothing more I can do. I don't want to play games. I'm a mother now, I have a corner office with windows, and I've worked hard to get my life together after he shredded my heart like a raptor. I can't—I refuse—to let myself crumble again.

I high-tail out of there, race through the grocery store, then go to my parents' house to pick up Lyric, which I should have done in the first place rather than hunting around for Blue. When my mother gets on me about how late I am, and how I should have called her, I don't have the energy to argue with her, tell her the truth, or make up excuses. I dole out the best apology I can, pack up my daughter and her tribe of stuffed toys, and drive home.

Lyric falls asleep in the car, and the absence of her usual chatter gives me the chance to re-compose myself. Unfortunately, the moment we step inside the house, the sight of Acorn wagging his tail and greeting us with Penguin in his mouth dredges up my heartache all over again.

Sometimes, I *do* hate Blue, but I still can't stop loving him.

CHAPTER NINETEEN

PIPER

"These are incredible. I think you found your calling." The two-page magazine spread of Josh modeling for an expensive cologne line is impressive. His expression and his body language are so confident and natural, it's hard to believe this is the same awkward teen boy I dated.

He rummages through the box on his living room floor between us, pulling out more photos. "Surprising, huh?" he says. "I enjoy it way more than I thought I would."

I hold up a photo of him with a beautiful female model that I instantly recognize. "Well, who wouldn't enjoy this?" I tease. "Is she really this perfect in person, or is this all photo editing? Tell me it's editing."

He laughs. "Nope, she's that perfect."

"Damn. It's so unfair." I put the picture on the floor next to the others and reach into the bottom of the box to pull out a few more photos while he flips through another magazine. The pictures I'm holding aren't professional photos, but appear to be candid photos of him at a party with some friends, and a few of him kissing a guy.

Kissing a guy.

Studying the picture with my brow creased, I decide they must be friends joking around, but my breath hitches as I shuffle to the next photo, which shows them half naked, making out, and clearly groping each other. Before I can truly grasp what I'm seeing, Josh snatches the photo from my hand and throws it back in the box, slowly shaking his head back and forth.

"You weren't supposed to see that."

Wow. Ditra called this way back in sophomore year of high school, and I told her she was crazy. She was right. Josh is gay. Or bi.

I swallow hard and try to meet his eyes as he shoves the lid back on the box.

"Josh...." I don't know what to say.

"I'm confused, Piper," he says in a low voice. "Have been for a long time."

I nod and touch his hand. "It's okay. I am, too."

So much makes sense to me now. This is why things never went further when we dated years ago, and why we've been strictly friends since we started spending time together recently. I haven't just been friend-zoning him because I'm still stuck on Blue. He's been friend-zoning me, too.

Damn. Maybe I'm just destined to never be in a normal relationship with anyone.

The brief moment of surprise and awkwardness fades away, and we let it. We resume our plans to make dinner and watch a movie. But when I yawn and tell him I should head home, he puts his hand on my arm to stop me.

"Can we talk before you go?" he asks.

"Sure."

He takes a deep breath. "I've been wanting to talk to you...I've just been waiting for the right time. But now that you know...yeah, I like guys. And women."

I'm not going to let this screw up my friendship with him. I need supportive people in my life, and he's been at the top of the list since we ran into each other.

"Josh... it doesn't matter to me who or what you like. You're my friend, I want you to be happy. My head is messed up, too. You know that."

"I know. And for the record, I think it sucks, because you deserve to be happy, and not be in love with some ghost of a guy."

I ignore his comment.

"So, the breakup you told me about? The one that messed you up? Was it a guy?"

He nods solemnly. "Yeah, it was. He's the first guy—the only guy—I've ever dated or been with. And you're still the only woman I've ever seriously dated."

"And I thought you were just a nice guy taking it slow with me because I was a virgin," I tease.

"Whoa... don't even think what you're thinking, Piper. I didn't not have sex with you because I wasn't attracted to you. I was. You're beautiful. I just didn't want to lead you on when my head was so fucked up. I wasn't going to let your first time be with a guy who wasn't a hundred percent committed to you in every way."

"Thanks." Visions of my first time flash before my eyes. The hair pulling, damp stone against my face, the rip and tear of clothes and flesh, the endless biting and sucking. Blood and cum on my lips. Those smoldering blue eyes....

I cross my legs to quell the tingling in my thighs. Any time I think of the intimate moments I shared with Blue my body becomes his again. My heart races. My legs wobble. I'll involuntarily lick my lips, waiting for his. Sometimes I swear I can smell the scent of smoke breaking through the barrier of my memories.

I miss him and how he made me feel so wanted. So loved. So alive.

I miss our little secluded bubble of love.

I miss him.

"Anyway, here's the thing. I've been thinking..."

I blink and nod, forcing my brain back to *now*. "Uh oh...."

"Just listen, okay?"

"Okay."

"I like hanging out with you. I love Lyric. I think you guys should move in with me. I'll help you with Lyric, you won't have to drop her off at your mother's every time you want to do something, I can take

Acorn jogging with me, we can just... I don't know. Be there for each other. Kinda co-life together, until we figure shit out."

This is not at all what I was expecting. "Um, what?"

"I have this beautiful house. I have four bedrooms. Three of them are empty, I don't even have furniture in them. I've got this huge backyard. I spent so much time and money on this house, and I don't want to give it up, but it's driving me nuts that it's so... empty."

I blink at him and he grins.

"Your place is cute, but it's small. You work on a snack table in your living room most of the time. You guys would have so much room here. I'll charge you the same rent you're paying now. We can share the kitchen. You buy your food, I'll buy mine. I've got a living room and a den so we can either hang out together, or separate, whatever you want. There's more than enough room for us to not be on top of each other."

He's right, this house is huge. It has rooms I haven't even seen. One of the bathrooms is almost as big as my bedroom in my apartment, and the other three are damn near close.

"Are you serious? You want us to live with you?"

"I'm dead serious."

"You didn't forget the cat, right? He has to come, too."

"I love Archie. Look at all the windows he'll have."

"I don't know, Josh. It's awfully tempting...." It is. We're slowly growing out of my current apartment, but everything I've looked at in nice neighborhoods, that's close to both my office and my parents' house, is almost double the cost.

"I do have one requirement, though," he says.

I cross my arms over my chest and raise an eyebrow. "I knew there had to be a catch."

"You have to be my date for public functions and when I visit my family, and when they come here. I promise not to grope you. Just hold my hand and smile and pretend we're dating. That's it. No other strings, we're roommates. No expectations, no lies, no hidden agendas."

Ah. He wants a decoy while he's half in and half out of the closet.

It's a small price to pay in exchange to live in a nice house and have a man in mine and Lyric's life, even if only as a friend.

"I guess I can do that. Will you do the same for me if I need a good-looking guy on my arm?" Finally, I could have a date for the company holiday party.

"Hell, yeah."

"What if you get involved with someone and want them to move in? Nobody is going to want to live here with me and a three-year-old and a dog and a cat."

He blows out a breath and shakes his head. "That's the last thing I'm worried about. I have no plans of getting involved or wanting to live with someone for a long time, trust me."

"What if I meet someone?"

As if.

"If you're dating someone and you want to hang out here, I'm totally down with that. I don't want anyone moving in, though. If you get to that point, you'd have to find a place."

"That's fair," I agree. "Can I think about it for a few days? This is a lot to absorb."

"Sure. I'm not going anywhere."

I already know I'm going to say yes, though. Josh is handing me the perfect situation on a silver platter: a fake boyfriend that I can hide behind while I wait for Blue to come back.

CHAPTER TWENTY

2003 - PIPER

"What are the chances we can have those new ad layouts by noon?"

I spin my chair around to face Dave, a thirty-something, average-looking account manager who's leaning casually against the doorframe of my office, wearing a smile on his face like he didn't just ask to completely derail my day.

"You know damn well I just got out of the Monday morning status meeting, Dave. You were there. That only gives me two hours to go through all these changes." I gesture to the project folder on my desk that has about fifty red sticky flags poking out of it.

"Don't kill the messenger. Production is pushing us to belt this out today. Do what you can." He walks off before I can rattle off a list of reasons why this process shouldn't be rushed.

"Dammit," I swear under my breath, wheel my chair across my office to open the window for some fresh air, then scoot back to my desk to tackle this new deadline. I switch on my desk radio to my favorite station and dive into the layout change list.

As stressful as my job can be, I love everything about it. I'm never bored, and the time flies by—a massive difference from when I worked as a receptionist, which seems like forever ago. I sing along softly to the radio as I work, glancing at the clock every so often to gauge the likelihood of me finishing by noon. So far, things are going smoothly.

I'm leaning over one of the documents, trying to decipher someone's incredibly scribbly handwriting, when a rock ballad playing on the radio rips my attention away. Dropping my pen, I snap my head up and raise the volume a little.

"Slayer of my heart,
Wish of my soul...."

Goosebumps spread over my arms, and my pulse beats rapidly in my veins as I stare at the tiny speaker in a state of disbelief.

I know those words. I know the sound of that guitar.

And I would know that voice—that unique, gravelly, sexy voice—anywhere.

Blue...

With my breath caught in my chest, I listen intently to the lyrics, and the voice, that captivated me so long ago, to the melody I still play on that tiny music box. Hot tears sting my eyes as the song nears the end, and I silently beg the DJ to come on and announce the band and song name.

"That was the new hit single 'Slayer of My Heart' by No Tomorrow that climbed to the top of the charts last week."

Holy. Shit.

My entire body is shaking from shock, and my heart is thumping wildly in my chest. This is real. Like really, really, *real.* I'm not suffering from some kind of stressed-out Monday morning hallucination. I just heard Blue—*my* Blue—on the radio, singing and playing guitar. And not just any song, but a song he told me he wrote for me. *About* me. The DJ just called it a hit single, on the top of the charts.

The edges of my vision blur as I stare at the radio. This is surreal. Like a dream. My head feels like a balloon—empty and floating off into a place so far out of reality that I can't reach it.

I press my fingers into my temples and close my eyes.

I take a deep breath.

A pop song comes on the radio next—a song that's on my aerobics playlist.

It grounds me somewhat. Brings me back from the shock.

When—how—did all this happen?

"How's that coming?" Dave pokes his head into my office and I quickly wave him away.

"Not now," I say abruptly, turning away to hide my state of anxiety.

Jesus. This can't be happening. I grab my water bottle and sip, taking deep breaths in between to try to calm the jitters quaking through me. Hundreds of questions fly through my mind like a whirlwind.

Shoving my project folder aside, I open up the search engine on my computer, type in *No Tomorrow band,* and within seconds my screen is filled with links to various web sites and articles, with the band's official web site the first result. I click on it and tap my finger impatiently on my mouse.

The page finally loads a large photo of the band standing in an alley, with Blue front and center looking hotter than an orgy on the desert, shirtless with a scuffed-up black leather jacket doing nothing to cover his inked-up six-pack abs.

Swallowing hard, I scan the text beneath the photo: Evan "Blue" Von Bleu, lead vocals and guitar; Reece Blackstone, backup vocals and lead guitar; Alex Oakley, Drums; Koler Simms, bass.

Evan Von Bleu.

I finally have the name of the father of my child and the man I love. How fitting that he has an exotic, sexy name. Somehow I knew there was no way in hell his name was going to end up being Evan Smith. Scrolling down further, I read.

No Tomorrow emerged from the grunge rock scene in early 2002 with their debut album, Things I Never Said. *The group's mix of dark and sensual lyrics coupled with Blue's distinctive raspy tone and effortless ability to hit a remarkable range of notes made them an instant hit. Singer/songwriter Von Bleu's sad and incredibly haunting vocals suck you right into his soul. The band often plays several acoustic songs during their live shows, which truly showcase Von Bleu's musical and vocal talents.*

I read on about a current world tour, top hits, and critic reviews.

When I click to the photos page, a deep pain hits my chest and radiates through my stomach. The photographs of Blue on stage, singing in front of thousands of people, tear me up just as much as the ones of him sitting alone on a tour bus, a cigarette dangling from his lips, notebook in his lap, with a faraway look in his eye.

I know that look so well.

My beloved, tortured Blue isn't homeless anymore. He's a popular rock star, with a web site and fans and articles written about his musical talents. It's clear from all this information he's wanted, loved, and respected by fans and peers.

But still alone. I see that.

Leaning back in my chair, I stare at his picture opened full screen on my monitor. His hair is blowing across his face, but I know behind it his eyes are royal blue and filled with wanderlust. I ache to reach out and touch him, feel the solidness of his body beneath my fingers, breathe in his scent, have his fingers grasping my flesh and his whisper against my ear.

An overwhelming longing for him washes over me, drowning me in memories of our time together, and dredging up the heartache that came with it. Seeing him again, even in photographic form, has torn apart the cracks in my heart, and my emotions are seeping out. My head throbs trying to process all this unexpected news, and nausea is roiling my empty stomach.

My focus has been hijacked, and it's impossible for me to function this way. Trembling, I gather up my paperwork and shove it back in its folder, turn my computer off, and grab my jacket and purse.

Dave appears at the other end of the hall as I'm locking my office door. "You're going to lunch? Are the layouts done?"

Flustered, I shake my head and avoid eye contact. "I'm sorry, I'm not feeling well. I have to go home."

"*Now*? I told you we need—"

"I'm sorry, but I need to go. Have Sue take care of it, or it'll have to wait until tomorrow."

Walking away from him, I know I just put a fault line in the foundation of stability and normalcy I've tried so hard to build in my life, but I'm powerless.

I drive to the mall, walk past the cinnamon bun place without stopping to get one—which is a first for me—and go straight to the music store. Fifteen minutes later I'm back in my car with the No Tomorrow CD.

"You're home early." Josh sits up on the couch, uprooting Archie and Acorn who were both using him as a bed. "You okay?"

Clutching the CD that I just spent two hours listening to while driving around aimlessly, I burst into tears. I recognized all the songs that Blue used to play in the park and in the shed. Back then he only actually sang three of them, but now they all have accompanying lyrics, and I swear he put our entire relationship into poetic words of heartache, love, and loss. Or maybe I'm flattering myself. Maybe some of those songs are about other women in his life, but my heart is telling me they're all about me, and us. I know our story, and these songs are dripping the blood of our relationship.

Josh shoots up off the couch and takes the CD, my bag, and my keys out of my hands.

"What's going on?" His hazel eyes search mine. "Were you in an accident?"

"No," I sob. "I'm fine."

"You don't look fine, Piper. You're having some kind of freak-out." He glances down at the CD and then looks back at me with skepticism. "Since when do you listen to grunge alternative rock?"

I kick off my shoes and fall into the big comfy recliner by the window. "I don't," I reply. "That's his band. That's him on the cover, the one with the longest hair."

"Him who?"

"Lyric's father," I say softly.

His eyes widen and he brings the CD closer to his face to examine the front and back. "The homeless guy?"

One night about a year ago when I was feeling particularly overwhelmed and frustrated with my feelings for Blue, I broke down and told Josh the entire story. He immediately turned it into a drinking game and we took a shot every time I said 'homeless' and 'but I really love him.' We were both trashed by the end of the night.

"Yes, apparently he's the lead singer."

"Holy fuck." He turns the CD over again. "You're telling me Evan Von Bleu, singer and crazy fucking mad talented guitar god, is your baby daddy?"

I roll my eyes and rub my hand across my pounding forehead. "Please don't say it like that."

A grin spreads across his face. "I've heard their music, they play it at the gym. He's got a voice like fucking smoky velvet. He's hot too. I'd be tempted, homeless or not."

"Josh, please!" I rip the CD out of his hands. "You're not helping."

"I'm trying to make you laugh. This is pretty messed up. It's kind of kickass, too. Lyric's dad isn't homeless, he's famous."

That tweaks up my anxiety even more, because I hadn't even thought of that part yet. My daughter's father has the potential of being a celebrity, and if he's in her life someday, that's going to affect her.

"He's not *really* well known, is he?" I ask. Up until today I hadn't ever heard of his band, and I listen to the radio at work a lot. They could be a one-hit wonder sort of band and just fall off the face of the earth in a year.

"Piper, you're holding a CD with his face on it. They're getting tons of airplay. You can't go near a music magazine without reading about his insane vocals and his crazy riffs."

Damn. How did I not know all this? How did Blue get to this place in life without me realizing it long before today? And why, why, *why* hasn't he come back for me?

"Josh, do you think it's possible that it was all a lie? Do you think maybe he wasn't really homeless, and maybe he never really loved me? What if it was just some...." My voice cracks and I struggle to find the right words. "Some kind of experiment to get song material? Maybe I was only a muse to him."

His face softens. "Piper, come on. I seriously doubt it. That's an awful lot of work just for creative research. The dude slept in a shed. And you're a sweet girl. I don't think someone could do something like that to you unless they were a supreme asshole with zero conscience."

"But he left the dog...why would he leave Acorn with me?"

He shrugs. "Who knows? Probably because he knew he was too messed up to take care of him anymore. Or he assumed having him would comfort you. Do I think the dog was part of some big act? No. Stop thinking like this, Piper. This isn't like you."

How many times have I heard those words in the past few years? If this isn't like me, what *was* I like? What *am* I like?

"I don't know what to think."

"Maybe there's nothing to think. You met a messed-up guy living a messed-up life, you did some messed-up things, he left in a messed-up way, you had a kid, and somehow he ended up where he is now and you're living in this messed-up situation with me and everyone seems pretty happy."

God. It sounds all sorts of crazy when it's spelled out. "It's *all* messed up," I say.

"Is it? Or is everything the way it's supposed to be right now?"

"I don't know, Josh. I need some closure, I think. You don't understand, he just left. I didn't get to say goodbye, I didn't get to ask why. One minute we were having the best night of our lives and the next he was gone. Then he leaves me a note years later that makes me even more confused. And now this! I find out he's a damn rock star? I need to talk to him. I need answers. And he needs to know he has a daughter."

"Are you sure that's what you want? What if he wants to meet her? Do you want to bring this guy into Lyric's life? Think of how confused she'll be."

His reservations are valid. Josh has been very protective of Lyric since we moved in and he took on the role Uncle Josh, and I love that he cares for her so much. He's been an amazing male figure in her life—especially since my father still barely speaks to me—but I can't keep Lyric a secret from her biological father if there's a way I can get in touch with him. He has a right to know he has a child, and if he wants to be part of her life, that's a bridge I'll have to think about crossing.

"Blue might be a little strange and difficult, but he's always been nice, and caring, in his own ways. I know he wouldn't do anything to hurt Lyric. I think he would love her."

"Really? Like he loved you and his dog?"

I glare at him. "Don't be a jerk. I think he was just really confused at the time."

"Nobody understands being confused more than I do, but he handled it like a first-class douche. I don't want you or Lyric getting hurt. I don't care who the hell he is."

"It doesn't matter to me who or what he is now. I still love him. And I believe he loves me," I say softly. "I saw the concert schedule on their website. They're going to be playing in Boston in two months, and I think I have to find a way to see him while he's there so we can talk."

He shakes his head. "Being in love with this guy has had your head fucked up for years. I don't think talking is going to do a damn thing or get you what you want. If I were you, I'd hire a lawyer, get a paternity test done for proof, and sue for child support. He's obviously got some money now."

Even after all this time, I know Blue would never question paternity. He would believe me with zero doubt. And besides, Lyric looks way too much like him for anyone to ever deny that she's his.

"Josh, really? Money is the last thing I want from him. You know I'm not like that."

He rubs the back of his neck in frustration. "All right," he sighs. "This goes against my better judgment, but one of the photographers I've worked with does a ton of band photography. Let me get in touch with him and see if he's got any connections to get you in front of this guy."

I perk up with renewed hope. "You'd do that for me?"

"I can't make any promises, but I'll try."

I jump up and throw my arms around him. "Thank you. You're the best."

"Don't thank me yet." He pulls away and rests his hands on my shoulders. "Your makeup is a mess. Why don't you go take a bath and I'll pick up Lyric. I have to run some errands anyway."

"Are you sure?"

"Yeah, it's no problem. I think you should regroup before Lyric gets home. You know she can tell when you're upset about something."

He's right—Lyric is very empathetic for a child. She dials right into the emotions of people and animals around her and wants to make everyone feel better. It's one of the many things I love so much about her.

The bath was supposed to relax me, but I sabotaged that by bringing the CD with me. I slid out the cover, which unfolded to show tiny printed lyrics and credits. On the last section of the foldout each of the band members included a short acknowledgement or dedication, and I read Blue's last:

For Piper, keeper of my heart, you'll always be my ladybug. Don't give up baby, I took a walk, but I didn't run away.

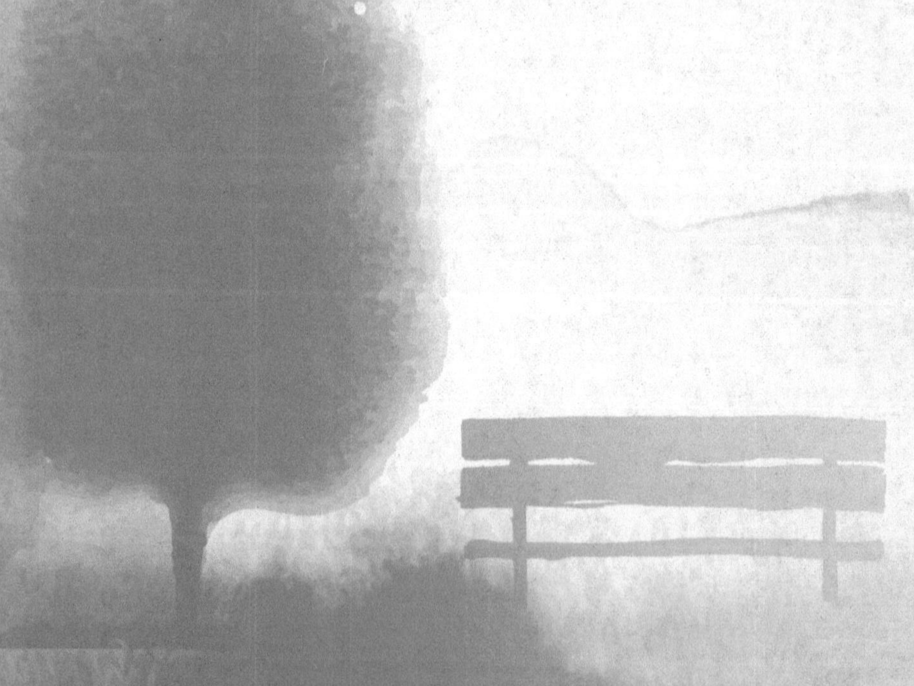

CHAPTER TWENTY-ONE

PIPER

The past two months have been a mix of both warp speed and dragging time. I haven't been sleeping or eating well, and my focus at work has once again been lacking. My brain is either too tired to function or my train of thought is constantly derailed with thoughts of Blue. I've been listening to his music practically non-stop, analyzing the lyrics, trying to decipher what they mean and wondering if they're a key to his feelings or just random words thrown together for the sake of a good song. I'm exhausted, and I'm disappointed in myself for getting so distracted with him again. I should be above this by now, shouldn't I? I'm older and more mature. I'm stable. I'm professional—most of the time. I'm a mother.

But damn, when it comes to Blue, I always short-circuit. As unsettling as that is, it's also undeniably exciting.

"Why can't I go with you, Mommy?" Lyric asks. She's perched on the bathroom vanity watching me put mascara on. She's obsessed with makeup lately and loves to put on lip gloss and eye shadow. I have to watch her or she'll make herself up when I'm not looking.

"Ditra and I are going to a concert, and it's just for grownups. But you're going to stay home with Uncle Josh and watch movies and eat popcorn and have lots of fun, okay?"

"Can I have ice cream, too?"

"You can have one scoop." How can I say no when she's inherited her ice cream addiction from me? I throw my mascara back into my makeup bag and plant a kiss on her nose just as Ditra appears in my bathroom doorway.

"Are you almost ready?" she asks. "We don't want to be late. It'll be a nightmare to find a parking spot."

Taking a deep breath, I nod and exhale. "Yeah, I think I am."

She picks up Lyric and settles her down on the floor, and we watch her happily skip off, most likely to find Josh downstairs.

"You look like you're going to be sick," Ditra says.

"I *feel* like I'm going to be sick."

Ever since Blue walked out of my apartment years ago I've daydreamed about seeing him again, and now that day is here. Josh pulled some strings to get VIP meet-and-greet tickets to the No Tomorrow live acoustic show in Boston tonight. With any luck, I'll be in the same room with Blue for the first time in five years. I've never been backstage at a concert before, but hopefully we'll be able to talk somewhat privately.

Unless he runs when he sees me. Or pretends he doesn't know who I am. Or…

"Piper?"

I shake my head and re-focus on Ditra. "Hm?"

"Stop freaking out. You're going to be fine."

"What if he ignores me? He might be too busy to even talk to me. He has fans now and I'm just a nobody."

She tilts her head. "Seriously? He mentioned you by name in the CD credits. He left a note in your car. The dude isn't going to ignore you once you're right in front of him. Plus, you look drop-dead gorgeous. There's no way in hell he's going to blow you off. And if he does? I'll throat punch him."

"What if he goes ballistic when I tell him about Lyric? There's going to be lots of other people there, right? I don't want to cause any kind of scene."

"I'm sure he'll be surprised but I don't think he's going to go ballistic. She's his daughter, and it's time for him to know she exists. You're doing the right thing telling him, no matter how awkward it is. That secret baby bullshit some women pull isn't cool. You're both adults. He'll be fine. Maybe a little shocked, but fine. She's a little girl, not a bomb."

I wish I felt her confidence, but I have no idea how Blue is going to react when he sees me. I don't know what kind of person he is now, or what frame of mind he's currently in with his life. He could be totally level-headed or off the rails.

He could be married. He could have other children. He could have a girlfriend.

Hell—he could have all of the above and Lyric and I might just be a massive inconvenience to him.

Then what?

For two months I've been rolling the scenario dice in my head and have come up with several outcomes, ranging from epic disaster to fairytale happy ending.

As Ditra drives us to the concert, I'm only half involved in our idle conversation. The other half of my mind is back to trying to manifest everything I've been dreaming of, focusing on the positives, like I did the day Blue disappeared. It didn't work then, but that doesn't mean it won't work now.

There's power in positive thinking. I've read about it, I've seen others do it and they got the results they wanted.

So can I.

I can be happy. I can have the life I've dreamed of. I can—

"Piper?" Ditra shoves my shoulder. "Snap out of it. No amount of driving yourself crazy is going to change anything. Please stop worrying. Let's just enjoy the concert. Do you have any idea how lucky we are to have tickets? This shit sold out months ago."

"I know." I wonder if the craziness of it shocks Blue as much as it does me. How he used to play for quarters thrown into a jar and now he's *sold out*.

Ditra continues to rattle on next to me. "Whatever happens after that, happens. You can't change it. But let's have fun and at least appreciate that this drifter dude you dated, the father of your *child*, went from playing on the streets to being a freakin' musical legend."

My stomach lurches. Blue? A legend? "I don't know about that, Dee."

She turns the car into the venue parking lot. "It's true. He's the real deal."

Legend. Real deal. None of that means a thing to me. He's the guy who made me a bracelet, bought me ice cream cones, snuggled with me as rain pattered against the tin roof, sang me to sleep, and ultimately stole my heart.

He's my first and only love. The legend of my very best memories.

❧

This is the fourth concert I've ever been to, and my first unplugged or acoustic performance. In a venue with other musicians and a huge crowd, that is. I watched Blue play unplugged, unhinged, unshowered, unhappily, uninhibited, and a million other un-things many times in the park and in the shed years ago. Back then it didn't have a fancy name, though. It was just what he did.

And now, as Ditra and I settle into our seats to the left of the stage, I'm shocked by the number of people filing into the hazy room all the while speaking to each other in hushed voices as if this is a library or they're in the graces of royalty.

I chomp my gum in fascination and watch all the fans, many wearing No Tomorrow T-shirts.

Leaning closer to Ditra, I whisper, "There are T-shirts."

"Do you want one? There's a guy out in the lobby selling them. We walked right by him."

I *do* want one, but how bad will that look when I talk to Blue later? Standing there wearing a band shirt like a starry-eyed fan? Which I'm not. I mean, I love his music and his voice and I've been listening to it all non-stop... but I'm not a fan in the traditional sense of the word.

I'm a fan of *him*. Of his mind and his heart.

This is so very complicated.

The overhead theater lights dim and people scurry like mice to take their seats as the stage curtain separates.

I'm disappointed when members of a band I don't recognize take the stage. I had completely forgotten about the opening act. My leg bounces with anxiety as they play songs I've never heard of, and I'm relieved when they finish and the curtain hides the stage again.

My teeth mash together in frustration. Does this really need to be so torturous?

After a few minutes, the heavy black curtain, deliberately torn, faded, and tattered, slowly pulls away to reveal the stage set up once again—still devoid of No Tomorrow.

The drummer, whose name I've forgotten, appears from the shadows and all but disappears when he sits behind his set. One by one, each band member enters the stage, and my heart pounds harder and faster, my eyes riveted to that shadowy, elusive entry point.

Waiting.

And there he is. Slowly sauntering, guitar in hand, to the stool and mic at the center of the stage, sandwiched between the other two guitarists. The crowd cheers and whoops, and he gives them the same humble, grateful nod he used to give the listeners in the park.

He looks so much the same, so much still in the world of his own head, that I almost expect to see Acorn sitting beside him up there on the stage. My chest heaves with deep breaths as a mix of anger and intense yearning clash inside me. How dare he sit there looking so normal—so untouched. For years I've felt that the scars I bear from his massacre of my heart must be visible to others in some way. Surely I don't smile nearly as much, or as brightly, as I once did. I no longer giggle at silly jokes. I can't read romance books or watch movies based on love stories anymore.

I'm changed.

But he looks the same. He's still insanely good-looking. Maybe even more so now as his hair is longer and fluffier and he's not quite as thin as I remember. His sparkling blue eyes are just as striking from my tenth-row seat as they were the last time I looked into them up close, when he kissed me goodbye, winked at me, and walked away.

The all-too-familiar lump of emotion forms in my throat.

He may have walked out of my apartment and my life, but he definitely has not walked out of my heart. Not by a long shot.

And as much as he's hurt me, and shredded my heart to bits, just the sight of him still draws me in, possessing me like the words of a favorite song that I can't not sing.

I feel like I'm about to combust in my seat as I grip the arm rests. I ache to walk up to him on that stage, see that beautiful smile he used to flash at me, and throw my arms around him. I want to grab his hand and run from this building with him. To the shed. To the place where we murmured undying love to each other over and over again and slept wrapped around each other, shivering from the icy drafts.

These people surrounding me don't know him. They know his voice and the sound of his guitar, but they don't know what his lips feel like, what his whispers sound like, what his body feels like.

They don't know he agonizes over every note and every lyric. They don't know how I listened and watched him with worry and love.

They don't know about ladybug myths and rain.

I do.

Tears well up in my eyes and my vision of him on stage shimmies, as if he's in an ocean of tears.

He lights up a cigarette with casual finesse as if hundreds of people aren't sitting here waiting for him. Not to mention I'm pretty sure smoking is prohibited in here. But when has he ever followed rules? Settling the guitar on his thigh, he leans forward slightly to adjust the mic, and I catch a glimpse of feathery blue in his wavy hair, and my mind and heart are transformed back in time again. When he was mine and I was his and all these movements and mannerisms were as comforting and familiar to me as an old childhood teddy bear.

Why did he leave me? Why has he chosen this life full of strangers to play for when he could be playing for me in all our special places, making me breathless like only he can?

"Are you okay?" Ditra whispers in my ear.

I nod, unable to look away from the man on the stage who's still got my heart in a vice, afraid I'll miss something—a smile or a glance my way. I wonder if he would just lift his head, not hide behind the hair falling across his face... if he would just look out at the crowd, would he notice me? Would our eyes lock like they did way back when in the park when we just *clicked*? Would he feel the wave of memories course through his veins like I am? The undeniable pull of fate? Would he miss my kiss and my touch—would he miss *me*—so much that he'll want to grab my hand and run?

I'd go. I'd sprint out of here with him without a second thought and run anywhere just to be with him again.

"Somehow he's even hotter, isn't he?" Ditra observes, breaking into my thoughts. "I guess he can afford to eat now. He's got some meat on him."

I noticed. I'm noticing everything.

I want to smack my best friend for also noticing and for pointing it out, because that means every other female in the room must be noticing and I don't want them to. I want Blue to be mine and only mine to look at.

But without introduction or warning, Blue's gravelly, tortured tone is filling the room:

> *We-eeeeee loved until it hurt,*
> *and we-eeeee, we broke each other's hearts.*
> *Believe me-eeee, every word I ever said,*
> *It was all I had, all I ever had to give.*
> *And I know, baby, I know, you shoulda had*
> *So much more.*
> *So much more....*

The lyrics, so seductive in their sadness, come to life on his lips and in his half-closed eyes. Blue has always sung as if the words were being torn right out of his soul and I'm relieved to see that neither time nor fame has changed that.

I've never witnessed such an intimate concert, not in person or on television. The stillness of the crowd speaks volumes of their respect and love for the band. We're all mesmerized, savoring every note and every word, waiting until the end of each song to clap and whistle in appreciation.

At the end of the third song, Blue finally looks at the crowd as if he's just realized we're here, and flashes a crooked, shy smile that I'm quite sure melted the hearts of every female in the room.

Me included.

"Thanks for being here with us tonight. We're honored to play so close to where we all grew up." He takes a sip from a glass that's sitting on the floor next to his stool.

Didn't he grow up in New Jersey? Hm. Maybe to him that's close?

The crowd claps softly.

"Once upon a time, I left my heart in New England," he continues, and my heart nearly leaps into my throat. Is he referring to me? Some other woman? Acorn, perhaps? "And I ain't never been the same."

He glances at Reece to his left, and they sing together in perfect synchrony.

Bloodstained tears, an angel without wings
Bury me in words, and steal my breath
Drag me from the depths of my tor-mented mind
Forget what I said, I've lost myself, I've lost my way
I walked so far but went nowhere in these shoes
I know nothing at all, but I once knew you
And, maybe, for a moment, you knew me too.

By the end of the concert, I'm a twisted mess of awe, heartache, and pride. Even if I had never known Blue personally, I would leave this theater feeling touched, forever changed by the band's talent, their obvious camaraderie, and Blue's charismatic stage presence. Tonight would be a memory I would cherish forever as something rare and special, as I'm sure most of the people surrounding me feel as well.

"That was amazing," I say to Ditra as we stand and slowly make our way to the center aisle. "His voice is incredible. Everything was incredible."

"It was definitely one of the best live performances I've ever seen. His voice is insane. And that other guy he sang with? Sheer perfection."

"I think that's Reece. I think they were friends in high school."

"I have a hardcore thing for him. I hope I can get his autograph backstage."

Just the word backstage sends me into an instant panic. Weaving through the crowd, we inch closer and closer to a guy with huge arms and a beard down to his chest who's checking VIP passes before allowing people to pass toward the hall that leads backstage. Ditra hands him ours and he quickly scans them and hands them back to us.

"Down there to the left," he says without making any eye contact.

"Josh is amazing for getting these tickets," Ditra exclaims when we're far away from Big and Beardy.

Halting, I pull Ditra off to the side so the people behind us can keep going. "I'm not sure I can do this. This is crazy, and kind of stalkerish, isn't it?"

"Piper, stop it. First, if you think I'm going to miss the chance of meeting these guys in person, you're nuts. Second, it's not crazy. You know him. You have a history. And a child. Remember?"

My shaking legs convince me to lean against the wall. "I know. I just feel like he's so out of my league right now. So much time has passed. I don't know him anymore, not like this. And I feel like I'm cornering him, coming out of nowhere."

"It doesn't matter. You need closure. And he needs to know he's a father. End of story." She grabs my arm and pulls me away from the wall. "Now let's go."

She practically drags me down the hallway to a lounge which is being guarded by a guy who looks almost identical to the first guy who checked our passes a few seconds ago. Big and Beardy Two waves us in and just like that, I'm standing a few feet away from Blue. Thankfully, he's got his back to the door and is engaged in a conversation with a small group of people and doesn't see me enter the room, giving me time to compose myself.

I didn't know what to expect for this meet-n-greet session, but I envisioned a room packed with people drinking, smoking weed, and trying to hook up with the band members while their music blasted in the background. In reality, it's nothing like that. The room is surprisingly quiet with fewer than twenty people chatting on bright orange couches or standing, sipping drinks and nibbling tiny sandwiches.

Ditra points to a bar and a table spread with food on the other side of the room. "I'm going to go get a drink. Do you want to come with me?"

I'm afraid if I put anything in my mouth I'm going to get sick. "No, I just want to get his attention and talk to him."

"Do you want me to go with you?"

I shake my head and run my tongue over my lips. "I think it's better if I approach him alone. I don't want him to feel ganged up on."

"Agreed. I'll be milling around trying to get Reece to notice me." She winks at me and dashes off with a sway of her hips. I shake my head, fluff my hair with my hands, and slowly walk over to Blue.

"Hey. Enjoy the show?" A huge wall of chest is suddenly in front of me, attached to a head of long black hair, an easy smile, and dark eyes.

I blink up at him, unable to find my voice. I wasn't expecting anyone to talk to *me*.

"Um, yes. Very much," I finally squeak out.

He raises his dark eyebrows as he lifts his beer bottle to his lips. "You don't sound so sure."

I smile reassuringly. "You just caught me off guard. It was amazing. You guys sound even better live than you do on your CD."

He grins with amusement. "I hope that's a compliment?"

"Yes, definitely."

"I'm Reece, by the way," he says.

"I know," I reply, wishing Ditra would get her ass back over here. Instead she's already off flirting with some random dude with a ring in his nose and a Mohawk, completely ignoring me. "I'm Piper...and I'm actually hoping to talk to Blue...."

His eyes narrow at me. "Piper? You're not *the* Piper, are you?"

Reece's question is completely unexpected. I can't picture Blue talking about me to his friends and bandmates. What I wouldn't give to be a fly on the wall to hear those conversations.

"I'm not sure if I'm *the* Piper you're referring to." I refuse to assume anything at this point. Even though my name is rare, it doesn't mean Blue hasn't met another Piper or two.

"The one he's been all fucked on for years?" Reece lets out a low laugh. "I guess I owe him fifty bucks because I bet him a few years back that you didn't exist and you were just one of his fucked-up hallucinations. But here you are."

I smile weakly. "Here I am."

He turns and yells across the room. "Hey, Blue! Look who's here."

My heart's no longer racing. I'm sure it's completely stopped. Blue turns slowly to Reece, and his gaze drops to meet mine, his eyes widening with surprise and disbelief. He turns back to the two women he was talking to, then moments later turns again to cross the room.

"Ladybug...." He says the nickname so affectionately I almost burst into tears. I force myself to not let that happen. I will not be the blubbering ex in a room full of people.

Reece watches us stare at each other, downs the remainder of his beer, then playfully smacks Blue on the back.

"I'll leave you two alone." He nods to me. "Nice meeting you. Glad to see you're real."

Not taking my eyes from Blue's, I reply to Reece absently, "Nice meeting you, too."

Blue lets out a low breath. "Holy shit. I never expected to see you here." A smile plays across his lips. "I've missed you. So fucking much."

"I miss you, too." My voice wavers over the words. "I never expected to find you here. Like this."

"Yeah. It's been a bit of a ride." He shoves his fingers into the front of his hair and pushes it back from his face. "So how are you? How's Acorn?"

It's the dog's name, that sweet, furry ball of love's name, that finally snaps me out of this surreal, polite cloud we're standing under. I raise my hand to slap him and he catches my wrist mid-air and yanks me tight against his chest. Holding me there, he bends his face down into my neck.

"You can slap the shit out of me, rip my heart out. Whatever you want. But not here." His lips brush across my ear, sending shivers up my spine and over my scalp. "I don't want your picture on every tabloid tomorrow with some nasty rumor attached to it. You're too good for that. Okay?"

I nod against his shoulder and slowly pull away to face his dark, sorrowful eyes. I imagine mine look the same.

"How could you?" I ask, keeping my voice low. "How could you just leave me like that? And your dog? What kind of person does something like that?"

"The kind who knows he can't be around good things without breaking them."

I have to give him credit for his ability to admit that straight to my face with dead-on honesty.

Choking back a sob that I refuse to let out, I shake my head. "No. You don't get to proclaim yourself an asshole and just walk away. It's completely unacceptable and shitty."

"You're right."

A rogue tear slides down my cheek. "You just left us. You took the easy way out."

He looks at the floor for a moment, as if he's letting the words sink in, then returns his gaze back to me. "There was nothing easy about leaving the only two things I care about."

I want to ask him why he did it then, if it was so hard, but this isn't what I want. For years I dreamed of this moment, and now it's heading straight into the direction I feared it would go. A place filled with anger and accusations and no closure, resolution, or new beginning at all. How on earth am I supposed to tell him about our beautiful, smart, adorable little girl in the midst of this awkwardness?

I can't help but notice a few people standing off to the side, stealing impatient sideways glances at us, and I realize I'm keeping him from fans who paid to spend time with him.

"I should go," I say softly. "But I have to tell—"

His hair flings over his shoulder as he shakes his head. "Don't go." He reaches for my hand and pulls it into his. "Not yet, okay? Have dinner with me. We'll talk." Hope flashes across his face—an expression I've not seen on his face many times before. "I know you're pissed off. But I don't think you came here just to see my band, or to slap me. Right?"

I relax my tense shoulders, despite the turmoil spinning up inside me. "No. I wanted to see you and talk to you."

"Then let's get out of here and do that."

Glancing around at the roomful of fans I ask, "Are you allowed to leave?"

"Of course." He smiles devilishly. "I can do whatever I want."

I study his expression before I answer, trying to gauge his intentions. Everything about him seems genuine. No alarm bells are ringing in my head. Nothing about him seems shady or deceitful.

And he's still holding my hand. In a roomful of fans, bandmates, groupies, and journalists. That must count for something.

"I came with Ditra, she drove me."

"Okay. I'll get you home later if that's what you're worried about. Or she can come with us."

"Er, I think I'd rather she not tag along. Let me find her and let her know."

He nods. "While you do that I'm going to say hi to a few people and sign some things so everyone's happy. Just come get me when you're ready and we'll take off."

The way he squeezes my hand before he releases it reassures me that everything is okay and I'm not making a huge mistake by going off with him. Maybe there's a way we can start over, after all. I may be jumping the gun, but if we still love each other, and if he accepts Lyric, then we could find a way to be together and make it work. People have gotten through worse circumstances and come out stronger.

It looks like Ditra gave up on her plan of hooking up with Reece because after scouring the room I find her still talking to the guy with the Mohawk. They've moved to a large chair in the corner and she's perched on his lap, touching his spikey hair.

"So? How'd it go?" she asks when I approach them.

"Good, so far. I haven't really talked to him much yet. He wants me to go have dinner and talk."

"When?"

"Now. Tonight."

"What are you going to do?"

"I think I'm going to go. Do you mind?"

She waves her hand at me. "Not a bit. I might be busy, anyway." She leans her head against the guy's head and the mother in me is petrified his hair is going to stab one of her eyes out. "How are you going to get home? Do you want me to wait around?"

"No, he says he'll get me home."

I ignore Mr. Mohawk's sudden obnoxious laugh, hoping he's just being a jerk and doesn't have inside info about Blue having a rep for handing out *I'll get you home* lines to various unsuspecting women. Ditra frowns and leans back up, straightening her shirt in the process which *somehow* has gotten all askew. "Are you sure? I don't want you abandoned in Boston in the middle of the night."

"I'll be fine." *I hope.*

"Okay, if you're sure. I'm going to hang around for a little while, too. You go have fun, be strong, and call me!"

"I will." I give her friend the side-eye. "You have fun, too."

Hand-in-hand, we walk across the street to the restaurant in the hotel that Blue and the band are staying in for the weekend. We sit at a quiet table in the back that Blue thinks should hide us from concert-goers.

We don't open our menus or ask each other what we're having.

We don't casually chat about the concert or the weather.

We stare at each other.

We hold hands across the table, like lovers do.

I concentrate hard to control the tremor of panic in my chest and take steady breaths. I knew it would be hard seeing him—exciting, confusing, emotional—but my body seems to have its own ideas. I have to shove away the fear and keep breathing or I'll start to feel sick. And I want to stay present with *him*, no matter how many directions my body wants to run.

"You're still wearing it." He thumbs the beaded bracelet. It's faded and tattered now, much like my heart.

"I told you I'd never take it off."

That makes him smile. "I thought you would have taken it off so you wouldn't be reminded of me every day after what happened."

I almost laugh. I have a much bigger and better reminder of him in the form of a tiny person with his same soulful eyes.

"What *did* happen, Blue? I thought we were happy. We had such a nice time that night."

"We did. It was one of the best nights of my life. Every second of us together is burned into my memory."

I stare at our hands, at his thumb caressing my knuckles. "I don't understand. Was it the apartment? Did it scare you? Did you think I was going to try to force you to move in? Give you an ultimatum? I wasn't going to. I was willing to accept the way you wanted to live."

"I know that."

Patiently, I wait for him to give me more of an answer. I refuse to keep prodding at him and making myself appear desperate. Even though I am—I'm absolutely desperate for an explanation, something to make me understand. The air is thick between us; the silence expands like a balloon about to burst. The waitress brings us water and he asks her for a few more minutes. Our hands are still clasped, resting against the unopened laminated menus.

"You wanted things I couldn't give you. You deserved things I had no way to give."

"Did I want to live together in my nice apartment? Yes. Of course I did. I wanted you out of the shed and in a nice, warm bed. I wanted you to have a bathroom and a closet of clean clothes. I wanted you to have a kitchen full of things to eat and drink. I wanted us to be able to sit on the couch and watch movies. I'm not going to lie; of course I wanted all of those things—that life—for both of us. Together."

He nods, and now it's his turn to fixate on our hands.

"But if given the choice," I continue. "I would much rather have you in my life, than to lose you. None of those things were worth losing you over. Not to me."

"You felt that way then, Piper. But in time you would've changed your mind."

I honestly don't think I ever would have changed my mind.

"Neither one of us knows that. Maybe I would have, maybe I wouldn't. Maybe *you* would have changed in time, Blue. Did you ever think of that? Look at you now. When you walked out my door you were a homeless street musician with a couple bucks in your pocket and a lost dog. You had nothing. Now five years later you're in one of the most popular bands in the country. A lot has changed, and you obviously did something to make that happen, and I don't understand why we couldn't have stayed together while all this was going on. I never would have held you back, I—"

His head snaps up. "Is that what you thought I was?"

I furrow my eyebrows together. "What?"

"A homeless, penniless musician with a stray dog?"

I shrug uncomfortably. "I guess so. Yes. But it didn't matter to me. I loved you for who you were, and how you made me feel."

"I never would have dragged you along on the ride to get here, Piper. You had a great job, a nice place to live, you were settling down. You had a *direction.*"

"So?"

"And I didn't. I was a fucking tumbleweed, a twisted-up mess of dirt and weeds bouncing around in the wind."

"That's a pretty harsh analogy."

"It's the truth. I couldn't be *still*, Piper. I know it sucks and I know it makes me a huge fucking douchebag. But at least I loved you and Acorn enough to know you were both much better off without me. And I guess it made me feel good, knowing you two were together. I knew you'd take care of him."

"I did. I still am. He's the best dog in the world." Acorn has taken care of me, too. He stayed with me on the bathroom floor when I suffered with morning sickness. He snuggled up on the bed with me when I cried myself to sleep every night. And he's been the perfect guardian and furry best friend to Lyric.

"He's okay?" he asks with a lilt of hesitation in his voice.

"He's great. Still dragging his penguin around."

Relief rides out of him on a long breath. "I'm glad. And you?"

"I'm good. Still at the same company, still living in the same town. Still have Archie. Still reading a book a week."

My heart blips when he winks at me. "And obviously listening to much better music."

Now. Now is the time to tell him about our daughter.

I pull my hand from his and take a quick sip of water. The glass is thick and heavy, damp with moisture, and it almost slips from my trembling hand. He takes it from me and places it back down on the cork coaster.

"Blue, I have to tell—"

"You ready to order? The kitchen is closing soon."

God. Flo is back, with her pad and pen in hand, with the worst timing ever in the history of time.

"How 'bout two cheeseburgers with fries?" Blue suggests, looking at me exactly the way Lyric does when she's excited about something. "Like we used to?"

I smile up at the waitress. "Two cheeseburgers and fries would be perfect."

"You got it." She scribbles on her notepad before scooping up our menus and walking away.

"I miss it here," he says wistfully. "New England."

"Where do you live now?"

"Still here and there and everywhere, only different now. Mostly in buses and planes and hotels. When we're not traveling, I share a condo with Reece in Seattle."

I'm relieved to hear he's in an actual residence and not living in a garage or in a cave of bats, but I was hoping he lived closer and not so far away.

"I'm so proud of you, Blue. Seeing you tonight on that stage, in front of all those people, was incredible. I always knew you were talented, but you've completely blown me away. It's just... wild."

"I guess."

"Are you happy?"

"No."

His answer surprises me and I tilt my head at him like a curious cat. "But why? You're living a dream."

"Someone else's dream. Not mine."

"Then what's your dream?"

He straightens the salt and pepper dispensers. Then he lines the bottles of ketchup and steak sauce perfectly next to the salt and pepper before he answers. "Being free. Flying like a bird. Not literally... but being weightless. Soaring above all the noise and the crazy. Gliding away from the storm."

"Can't you do that? I'm assuming you have the money now to go on relaxing vacations... or to pay people to handle stressful stuff for you?"

"I wish it was that easy."

"Are you enjoying it at all? Writing songs, bringing them to life for millions of people to love? You had the entire audience under your spell tonight."

"That part, yeah. It's all about the music and the words for me, you know that. It's the other crap, the never-ending circus of bullshit I can't stand."

"I guess that sort of comes with the territory?"

"Yup."

Our food arrives and we eat in silence for a few minutes before he puts his burger down and looks up at me.

"I didn't want to hurt you, Piper," he says. "Back then...."

Swallowing my food, I nod. I know his words are true. I may not understand him, but I believe him.

His steely cobalt eyes practically hypnotize me. "I meant what I wrote in the note. You're in my veins. You're what makes me tick. You've heard the songs. You know I'm not getting over you."

I sway under his gaze and the weight of his words. Words I've waited for and wished for, for what feels like forever. Words that feed my starving heart.

"Do you want to?" I ask.

"No, babe. I really fucking don't."

The sound of my heartbeat whooshes in my ears. My voice comes out just an octave above a whisper. "Good. I don't want you to."

A silent agreement passes between us. It's not spoken, but I heard it. I *felt* it. We didn't read the fine print, we didn't take time to think it over, we just signed on the dotted line with our hearts and our desires and the deal was done.

CHAPTER TWENTY-TWO

PIPER

One minute I'm eating a hamburger and fries and the next I'm walking down a long corridor toward Blue's hotel room with my hand tightly clasped in his. The zig-zag pattern of the carpet makes me dizzier and dizzier with each step.

Or maybe it's from walking up four flights of stairs because Blue *doesn't do elevators.*

But most likely it's because I'm having an anxiety attack. Because I haven't told him about Lyric yet. Not before he asked me to come up to his room to talk, and not as we hoofed up the stairs.

And certainly not now, standing in front of the door as he swipes the card reader. It doesn't exactly feel like the right time. He's happy. I'm happy. Feelings of awkwardness, heartache, and guilt have been shoved into the closets of our minds, waiting to jump out again during a fight someday in the future like emotional boogie-men.

Once we're on the other side of the door, he releases my hand and cups my cheek with his warm palm. His smoky eyes linger on mine, then lower to my lips. His thumb moves across my cheek to the target of his gaze.

My breath catches when he pushes his thumb past my lips, forcing my jaw open. His mouth comes down on mine, kissing me deeply, filling my mouth with his tongue with his thumb still pressing my bottom teeth. Weakening, I lean back against the door and his hard body leans perfectly into mine. Familiar calloused fingers dig into the flesh of my waist under the material of my shirt.

I missed this so much. All of this that's him. The rough demands of his touch, his passion, his torment and his words. His scent—oh how much I missed his woodsy, smoky, mint-tinged scent. I love how his touch instantly jump-starts my body back to life. My heart is racing. I'm practically panting with want for him. I want him to throw me on the bed and brand every inch of me. I want to touch him, explore all his new tattoos and his thicker body.

As he slowly drags his thumb from my bottom lip to my chin, his eyes burn with lust watching the wet path of his finger.

"Been waiting all fucking night for that," he says hoarsely.

My legs are wobbly with desire when he tugs me farther into the large, posh room, and I'm still intoxicated from his kiss when I teasingly ask, "Was it worth the wait?"

I didn't know my comment was the equivalent of giving a hungry wild animal even the tiniest taste of meat.

With mind-spinning speed, he captures me in his arms and throws me down on the king-sized bed. He lands hard on top of me, his size and weight nearly knocking the wind out of my lungs.

We kiss like two people who have been doing nothing but thinking about kissing each other for the past five years—rough, wild, desperate and wet. We're a tangle of lips and tongue and hands yanking off clothes.

In the midst of it all I manage to gather my wits and separate my lips from his long enough to attempt to tell him what I came here for.

"Blue, we should talk...."

He hovers above me with his messy hair hanging down into my face and stares at me with a veil of denial already in his eyes.

"Don't say it, whatever it is, Piper. I don't want to hear it if you have a boyfriend or a husband—"

I reach up to stroke his stubbled cheek. "No. Not at all. It's not that—"

His lips touch mine again, soft now, almost pleading. "Good. Me either. We'll talk later...."

"But—"

His warm lips slip across my throat, and his teeth nip a trail, leaving his mark. "Shh...."

I shouldn't give in to his shushing me, no matter how much we want each other. I should sit up and force him to listen to me so I can tell him about our daughter before we go any further physically or emotionally. And if the realization that he has a child doesn't wreck him and cause him to have a meltdown, *then* we can ravish each other all night long, and hopefully move forward.

I open my mouth to protest, but he moves his lips back up to mine, kisses me in that desperate way that weakens me.

"I can't talk, Piper. Or think," he says softly, then brushes his lips across mine again. "Just let me get lost in you... please."

I've never been able to resist or deny him. My body craves his. My heart beats in perfect tune with his. My soul meshed with his the day we met. I need and want to get lost in him, too. More than anything.

So I give in, and I shush.

For now.

My silence doesn't last long. Faint sighs and throaty moans soon drift from my lips in response to his hands and mouth reclaiming every inch of my body. Each time I reach for him, he pins my hands back down on the bed and immobilizes me with deeper kisses, imprisoning me between his strong thighs. I ache to touch him, dig my nails into him, to feel that he's real and not another one of my many dreams.

"Don't move," he says gruffly, climbing off the bed. I'm all eyes and quivers watching him unbuckle his leather belt and kicking off his black combat boots to step out of his jeans.

"Do these expire?" he asks, holding up a crumpled foil condom he just pulled from his wallet. The same wallet he had when we first met.

"I'm not sure. How long has it been in there?"

"Years. Since us."

I lean up on my elbows. "You haven't used it?"

"For what?"

"Um, for safe sex?"

He grabs my foot, lifts it up to his bare chest, and removes the strappy heel. Heat floods between my thighs when he bends down to plant an open kiss at the arch of my foot.

"I haven't touched anyone," he says, repeating the same erotic actions with my other foot. "Don't you get it, Piper? You're it." Placing the condom between his teeth, he hooks his fingers in the waistband of my jeans and yanks them over my ankles.

I blink at him, disbelieving. It's been easy for me to not be with another man. I've dated very little over the past few years and none of those dates ever led to sex. Sure, a few guys tried, but I always sabotaged the moment. Besides, I work long hours and spend all my free time with my daughter or walking Acorn. I don't have time to start a serious relationship. As unconventional as it is, Josh and I have a friend-lationship that works for us on a non-physical level.

But how could Blue possibly be celibate for so long? It's unthinkable. He's a guy. A very good-looking and extremely sensual one. And he's a musician. Women love musicians, especially sexy, dark, brooding ones like him. We're inexplicably drawn to them, like chocolate or coffee or diamonds. We want to fix them. We want to be the *one*. The one to change them, the one to win their hearts and stop their wandering ways. The one who makes them forget all other women. We want to be the *it*, as he said.

I have no idea how four-foot-eleven, one-hundred-pound, boring me could possibly be anyone's *it*.

"You're serious?" I ask.

Standing at the foot of the bed, he tears open the foil and rolls the latex over his shaft with the city lights from the window behind him illuminating his shape in the dark room. Wild and wavy hair tumbles over his shoulders and the feather catches the light, glinting with iridescence. Such a bittersweet symbol of his beloved bird, tethered to him, without the freedom to soar.

He leans over my body, between my spread thighs, and grabs my throat, pulling me up to him.

"Shhh...." He kisses me, one hand still closed around my throat, while the other reaches between my legs to stroke my wet lips. He hums with desire when I spread my thighs wider, inviting him in.

Begging him, is more accurate.

His name is all over my lips when two skull-ringed fingers thrust inside me and begin expertly stroking, zeroing in on all the right places, just like he used to. The span of his hand clenched over my throat tightens slightly, capturing the vibration of my moans against his palm.

"I missed you so fucking much, Ladybug. Every day. Every night."

I'm close to delirious with want—wanting to give him everything, wanting him to take everything. Wanting him to never leave again. Wanting to stay in this moment forever. Wanting to forget, wanting to hope.

I drop my head against the bed when he releases his hold on my neck so he can grab my legs and swiftly flip me over. I'm dragged to the edge of the bed, lifted up onto my knees, and spread wide before him. He inches his hand lightly up my back, skimming over the goosebumps, and grabs my hair, twisting it around his hand and tugging my head up and backward to meet his mouth. His hips slam hard into my ass, driving his cock balls-deep into me. He growls against my mouth like a wild animal when I arch my back, angling myself to take him deeper. My walls stretch around his thick cock, my fingers clench the bedspread. He sucks my tongue into his mouth, moving his free hand across my belly, up to cup my breasts, squeezing my nipples into the channel of his fingers. The heat coming off his body is like a fire enveloping us and our bodies, slippery with sweat, slap against each other. I'm spinning into euphoria, falling fast down the rabbit hole, going back to that exquisite place where there's no time, no place. There's just *us*.

I break away from his lips, gasping for breath and whimpering as orgasms quake through my body. His ab muscles tense deliciously against the small of my back, his breath quickens, and I feel his body pulse inside me.

Leaning his forehead against the back of my head, he rests there, catching his breath before slowly pulling out and rolling onto his back next to me. I crawl into his outstretched arm and rest my head against his chest. I trace small circles over his stomach with my fingertips and watch his muscles dance beneath my touch.

His voice, soft and deep, is melodic in the dark quietness of the room. "I know I show it in messed-up ways, but I really do love you," he says.

"I know, Blue. I never doubted that."

His heart beats wildly under my head. He moves his hand lazily up and down my arm. I can feel him thinking.

"Do you love me, Piper?"

I sit up to face him, even though we can barely see each other in the dark. "I love you more than words can say. I never stopped, not for a minute."

He gently squeezes my shoulder. "I'll be right back." He rises from the bed, disappears into the bathroom for several minutes, then comes out with a white towel wrapped around his narrow hips. Next he goes out on the balcony and lights up a cigarette, and I watch him smoking and looking out over the city.

I wonder what he's thinking about.

I wonder what I'm doing here.

I wonder why I'm so afraid to tell him why I came here.

I wonder where we go from here, and from there, when I tell him.

I *have* to tell him.

While he's smoking I find my way to the bathroom and wash my face and fix my major bed-head. I sit on the edge of the Jacuzzi tub and stare down at my shiny pink-tipped toenails, trying to regroup my brain. I didn't think we'd go from zero to sixty tonight. I should have slammed on the brakes before things careened straight to his bed.

When I come out of the bathroom, he's lying on the bed, propped up on a pile of stark white pillows. It's odd seeing him in a room surrounded by lamps and furniture and television remotes.

"You have a glass shower and a huge jet tub," I say.

"Weird, huh?"

I crawl onto the bed next to him and he pulls me up against him, wrapping his tattooed arm around me as if we've never been apart.

"You deserve to have nice things."

"To me it's just stuff that water comes out of."

I giggle and turn to kiss him. "You're adorable."

"I want to try again."

The smile slowly fades from my lips. Not because I'm not happy, but because I'm confused and unsure.

"What do you mean?"

"Us. We could try again, right?"

"Yes. We could." I swallow hard over the lump of cautious excitement in my throat. "I mean, I want to. Really. Things are a lot different now though..."

I place the first breadcrumb down and hope he follows it.

"I know. But we could do it. I could stay with you when we're off tour. And we could still see each other when I'm touring. We could fly to each other."

I went from dating a guy who lived in a shed to a guy who now tours and flies around the world. It's hard to grasp he's the same guy. I wonder if I would fit into his new, exciting life, or if I'd feel totally out of my element with him.

But when I move the layers of his new lifestyle to the side, Blue *is* the same. He's still quiet, honest, and passionate. He still makes me feel like I'm the only woman on the planet that exists in his eyes. He walked away from a room full of paying fans to be alone with me—just like he walked away from the listeners in the park to come sit with me years ago.

In his own way, he's incredibly romantic.

He's still *my* Blue.

Having money, a band, fans, and a busy schedule hasn't changed who he is or the things I love about him. I don't see any sign of a man who has turned into a player or who hops from woman to woman. It might take a while, but I could accept his career and everything that comes with it as long as it doesn't change him.

"That's true," I finally say. "We could find ways to make it work. Lots of people do it." My mind tries to wrangle how I'd work that out between my job, a four-year-old, and two pets. Blue isn't the only one who's living a different life now. My life is completely different, too, and he knows absolutely nothing about any of it. Just as I would need to accept his new life, he would also have to be willing to accept mine.

And most of all, he would have to accept our daughter. Unconditionally.

"My drummer's got a long-term chick. They work it out."

We reach for each other's hands at the same time and entwine our fingers together. "I've been thinking about you a lot, Piper. I was blown away when I saw you tonight. It's like fate brought you back to me. I even dreamt about you a few nights ago. And now you're here and it's like we were never apart. I think I can do it right this time. I'm flat out with the band and writing new songs and all that other shit, but I'll make time. I can be better now."

"There was nothing wrong with you before," I interject.

"No, there was and I know it. I was tumbleweeding all over the fuckin' place. I had all kinds of shit in my head and I could never get the words or the notes right and everything else just spiraled and it was just too much and that's why I got headaches and felt sick. But it would be better now and we could be together. I'm leaving tomorrow night for the next show, but you could come with me." The frantic speed of his words and his overly excited tone is sweet yet equally alarming. "I'll make sure we have a room with a big tub and lots of soap and towels and we'll have a big bed like this one. And you can come to the show every night and watch me like you used to in the pub, remember? I used to love that, looking out at the crowd and seeing your big beautiful eyes watching me. We could have cheeseburgers every night and we can fall asleep together in a real bed, just like you wanted." His arm tightens around me, as if he's pulling me into this scenario with him. "We could be together again, me, you, and Acorn."

When he finally pauses to take a breath, I jump in.

"I wish I could do all that but I have to work, Blue. I can't just take time off without any notice. I want to. More than anything. But I'd have to put in vacation requests with HR. I have over a month of vacation time but I can't just take off whenever. We can still make plans, though. You'll have to let me know your schedule and we'll see what we can make work and talk about everything else."

"Oh. I forgot about all that." His tongue piercing clicks his teeth. "It's okay. As soon as we can, we'll get together. And I can call you. Every day. I have a phone now."

I nod enthusiastically, trying to figure out how I can bring up Lyric in this conversation without ruining the moment. "Definitely. We'll take it day by day. No pressure."

Squinting, he rubs his fingertips across his forehead. "My head is killing me. I'm so tired. I can't remember when I slept."

"You need to get some rest. It's late."

He rolls onto his side and curls his body around mine. "Sleep with me and we'll get you home in the morning. I won't be able to sleep if you leave."

Shit. I should have gone home hours ago, or at least called Josh, who must be worried out of his mind right now. I feel like the worst mother in the world. I've never let Lyric go to bed without telling her I love her. Ever.

"I need to call my roommate."

He nods, already drifting off to sleep, too tired to ask questions. "Okay, then come sleep with me," he mumbles into his pillow.

I use the phone on the desk across the room rather than the one closer to the bed, and Josh answers on the second ring.

"Jesus Christ, Piper, where the hell are you? It's two a.m."

I cringe from the receiver. "Calm down, please? I'm with Blue."

He scoffs down the line. "What a surprise. I saw this coming a mile away."

"Josh, please," I whisper loudly. "Is Lyric okay? Is she awake?"

"She's fine, and no, she's not awake. I put her to bed hours ago. I've been sitting here watching Project Runway worrying about you."

"I didn't get to say goodnight to her. Was she upset?"

"No, she just kept asking when you were coming home and if she could have more ice cream."

"Shit. I feel terrible."

"When are you coming home?"

"Tomorrow."

He lets out a frustrated sigh. "I hope you know what you're doing."

Nope. Not at all.

"So I guess he took the news well?" he prods.

"I didn't tell him yet."

"Are you going to?"

"Yes. In the morning. This is really hard, Josh. He's so happy to see me. You don't know him, not much makes him happy and excited like this. I just wanted us to enjoy some time together."

"I have a bad feeling about this. Don't make me regret getting you those tickets, Piper."

"Ugh. Really? Why are you being like this? I'm an adult."

"Yeah and the first night you go out to see your ex you don't come home and completely blow off your kid. This guy just fucks you all up."

"He doesn't fuck me up. And I didn't blow off Lyric. How dare you say that to me? This is the first time I've gone out at night in months! I just lost track of the time."

"I'm not going to argue with you—I'm going to bed. I'll see you tomorrow," he says. "And don't worry about Lyric, I'll make her breakfast and keep her busy until you get home."

"I *do* appreciate you taking care of her for me. I'm sorry I made you worry. I just need a little more time with him."

"Just be careful." He ends the call and I slowly put the phone down, feeling my happy bubble slowly deflating.

Sighing, I crawl under the covers with Blue and cuddle up against his warm body. He presses his lips to the top of my head. "Don't go," he says sleepily.

"I'm not going anywhere. I promise," I whisper, rubbing my hand back and forth across his warm back.

Tomorrow morning I'll tell him about Lyric. After we've both gotten some sleep and have absorbed our decision to be together again. To try again. I don't let my mind wander too far into the future. I won't let myself worry about being in a relationship with a rock star. Blue is the same person he used to be. He's humble, unfazed by his new life. I can see it so clearly—our future—as I envisioned and hoped for. We can be a family. We can be happy. We can put the past behind us, leave his demons in the dust.

> *We are the myth, of love and lore*
> *Of visions and gem-painted bugs, forever and evermore*
> *We are faith and hope and dreams come true*
> *We are one and two and there is no one but you.*
> *No one but you....*

The lyrics of Ladybug drift through my exhausted mind. Blue is a poet, a dreamer. Loyal to love and forgiving of its madness. We'll be fine, the two of us, and our whimsical little girl.

> *Mend my shredded wings, lend me your heart*
> *Fly with me, there's nothing to tear us apart....*

CHAPTER TWENTY-THREE

PIPER

8:06 a.m.

I yawn at the digital clock on the nightstand. It seems like just a blink ago it was three a.m. Last night's activities cycle through my memory like a slow, out-of-focus slideshow.

Blue on stage, with his band, surrounded by fans.

The way his voice and his lyrics slammed through my chest and into my soul.

Cheeseburgers.

Love.

His hand in my hair, his body buried in mine.

The hope.

Waking to slow, sweet kisses with the rise of the sun.

Him in my mouth, his moans and lusty eyes.

The promises.

A sensation creeps over me, similar to that feeling I get when I forget to put my watch on, and then for the rest of the day my wrist feels strange and oddly amputated.

Blue isn't in bed with me. I'm a wrist without a watch.

My back and neck ache in protest when I sit up and stretch my arms high up over my head. I'm not used to sleeping all tangled up with another person. Or being stretched and bent and bit and sucked.

On my way to the balcony, I pick his T-shirt up off the floor and slip it over my head, then slowly slide the glass door open to step out into the warmth of the sun, which doesn't wake me as much I hoped it would.

I desperately need a latte to fight off the lingering brain fog from lack of sleep. In fact, I could probably use a gallon to help me get through the interrogation I'm sure I'll be enduring from Josh and Lyric when I get home. But first, I need to use the bathroom and take a long hot shower. Then we can have breakfast in the café in the lobby and figure out how I'm getting home and where we go from there.

And somewhere in there, we need to have a serious talk.

When I step back inside he still hasn't come out of the bathroom. My bare feet pad silently over the plush carpet as I cross the room to the marble tile hallway that leads to the bathroom. Pausing, I turn my ear toward the heavy door. There's no sound from the other side.

"You okay?" I call out awkwardly.

No answer.

"Blue?"

A cough. "Gimme a sec, babe...."

While I wait, I tidy up the room, which other than our clothes all over the floor, is surprisingly neat. Two large suitcases are on the floor with their lids open, exposing his wardrobe of jeans and T-shirts. And cigarettes. Lots and lots of cigarette packs.

Five empty water bottles and two empty liters of lemon soda line the top of the dresser.

Even though I know a maid will be coming shortly, I make the bed and smooth the wrinkles from the comforter, then sit on the edge with my feet dangling, waiting for him to come out. I'll be upset if he decided to soak in that huge tub without me.

A cold chill suddenly courses through me. What if he changed his mind about us and now he's hiding from me, devising an escape plan like he did five years ago, but now he's got himself cornered in the bathroom with no way out?

No. That's ridiculous. He wouldn't do that.

I exhale a steadying breath, growing more impatient and worried, and search for the television remote, hoping to distract myself. Instead, a book on his nightstand catches my eye, and I realize it's one of his notebooks, with the pen I gave him for Christmas years ago sitting on top of it. The pen brings a smile to my lips. He kept it, and he's using it. Which means it must remind him of me. Curiosity gets the best of me, and I pick up the notebook and flip through the pages.

The pages are filled with nothing but harsh jagged scribbles.

My mind races back to the shed, to the first time I noticed the pages of scribblings. But I saw him on the floor, with one of these books, writing and tearing the pages out, throwing them around the room, then starting all over again. I distinctly remember him telling me he was trying to get the words right. He was distraught, literally agonizing over the words and the notes.

What words? Where are the actual words?

And why were there stacks of these exact books piled in the shed of the old house?

I finger the notebook, trying to make sense of it, but I'm clueless.

What is he doing?

Taking the book with me, I walk back to the hallway and knock softly on the door.

"Blue? Are you okay? I need to use the bathroom." I wait. I hear a faint rustle. "Can you come out? We really need to talk before I leave."

Nothing.

I debate opening the door. We're definitely nowhere near sharing bathroom activity status, but worry soon takes over any fears of humiliation. Turning the knob, I push the door open a few inches.

I wish I never had.

In fact, I wish I had never come here to begin with.

The sound of the notebook falling from my grasp to the floor startles him, and our eyes meet for a quick second before I turn and run back to the bedroom with my hand over my mouth, suppressing the screams threatening to rip from my body.

Hot tears well up in my eyes and slide down my cheeks as I

frantically pull on my clothes, and he stumbles out of the bathroom, still holding the needle that was inserted in his vein just a few seconds ago.

"Piper, wait...."

"Get away from me," I cry, pushing past him to get to the door. I have to get out of here, away from him and his horribly bloodshot eyes and swollen vein. I'm spun around when he grabs my arm, and I can't avoid his eyes, those beautiful blue eyes I love so much, now wild, spacey and unfocused. Nausea bubbles up in my gut like acid. Sobbing, I wrench my arm free from his grip. "Don't touch me."

"Please." He sways toward the wall, drops the syringe onto the floor, and almost falls on his face trying to pick it up.

Devastated at the sight of him this way, I shake my head in horrified disbelief. "I thought you were clean. You told me you were better. What the hell are you doing to yourself?"

Like a zombie he stumbles forward, arms outstretched, and tries to pull me into his arms. "Baby, I'm better. I'm much better. I just need a little sometimes. To get through all the shit." He holds his arm toward me. "Look, there's not even a lot of marks. See? It's only when I'm tired and I can't sleep and I can't think..." He rakes his fingers through his tangled hair. "I just need to get it all to stop sometimes. That's all. I'm fine." A demented smile slashes across his face.

I back away from him. "You're not fine, Blue. And you're scaring me. I-I can't see you like this."

And I can never, ever, let my daughter be around someone like this.

Gasping for breath through the sobs wracking through me, I run from him, down the ugly hall to the elevator, where I stab the down arrow on the panel repeatedly. The chrome doors slide open just as Blue appears at the end of the hall, yelling my name. Tearing my eyes away from him, I step into the elevator before he catches up to me and back myself into the corner just as the doors close me in like a vault. An older woman already occupying the elevator eyes me with an expression of great concern while I hunt through my bag for a tissue.

"Excuse me, miss, are you all right?" she asks when the elevator starts to descend.

I nod and wipe at my eyes with a ragged tissue I found at the bottom of my purse. "Yes. I-I just had a fight with my boyfriend."

She *tsks* and shakes her head. "Men are bastards," she mutters. "And not worth your tears."

Words of defense sit at the tip of my tongue, but I can't let them out. She could very well be right. Maybe all men really are bastards, completely lacking the ability to get their shit together and forever destroying all the good things in their lives and breaking every heart they claim to love into a million pieces.

I'm done. I gave him my heart and my body and my trust and he threw it all away in a matter of hours. *Hours.*

I'm shuddering with emotional overload. All I want to do is get far away from here, home to my little girl and the safety of my gay fake boyfriend. I can't get the vision of that needle in Blue's vein out of my head. Or the way he was leaning back against the tile wall, eyes closed, lost to me, lured into an affair with heroin.

As soon as the doors open, I bolt out of the elevator and head straight for the concierge's desk in the hopes of getting a cab, but out of the corner of my eye Blue appears from the stairwell doors looking like a savage with his jeans unbuttoned, barefoot and shirtless, all abs and ink and lipstick kiss smudges on full display.

It's a miracle he managed to run down four flights of stairs while high as a kite without falling on his ass. Spotting me, he quickly closes the space between us and grabs my hand. "Don't go," he begs, trying to catch his breath. "Please."

"Look, you need to go back upstairs." I glance around the lobby to make sure no one has recognized him. "You're a mess."

"I don't give a fuck. I'm not losing you again. Come back up with me." His bloodshot eyes plead with me, and I hate myself because I'm close, so close, to giving in.

I squeeze his hand tighter in mine, because I truly don't want to let go of any part of him. "Blue, I can't do that. I'm sorry."

He blinks hard. "I'll go to rehab. Okay? I'll get off the shit again."

"You should do that. Definitely," I agree.

"I don't want to lose you."

I shake my head and choke back more tears. "I don't want to lose you again either, but I can't do this. This is too much for me. All of this is just way more than I can deal with right now."

"I thought you loved me," he accuses angrily. "You said you loved me."

I lead him away from the center of the lobby, back down the hall leading to the stairwell. "I do love you," I say softly. "I always will. But you need to deal with this. Permanently. Before we can ever try to start again."

"I will. I promise." He staggers closer to me. "Just don't go. Don't do this to me."

I take a deep breath and cross my arms, hugging myself. "We have a daughter," I blurt out. "She's almost five years old. That's why I came to see you when I found out your band was playing here."

His eyes widen like saucers then squint to thin slits. "What? When? How?"

"I found out a few weeks after you went to get bagels."

His face contorts with severe confusion. "A baby?"

Not once did I ever expect to be having this conversation with him while he's stoned out of his skull, and it's making me want to smack him, because this should be the most important news of his life. "Yes. A baby," I repeat.

"You never told me."

"How could I? I had no way of finding you. I didn't even know your real name!"

He leans against the wall and runs his hands over his face. "I don't believe this," he mumbles. "I'm way too high for this heavy shit."

"Well, obviously."

"I'm so fucked. *So fucked.*"

My heart breaks watching him slide down the wall until he's sitting on his heels, rocking. "I tried to find you after you left. I looked for you for months. Every weekend I went to every damn park in the tri-state area looking for you."

I can see on his face he's a million miles away, not even hearing me. Finally, he looks up at me. "A girl?"

"Yes. She's adorable. She has dark brown hair, and eyes the same color as yours. She's smart, and inquisitive, and caring. You'd love her, Blue. Everyone does. Her name is Lyric."

"Lyric," he repeats. "That's such a cool fucking name."

I kneel down on the floor next to him. "I didn't want to tell you like this. I should have told you last night but... I don't know. I was scared, I guess. But that's why I came here to see you. I wanted you to know you have a daughter. And someday—when you're really better—you can see her. If you want to, you can be part of her life. But not like this."

"No. I can't."

I nod in agreement.

"Ever," he adds.

"What?"

"I can't do that...be somebody's father. I couldn't even take care of my dog."

"Blue—"

He rises to his feet, and I do too, but he hangs his head, hiding behind the hair hanging over his face. "I'm sorry, Ladybug, you know I can't do that. Look at me. I'll never be good for that little girl. I'm just a worthless piece of shit." He reaches into his pocket and comes out with a wad of cash, thrusting it at me.

I push his hand away. "I'm not a hooker, Blue."

"It's for her. To take care of her."

Despair settles into me. "We're fine." I blink back tears, resigning myself to the end that's now our unexpected reality. "You should go back upstairs before someone sees you like this. Drink some coffee or go to sleep or do whatever it is you do when you get like this. I need to go home."

Still not looking at me, he nods and shoves the cash back into his pocket. That's when I notice the tiny ladybug tattoo on the side of his wrist, and it nearly cracks my heart wide open. Tentatively, I reach out and gently touch his arm.

"Please take care of yourself," I tell him, and that's all I really want. Is to see him better. Truly better, in every sense of the word.

He closes in on me and pulls me into a desperate embrace, and we cling to each other for a long time, and God, how I wish things were different. I would have done anything to try again, to finally start over with this man I love so much. We were so close to getting there.

He cups my face in his hands, gently wipes his thumbs across my cheeks and kisses me so soft and so deep, I swear he's trying to crawl right into my heart. What he doesn't realize, is that he's already there.

> *And that postcard I sent you*
> *With the pretty little picture on the front*
> *And all those words I wrote on the back*
> *Sincerely yours, see you soon, and all my fuckin' love*
> *You got it too late, you were already gone,*
> *And there was nothing else I could do.*

I hug him tight, my lyrical, dark, beautiful love.
And then I let go.

CHAPTER TWENTY-FOUR

PIPER

Mondays can suck it.

It's not even Monday, it's Wednesday. But I didn't come into work for two days, so now my Wednesday is masquerading as a Monday.

I'm wading through no fewer than a hundred emails when my desk phone beeps, signaling a call from the front desk receptionist.

I press the speaker button. "Hi, Marybeth."

"Hi Piper, you have a visitor."

My eyes quickly glance over my calendar, but I don't see any appointments noted. "Is it a salesman? If it is, I'm too busy to meet with someone today."

"I don't think so."

"Well, who is it?" I ask with frustration. Did she forget her job is to find out the names of callers and visitors?

"Um, I'm not sure but he looks just like the guy from the band No Tomorrow. He's in the lobby. Oh my Goddddd."

My heart immediately starts to gallop. *Blue is here.*

"I'll be right there."

A million thoughts race through my mind as I walk down the corridor toward the lobby. It's been two weeks since Blue and I parted at the hotel, and my wounds are still raw. I finally broke down and took two days off as mental health days, to attempt to catch up on weeks of no sleep and to spend extra time with Lyric. Today I feel slightly better. Or at least I did until Blue showed up unexpectedly.

But as I round the corner to the lobby, it's not Blue waiting to see me at all.

It's Reece.

"This is a surprise," I say.

When I met him the night of the concert he looked the part of a grunge guitarist with messy greasy hair, a few days of facial hair, torn-up jeans, and an old band T-shirt. But today, he looks like he just stepped off a Hollywood movie set. His long dark hair is neatly tied back and a pair of aviators sit on the top of his head. A charcoal black Henley shirt stretches over the biggest biceps I've ever seen. He looks exotic and confident and rich. Most of all, he looks healthy and well-rested. A stark contrast to how exhausted Blue looked.

"Yeah, sorry to show up unannounced. Can we go somewhere and talk?"

"Of course. There's a courtyard outside."

"Perfect."

"Is Blue okay?" I can't fathom why his friend would be here, unless something terrible has happened, and I'm already queasy with worry.

"Yeah, he's... he's being Blue."

"What does that mean?" I ask as we reach one of the picnic tables.

He leans against the table and grins down at me. "He's pretty fucked up about everything."

"Well, so am I."

"Totally understandable."

"Has he gone into rehab?"

"Not yet."

"Not yet?" I repeat. "He was doing heroin in the bathroom. Did he tell you that?"

"It's not new, Piper. He's had issues since high school."

"I know. Which is why he should really be seeking professional help."

"He will. He's not ready yet. And I agree with you, he needs to get clean, but he has to want to. Otherwise, he'll be doing this again in a few months. Just like he always does."

That doesn't sound promising at all.

"I don't even know what to say. Do you do that stuff, too?"

"Me? Fuck no. I'm straight as an arrow."

I shake my head and stare off down the street, toward the park that I can't even bear to go to anymore because it's a graveyard of memories.

"So why are you here?"

"He told me about the baby. And I wanted to talk to you about it... make sure you and the baby are okay."

"Did he send you here?"

His head moves back and forth. "No. I came on my own. I found your information in his wallet."

"You went through his wallet? That's pretty invasive, don't you think?"

"You think I care?"

"Apparently not. And she's not a baby anymore, she's almost five years old. Her name is Lyric."

"I heard. He's friggin' in love with her name."

"That's great," I say sarcastically. "Sadly, she doesn't have his last name, because I had no idea what the hell it was. And trust me, I know that's my fault because I'm obviously a terrible decision maker when it comes to men."

"Nah. Blue's just an odd dude. Always has been. And you can change her birth certificate, now that you know. It's no big deal."

The thought of changing my sweet little girl's last name to that of the lead singer of a grunge rock band with a drug addiction scares the shit out of me.

"Maybe someday," I reply. "When she's old enough to understand, I'll let her decide what she wants to do."

He nods. "Fair enough."

This is awkward and uncomfortable and I'm sure my inbox is piling up as we speak, so I make a show of checking my watch. "I really should get back to work..."

"Are you a single mother, then?"

My eyes narrow. "I hope you're not planning on asking me out, because I'm definitely not going there."

He lets out a deep laugh. "I'd love to, sweetheart, but you're off limits." My cheeks heat with embarrassment. "What I was trying to ask is if you're raising her alone? Do you need help? Daycare? Money? Any medical problems?"

I don't know if I should feel flattered or offended by everything that just spilled out of his mouth.

"As you can see, I'm employed and I do have health insurance. I'm single but I have friends and family to help out. Lyric is very well loved and cared for. You can tell Blue we don't need anything from him. You can tell him his dog is still fine, too."

"You can drop the defensive act. I'm here as a friend, not your enemy."

"I'm sorry. I'm just having a rough couple weeks. It's...." My voice trails off and I let out a bewildered sigh.

His expression softens. "It sucks to be in a toxic relationship. Been there."

My lower lip trembles defiantly. "I'm not in a toxic relationship with him or anyone. We're not in an anything."

He touches my chin and tilts my head up, forcing me to look at him. "Trust me, Piper. You're in a toxic relationship. He's the father of your kid. You're always going to be in a something with him. Whether you like it or not."

Shit.

"I have a kid with my ex. It's hard, but we make it work. I make sure she has everything she needs." He pushes his body off the table and levels his brown eyes on me. "Blue ain't me, though. He can't deal, ya know?"

"Unfortunately, yes. I *do* know."

"He cares about you. That's a first for him. And since he's too fucked up to deal with it right now, I'm just trying to be a good friend. To make sure his kid is all right."

"She is. She's happy, she's super smart, she's a lot like him."

He sticks his hand in his back pocket and hands me a card. "Let's hope she's not too much like him. My number's on the card, and I wrote his on the back, in case you don't have it."

Reluctantly, I take the card from him and shake my head. "No. He didn't give it to me."

"You're better off calling me. He never answers his."

"I'm sure we won't be needing anything, but I appreciate it. You're a good friend."

He winks at me. "Someone's gotta be."

After he leaves I ignore the stare from the receptionist and return to the privacy of my office. I have an overwhelming gut feeling that this definitely won't be the last time I see Reece Blackstone.

A month later an envelope is delivered to my office, with a thousand dollars of cash inside, and a note from Blue:

Ladybug,

I'm sorry I fucked up. Again. You see my pattern? This is me. I can't stop thinking about you. I wish we had more time together before it all went to shit. I wanted to start over. I love how you love me and I love how you hate me. Don't feel bad. I need your hate and I need your pain just as much as I need your love. It fuels my fight like nothing else. I wish it didn't hurt you. I hope I'm worth it but I'm probably not. I'm sending you money for Lyric. I love that name. I know you named her for me. I'll send you more when I can. I waste a lot of money on shit I shouldn't do. But now maybe I won't do that anymore. Someday I'll be better. I hope someday we can try again. I miss you. I fucking ache for you, really.

I love you.

~ Blue

I close my door so my co-workers can't see me crying at my desk, and then I re-read the note multiple times. I do this every time Blue leaves me a note—I read it over and over and get more upset and fall more in love and by the end of the day, I've memorized his words and I'm even more confused and pulled deeper into this abyss with him.

As much as I hate to admit it, maybe Reece was right, and this *is* a toxic relationship. Has knowing Blue ever not given me both the best and the worst parts of my life? No. My life pre-Blue seems like another life altogether. What did I think about before him? What did I love before him? What did I look forward to before him? What made me cry before him?

My mind blanks. I can't see the answer to these questions.

I tuck the envelope of cash and the note into my bag, wondering what he was thinking, sending this amount of cash through the regular mail. It's unheard of and I'm surprised it didn't get stolen. The missing return address on the envelope doesn't go unnoticed, nor the absence of his phone number. Does he not have an address or a phone again? Or does he not want me to be able to contact him?

For the rest of the day, that little tidbit continues to irk me. How I have never been able to contact him. How he was able to disappear, nameless and address-less—for years! If I hadn't heard his song on the radio that day, who knows how long it would have been before I ever saw him again. Years? Maybe never.

Lyric is a chatterbox all through dinner, describing a new girl in her pre-k in great detail. Apparently the little girl is missing a finger after an unfortunate accident. Usually a very quiet child, certain things possess Lyric's attention and it will sometimes take days or weeks for her to move on from them. I have a feeling this missing finger is going to be an obsession for a long time and I pray she's not making the poor girl uncomfortable.

"She's my best friend now," she announces at bed time.

I tuck her in and plant a soft kiss on her cheek. "That's very sweet.

She's lucky to have you as a friend because you're fun, and smart, and caring."

"I'd give her one of my fingers if I could, Mommy. I don't need them all, do I?"

Stifling a laugh, I raise her little hand to my lips and kiss her fingers. "I think you do. In case you want to play piano someday."

"But what if *she* wants to play piano someday?"

"Well... I'm sure she still can. It will just be a little bit harder for her."

"Then I really don't need all of mine," she protests.

"Sweetheart, you don't need to worry about your friend's fingers. I'm sure she's just fine. Anyway, I think Acorn would like you to have all your fingers to pet him with."

At the mention of his name, Acorn lifts his head from his favorite nighttime napping spot at the foot of her bed. "See?" I say. "He heard us talking and he agrees."

She giggles. "You're silly. He didn't say that. He said I can pet him with any or no fingers or I can pet him with just my eyes and he'll feel it inside."

Acorn wags his tail, and I'm sure it's true, he wouldn't care as long as he was getting attention. I'm touched that Lyric seems to understand that—that there's different ways of loving someone, and different ways of accepting the kind of love they can give.

After Lyric has fallen asleep, I get ready for bed, but I don't go to sleep. Instead, I take Reece's card out of my wallet and dial the number written on the back before I have a chance to change my mind.

It rings four times, and I'm just about to give up and end the call when he answers.

"Yeah?"

My heart jumps at hearing his deep, scratchy voice.

"Blue..." I swallow hard. "It's me."

There's a long pause, then the sound of a lighter clicking, then a deep inhale and exhale of breath. I can almost see the smoke drifting from the tip of his cigarette.

"Are you there?" I say.

The click of metal against teeth. "Yeah... just surprised."

"Reece gave me your number. I hope that's okay."

I can hear his lips wrapping around the cigarette. *Inhale, exhale.*

"Sure."

I can't tell if he's glad or pissed that I called, so I babble. "I got the money you sent; it came today. You didn't have to do that, but thank you."

"Don't thank me, babe." The hoarseness of his voice calling me *babe* sends a tingle of heat through my thighs.

"I just wanted you to know I appreciate it."

"It's weird talking to you on the phone. You sound so little."

I let out a laugh and clutch the phone tighter. Vendors and clients tell me at least twice a week that I sound about fourteen years old over the phone, which is I why I try to use email as often as possible.

"Does that bother you?" I ask.

"No. It makes me wish you were here."

My eyes close as his words sink down into my heart.

Clearing my throat, I pull a pillow onto my lap and lean my elbows on it. "Where are you?"

"Seattle. For a week, then we head back out."

"More concerts?"

He sighs. "Yeah."

"You sound tired."

"So do you."

"I haven't been sleeping very well lately."

"Because of me?"

I chew my lip. "Because of what happened."

"Do you remember how we used to listen to the rain?"

"Of course I do," I reply softly. We used to spend hours making love in that tiny shed, then cuddling under the blanket, listening to the rain falling on the tin roof.

"Those were my favorite days," he says. "I loved the quiet of it. Just me and you. I think about it a lot."

I remember. I loved it, too. He seemed happy then, and much less restless, but I don't trust myself to say anything, because he's the one who left and put an end to our time together.

"How are you doing... with everything? Are you getting help?"

He lets out a short laugh. "I've been smoking a joint laced with opium and drinking J.D. since you called. So, no."

My stomach sinks like a lead ball. "Blue... why are you doing this to yourself?"

"I don't know. This is what I do."

"But you stopped. You weren't doing all this when we were together. You told me you never wanted to go down this road again."

"I didn't." His tone deepens with frustration and anger. "Sometimes this road is easier. I know you don't understand."

"You're right, I don't. Help me understand, then. I'm trying."

The clink of a bottle against glass sounds in the background, then the swirl of liquid over his lips and the gulp of his throat.

"It's like living with a monster in your head, Piper. And it just fuckin' owns you, consumes you, bleeds you, tortures you. It doesn't let you sleep. It doesn't let you be happy. It doesn't let you trust. So you do what it says just to shut it the fuck up, to try to get just a tiny amount of peace, and then it starts all over again."

Emotional grief for him spreads through me, twisting my stomach into knots and sending tears to my eyes. I wish I could go to him, somehow take this away for him. I wish I could overtake the monster inside him, and hide him away so it could never find him again.

"I'm sorry," I say softly. "I wish I could do something to help you."

Something slams on the other end of the phone. "You can't. And the more you try, the worse it'll fucking be. I warned you, Piper. I told you we'd destroy each other. You'll kill yourself trying to save me and I'll kill myself trying to make it right and in the end the monster will kill us both. Don't you see? We can't win this."

"Evan, don't get mad. You *can* win. You were winning. I just think you need to find the right help—"

"*Evan* again. Always dragging him back in." More banging sounds come over the line, and his words are starting to slur.

"It *is* your name. And I like it."

"You like it because it's not me."

"That's not true. It *is* you. I think it reminds you of who you were before you got like this."

He scoffs. "Don't try to play shrink, Ladybug. That's really not a place you want to put yourself."

His rollercoaster mood and tone is giving me whiplash, so I decide to quit while I'm ahead rather than agitate him any further. The last thing I want is to make him get higher or drunker tonight.

"Blue," I begin softly. "I don't want to fight with you. I called you to thank you. That's all."

And because I miss you. And I wanted to hear your voice. And for once, I wanted to be in control.

"I don't want to fight either. I'm so fucking tired of fighting everything. It's beating me down."

"I know, and I don't want you to feel that way. Please try to get help. I'm so worried about you."

"Come see me, then."

"What?"

"Come out here and stay with me until I leave. We can talk."

"We're talking right now," I point out, thrown by his suggestion in more ways than one.

"We are. But I can't stop thinking about how delicious you taste."

"Blue...."

"What? I want more of you. When I'm lost in you, everything else goes away."

"I'm not entirely sure that's a healthy situation for either one of us."

"Everything we want is bad for us in some way, Piper. Come see me."

My heart leaps to say yes and wants me to run straight to my closet and grab all the cute clothes and hop on a plane to re-capture the night we shared a few weeks ago—before the shit hit the fan. But my brain is screaming no, no, no. He's still on drugs. He's messed up right now on the phone as we speak. Tomorrow he might not even remember asking me to come see him, or he could disappear before my plane lands and I'll be stranded in Seattle.

"I wish I could do that, but I can't. Like I told you, I can't just take off work last minute. And even if I could... I have Lyric to think about and you're still messed up." I try to word it as gently as possible. "I don't think it's a good idea for us to see each other when you're using."

"Could you maybe get someone to watch her? And you come see me? Then you could only miss one day of work. Like fly out here Friday, spend Saturday with me and go back on Sunday when I leave."

He's right, I totally could do that. But I'm disappointed he immediately wants me to leave Lyric home. Even though I'm not ready for them to meet yet, it hurts that he hasn't asked about her at all during this conversation. I had hoped he would be curious about her, maybe ask me to send him a picture. *Something.* I'm grateful he sent money for her, but that may be all he'll ever do, and I have to accept that. I refuse to push Lyric on a father who doesn't want her and risk her getting hurt. She deserves better than that.

I don't let my heart sway me into another heartbreak. "I can't see you when you're using drugs."

"Okay. So I won't do anything while you're here. I'll be high on you, nothing else."

I lean my forehead onto my hand and close my eyes, wishing this wasn't so hard.

"So we have a great day together, then we both leave, and you go back on tour and get all fucked up and I come home with a broken heart. Again. And I won't know when I'm ever going to see you. Again. And I'll worry about you constantly. I'm sorry, I can't do it."

I hear the click and spark of the lighter again, the suck of air, and I'm pretty sure he's getting high again.

"You're right." The sexy confidence he had a few moments ago has been replaced with sadness. "I can't do that to you. I'm sorry, babe, for being such a fucking mess."

"I'm sorry, too."

"After the tour, I'll get in a program, okay? I promise."

"Okay..."

"I mean it, Ladybug. I'm gonna try really hard this time."

I sigh. "Okay." I can't say anything else. My heart hurts too much.

"Will you tell me you love me?"

"Of course." I take a death breath and swallow over the tightness in my throat. "I love you."

"Will you think of me when it rains?"

"Yes. I always do."

"I want you to go to sleep, okay? Don't think about the bad stuff. Think about how much I love you, and how much I want you, and no one else. No matter what, that's always going to be true."

That much *is* true. And that's what scares me.

After we hang up, Acorn shows up at my bedroom door with Penguin in his mouth, and jumps up on the bed to cuddle against me. Blue might be a mess, but without him I wouldn't have the love of two of the most precious little beings in the world.

CHAPTER TWENTY-FIVE

PIPER

"Morning."

I smile at Josh as he enters the kitchen and makes a beeline for the coffee maker.

"Hey. What time did you get home last night? I didn't hear you come in."

He pours coffee into his favorite mug and leans against the kitchen counter. "It was late. Like two a.m."

"Ooh. So the date went well?"

He shrugs. "Eh. She was okay."

Putting my book down, I look at him across the room, wearing gray sweatpants and a white V-neck T-shirt. The front of his blond hair is longer now, hanging down almost to his eyes, and it makes him look edgy and sexy. He's been doing a lot of photoshoots lately and even landed a hair product commercial not too long ago.

"Just okay?

"She has a lot of shoes."

I raise an eyebrow at him. "Do you feel threatened by shoes?"

"No, seriously, Piper. She has about a thousand pairs of shoes. She collects them. She has an entire room in her condo just for shoes. They're all sorted by color and heel height. It was scary."

"Well it could be worse. She could collect dolls," I tease.

"I would've jumped out the window. I love fashion, but having that many of anything isn't normal."

"It's expensive, too."

"No doubt. They were all expensive brands. I don't know how she can even afford that many shoes."

"Maybe she steals them."

He gulps the last of his coffee and puts his mug in the dishwasher.

"I'm not going to see her again. I tried. She's nice but I think she's got hoarder potential or at the very least will run me into debt in six months flat."

"You do realize you have double the dating pool and you still can't find someone you like? Maybe you're being too picky?"

Shrugging, he looks out the window into the backyard. "I'm not settling for someone just to be with someone. I'm happy. I have friends, I have family, I have you and Lyric. I don't need a shoe hoarder or a guy who wants me to call him Daddy. I'm all set." He turns back to me. "Where's Lyric?"

"She's in the playroom with Acorn doing that puzzle you gave her."

"Have you been online this morning? Read any of the entertainment news?"

I narrow my eyes at him, suspicious of his random questions. "No... I haven't been on my laptop yet. Why?"

"You might want to. Looks like your boy's on a bender."

"What are you talking about?"

He just shakes his head. "Go look. I'll be out raking the backyard if you want to talk."

Dread sends a feverish chill through me as I check on Lyric and then retrieve my laptop from where I left it on the coffee table last night. Sitting on the couch, I pull it onto my lap, wait impatiently for the dial-up to connect, and then open up my AOL account. I click on the Entertainment section and there it is.

The beginning of the downfall.

Thousands of Las Vegas concert-goers were disappointed and rightfully outraged last week when No Tomorrow front man repeatedly botched his own lyrics, cursed at fans, and stumbled around on stage in a clear state of intoxication before walking off stage mid-concert and refusing to come back.

Sources confirmed Von Bleu then disappeared with no contact for four days and was found wandering incoherently in the desert. He is currently hospitalized for dehydration and exposure but is in stable condition.

Back-up vocalist Reece Blackstone publicly apologized to No Tomorrow fans for canceling the last three shows of the tour and claims Blue has been suffering a breakdown from extreme stress coupled with a recent shoulder injury. He advised that Blue is receiving treatment and they will resume working on their new album soon.

There's a video alongside the article, and I immediately regret clicking on it. Like a train wreck, I can't look away from the ugliness of it. Even though I just read the details of his behavior, seeing him so out of control on stage, a complete disheveled drunken mess, barely able to stand or speak—let alone sing—is devastating and cringeworthy. Fans are yelling and booing at him, and I can understand why. The man stumbling around is nothing like the soft spoken, charismatic vocalist they came to see.

I want to bleach my brain. The videos and photographs make me nauseous on so many levels. And that whole disappearing thing. Just the thought of him walking into the desert, most likely with nothing but his guitar and his backpack, is disturbing.

Worried, I chew my thumbnail while I try to process my thoughts. I want to call or email Reece and make sure Blue is really okay, but he may tell me things I don't want to hear. I'm not sure I can be trusted to stay away if Reece tells me Blue is in a lot worse shape than this news article is letting on. And then what? Do I fly out there to see him? Get dragged further into this spiral of push and pull with him? If he's this much of a mess, it will destroy me to leave him. I'll want to bring him home with me and try to fix him. And him? He'll probably fight me like a wild animal and ricochet between making me leave and begging me to stay. But other than Reece, who else does he have? What if he needs me?

I open up my email program and search for Reece's email address, which I added to my contacts the day he came to talk to me and gave me his card.

"Mommy?"

I look up from the screen. Josh holds Lyric in the doorway. Acorn is beside them. "Uncle Josh is gonna teach me to plant flowers. Will you come, too?"

I hover my fingers over the keyboard for a few seconds, and then I exit out of the email. Standing, I smile at my beautiful baby girl. "I would love that," I reply, catching Josh's slight approving nod.

I need to focus on the good things in my life, and they're all right here in front of me.

CHAPTER TWENTY-SIX

PIPER

Immersing myself in work is what I do. I don't even take a lunch break anymore. I eat at my desk over my keyboard, sometimes calling my mother or Ditra for a quick chat before I throw myself back into the never-ending to-do list of my day.

The rest of my time is spent with Lyric. Reading to her, taking her and Acorn to the park. Letting her help me get dinner ready. Watching television with her and Josh, until I finally fall into bed completely exhausted. The next day, I do it all over again.

As long as I keep myself busy, I'm not falling apart missing Blue, or working myself into a worried frenzy reading about his debauchery. There's been a lot of crazy in his life lately, unfortunately. His life and career have been up and down like a seesaw. When I read about the ups, I silently cheer for him. I print out the articles, the interviews, and the photos. I hide them all away in an old steam trunk in the basement, along with all of his albums, band T-shirts, and memorabilia like concert tickets I've purchased over the years. All of this I hope to give to Lyric someday so she has pieces of her father's life and accomplishments. Regardless of anything else, he's an amazing musician—an icon in the grunge rock era—and I'm immensely proud of him for that. I hope all his accomplishments will help Lyric overlook his less than favorable moments. Like drunken tantrums on stage and disappearing into the desert.

It's nearing five o'clock on Friday night, and I'm almost done updating the production schedule when my direct line rings.

"Good afternoon, Piper Karel."

Silence.

"May I help you?" I ask.

"Hey, you."

At the sound of his deep voice, my heart flip flops like a trained dog under his command. It's been a year since we last talked, although I'm not really sure I can call that a talk at all. He called me drunk in the middle of the night, distraught and mumbling about voices and darkness and pain and how much he missed me and birds and things I couldn't even begin to comprehend. I listened to him until the sun came up. I tried to calm him and bring him down from whatever mental trip he was on. Suddenly he stopped talking, and I held the phone to my ear for a full ten minutes, waiting and listening, and softly saying his name. Worried, I hung up and called Reece, who confirmed that Blue had passed out on his bed, still with the phone in his hand.

I, unfortunately, didn't get to pass out and sleep that particular night a year ago. I had to get my daughter ready for school and head to a grueling Monday morning at work.

"Hi," I say.

"You're mad at me. I can hear it in your voice."

"And you sound sober."

"I am. But it's still early," he jokes.

"That's not funny, Blue."

He clears his throat. "I know. You're right. I'm two weeks sober, actually."

"That's great." I force myself to sound positive, but I've heard this before.

"I miss you, Ladybug. I think about you all the time."

"I miss you too. You know I do."

"How's Lyric?"

I lean back in my chair and spin it toward the window. "She's great.

She loves school, she's making friends. She loves to read. She's reading books way ahead of her grade level."

"She got that from you. I got the pictures you sent me. She's adorable."

"She is."

"How's Acorn?"

"He's doing okay. He's got cataracts now, and he doesn't hear very well anymore. He limps sometimes. The vet says he has arthritis. He's still happy, though. Lyric just loves him to pieces. They're inseparable."

"You're a great mom, Piper. To both of them." He pauses. "I don't know what I'd do if I didn't know you were taking care of them."

I want to tell him I didn't have a choice, because he abandoned me with both of them. But I don't, because I know he's incapable of taking care of anyone—himself included.

"Well, I love them. So it's easy." I glance at the clock on my desk. "I hate to cut this short, but you caught me just as I was about to leave the office. I have to pick up Lyric at a friend's house."

"Can I call you tonight at home?"

"If you want to. But if you forget, I'm not going to call you." We played that game last year. He'd email me and tell me he was going to call, and I'd sit and wait. And wait. I'd lose patience, give in, and call him and he'd either be out or inebriated in some way, and I'd feel like an idiot for waiting around for him.

"I won't forget. I promise."

I think about him as I drive across town. He sounded good today, like he did years ago. I know better than to get my hopes up, though, because we've been here before.

So many times.

As soon as Lyric's in the car, I push Blue out of my mind to focus on her. I refuse to let him crawl back into my head and my heart and distract me from all the important things in my life.

I take Lyric to the diner for dinner. We have grilled cheese and share a milkshake while she tells me all about her day. Later, we put our pajamas on and sit in my bed watching Disney movies like we do every Friday night.

At ten-thirty my phone rings, and I pick it up before it wakes Lyric. She has fallen asleep beside me.

"Wow, you called," I say, smiling with surprise.

"I'm trying to live up to my promises."

"This is a good start."

"How was your night?"

"The usual. I took Lyric to the diner, we took Acorn for a short walk, then we watched television. Exciting, huh?"

I wonder what rock stars do with their time. I doubt he sits around watching television.

"Honestly? It sounds nice."

"It *is* nice," I agree. "So what about you? Where are you now?"

"I got home last month."

"I heard you did a tour in Europe?"

"Yeah, it was wild. The fans are crazy over there, they're so passionate. And the food is fucking amazing. I got some new ink while I was there, I found a killer artist. I'll send you pictures if you want to see."

"I'd love to see."

Lyric stirs next to me and pops her head up. "Mommy. Is that Gramma?"

"No, it's a friend of mine."

"Can I say hello?"

"Not tonight."

"Wow. That's her?" Blue asks.

"Yup. That's her. Can you hold on for a few minutes while I take her to bed?"

"Yeah. Of course."

I lay the phone on the nightstand. "Let's get you in your bed, okay?"

"Can't I sleep with you tonight?"

"Mommy's going to be on the phone for a little while so you should sleep in your own bed." I jump off the bed and hold my hand out to her. "Let's go brush our teeth."

It takes me fifteen minutes to get her ready and into her own bed, and it hurts my heart when she asks me again who I'm talking to. I tell her again it's a friend. Not telling her who it really is feels like a betrayal, but I'm not ready to tell her about Blue yet. Lyric has never asked me where her father is, or who he is, but I know as she gets older she'll be asking those questions. I have no idea how I'm going to tackle that.

"You still here?" I ask when I'm back in my bed with the phone.

"Yeah."

"I'm sorry that took so long."

"It's fine. I'm a little wacked hearing her voice for the first time."

"How did that make you feel?"

"Um... a lot of things. Surprised and sad, but glad, too. Her voice reminds me of yours, so soft and cute. Does she know anything about me?"

"I was just thinking about that actually. She doesn't. She's never asked. But she's almost six now and sooner or later she's going to have questions."

"What are you going to tell her?"

"Honestly I don't know. I'm just going to tell her you moved away. When she gets older I'll tell her more. I guess someday you and I can figure something out together."

"Okay. I'm not ready yet but someday."

I hear him inhale and I hope it's a cigarette and not a joint.

"Someday I'd like to get to know her. It's up to you, though. I know I don't deserve anything."

"Blue, don't say that. She's your daughter and I want you to have a relationship with her, but as long as she's under eighteen, I don't feel comfortable with her being around you if you're still partying. I won't let you yo-yo her like you do to me."

"Understood. And I agree. I'm not an idiot, I know I'm not good for her. But it's on the list of things I want to work on."

"You have a list?"

"A list of things I want to unfuck in my life."

"Well, that's a step forward, right? How's it going so far?"

He laughs. "You tell me. You're the first thing on my list."

"I'd like to be flattered but that's not really a compliment," I tease.

"Being on the top of your 'things I fucked up' list."

"It's a long list."

"I'm not surprised."

"All kidding aside, I fucked up with you the most. And I hate that, Piper, I really do. I keep wondering what would have happened if I'd stayed."

A pang hits me in the chest. "Blue... let's not talk about that. You're trying. And I'm trying to let you try. So let's not dwell on the bad stuff."

"Deal."

I pull the comforter up to my chest and get comfy against my pillows. "But... I do want you to tell me where you went that day you left. Did you go back home? To Jersey?"

"No. Don't take this wrong, but I wanted to get as far away as possible. Not from you, but just... away. I can't explain it. So I headed for the west coast. I had some friends back there, and it was warmer and I thought it'd be cool to play guitar by the water, ya know?" The sound of liquid pouring is in the background. "That's iced tea, by the way," he says, as if he's reading my mind. "So I was making my way across the country and I ran into Reece at a bus terminal. I hadn't seen him in a few years."

"You knew him when you were younger, right?"

"We went to high school together. And we shared an apartment for a while. He was a kickass guitarist back then and we wanted to start a band but his bitch of a girlfriend at the time wouldn't let him do shit. That's when I said fuck it and I took off. When I ran into him at the terminal he was playing in a fucking wedding band and I was like dude, you're too good for this shit, let's start a band and rip this town up."

"That's how No Tomorrow started?"

"Yeah. The other guys had just come out of some sucky-ass band. We had a rocky start but somehow we got lucky and ended up here."

"That's pretty crazy. But wow, look at you guys now."

"Yeah, look at me, fucking the band all up with my shit," he says sarcastically.

"How's all that going?" I'm almost afraid to ask. The press has been hard on him. Every detail captured, every one of his drunken tirades, fights with band members, and other seedy gossip plastered all over the tabloids and internet.

He blows out a breath. "It's good and bad. None of us are saints, we've all had our moments. Mine of course have been way more frequent and disastrous. There's some bad blood still flowing. We're taking a break for a few weeks then we're gonna hit the studio and work on some new material."

"Every band goes through rough times, not just yours. And I'm not going to lie, you pissed off a ton of fans. I'm sure the rest of the band wasn't happy about any of that. I saw the videos and read the articles. It was pretty bad, Blue. But... you're trying to make it better, that's what's important now. You sound happy. It's been a long time since you sounded so...normal."

"Normal? Me? Never gonna happen, babe. But talking to you is the closest to happy I get."

My defenses melt like butter. "It makes me happy, too."

"I really fucking miss you. I know you're so sick of my shit. And I know you probably wish I'd just leave you the fuck alone. I try to, but it never works."

"No," I say, cringing at how fast I said it. "That's not what I want. I've never wanted that."

He takes a deep breath. "You want to tell me what you *do* want?"

My ovaries scream his name. "No, I don't."

"It's me, isn't it," he teases in his wicked, sexy voice.

I laugh, even though I don't want to. "Ego much?"

"No, it's not ego. Just wishful thinking."

A moany sound of frustration comes out of me. It's totally not fair that he does this to me.

"Fuck, baby if you keep making noises like that I'm gonna lose my mind over here."

"You're so bad, you know that?"

"I know. I also know it's what draws you to me."

I twirl my hair around my finger nervously—a childhood habit that Lyric has picked up as well. "Really? Is that what it is?"

"It's part of it."

"So what draws you to me, then?"

He exhales, and his voice is raspy with smoke when he answers. "Your innocence. How unconditionally caring and loyal you are. And your hot little body."

"My innocence didn't last too long once you came along."

"It's still there. A little tarnished, maybe."

"By you."

He hums on the other end of the line. "Only by me?"

I know what he's asking, and I'm tempted to lie and let him believe I've been with other men. In a way, I want to knock him out of that place in my body he claimed and still owns. I know he likes it and it turns him on—to be the Highlander of my vagina, the only one. But I hate to play games and manipulate people's emotions, so I tell him the truth.

"Yes, only by you. Happy now?"

"Very."

"And you?" I really don't want to know, but it's human nature to ask questions. Even the ones I truly don't want the answer to.

"I might've fucked a hole in the ground while I was walking around in the desert. I was pretty wasted and having all kinds of messed-up hallucinations."

I laugh at him. "You're an ass."

"It's true. But other than that, I've been having a great time fucking myself."

"Can you be serious? I was honest with you, Blue. You can just tell me the truth." Yes, I'm practically begging the man I love to tell me how many women he's been with since the last time we were together.

"I swear to God I'm telling the truth. You want brutal honesty? I jerk off on one of the pictures you sent me and I come all over your face."

I'm totally horrified but also strangely turned on. "Oh my God! Isn't that messy?"

"Not really. I put it in one of those clear plastic sleeves. I bought a case of them so I just throw it out and put your picture in a new one every day."

"You are so twisted. I can't even tell if you're kidding."

He laughs with me, and it's so good to hear him happy and joking, even if he's being an ass. I can't remember the last time he acted sexy and flirty with me, but I've missed this side of him.

"Ya know what, Piper? If you're the one that's got a hold on me? Then that's it. I can go without sex if I have to. Maybe that makes me weird, I dunno. The way I look at it, I've always been too much of a fucked-up mess to give you any kind of normalcy, but I can give you my heart and I can give you my body. We've had a shit ton of ups and downs, but I've always believed that we're not over. So no, there's no one else."

Hugging my comforter tighter to me, I lean my head into the phone and quietly sob. Life and love can be so cruel and beautiful and utterly confusing. This isn't the love I dreamed of as a little girl. This isn't the whirlwind romance I swooned over in books. There's no sparkly ring, no wedding bells, no husband holding our baby in the delivery room. But what we have is a *real* love. It's dark, and ugly; raw and passionate. It brings pain and it brings happiness and everything in between. This love—*our* love—is a love that never dies. It withers in the dark and comes back to life again under bright moments even stronger than it was before.

I wipe my cheeks with the back of my hand. "For someone as fucked up as you are, sometimes you're really kinda perfect, too."

"I guess I have my rare moments..."

"You do."

"You're the only one that's ever looked past the dirt to see the flowers, Ladybug. That's why I can't let you go."

How does he somehow manage to say the right things?

"I really wish I could hug you right now," I whisper.

He's quiet on the other end, and I worry I've said too much and wrecked his good mood. But then he answers. "Maybe we can work on arranging that. I can't promise I'll let you go, though."

God, I'm in trouble. He's bulldozing his way right back into my heart again.

CHAPTER TWENTY-SEVEN

PIPER

I feel like someone injected a rainbow up my butt. I can't remember the last time I've felt so happy, so hopeful, and so excited for each new day to start. I've started going to the park again, because now I can think about Blue, and I can visit our memories without falling apart. I can smile at the ghosts of our past that still linger under the old bridge, and not run away from them.

Four weeks of talking on the phone for hours every night coupled with pages of heartfelt emails has changed us. We've rebuilt our friendship, and are creeping toward more. I won't jinx it by putting a label on what we are.

We video chat on the weekends, and he plays guitar and sings for me—all shirtless and sexy and swoony and I feel like the luckiest girl on the planet. One night after Lyric went to bed I put Acorn in front of the web cam so Blue could see him, and he started to cry. When Acorn heard his voice, he ran around in excited circles with his penguin in his mouth.

We've talked about spending a weekend together, and we're figuring out what would be better—me flying to him, or him coming to see me. The best part, the most shocking part, is his new willingness to meet Lyric if things go well between us after a few months. If—and only if—he remains clean. The plan to meet Lyric was entirely his idea, which is huge. *Huge!*

I'm going to be very cautious with Lyric, though. Meeting her father will be confusing for her, and life changing. It's a big commitment on Blue's part that will require a lot of patience and I'm not sure he's ready for all of that yet. In the meantime, I've slowly made Lyric aware that I've been talking to a 'friend' every night, to ease her into the idea of me having a man in my life other than Josh.

Tonight I make spaghetti and meatballs for dinner, and we eat together —Josh, Lyric, and I, which we try to do a few nights a week. Growing up, my parents always insisted we eat dinner together as a family every night. Now that I'm older I can look back and see how important that was—to have that stability with loved ones every day. I want to give Lyric the same.

After dinner Josh leaves for a date, Lyric works on a Lego castle she's been building for the last week, and I do forty-five minutes of aerobics in front of the television. Before heading upstairs to shower, I check my email and see I have one from Blue.

> *Piper,*
> *I feel like shit tonight. It's just a headache but I'm gonna hit the sack early.*
> *I hope you had a good day, beautiful.*
> *I'll call you tomorrow night.*
> *Love,*
> *Blue*

I reply:

> *Blue,*
> *I'm so sorry, I hope you feel better! Call me if you can't sleep, I don't mind if you wake me.*
> *I miss you bunches and love you always.*

> *Kisses,*
> *me*

"I missed you last night. Do you feel better today?"

"My head is still fuckin' rocking. I missed you, too, babe."

"I wish you didn't still get these headaches."

"Me too. They're gettin' old. Tomorrow I'm going to look into flights, if you're still okay with coming here? You can meet the guys, see where I live. We'll go out to eat, look at the local sheds. All that happy stuff."

I laugh at his shed joke. "I'm totally fine with that. Except the shed part."

I'm looking forward to seeing Blue's condo and be in his world. I've often wondered what kind of decor he's into, what color bedspread he has, if he has any photos on the wall. They're such simple details, but will mean so much to actually see.

"And I'll let you decide if you want to stay at a hotel or stay here with me. Or I can stay at the hotel with you. Whatever'll make you happy, I'm down with. I'm paying for it, so don't even try to argue about it."

"If you insist. Let me think about the hotel thing. Once we figure out dates, I'll let HR know. I'm sure my mom will love having Lyric for a weekend, and Josh won't mind taking care of the pets for me. He's home most of the time."

I hear the click of his piercing against his teeth. "Who's Josh?"

"My roommate? I've mentioned him a hundred times."

"You never said it was a guy."

My brain cells spin around like the Windows hourglass. I'm positive I told him about Josh quite a few times over the years. "Um, I kept saying Josh. That's a guy's name."

"You never told me that." His voice is flat, almost cold now, and completely different from a few moments ago.

"I'm sorry, I just thought you knew."

"So where does *Josh* sleep?"

"In his room. Blue, there's nothing going on if that's what you're thinking. We've been friends since high school. And he's gay. Well, bi. Whatever. But we're strictly friends. We've been living here with him in his house since Lyric was three years old. I don't know what I would've done without him, to be honest."

"It's his house?"

"Yes. It's huge. We all have our own bedrooms and bathrooms and there's a big fenced-in yard and a swing set. It's perfect for Lyric and Acorn."

"So you guys are all living together like a family in his big house?"

His voice rises with each set of questions, and I can picture him running his hand through his hair and pacing around the room. I'm clueless as to why he's suddenly getting angry about my living arrangement. I know I've mentioned it to him many times and I can't understand how he could have forgotten.

"Well, yeah, I guess if you want to put it like that, then yes. Josh has been great helping me take care of Lyric over the years. He takes her to school sometimes, he spends a lot of time playing with her. She thinks of him as an uncle. He's a good guy, and she's crazy about him."

There's a long silence on the other end, and I wait patiently, hoping that's the end of this conversation and we can go back to planning our weekend together. Unfortunately, the silence continues, reaching into awkward proportions, until I have to put an end to it.

"Is something wrong? You sound like you're getting mad and I don't understand why."

"I don't know. I'm not sure how I feel about all this. With this guy."

"There's nothing to feel. He's just a friend who offered me an amazing place to live. My apartment was way too small for myself, a toddler, a cat, and a dog. I was having a hard time finding something bigger that was also in a nice neighborhood, close to my family, and close to my office. I was doing my best. I wasn't expecting to have a dog and a baby, remember?"

I probably shouldn't have added that last part, but he's starting to upset me with his mild insinuation that I'm doing something wrong.

"Oh. So some other fucking guy just gets to have my chick, my kid, and my dog? And I'm not supposed to be pissed about that?"

"Nobody has your anything, Blue. You left, remember? I was alone and doing the best I could to give Lyric and your dog a nice home. Excuse me for not getting your permission, but I had no damn idea who or where you even were!"

I've never seen him act like this—tossing out accusations and walking the line of jealousy over another man being in mine, Lyric's, and Acorn's life. Has it taken all these years for him to regret his decisions?

"Why haven't you moved out? You must make enough money now to get your own nicer place. Especially with the money I send you every month."

"Because this is our home. I have no reason to leave. And please don't throw money in my face. You don't send it every month for one thing, and when you do, I put all of it into an account for Lyric for when she's older."

The telltale spark of the lighter is heard, then an angry inhale. "I don't like you living with some fucking guy who I don't even know. And how do I know what else you're keeping from me or what else is going on?"

"Don't you dare!" I seethe, fed up with all of this craziness. "I'm not keeping anything from you, and there shouldn't be any issue over Josh at all. If it weren't for him, I never would've seen you that night in Boston. He's the one who got me the tickets."

He scoffs. "You want me to thank him, Piper? Pay him back for the tickets? I'm sure you regret that whole night, anyway."

My blood starts to boil and now I'm the one pacing my bedroom, from the door to the window and back again.

"What is wrong with you tonight?" I ask. "Why are you acting like this? Josh is a friend and that's it. And no, I don't regret that night, even though it turned into a total disaster."

He says nothing. I want to cry and throw something across the room.

"I'm gonna go," he mumbles.

My stomach drops. "You're just going to leave things like this?" I ask tearfully.

"I don't want to talk about this anymore. I need to go do things."

"What?" My voice catches in my throat and it takes me a few seconds to recover. "What things?"

"I just need this to stop. I have to go for a jog. There's a lake I like to jog to and I want to go before it rains. I should do about ten miles."

I pull the phone away and stare at it, then put it back to my ear. "What are you talking about? It's late." He's three hours behind me, making it ten p.m. there, which is late to go for a ten-mile jog around a lake.

Isn't it?

"It doesn't matter what time it is, Piper. I just want to jog."

I let out a massive sigh of mental exhaustion and close my eyes for a full five seconds. His erratic mood swing is confusing me, and I don't want to fight with him, especially when things have been so perfect. I need this to stop, too. I'm not going to go for a jog, but I'm definitely going to go to bed and hope for a better tomorrow.

"Okay," I say. "Do what you need to do, then. It's late and I have to work in the morning."

Questions sit at the tip of my tongue, but I suck them back. I won't ask him if he's started doing drugs again. I won't make him feel like I'm doubting him.

"I'll call you tomorrow."

Click.

Did he just hang up?

Without saying goodbye or I love you?

He did.

Crying, I sit on the edge of my bed and cover my face with my hands. I'm tempted to pick up the phone and call him back and somehow undo what just happened and go back to happiness and normalcy. Past experience has taught me that if I force him to talk, he will just put walls up, though, and that's the last thing I want to do. He'll end up walking fifty miles tonight and end up God-knows-where.

A scratching sound breaks through the sound of my own sobs. Acorn is pawing at the bed.

Smiling weakly, I pat the bed next to me. "Come on up, pupper. We'll go to sleep."

He whimpers and rests his chin on the mattress, lifting one paw up.

"Come on," I say softly. "Let's go to bed."

He whimpers again, lifts one front paw, then puts it back on the floor, then lifts the other paw, only to put it back down. His big brown eyes stare up at me and I realize he can't jump up. Frowning, I bend down and gently lift him onto the bed, and I curl up next to him, my face close to his, nose to nose. I stroke the soft fur of his forehead and watch his eyes close as he falls asleep. So many times this dog has comforted me, kept me warm when I shivered in the shed, kept me company on my loneliest days. People should be more like dogs—with unwavering and unconditional love no matter what. Always happy to see us, always grateful to be with us, never hurting us.

Tomorrow I'll ask Josh to build a ramp next to the bed for Acorn, and Blue can screw himself if he doesn't like it.

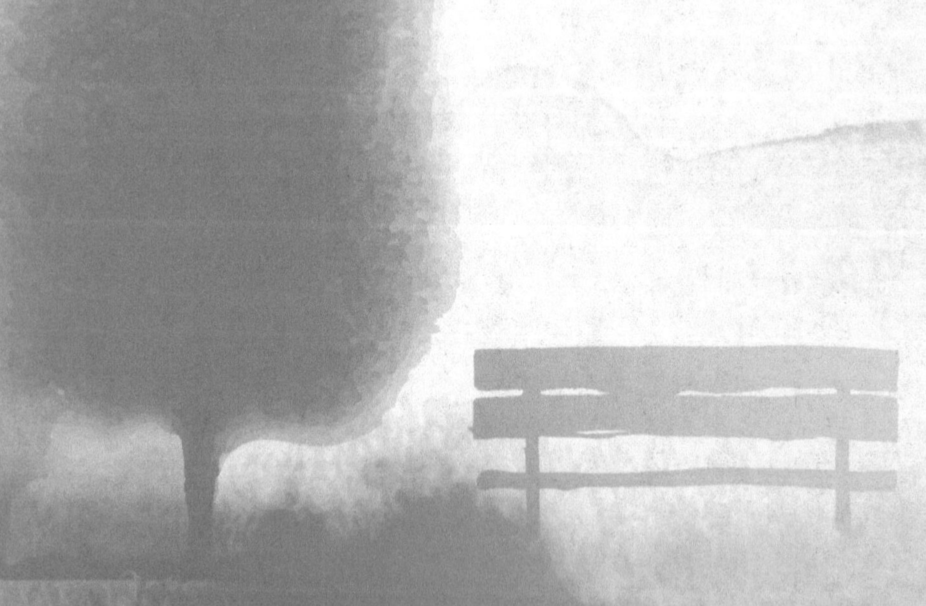

CHAPTER TWENTY-EIGHT

PIPER

Two days.

Forty-eight hours.

Give or take a few hours, minutes, and seconds.

That's how long it's been since I heard from Blue. That might not seem like a long time to some, but it is after talking to him for hours every single night. That time with him has become an incredibly bright spot in the day, something I need to help me get through the day like a morning coffee.

I called him once, and emailed him twice—with no answer from either, and I can't even describe how upsetting that was. I've picked up the phone to call him again at least fifty times, and I've chewed my fingernails to stubs debating whether I should call Reece to see if Blue's okay.

But I don't want to be *that girl*.

I've been that girl in various degrees for the past few years and I swore I'd never let myself be that crying, speed-dialing, crazy-ass message-leaving person again.

It is so very hard, though, to miss someone—to ache for them emotionally and physically. Blue has turned me into just as much an addict as he is.

Unfortunately, there's no rehab program for love. Ditra has urged me a million times to date, have sex with other men, and hopefully fall in love with someone else. But to me, that's a rebound. Or a distraction. I can't get involved with another guy *hoping* I'll love him more, want to be with him more, and will eventually get over Blue. What if I never get over him? That wouldn't be fair to anyone. I've always chosen to just be alone, keep myself as busy as possible, be the best mother I can, and try to put him out of my mind.

Does that work? No.

Especially when I have to look at a little face every day that looks so much like him. And another little face that comes with a wagging tail.

I have a feeling that even if I didn't have Lyric and Acorn, I'd still be thinking of Blue every day and waiting for our time to come.

After three days of Blue being MIA, my phone rings in the middle of the night, jarring me out of a sound sleep. Before I even answer I know it's him and I already know he's going to be a mess.

"Hello?"

"Ladybug, it's me." My ear is filled with his deep, scratchy voice. Not his sexy, lemme-drop-my-panties-at-the-sound-of-it voice, but his exhausted, wasted, slurry voice.

I sigh loudly. "What are you doing?"

"I've been so messed up, man. I meant to call you but I just couldn't deal with it."

"Don't call me man, please."

"Sorry." The sound of him puffing on who-knows-what fills the next few seconds. "I'm sorry, babe. I just—I just I don't even know. I've been so tired and I can't sleep for shit and my head hurts and I couldn't find my shirt and I had so much to do but then I just had to just get away from all the noise and all the fucking people just talking and talking and talking and I just wanted to stab my own ears. Do you know what I mean?"

"Not really..."

"I know...because you're always so good, and you're so...clear. Ya know?"

I *don't* know. I wish I did.

"Blue, I've been really worried about you. Do you have any idea how much it upsets me when you just stop calling and emailing and I have no idea what's going on? You could at least send me an email."

"I'm sorry. Don't be mad, okay? I hate when you're mad."

"I'm not just mad, I'm hurt and I'm disappointed. And I worry."

"I am too. About the guy and all that shit... it's got me all fucked up. It's like he's in my life and *I'm* not even in it."

Sitting up, I turn on the lamp next to my bed. "Listen to me," I say softly. "You have nothing to worry about with Josh. He's just a friend. I've never even kissed another man since I met you, and I don't want to. I only want to be with you."

"I dunno, babe. I can't deal with anything. Life. The band. All the fucking clouds. I just wanna sleep and walk and maybe sleepwalk. I want to fly." He starts to laugh and cough. "I don't know what the hell I'm saying. I'm thinking of learning a different language. I really just want to learn new words. Better ones than what I've got now."

That sinking feeling of dread starts in my gut, spreads up to my chest and settles as a thick lump in my throat. Every minute of this phone call is slowly eating away at the happiness and hope that I felt for the past month.

"Have you been drinking? Tell the truth, please."

I hear the clickity clack of his piercing. "Come on...." His voice drips with desperation.

"Just tell me."

"Yes."

"What else?" I ask with a shaky voice.

"Piper..." he pleads. "Don't."

"Tell me."

"Everything. All the usual," he admits. "I didn't mean to. I just wanted to numb everything out for one night. That's it. But then I couldn't sleep and the night just didn't end."

"You *know* you can't do that," I say. "You know you can't stop once you start."

"I thought I could this time. I really fucking did, babe. But man it just felt so good...."

"Stop it!" I scream. "I don't want to hear this." The tears I've been trying to hold back spill from my eyes and I hurl one of my pillows across the room in frustration. Waves of nausea quake through me as the reality of it all sinks in. He's just thrown all his progress away. He ruined his chance of meeting Lyric any time soon. And he's once again disintegrated the foundation we were building.

"Hey, I'm sorry—"

"You're not sorry! You keep doing this to yourself, and to me! What's wrong with you, Blue? Why do you have to destroy everything when it's finally getting good? You do this *every time*. Is this some kind of game to you?"

"Games are fun, Piper. This is the furthest thing from fun. What the fuck?"

"I can't believe you did this again and I fell for all your promises again. I am so stupid!"

"I'll stop. Okay?" he says with exaggerated optimism. "Give me a week. Two weeks, tops. I'll be better. I promise."

"You're lying! You've said this all before. You're never going to stop."

"I'm trying. You don't know what it's like...to feel like this and not be able to just feel normal. You just don't fuckin' get it. You live in your perfect little elf life—"

"Excuse me?" I ask. "What perfect life do I have? I have some guy who's been jerking my heart around for years! I work my ass off every day! I've been single since the day you disappeared and ya know what? It sucks. I'm lonely. I wanted to be married and have a family and instead I'm all tangled up in this mess with you because I don't know how to forget you." Tears stream down my face as I yell at him. "Do you think I wanted to raise a kid alone? Do you think I want to play house with my bi friend? Do you think I like carrying your poor dog up and down the stairs because he's too weak to come upstairs by himself?

How do you think it feels that both my sisters are married, they go on vacations, and they have all sorts of future plans and I have *nothing*? Do you even care that my father barely even speaks to me because I got pregnant and abandoned by some homeless guy who fucked me and then ran off? No, Blue, I don't have a perfect little life at all! I'm stuck in an abyss because I love you and you keep stringing my dumb ass along and I *let you* because I keep trying to believe in you. And ya know what? You're not worth it."

My temples throb with anger and my throat is raw. He's finally pushed me to my breaking point and I can't take any more. All the confusion and heartache and false hope is overwhelming.

I can hear him breathing hard on the other end of the phone. "Wow." His voice is strained when he finally talks. "That's how you feel? About everything? About me?"

I wipe my nose with a tissue from my nightstand. "Yes." I know I'm hurting him but I'm beyond caring right now because *I'm* hurt and I don't know how to make it stop.

"That's really fucked up. I thought you loved me and now you tell me I'm not worth it? Fuckin' great."

"I do love you! You know I do. Why else would I keep trying with you? Who else would put up with this? The problem is you're in love with getting high. You love drugs and alcohol more than you love me."

"No."

"It's true! Every time you do this you know you're going to lose me but you still do it. You just don't care! You treat me like I'm disposable. You take advantage of me because you know I'll always try again. You always have!"

"Fuck you, Piper. You don't understand a fucking thing about me."

His words are like a sword straight through my heart. I've tried so hard to understand him. I've tried to be patient and forgiving and it's gotten me hurt over and over and over again. Even now, he's so messed up I don't even think he's comprehending the gravity of this conversation at all.

"Ya know what? You're right. I don't understand you," I cry. "And I'm sick to death of trying! I don't want to do this with you anymore.

You can go get high and get fucked up and destroy your life and your career, I don't care anymore! I don't want you to ever call me again. Do you hear me? I want you to get out of my life for good."

"Piper...."

"Go to hell!"

I slam the phone down so hard the plastic handset cracks and a small piece flies across the room. Burying my face in my pillow, I cry harder than I've ever cried in my entire life. I cry until I can't catch my breath and my ribs ache and my eyes swell and burn. I cry until there aren't any more tears and I choke and shake with emptiness.

Why isn't my love for him enough? Why does he need to get high? How can he tell me that all he wants is for us to be together and then turn around and throw it all away for something as meaningless as drugs and alcohol? It makes zero sense to me.

Like a zombie, I go into my bathroom and fill a small paper cup with water and slowly sip it while I stare at myself in the mirror. My reflection confirms I look exactly how I feel inside.

Broken. Exhausted. Hideous.

I've never said such ugly words to anyone, and I wish I could take them all back. This isn't me. *This isn't me.* I'm a good person. I don't deserve to be treated this way and I hate how horribly I just treated the person I love most, because I don't feel like he deserves it either. Something is just *wrong*.

I crawl back into my bed, but I can't escape into sleep. My brain won't rest, it keeps playing our conversation on repeat, dredging up more tears. My head pounds with intense pain and feels like it might explode. I go back into the bathroom and swallow three Ibuprofen and a decongestant. I put a cold cloth on my head, but nothing eases the pain in my head.

Or in my heart.

The morning sun filtering through my gauzy curtains does nothing to cheer me. Today isn't a bright new day like the ones I woke up to when things were going so perfectly between us. Hours have passed since I hung up on him, and I truly thought he would have called and at least attempted to make things better. Isn't that what he should be doing? Apologizing? And I'd apologize, too. I'd tell him how sorry I am and how much I love him. It's true I don't understand him. But I *know* him, and I'm sure he ran to whatever drugs he has as soon as he hung up the phone, to numb himself from all of this rather than face it. I guess the choice for him is never between me or getting high—his choice is always to escape.

CHAPTER TWENTY-NINE

PIPER

This month's child support check came today with a folded note in the envelope. I recognize the thin paper—the same he writes all his notes on.

I don't unfold it. I put the check in my wallet to take to the bank, and I take the note upstairs to my room.

Do I want to read it?

I'm not sure.

I could shove the note in a drawer and forget it.

I could rip it up and flush the tiny pieces.

Or I can open it and see what Blue has to say.

Of course that's what I do.

Dear Piper,

I'm trying to do what you asked and stay out of your life. I know that's what's best for you and Lyric. Everything you said is true. I'm not worth any part of you. I wish I was worth your love and care. I've never understood what you see in me. I've never understood why someone so beautiful and sweet would let me touch them. That's why I can never keep my hands off you.

Every touch of you is like a gift, something rare and precious I know I shouldn't have. But I want it. I want you. I have from the first day I saw you in the park. You asked me what's wrong with me, why do I wreck things, and the answer is I don't know. Something is wrong with me or maybe this is just who I am and that makes this normal for me and there's nothing wrong with me. Whatever it is, I fuck things up and I hurt you and I'm sorry. I know you don't believe me but I never want to hurt you. I want to give you everything. I want to make you the happiest you've ever been. I don't want to be your favorite regret or your worst memories. I want to be someone you and Lyric can be proud of. I'm trying. I promise you with every part of my heart and soul I'm trying so hard and I'm so tired but I'm not giving up. You be strong and I'll be strong and someday, we'll get this right.

Not a day goes by that I don't ache for you and dream about you. I'd love to tell you to find someone to love you and be happy but I can't do that, Ladybug. I'm selfish when it comes to you. You're all I have and all I love and I can't give you up. Try not to give me up, either.

I love you like no tomorrow,

~ Blue

That familiar ache burns in my stomach and spreads up to my chest, then to my throat. All I want to do is call him and tell him how much I miss him. I want to tell him I don't care if he drinks or does drugs or walks halfway across the planet. If we love each other this much, we should be together no matter what.

Maybe I've been too hard on him, expecting him to be some kind of perfect that doesn't exist. Lots of people have addictions and they still have careers and relationships. If I'm patient with him, maybe we can find a way to overcome it and he'll quit for good. It would be so much better than this. There's no reason we can't work this out together.

I grab my phone and dial his number.

"Mom?" Lyric pokes her head through the doorway. "Are we taking Acorn for his walk?"

And there it is, my adorable, sweet, world of reason.

Smiling, I press the end call button on the phone before Blue answers.

"I was just coming to get you," I answer, folding the note back up and putting it in my nightstand with all the others I have saved over the years.

I hope you're right, Blue, and someday we get this right. For all of us.

CHAPTER THIRTY

PIPER

Do you think you broke my heart, baby? Do you think I laid down and died?
You ripped my soul out, darlin', did you think I didn't care?
If you thought you knew me, take a look around
I don't even know me, and I'm sick of the lies,
Sweet insanity, where the fuck have you been?
You know you've always been my best friend
You showed me heaven, baby, now I'll show you hell.

I grip the steering wheel and Ditra leans forward and changes the radio station to something else.

"I'm so sick of his lyrical tantrums." She sighs and puts her bare foot up on my dashboard. "He needs to get over it and get his shit together already."

"I don't want to talk about him," I reply, and I don't. I don't even want to think about him.

"Billy saw them in concert last month and said they killed it. He loves these harder rock songs on their new album. I guess it's true that agony breeds creativity." Billy. Also known as Mohawk Guy. He went home with Ditra that night of the concert and never left. Turns out he's a nice guy. Smart, too. He's a video game developer making six figures.

He doesn't have the Mohawk anymore, thankfully. His hair is shoulder length now instead of sticking a foot off the top of his head and he's actually very good looking. He and Ditra are crazy about each other and have even talked about getting married soon.

I never thought Ditra would be the one to fall in love and get married and I'd be the one single one.

I park the car in front of the café, Ditra puts her shoes back on, and we go inside. Our Thursday night ritual has been sporadic over the years, but we still do our best to get together as often as we can, whether it's for dinner, or to grab a latte and pastry like we're doing tonight.

"How's work?" I ask once we're settled at our table.

"Crazy busy. I referred Boner to a male masseuse."

"Finally! You should have done that weeks ago. It's so gross and inappropriate."

She bites into her apple streusel and nods as she chews. "It happens sometimes when you give people a massage. They get a little emotional, they get a little turned on. It comes with the territory of putting your hands on people. But he took it to a whole new level. I can't have someone with a monstrous dick having a boner every damn week and staring at me like it's my fault or something." She shudders. "In all the years I've been doing this he's the only one who's ever grossed me out."

"I'd probably get turned on if you were massaging me, too," I tease.

"You should let me give you a massage. I can see your stressed-out shoulders from here. Are you using the ergonomic keyboard I bought you?"

"I can't type on that thing to save my life." I tried. Really. But the big split in the center of the keyboard and the angled keys drove me crazy.

"It takes a while to get used to."

"I can't do it. I went from typing ninety words per minute to ten words per minute. It was messing up my productivity big time."

"Then you should do the exercises I showed you."

"I have been," I lie. Ditra is all into body therapy and likes to use me as her guinea pig, which I don't mind because it makes her happy. The keyboard was a disaster, but the back cushion she gave me for my office chair is amazing.

"You said you wanted to talk to me about something tonight. Is everything okay?"

I nod. "Nothing's wrong. I've just been doing a lot of thinking and soul searching. And I think it's time for Lyric and me to get our own house."

She lets out an odd laugh. "You're kidding."

"No, I'm serious. I think it's best for everyone involved. Why? You don't agree?"

"You're not going to believe this. I have something for you," she says, pulling her leather purse into her lap. She fishes around and comes out with a folded piece of paper that she slides across the table at me.

"This better not be another dating site," I say, leering at the paper like it might bite me.

"It's not, I promise."

I'm surprised to see it's a real estate listing for a small bungalow style house. I glance over it quickly—three bedrooms, two baths, small yard, cute porch on the front, lots of flowers. It's perfect.

I smile, but feel surprised and slightly confused. Although I suppose I shouldn't feel that way. Ditra's my best friend. I'm sure, just like me, she also was starting to think that it's time for me to spread my wings.

"It's the house directly behind ours. My backyard touches that backyard. As soon as I saw the for-sale sign go up a few days ago, I thought of you."

"It's like you read my mind. I've been debating getting my own place for months. It's a hard decision to make. Josh and I are so close, and Lyric loves him."

"This house would be perfect for you," she says. "I love you. And Josh. It's great that you guys are such close friends. But you both need some kind of kick in the ass. You're using each other as a crutch to avoid getting involved with other people. You guys have taken friends with benefits to a bizarre extreme."

"I don't know about that...." I say, even though I know she's right.

"It's true. And I'm not sure it's good for Lyric now that she's getting older. She pretty much views Josh as her father."

I shake my head and break my sugar cookie into four pieces, dipping one piece into my latte. "No, she doesn't. She knows Josh isn't her dad. He's like an uncle to her."

"She thinks you two are basically married. She doesn't understand. I think it's going to give her a warped idea about relationships."

I think about that for a moment, and I can understand why Ditra is concerned. I would never want Lyric to be negatively affected by anything I do.

"You're thirty, Piper. Even though you still look twenty, but I'll bitch about that later. But as your best friend, I want you to have more in your life. You should be dating. You should be getting over Blue and not living in la-la land with Josh. And Josh is another story. I think he's afraid to commit because he doesn't know if he prefers dick or pussy and he's afraid he's going to choose the wrong one."

"Ditra! That's horrible." She's right though. I know it and Josh knows it. Everyone knows it.

"I'm being honest."

"I know."

"I just really want to see you happy and I feel like you're letting so much of your life slip away because you're not letting yourself move on. You've been using Josh as a safety net for too long. As you well know, I dated a lot of guys and I figured out what I liked and didn't like and I knew what I wanted."

"And you knew you wanted a guy with a Mohawk and a ring in his nose?"

"No. I knew I wanted a guy who makes me laugh, doesn't want kids, doesn't mind that I'm kind of messy, has a good job and isn't a lazy ass, and looks at me like I'm the only girl in the world. That's what I found."

She *did* find that. Billy really is a great guy that was masked behind some strange decor. I'm glad my night of hunting down Blue turned into a happily ever after for them.

I wish I had been as lucky.

She taps her fingernail on the real estate listing to bring my attention back to it. "Now about the house. I have the details on it."

I smile at her and take a deep breath. While I planned to tell her I wanted to start looking at houses, I had no idea I'd have one put in front of me so quickly. "Okay, I'm listening."

"I went over to look at it and it's beautiful. Everything's been updated—all the appliances are new, it's got granite countertops, hardwood floors, all the bathrooms have been redone. The basement is completely finished, too, with another half bath. It's like a brand-new house. It's small, but it doesn't *feel* small. It's very open. And, it's close to your office and Lyric's school. And me. Did I mention that?"

"It sounds really nice. I'm not even sure if I can afford this, though. I haven't gotten that far yet."

"You'll probably qualify as a first-time home buyer. You make great money. Do you have a bunch of credit card debt?"

"No. I only have one credit card I owe about two hundred dollars on. That's it."

Her mouth hangs open. "That's nothing! You should see mine. If you have a little money for a down payment for a mortgage, I'm sure you can afford this."

I chew my lip. The house *does* sound perfect.

"I wasn't expecting to have to take the next steps so soon."

"This is fate, Piper. It's too good to pass up. You'll be so close to me if you bought it! It would be awesome. You could come over for dinner, or I could walk over and visit you. Wouldn't you love that?"

"It *would* be nice. We could go walking together."

"Yes! I know Josh helps you a lot with Lyric. Billy and I are more than happy to help you. We can babysit, I can pick her up if you have to work late. Just because we don't want our own kids doesn't mean we don't love Lyric and don't have a blast spending time with her. She's like our pseudo-kid."

"You guys are great," I reply. "I promise you I'll think about it."

"Will you look at it tomorrow? I talked to the realtor and she said if we call her, she'll meet us there. She lives nearby."

She's being pushy, but that's because she knows I'll probably drag my feet about this. I'm still a little shocked at hearing myself referred to as thirty.

Thirty

Thirty!

Lyric is almost eight years old now. Where the heck have the years gone? Ditra is right, I've let years just go by, throwing myself into work and momming and riding the rollercoaster with Blue. It's been close to three years since I told him to get out of my life, and that's exactly what he did. Other than sending a check every month, and that note last year, I haven't heard from him. No more notes, no emails, no drunken calls, no sweet sober calls.

There are angry lyrics, though, which I know are directed toward me.

Picking up the paper, I nod across the table at my best friend. "Can you call the realtor? Let's take a look at this house tomorrow afternoon."

She squeals with delight. "Yes!"

CHAPTER THIRTY-ONE

PIPER

"You're moving?"

I turn from my closet door and nod at him. "Yes. I put in an offer yesterday and it was accepted. It's a great house, Lyric loves it, too."

"She loves it *here*. I thought you did, too. Did something happen you're not telling me?"

"No, of course not. I just think we've worn out our welcome here. Do you realize we've been living here for five years?"

He shrugs his wide shoulders. "So? There's no time limit, Piper. I told you that when you moved in."

I sit on the bed and tuck my legs under me. "I know, and we've loved living here. I feel like it's time for me to be on my own and not be leaning on you."

"Leaning on me?" He sits beside me on the bed. "I never thought you were leaning on me."

"Yeah, I have been."

He shakes his head and his blond hair falls across his eyes. "If you were, I don't care."

"I care."

He searches my face, and I see confusion—even sadness—in his. A pang hits my heart. I didn't think he would be upset about me moving out. I thought he would be happy for me, maybe even relieved to have us all out of his house. Especially since Acorn has been having accidents all over the cream-colored carpet. Josh has never acted mad about it, he's always been understanding, and even helped me when I rented a big carpet cleaner. It must bother him, though.

"I don't want you guys to move out. I thought we were like a family here."

"We are," I assure him, touching his arm. "And we love you so much. But on the other hand, we're not a family, Josh. We're pretending to be one. We go to dinners and movies, we sit on top of each other on the couch at night, we cook together. I've been posing as your girlfriend and you've been posing as my boyfriend. It's probably really confusing for Lyric."

"I don't think that's true at all. She's safe and loved. She's happy."

"Yes. That's all true. But I do think us living together could be confusing for her now that she's getting older, and I think it's confusing for *us*, too."

"*Life* is confusing. Just go with it."

I smile. "It is. But I'm starting to think it doesn't have to be. At least not this much. Look at us. We've spent the last five years in a state of massive confusion, together and individually. I think I need a new beginning of sorts. I think you do, too. Does that make sense?"

He rubs the stubble on his cheek. "It does. But I still don't want you guys to *leave*." The last word takes on a note of anguish, as if the thought is ridiculous and unthinkable for him.

"I know. We'll still see each other, Josh. I don't want this to ruin our friendship. That would kill me. I still want you in our lives. Just in separate houses."

"Are you kidding? You're not getting rid of me that easy. I still expect you guys to come over once a week and eat my latest culinary experiments."

I smile with relief. "Of course we will. What would I do without my weekly stomach ache?"

Leaning across the space between us, I put my arm around him for a hug, and he hugs me back tightly. I close my eyes and sigh against his shoulder. It's going to be hard not seeing him every day, because he's been my safe, consistent place for a long time.

I pull away a little, but linger my hand on his muscular shoulder. It feels good to have a man's arms around me again. To smell his cologne. He gives me a bittersweet crooked smile, then leans down and presses his lips to mine. When I squeeze his shoulder in response, he touches my cheek, tilts his head, and kisses me deeper.

After a few moments, he pulls back a fraction, perhaps waiting for me to push him away. I don't, and he kisses me again. Something deep inside me snaps like a thin unraveling thread, and I get lost in his soft kisses. I move my hand down his arm, slowly sliding my hand under the sleeve of his shirt, feeling the smooth, hard muscle. Gripping my waist, he pulls me until I'm sitting on his lap. I wrap my arms around his neck and kiss his full lips.

Blue's face flashes behind my eyes, and guilt comes with it like roaring thunder in my head. He shouldn't be here wrecking this sweet moment. He has no business invading my life. But he is. And it makes me hate him and it makes me miss him and that makes me hate myself.

Josh whisks my attention back to him by raining warm, soft kisses from my lips down my neck, inching toward the valley of my chest.

Cupping his face in my hands, I coax him back up to my lips and he kisses me with growing hunger.

"What are we doing?" I whisper when we break away for air.

"I've been wanting to do that for a long time." He kisses me again.

I can't deny the sparks between us. But whoa—*Josh?*

"I'm... I'm surprised," I reply.

He lets out a sigh and strokes his hand across my cheek. "Yeah, me too. So look, once you get settled in your new house, and we're not all up in this roommate situation anymore... Why don't we go on a real date? See what happens?"

I part my lips in speechless shock. I didn't see this coming.

Not. At. All.

I shake my head in an attempt to rattle my brain into working order. "Okay. Yes. Let's try that."

He kisses me once more—a deep kiss meant to sweep me off my feet and give me lots to think about.

Suddenly, Josh isn't my consistent place anymore. And my plan to un-confuse my life may have just gone up in smoke.

CHAPTER THIRTY-TWO

PIPER

"Mommy? Mom?"

Lyric is standing next to the bed in her PJs, tears on her face. Cold fear rushes through me and I instantly bolt up.

Lyric never cries.

"What's wrong? Are you okay?" I scan her from head to toe, searching for blood or bruises.

"It's Acorn. He won't stand up and he's breathing funny."

Oh, no.

I jump out of bed and follow Lyric to the living room, where Acorn is lying on the floor, panting heavily. Normally, he sleeps in either my bedroom or Lyric's. He must have come out here sometime during the night. One of the things I love about our new house is that it's a one-story ranch. Acorn can get to all the rooms without being carried.

Kneeling down, I pet him and gently run my hands over him, alarmed at how thin he seems to suddenly be. "What's wrong, buddy? You want to get up? Have breakfast?" I use the words that usually excite him and get him up and moving, but he's not budging.

"Is he sick, Mommy?"

I put my arm around her and kiss her temple. "I'm not sure, honey. I think I need to take him to the doctor."

I try to lift him up to stand, but he wobbles and falls back down.

"It's okay, pupper." I kiss the top of his head and he licks my cheek. Biting my lip, I fight against the tears burning behind my eyes. I love this dog so much. He's like another child and the thought of losing him is breaking my heart.

"Honey, why don't you sit with him and pet him really nice while I go call the vet, okay?"

She's already bringing his food and water dishes and penguin over to him, and plops down next to him, arranging everything within his reach while talking softly to him. His tail thumps weakly and he rests his head on her knee.

From the kitchen I call the vet and get an appointment two hours from now. Next I call Ditra and ask her if she can come over and hang out with Lyric while I take Acorn to the doctor. Thankfully, it's Saturday and Dee tells me not to worry and she'll be over in about an hour.

I've been in the waiting room, which is nicer and more comforting than my doctor's waiting room, for three hours. Decorated like a farmhouse living room, with oversized brown leather couch and chairs, an electric fireplace, and vintage photos of dogs and cats on the walls, it's very homey. In the corner is a credenza with a coffee maker, tea, water bubbler, and free homemade cookies. In any other situation I'd be all over those cookies, but I'm too worried about Acorn to indulge in snacks. Instead, I sit in one of the big overstuffed chairs sipping water and trying to read a new book on my e-reader.

"Miss Karel?" I look up at the tech who's appeared in the doorway. "Do you want to come with me and speak to the doctor about the tests?"

I want to scream *yes* right in her face, but instead follow her down a long hallway with paw prints and numbers on the doors. She takes me to paw number five. Acorn is lying on a thick blanket on the floor, looking even more worn out than he did when we first got here.

"The doctor will be right in."

I nod, planting myself on the floor next to my dog.

I smooth the fur from his face and whisper to him. "I missed you, pupper. Did they take all kinds of pictures of your insides back there?" A red bandage is wrapped around his front leg from where they took blood. I know Lyric will ask many questions about that when we get home.

The door opens and I can see a pair of black shoes a few feet away from me, but I don't look up. I don't want to hear what I know is not going to be good news. The vet's tense energy is thick in the air and her mood seeps into me.

"Miss Karel?" she repeats.

I finally look up, because that's the polite thing to do, even though she is going to destroy me in a few seconds.

"I'm so sorry to keep you waiting. We ran a lot of tests and X-rays. We won't have some of the blood test results in until Monday, but unfortunately what I've seen so far isn't good." She looks at her chart and I want to tear it out of her hands and throw it in the trash. "I'm quite sure it's gastrointestinal lymphoma. There is also a large mass in his chest. Judging from the length of time he's been in your care plus the condition of his teeth and other physical factors, I'm guessing his age to be approximately sixteen years old. I'm afraid due to his age and the location of the tumor, it's inoperable. And the gastro lymphoma is obviously wreaking havoc on his body. He's lost a lot of weight. You indicated he hasn't been eating well and has had diarrhea...I'm very sorry."

I blink at her, because just a few short months ago, my dog was perfect and happy.

"But he only just started showing those symptoms a few months ago. I didn't know it was anything serious, I thought it was just old age. Up until today he still seemed happy."

"Unfortunately, this is how these things usually present. It is very hard to tell if an animal is sick. They hide it well. They cannot tell us what's wrong. There is really nothing you could have done to prevent this, Miss Karel. He just had his annual check-up a year ago and there was no indication then that he was ill. In fact, he was in remarkable condition considering his age."

"Wh-what about chemotherapy?"

"I'm sorry. The disease has progressed too far. I don't think it will improve his quality of life or keep him with us any longer. I'm so sorry, Miss Karel. I know how much you love him and how hard this is. We'll have more results on Monday but I really think you have to think about end of life."

I tighten my fingers in Acorn's fur. *End of life?*

"What do you mean?"

She kneels on the floor beside me. "He doesn't have much time left. This cancer is very aggressive. He'll start to decline rapidly."

"Will it be...terrible for him? Will he be in pain? And get sicker?" My voice shakes asking these horrible questions.

The sadness in her own eyes gives me all the answers I need. "Unfortunately, he will get very sick. If he were my dog, I wouldn't want him to go through that. I would want him to pass peacefully."

I nod and blink back tears. "Could I take him home and think about it for a few days? Let my daughter be able to say goodbye?"

"Of course. In the meantime I'll prescribe some meds to make him a little more comfortable. You just call us whenever you're ready and I'll be here. My cell phone number will be on your paperwork when you check out. If you need to speak to me, for any reason, please just call me."

"Okay. Thank you."

"I'm so very sorry. He's a wonderful dog."

"He is," I say, looking into his big eyes. "He really is."

A vet tech helps me put Acorn in the back seat of my car on the blanket that's been his for years. As soon as we're alone I crawl into the back seat with him and cry my eyes out. Acorn paws at me and licks my face, and I feel awful for falling apart on him. I should be stronger than this. I should be stronger for *him.*

"I love you so much," I whisper to him. "You're such a good boy." His wagging tail makes me cry even harder. This isn't fair. Life is so confusing and unfair and hard. I don't want to say goodbye to this sweet dog. I want to hold on to his unconditional love forever. This dog has given me the only love that has never let me down. He's never left me. He's never been a confusing mess. He's so much more than just a dog. But I cannot stand the thought of him getting sicker and being in any kind of pain. If letting him go on to his next journey is the last act of love I can show him, then I'll force myself to do it, no matter how much it hurts me to do so.

When I get home, Ditra lets me cry on her while Billy keeps Lyric occupied. When they leave, Lyric and I gently take the bandage off Acorn's leg and I explain to her that he's very sick and needs to rest. I'm not ready to tell her yet that he'll be leaving us. She's tired and worried, and has asked if she can sleep on the couch in the living room with him. I want her to have this time with him so I pile the couch with pillows and blankets and put her favorite movie on.

After they've fallen asleep I kiss them both and then go to my room to take a long, hot shower, hoping to wash away the heavy burden of sadness I feel, but it doesn't work.

I call Josh, not expecting him to answer since it's Saturday night, but he answers on the second ring.

"I was just thinking about you," he says when he picks up. "I'm eating the ice cream you left in the freezer."

"I need to talk to you."

"Hey. Are you okay? You don't sound right."

"No... I'm not."

"Christ. What did that asshole do now?"

"It's not him, Josh. It's Acorn. He's really sick. He has cancer."

"What? When did this happen? I just saw him two weeks ago when you moved and he was fine."

"I know. It happened so fast. I can't believe it. I'm going to have to put him to sleep, and I just don't know how I'm going to tell Lyric or how I'm going to get through this..."

"Piper," he says softly. "I'm sorry. I love that dog."

"I know you do. My heart just hurts."

"I'm gonna come over."

"Really? Can you?" We haven't had a chance to see each other since

I moved into the new house. We haven't talked about the date he mentioned, or the kiss we shared, but I would love to see him right now.

"Yeah. I'll be there in half an hour."

"Come in the back door. Lyric's asleep on the couch."

"Got it. See ya in a few."

I wait in the kitchen for Josh to arrive, and we quietly go to my bedroom and close the door halfway so we don't wake Lyric. He immediately pulls me into a hug.

"You're so sweet for coming over," I say, looking up at him. "Thank you so much."

"Stop. I'm always here for you."

I lean up to kiss his cheek and then pull away to sit on the bed, and he follows me. "I don't know what to do, Josh. This is the worst decision I've ever had to make. I mean, this is his *life*."

"What did the vet say? There's really nothing they can do? Chemo?"

I shake my head. "No. It's too far gone and he's too old. She thinks he's sixteen years old. I honestly had no idea he was that old. Blue told me he had him for two years so I just assumed he was two years old when I met him."

"That *is* old for a dog, Piper. And he's had a good life. You treat that dog like he's a baby."

"I know... I just don't want to do the wrong thing."

He reaches across the bed and holds my hand. "What does the vet think you should do? What does your heart tell you to do?"

"She said if it was her dog, she would let him go before he gets worse. And my heart wants to keep him because I'm selfish. I also want him to go peacefully and not suffer for weeks or months."

He nods. "I think that's the right thing to do. And think of Lyric, you know how sensitive she is with things like this. I don't think she could handle watching him get worse. She loves that dog like crazy."

"I know," I say tearfully. "But how am I supposed to tell her I'm taking him away forever?"

"She's a smart kid, Piper. She'll be upset, but I think she'll understand." He pauses and locks eyes with me for a few moments. "We can tell her together, if you want."

"Would you do that with me? I think hearing it from both of us would be better for her." Having him here with me, being so understanding, is making me doubt whether I made the right decision by moving out. Josh may not be Lyric's father, but he's the closest thing she's had. Now I'm not sure if pulling her out of his life was right or wrong.

"Of course I'll do that with you. I love Lyric," he says, then adds, "I love all of you."

The way he says *all of you* makes my heart clench. I'm not sure what's changing with him, but there's definitely something going on.

"We love you, too."

His gaze drops to our hands. "I think I've been falling for you," he says. "And I've been in denial about it for a long time."

I hold my breath for a few seconds. Let his words sink in. Then I slowly exhale.

"Oh." It's all I can manage to say because I'm not prepared for this on any level today. Or any day, really.

"I knew you were in love with Blue and I didn't want to get in the middle of that. I've been trying to figure out my shit at the same time, but when I think about what I really want? I want what we had. Me and you and Lyric and the pets."

"Josh...."

He looks at me. "When I kissed you, it felt right. For me. How did it feel for you?"

My body buzzes with nervousness and I swallow hard. "Surprising," I answer. "But good, too. I guess I wasn't ready for it. And to be honest, I wasn't thinking about you in that way, so it kinda spun my head around."

"Fair enough. *Could* you think of me in that way?"

I take a good look at the man in front of me. He's changed a lot since we dated when we were kids. He's not the shy nerd anymore. The man sitting on my bed is, quite frankly, gorgeous and confident. Not only does he have an amazing muscular body and perfect *GQ* face, but he's a truly great guy. He's caring, affectionate, patient and family oriented. He's intelligent and has a great sense of humor. He's stable and normal—which is a huge plus.

But he likes men, too. That's certainly not *abnormal*—just something different for me to think about. I admire that he's capable of caring about and being attracted to people for who they are and not for what's between their legs. It does make me feel insecure that he's been intimate with men, though. I can't help but wonder if he's physically attracted to me, and if I would be enough for him when it comes to sexual intimacy.

I lick my lips and try to answer as honestly as I can. "I think I could. I think I'd need some time, but I do think it's maybe possible. I'm attracted to you and I care about you and...."

He kisses me before I can finish, and again, I'm not ready. I want to be, and I think someday I could be. But tonight, I'm too worried about my dog and my daughter and a phone call I'm going to have to make tomorrow to give a hundred percent of myself to Josh. And I don't want to give less than my all to anyone.

I pull away, and he touches his finger to my lips. "Don't say it." He grins. "I shouldn't have done that. I know you're not ready. I just want to show you I know how to kiss now." He flashes me a joking smile.

"You definitely know how to kiss now. No worries there," I assure him.

"I won't push you, Piper. I promise. When things finally do settle down, I'm taking you on that date and we'll see how we feel."

I nod and smile softly at him. "I'd like that."

We lie on my bed together and watch a movie, and he falls asleep next to me. I snuggle against his arm and watch him sleep. I like how content he looks, and I like having him next to me. I feel safe, and comfortable. This is something I could see myself getting used to and being happy with.

If I could forget Blue.

CHAPTER THIRTY-THREE

PIPER

This morning was one of the worst of my life. Telling my daughter that her very first best friend was going to be leaving us soon was absolutely heartbreaking. I'm grateful Josh stayed overnight and was here with me when I told her, because he was able to help explain how Acorn would be going to sleep forever and be a doggy guardian angel much better than I could, and he was able to talk to her without crying. I could barely get two sentences out without breaking down.

After Josh leaves, Lyric somewhat recovers and decides to work on a huge jigsaw puzzle on a board in the middle of the floor. I grab my phone and go out on the back porch to call the person I vowed to never call again. It takes me at least fifteen minutes of staring at the phone and pep-talking myself to finally dial his number.

The first time I call, it goes to voicemail, but I don't leave a message. I hang up and redial, and this time he answers.

"Yeah?" he says, and I have no idea if he has caller ID and knows it's me.

"It's me."

There's our notorious minute of silence that our random phone calls always seem to start with. I wait for it to end.

"Ladybug." He clears his throat. "Wow."

"Hi."

"Hi." He pauses. "Damn, just hearing your voice again... it's making my heart pound like fucking crazy."

Mine too. But I won't tell him that.

"I have to tell you something."

"If you had a baby without me I'm gonna be really mad."

My teeth grind together. "No. This is serious."

"I was being serious, babe."

"Don't call me babe right now, please. I just need to get this out." Hearing his voice only amplifies my emotions. I'm trembling and on the verge of tears for the hundredth time in the past forty-eight hours. Still, after all this time, he has that same heart-fluttering, time-has-stood-still effect on me.

"Okay," he says. "I'm all for getting it out. Whatever *it* is."

"Acorn has cancer. It's untreatable. He's very sick and I'm going to have to put him to sleep. And I thought you should know in case you want to be there. To say goodbye."

He exhales deeply on the other end of the line. "Fuck," he says. "Fuck. Fuck. *Fuck*."

"I'm sorry, Blue. He got sick in a short time, and I just didn't know. Up until recently he's been happy and playful. He was having some trouble with the stairs and jumping on the furniture, but I thought it was old age. A few weeks ago I bought a new house with no stairs so it was easier for him to get around. I just..." I gulp for air as a sob escapes me. "I did everything I could to give him a good life. He's the best dog in the world and we love him so much and I just wish this wasn't happening..."

"Piper..." he breathes. "That's why I left him with you. Nobody loves like you do."

I choke and sniffle. "Yeah, well, a lot of good that's done me. All I do is get my heart broken. I spent the morning trying to explain to our daughter how this dog that's been her best friend since the day she was born isn't going to be here anymore."

"Fuck, babe. I'm so sorry. Is she all right?"

"I think so. I don't know, really. She's a very caring little girl, but sometimes she gets quiet and I don't know what she's thinking."

"I'll be there. Tell me when and where."

His answer sets me back a step. I wasn't expecting him to actually want to be there. I thought he'd be upset, and I thought I'd hear him run to the nearest bottle and then hear him fall apart on the other end of the phone. I wasn't prepared for him to sound so together.

"I have to talk to the vet first. Can I email you the information? It will be soon though. Probably next weekend."

"I can make that work. You can call me with the info, though, you don't have to email me."

"I'd rather just email it to you."

"C'mon, Piper. Don't be like this. I miss you. We're both upset... we can talk."

Closing my eyes, I count to five to give myself time to *not* let myself open up to him again.

"I don't want to talk. I'm just trying to do the right thing."

"So you won't even talk to me? That's it?"

"Yes."

Click, click of his tongue bar.

"All right, then." Frustration and disappointment deepen his tone. "I'm not gonna beg. I'm glad you called. I want to be there. Does he need anything in the meantime? Medicine? I'll send you some money."

I don't think I'll ever get used to the fact that Blue has money now. And probably a lot of it. To me, he's still the cute guy playing in the park getting coins tossed in a jar who insisted on buying me an ice cream cone. And I'm still the girl who didn't give a crap about any of it and only wanted to be with him. No matter what.

"Thank you, but I'm okay for money."

"I want to send something. Maybe you can take Lyric someplace special or buy her something to kinda cheer her up? Maybe we can buy her a locket to keep a bit of his fur in? Or a picture of him? I dunno, I'm not good at this shit."

For the first time, he just referred to us as a *we* regarding Lyric. We as in parents together of this little person. I sit in one of the wicker chairs on the porch and watch a wind chime blow lightly in the wind while I try to process how his words make me feel.

Confused. Leery. Hopeful.

The locket suggestion is also a surprise—one I wish I had thought of myself.

"The locket is a really sweet idea. I think she'd love a picture of him to wear around her neck. I'll pick one up for her. I really have to go now, I don't want to leave her alone for too long when she's upset."

"Got it. I'm sorry, Ladybug. For everything-"

I don't let him finish. "I'll email you when I have the information. Goodbye."

I end the call and yank my hand away from the phone before I change my mind and call him again. It's been almost three years since we last talked. *Three damn years.* Our feelings for each other should be gone. People break up, they move on; they stop loving and wanting each other. Why can't we do that? What's wrong with us that we can't just end?

"Why would you ask him to come out here? Why get this shit all stirred up again?"

Josh's broad frame fills my bedroom doorway. I knew he was going to react like this, which is why I waited until the last minute to tell him.

"It's the right thing to do," I reply, sitting on the chest at the foot of my bed to pull on my sneakers.

"I think it's a *dumb* thing to do."

"He loves Acorn. He deserves a chance to say goodbye."

"He dumped him. That was his goodbye."

"Will you stop, please?" I ask, rising to my feet. "This is hard enough on me already. I don't want to see him, Josh. It's going to open up all the old wounds again. I know that. But I also know how much

Acorn means to him. I don't expect you to understand it. People deserve closure, and so do animals."

He shakes his head. "I think you're being way too nice."

"Well, that's me."

"Let me go with you, then, and have Ditra come here and stay with Lyric. If I go with you at least you won't end up in bed with him. I won't even go in, I'll wait in the car for you."

I glare at him. "I can't believe you just said that to me. And Lyric asked for you to stay with her tonight while I did this. She wants you to tell her the rainbow bridge story again. Ditra doesn't know anything about that."

"I said it as your friend, Piper. Not as someone who's interested in dating you. Blue makes you do dumb things."

His comments hurt regardless of how he meant them. "As my friend and someone who supposedly wants to date me, I'm offended that you don't think I'm capable of not sleeping with him without you babysitting me."

His shoulder lifts in a shrug. "Are you?"

I hope so.

"Yes," I reply. "Now please stop this."

He follows me out to the living room where Lyric is sitting on the floor with Acorn reading a book to him. My heart shatters in a million pieces.

"Okay, sweetheart. It's time for me and Acorn to go for a drive to the special place," I say in as upbeat a tone as I can.

"To the bridge?" she asks.

"Yes." To an imaginary bridge that takes pets up to heaven that I want to believe in just as much as Lyric does.

I do my best to hold back tears and keep this experience positive for Lyric, like I read about on a website for how to help children with losing a pet or family member for the first time. It's not easy when I'm overcome with grief myself.

After Lyric says her sweet and heartbreaking goodbye, Josh helps me put Acorn into the back seat of my car, gives me a hug and a kiss on the cheek, and then I'm driving across town, tempted to turn around at every red light. I wish I really was driving Acorn to a special bridge somewhere serene and pretty with rainbows in the clouds and not to a sterile veterinarian's office. I keep glancing at him in the rearview mirror, singing happy songs to him, and he meets my eyes in the mirror. His eyes have lost their spark. He is bone thin and looks exhausted. I know I'm doing the right thing for him, even though it feels awful.

The vet scheduled me for the last appointment of the night, so we wouldn't feel rushed. I pull into a parking spot and reluctantly get out of my car and open the door to the back seat. The slam of another car across the parking lot vaguely catches my attention as I lean in to lift Acorn, and when I turn around the unmistakable figure of Blue, his familiar gait, hair blowing in the wind, comes toward me across the dark lot.

Wordlessly, he takes the dog from my arms and holds him against his chest, bending his face down to kiss the top of Acorn's head. Acorn immediately perks up, tail wagging, and licks Blue's face.

I can't watch this reunion. I can't watch Acorn summon up energy to love on Blue when we're going to be ending his life just minutes from now. Turning away, I close the car door, wishing I could also shut out the sound of Blue talking softly and Acorn's happy whimpers.

"Piper..."

I refuse to turn around. I don't want him to see me crying, and I don't want him to see I still care about him.

"Piper, look at me."

I turn, but avoid making any eye contact with him. "Let's go inside," I say, reaching out to touch Acorn's back. "You can sit with him for a little while."

He follows me inside, and the receptionist takes us to a private room, advising us to press a button on the wall when we're ready for the doctor to come in. There's no exam table in this room, just two large leather chairs that match the ones in the waiting room, a big soft dog bed on the floor, dim lighting, and an electric candle lit on a small table in the corner. I can't help but wonder how many sweet furry souls say goodbye in this room.

Blue gently sets Acorn on the bed and sits cross-legged on the floor next to him.

"He looks so old," he says, shaking his head slowly in disbelief.

I sit on the other side of Acorn and we pet him together. He's breathing heavier now, and his eyes have closed. "He *is* old."

"Can I tell you something?"

Nodding, I grab a box of tissues from the table and put it in front of us.

"I found him when he was a little tiny puppy. I was walking around in the woods, getting high, and there he was. All alone."

"Wait... I thought when I met you, you told me you had him for two years?"

"I said we'd been *traveling* for two years."

That was so long ago I can't remember the exact words he used. All this time I thought he found Acorn as an adult dog while he was walking from state to state.

"I took him home with me and my dad had a shit fit. We were already on bad terms cuz I was such a fuckup, and the last thing he wanted was an animal in the house. He told me to get rid of the puppy or get the hell out of his house. I refused to give up the dog so he kicked me out. I had nowhere to go, so I took the puppy to the shed in our backyard. It was freezing, and I was hungry, and I begged my father to let us come in and he fuckin' refused. Even with my mom begging him to let me in. I ended up living in the shed with Acorn for six months until I moved in with a friend. I didn't even have a job so I couldn't afford to buy him real dog food or toys, so I just fed him what I was eating and gave him an old sock to play with." A tear slides down his cheek as he strokes Acorn's ears. "He was such a cool little dog. He never barked or chewed anything up. He seemed happy just hanging out with me, and he loved when I played guitar and sang. He'd sit and watch me for hours when I played, and he'd fall asleep with his head on my leg and I'd keep singing and playing. He was the first real friend I ever had." He wipes his hand across his cheek. "And you told me he was Lyric's first best friend, too. I kinda feel like he's this little guardian that came into my life to take care of me and the two people I love."

Swallowing over the lump in my throat, I reach across the pillow and touch his hand. "I think you're right," I say softly.

"Do you think he forgives me? For leaving him?" His voice is strained with emotion.

I nod slowly. "I know he does. I don't think he ever thought you left, Blue. I think he knew you lent him to us."

Tears fall from his cheek and onto Acorn's fur. "I hope so," he whispers.

I watch as he says goodbye to his dog, and I can't help but wonder if him staying in the shed with Acorn when he was just a teenager messed him up and that's why he repeated it later when he was older.

After we've said our goodbyes, we stay with Acorn until the very end, and the vet leaves us alone for a few more minutes. Blue immediately pulls me into his arms, and we cry together, burying the hatchet to cling to each other in grief. When it's time to leave, we walk out into the parking lot, silent and emotionally drained. He walks me to my car, lights up a cigarette, and stares up into the star-speckled black sky.

"That was officially one of the worst moments of my life," he says. "And I've had a lot."

I lean against the back of my car and breathe in the cool air. A deep pain has settled in my chest and in the pit of my stomach.

"Thank you for letting me be here. It feels right." He exhales a plume of smoke. "That we did it together."

"I think so, too."

He puts out his cigarette on the bottom of his boot and shoves the butt in his back pocket, just like he used to do.

Some things never change.

Shoving his hands into the front pockets of his jeans, he steps closer to me and I can feel him looking me up and down.

"What's made you so distant, Ladybug?"

I cross my arms over my chest. "*You* did."

He steps closer. Too close.

"That means I can undo it."

I refuse to look up at him. I'm not going to fall into the hypnotic trap of his dark eyes again. I know my weaknesses when it comes to him. It may have taken me years, but I'm smarter now.

"You can't," I reply.

He bends his head down close to mine. "Wanna bet?" he whispers next to my ear.

I smack my hand into his chest. "Stop it."

He sighs and rocks on his heels. "I'm only here for one night. Tomorrow afternoon I fly back out."

"So?"

"So let's not waste it. I haven't seen you in fuckin' years."

"That's your own fault. You wrecked everything. I'm not letting you do it again."

He reaches out and touches my face. "I miss you, Piper. We just went through something horrible together. Don't you feel the same? Don't you want to spend time with me?"

"I do, Blue. But I also value my sanity now."

He continues to caress my cheek. "Sanity is overrated, baby."

He kisses my forehead. Then the tip of my nose. And then, my lips.

We kiss soft and slow, tasting each other, remembering each other. His tongue dances over mine, hints of metal and smoke fill my mouth. He has always been my favorite flavor. Grasping my waist, he lifts me up onto the trunk of my car and moves between my legs, not breaking our kiss. I wrap my thighs around him, my arms around his neck, and welcome the hardness of his body against mine. He's like riding a bicycle, the balance, movement, and fit is instantly perfect and familiar.

After a few minutes I pull away for air and press my lips against his chest exposed by the V-neck of his shirt. "Why can't I forget you?" I whisper more to myself than to him. "I don't want to want you anymore."

He threads his fingers through my hair, pushing it back from my face and tilting my head up to his. "Come back to my room with me."

My thighs tighten around him, contradicting the words I'm going to say.

"I can't do that."

He moves his body against mine, and I can feel every inch of him—

hard and hot and tantalizing—between my thighs. My body quivers and heats in response, wanting him closer, with nothing between us.

"We don't have to do anything. Just let me hold you. I want to fall asleep with you like we used to. I'm so tired, Piper."

Closing my eyes, I rest my cheek against his chest and listen to the soft thump of his heart. I can't go with him. I have to go home to Lyric, and to Josh. Isn't that where I belong now?

"I can't, Blue."

His muscular arms encircle me like a vice. "Don't leave. I'm gonna fall apart without you tonight. I don't want to be alone, and I don't want you to be, either."

"I have to go home to Lyric. This has been really hard on her, too."

"I know." He leans his head against mine. "I know it has. Can I come with you?"

My stomach jumps into my throat at the thought. "No. Blue, I—"

"You don't have to tell her who I am. Tell her I'm an old friend."

Lyric is definitely smart enough to know I wouldn't be running into an old friend at the vet's office and bringing him home with me.

"That's not a good idea."

He pulls away and stares down at me, his eyes transitioning to a darker, midnight velvet blue.

"You told me you bought a house. You don't want me there, do you?" he asks. "Why?"

I chew the inside of my cheek, trying to find the right words, but there are none. "Josh is there with Lyric. He's waiting for me."

The corner of his mouth twitches. "Josh your roommate? You still live together?"

"No, we moved out of his house."

His eyes narrow as understanding trickles in. "So something's going on with him now?"

"I don't know," I say softly. "But there might be."

His chest expands, and he backs away, turns in a circle and then looks back at me. "My fucking dog just died. He's in a freezer right now, Piper. And you're telling me you still want me, but there's someone else? You're letting him come between us?"

"He was my dog, too," I remind him. "And you have no right to do this to me. I gave you so many chances, Blue. I gave you my heart a million times, and every single time you broke it. You always let me down. You let drugs and alcohol come between us and destroy your life. At least Josh is a *person*."

He scoffs. "I've never let a person come between us. That's way worse."

My heart twists and sinks like an anchor. "You told me there's never been anyone else."

He whips out a Zippo lighter and snaps it open to light another cigarette. "I said that years ago."

I jump down from the trunk of my car. "So, you've been with other women?"

That really shouldn't surprise me at all. I couldn't expect him to stay single and celibate forever, especially when I told him I never wanted to see him again. Of course he moved on, just as he should have. *Just like I should have.* I have no right to feel jealous or betrayed in any way at all.

But I do. Terribly so.

"I'm going home," I say, not waiting for him to answer. "We're both upset about losing Acorn and if we keep talking, we're just going to hurt each other."

With a hard stare, he takes a long drag on his cigarette. "Yeah. Apparently so."

I walk around the car to the driver's side door, and he talks to my back. "I've been clean for six months. Can't you tell I'm better?"

When we talked on the phone the other day I could tell something was different, but I thought it was just the shock of me calling him and telling him about Acorn that had subdued him.

Standing in front of my door, I turn to him with my car keys in my hand. "I'm glad, Blue. But it doesn't change anything else."

His hair flies around his shoulders as he shakes his head. "You're wrong, Piper. It changes everything."

I unlock my door, listening to his boots on the pavement walking in the other direction. "We're not over, Ladybug," he calls over his shoulder. "And I haven't been with anyone else. You're it."

I sit in my car for a long time, crying for the dog I'm not going home with and regretting how Blue and I are leaving things. Once again we've left each other in limbo, with no closure, no parting on good terms, no understanding of where we stand. I don't know how to find any kind of peace with him and move forward.

Suddenly my car door is thrown open and I jump and yelp in surprise.

"Get out of the car."

My chest heaves up and down with fear as I look up at him leaning one arm on the top of my car and the other on the top of my window.

I let out a breath of relief that it's him and not a lunatic carjacking me.

"Please, Blue, just go away."

"No. We're not doing this again. This is the kind of shit that sends me straight into a bottle or makes me snort lines all night and I'm not doing it. I'm not waiting another two or three fucking years to talk to you again, either. Get out of the car or I'm coming in there. Your choice. And don't forget how much I love car sex."

"Blue—"

He grabs my arm and tugs me out of the car. I stare at him like he's lost his mind. "Why are you acting like this?" I demand. "I have to go home."

"Because I want to talk to you. You wouldn't talk to me on the phone, and you refuse to come with me to talk in private. So now we're going to talk here in the middle of this fucking parking lot because I'm not leaving without talking to you."

"Okay." His demanding attitude has my interest piqued, and my inner romance fan is swooning and begging for more.

"The past six months have been really hard, Piper. Withdrawals, crazy mood swings, feeling sick all the time. I wanted to freakin' crawl out of my own skin. I got through it, though, and you want to know how?"

I nod. "Yes. Tell me."

"Thinking about you and Lyric. You're what got me through."

"I don't—"

"I want you back. And I want to meet my daughter. I'm thirty-four, Piper. Thirty fucking four. I've fucked up a ton of shit. I've lost literally years of my life being high or running away from something that I can't even see or explain. I don't want to do it anymore. I want you, and my kid, and my band." He grabs my hand. "I wanted my dog too, but I'm too late. I won't be too late for you and Lyric."

"Evan...."

"I'm not kidding, Piper. This is all I've been thinking about since you told me to fuck off years ago."

I feel incredibly small and vulnerable all of a sudden. Stripped of all the strength I've built up over the years and attempted to enforce tonight. His words have gutted me, and I'm not sure if it's because I'm already broken over losing Acorn, or if the exhaustion of wishing and hoping for Blue to get to this place for so long has finally taken its toll.

I should be jumping up and down with excitement. Or telling him no; it's too late for us. But instead I feel numb and unable to feel much of anything. It's as if a thousand bees have taken up residence inside me and are buzzing, buzzing, buzzing, drowning out everything and making my entire body tremor with an odd, unfamiliar energy.

He squeezes my hand. "Say something."

"I'm not sure what to say."

A car door opening and closing, then an engine starting sounds behind us, and a few seconds later the car's headlights shine on us as it pulls out of the parking lot. A quick glance reveals it's Dr. Simon leaving—the doctor who slid a thin needle into my dog's fragile vein and then promised they would handle him with love and care until his remains were ready for me to pick up in a mahogany urn Blue and I picked out.

How odd, and incredibly sad, that the first thing we ever picked out together was a cremation urn. Not a couch, or dishes like most couples.

"Are you sure you don't feel this way because you think I'm getting involved with someone else?" I ask.

"I just found that out ten seconds ago, Piper. So, no."

"Are you involved with someone?"

"No. Never."

"Did you sleep with someone?"

He takes a deep breath. "There was one night years ago at a party, I was wasted off my ass. I don't think anything happened. I kept pushing her away…I didn't want her. I'm pretty sure I blacked out."

The thought of him possibly with another woman is like gasoline in my veins, burning through my limbs and exploding in my heart.

"*I* definitely haven't been with anyone." My tone is accusatory and bitchy but I'm not sorry.

"But you care about him. He's important to you. I can see it in your eyes."

"Yeah…I care about him a lot. He's a great guy. There's the possibility to have something real with him. But…" The muscles of his jaw clench and I stare off at the road for a few seconds then return my gaze to his. "I'm still in love with you."

His body closes in on mine, pushing me against the car. "I know you are."

"You are *so* bad, Blue."

His face is in my hair, his warm lips moving against my ear. "I didn't even get a chance to tell you how beautiful you look," he whispers. "It's like you don't age at all. You still look twenty-one years old to me."

"Hm... so you like younger girls?" I tease, slipping my hands under his leather jacket.

Our lips meet, and linger, touching softly, breathing each other.

"I like *you*," he says under his breath. "Can we get the hell out of this parking lot? I have a suite at the hotel. We don't have to spend all our time outside anymore."

"I can't. Not because I don't want to, Blue. I *do* want to spend more time with you. But I need to get home to our daughter."

He lets out a low, drawn-out groan. "You're right," he agrees. "She needs you. Can you call me later tonight? After she's in bed? Or is he staying the night?"

"He absolutely is not spending the night."

"Then call me later when you can."

"All right." I relent. "I'll call you... but I really need to do some thinking about everything. You have to slow your roll a little."

He laughs. "Look at you with the badass lingo. You're so cute."

His smile ebbs away some of the sadness in my heart, and I love him the way he's been tonight—so open with all his emotions, driven and communicative. A little pushy? Yes. But that's okay.

The question is: how long will he stay this way?

CHAPTER THIRTY-FOUR

PIPER

My life always seems to be in some stage of effed up. I'm not even sure why. I think I'm a pretty normal person just trying to live a normal life. I stay in my bubble. I try to do the right thing. I do my best to treat others well. But I still find myself in stressy positions that I had no intention of getting into.

Like having to face Josh at my house after just seeing Blue.

When I get home, Lyric is on the couch with her favorite stuffed animal and about five books scattered on her lap. Josh is on the other end of the couch with his laptop. I kneel down next to Lyric and kiss her forehead.

"How's my girl?" I ask.

"Did Acorn go to the rainbow bridge?" she asks solemnly.

"Yes. He's an angel now."

Tomorrow I plan to wrap up the locket with Acorn's photo and a tiny piece of his fur and mail it to her. She believes in angels and Heaven. I know it will mean a lot to her when it arrives. She'll cherish it. In her sweet, innocent mind, she'll believe that it came from him.

She picks up one of the books and points to a little girl playing a harp. "I want to do this," she says.

"Read this story?" I ask.

"No," Josh says, shutting the lid of his laptop and putting it off to the side. "She wants to play the harp."

"Can I, Mom?"

"Wow, the harp?" I exclaim.

"Yes, like an angel," she answers.

I wonder if she has her father's musical talents, and now I can't wait to find out. "Of course you can. I'll find out where to get you one. Do you want to take lessons, like with a teacher?"

She nods excitedly. "Yes."

"Okay. I'll find out everything as soon as I can. I think it's a really neat idea."

Josh hangs around while Lyric gets ready for bed, and I'm dreading the questions I know are coming. My head hurts from crying, and I'm exhausted and depressed about Acorn. The last thing I want to do is talk to anyone right now. I just want to crawl in bed and escape from everything.

"Was it peaceful?" he asks as I straighten out the living room and put Lyric's books back on the bookshelf. "For Acorn?"

The ache returns to my chest as the vision of Acorn closing his eyes for the last time passes through my memory.

"He just kind of went to sleep. It was very quick. And just really sad."

"At least he didn't suffer. He was a good dog."

I nod and head to the kitchen with an empty glass that was next to the couch. Josh follows me and leans his shoulder against the door frame, watching me fill the dishwasher.

"Did he show up?" he asks, trying to sound casual. Archie wanders in and sits in the middle of the floor, observing us with a smug expression.

"Yes."

"And?"

"And we talked," I answer.

"Your lipstick is smudged."

I automatically touch my lips and wipe the corners.

"I was crying, Josh, and blowing my nose."

"And kissing."

My frustration jacks up. "Do you see a ring on this finger? Nope. Am I in a relationship with anyone? Nope. Do both of you put me in impossible, awkward situations because you don't know what you want? Yup!" I push past him on my way back to the living room.

"I was trying to be patient by asking you out on a real date, Piper."

"I know, and I appreciate that. I really do. But kissing me totally came out of left field and you know that."

"I thought you liked it. I thought maybe you felt the same way."

"I did like it. And to be honest, I'm really not sure how I feel about anything or anyone right now. I was open to going on a date with you to see how we felt about each other... to see if we could be more than friends."

"Was? As in not anymore?"

"As in I have no freakin' idea! Did you guys like plan this? To make me mental and sandwich me in your fuckedupness?" I snatch a blanket off the floor and fold it before draping it over the back of the couch.

"So he's trying to weasel his way back in?"

"I don't know." I run my hands through my hair in exasperation. "He wants to meet Lyric."

Josh leans forward and shakes his head in disbelief. "Seriously? All of a sudden now he wants to be a father? What's he going to do? Take her to a kegger? Drag her around on tour? Spend the day with her then disappear until her eighteenth birthday?"

"All valid points," I agree. "And definitely things I'm going to consider. But he *is* her father and I'm not going to keep my daughter from meeting her father. That's not fair. She'll resent me someday if I do that, and I'd like to keep my relationship with my daughter in a healthy place so we don't end up like me and *my* parents."

He crosses the room and grabs his coat from the closet by the front door. "I guess you're right. I don't want to see either of you get hurt, Piper, that's all. I'm gonna leave the ball in your court. Your head's always been a mess over him. I thought that shit was in the past, but now it seems like it's back. Am I right?"

I slump into the couch, feeling defeated and shitty. I don't want to hurt Josh's feelings. That's the last thing I'd ever want to do. But I can't deny that deep inside, my heart is peeking out of the darkness hoping for Blue to come mend all its broken pieces forever.

"I'm not really sure. I told him the same thing, for the record. I also told him about you. I'm not playing games or lying to anyone."

"I know you're not. That's not you." He shoves his arms in his jacket. "I'm gonna hit the road. I'll call you in a few days."

"Thanks for staying with Lyric for me. It really means a lot to us."

"Anytime," he says as he walks out the front door. I immediately get up from the couch and lock the door behind him, then go down the hall to my room, checking on Lyric as I pass her room.

The house feels empty without Acorn. Even though he was such a quiet dog, there's a strange, lonely silence where he once was.

"You called. I was starting to think you were going to blow me off."

"I almost did," I admit, stretching out across my bed. Archie pauses licking his paw to glare at me for the intrusion.

"Ouch. Brutal honesty."

I sigh with exhaustion. "Sorry, but it's true."

"So what made you decide to call?"

Stupidity, most likely.

"I didn't want to leave things just hanging. It drives me crazy when we do that."

"Me too. We do it too much."

"It's definitely a pattern."

"How's Lyric?"

"Sad, but she seems okay. She told me tonight she wants to learn how to play the harp."

"The harp? Shit, that's a lot of strings to tune. Do you think she's serious?"

"Lyric is always serious."

"There's a chick who plays the harp on our tour for one of the song intros. I could ask her what kind to get an eight-year-old."

"That would be great because I'm clueless. She wants to take lessons."

"Would you let me buy her the harp and pay for the lessons?"

"You don't have to do that. I can—"

"I want to. You have to let me start somewhere, Piper. You don't even have to tell her, but for fuck's sake let me feel like I'm doing something for my kid."

My defenses start to rise, but I'm unsure if they're valid. In some ways, he's treading on my territory, and I'm protective. Other than sending checks, he hasn't ever been involved in Lyric's life. Letting him help make decisions and pay for actual things is going to take some getting used to. While it's not entirely unwanted or unappreciated, it's foreign ground for us. Lyric has always been just *mine*.

"Okay," I reply. "I'm just not used to this. If you'd like to pay for it, then I'm fine with that."

"Thank you. What do you think about me meeting her?"

Geez. He's not beating around any bushes tonight.

"Do you really want to talk about that tonight?"

"Yeah."

I thought we'd ease into this conversation slowly, maybe talk about his band and my job and casual life things before diving into child visitation.

"Are you sure that's what you want? You've never wanted to see her before, so I'm sorry if I sound skeptical about all this."

"I get why you feel that way. I'm clean now, and I'm trying to get my life together. She's my family... and when I think about that, it's big. She's probably the only child I'm ever going to have, and she's eight years old already and I barely know anything about her. The pictures you send are great but I want to see her and talk to her, ya know? In person. What have you told her about me?"

"Nothing."

"What do you mean, nothing?"

"Nothing. She's asked if she had a father twice I think, and I told her you moved far away and she's never brought you up again."

He's quiet for a few moments. "Does she listen to my music?"

"Blue, she's only eight years old. She's not listening to grunge rock songs about sex and heartache and drugs and depression. She doesn't listen to music much, but she likes Colbie Caillat and Britney Spears."

"Ugh," he groans. "That's awful."

I laugh. "Well, it is what it is. She's a girl."

"You really think that badly of my music?"

"I don't think badly of your music at all. All I have to do is listen to it to know exactly how you're feeling about me," I tease.

He lets out a short laugh. "Very funny."

"Seriously, I do love your music, even though I don't fall all over you about it. Your lyrics are deep and raw, it's the kind of music I want to blast at full volume and do ninety miles per hour listening to, just rocking out."

"Hell yeah, baby. Now that's more like it."

"I'm going to have to talk to Lyric, and slowly introduce her to the idea of having a father. I can't just say, hey guess what? Your father has materialized out of nowhere and wants to start seeing you."

"True. I don't want to scare her. I want her to like me."

"You have to understand this is all new for me. I haven't introduced her to anyone. The only guy friend of mine she's met is Josh. I'm a bit of a wingnut as a mother, I just take things one day at a time. Thankfully, she's very easygoing and self-sufficient in a lot of ways so she makes parenting easy. If she was one of those demanding, tantrum-throwing, dramatic, clingy types I probably would be a total fail in the mother department."

"Don't be hard on yourself, Piper. I think all parents guess their way through it."

"I don't know. Like I said, she's usually very easy but a sudden *dad* in her life might freak her out a little."

"You'll be there, right? The first time I meet her?"

"Of course. I'm not going to just let my daughter go off with a stranger."

Not the best choice of words.

"Hey, I'm not that strange," he teases, flicking his lighter in the background.

"I didn't mean that like it came out, I just mean she doesn't know you. So to her, you're a stranger and she knows she's not supposed to talk to or go off with anyone she doesn't know for any reason."

The strumming of his guitar drifts through the phone, and the sound instantly puts a smile on my face. I miss hearing him play.

"I know you didn't mean it that way, Piper."

I sit up and run a hand through my messy hair. "I'm going to ask you for one thing."

"Okay."

"I would feel better if we wait about two or three months before you meet her."

The strumming pauses, then starts again. "And the reason for that?" he asks.

"There're a few reasons. The first is that she'll be on summer break then. She's doing really good in school right now and I don't want to do anything that might disrupt her. The second is you said you've been straight for six months, and given your track record, I'd feel more comfortable if you were clean a few more months. I'm not trying to throw the past in your face, Blue, but I have to be careful. I can't let you come and go like a revolving door with our daughter. You need to be absolutely, one hundred percent sure that you can commit to some kind of stable relationship with her."

The strumming stops. "I really fucking love you, Ladybug." His voice is husky and dreamy.

A small laugh slips from me. "Um... that's really sweet but also a totally random response to what I just said."

"I know. It's just the way you love her, the way you loved Acorn, the way you've always loved me. It's so powerful and intense. It makes me feel lucky... and proud that you're her mother. I can just tell you won't take any shit."

"I won't, Blue. Not when it comes to Lyric."

"Then three months it is. That gives me time to try to figure out how to be the cool dad."

"You already *are* the cool dad. She's going to be fascinated with your long hair, your tattoos, all your jewelry. She's very artistic like you."

"She sounds awesome," he says. "I can't wait to meet her."

He genuinely sounds excited and sincere. I'm hoping all the crap from his past stays in the past and doesn't creep back up to ruin this for him or for her.

A faint, wandering melody fills the silence for a few minutes. I close my eyes and get lost in it, just like I used to. I'm taken back to the park, to his sexy smile, to falling in love with him. I wish we could go back to that time.

"Do I have to wait three months for you, too?" he asks.

"Oh, Blue," I say with a small amount of exasperation. "What am I going to do with you?"

"What do you *want* to do with me?"

Where to start? So many things...

"That's a hard question to answer. I've tried to spend the last three years detoxing myself from you. Just like you said you went through withdrawal and felt sick and depressed? That's how it felt for me, too, trying to get you out of my head, not letting myself call you like a psycho or email you or sit and cry over you."

"Babe... I had no idea you were going through that. You've never told me you felt like that."

"I did. And it wasn't the first damn time, either. I've let myself get in that place over you a lot and it makes me feel like a fool. My friends and my family think I'm a dumbass, a doormat, for allowing you to come back into my life after you disappeared the first time. And then you hurt me *again*."

"You're not a doormat, Piper. I've never thought of you that way and I never wanted to hurt you. I was just fucked up."

"That's really not a good excuse."

"I know, but it's all I got. I don't know how to make you understand that I don't know why I constantly fuck things up."

I want to pull my hair out in frustration. "How am I supposed to trust you then? If you don't even know what the heck goes on in your own head? How am I supposed to trust you with our little girl?"

"Because I'm trying. And I'm not letting drugs and alcohol stir up the mess in my head. I feel *good*, Piper. Better than I have in a long time.

I'm writing new songs again, we have a tour scheduled, the band is getting along great. Things are all falling into place."

"That's all great, and I'm proud of you. I just don't want to get hurt again. I'm petrified of it."

"I know you are, and I don't fucking blame you. I just... I can't let you go. We belong together."

I wonder if because we both feel that way that means it's right? Is there some cosmic rule that if two people feel they're meant to be together, then they should be together no matter what? Or sometimes do we have to walk away from the person we believe we're meant to be with? And if we do... does that feeling that we're missing our true other half ever go away?

I wish there was a way to get these answers.

"My aunt used to say something to me when I was younger," he says softly. "She used to say, don't listen to the voices in your head, listen to the voice in your heart, and you'll always be okay. That's what I'm trying to do."

The voice in my heart has always spoken Blue's name. *Always.*

I finger the beaded bracelet on my wrist, just inches away from my ladybug tattoo, and one of my favorite memories plays out in my mind:

"There's a myth that if a man and a woman see a ladybug at the same time, they'll fall in love."

"No... I didn't know that."

"We just looked at yours at the same time."

"That doesn't count. It's a tattoo. It's not a real ladybug."

"I guess we'll find out, won't we?"

Did that playful conversation seal our fate? Do we ever really know when *it* happens? That moment where we know, that *this* person, is our person?

"Can we take it slow?" I ask. "And see how things go?"

"We can try, Ladybug. But I think you know there's no such thing as slow with us."

That might be true, but I'm going to do whatever I can to keep everything at a snail's pace with him.

CHAPTER THIRTY-FIVE

PIPER

"Ooh, we're going over there," Ditra says as we walk from our favorite small Italian restaurant to my car.

"Where?" I follow her tipsy gaze. She had a few too many glasses of wine over dinner and I really want to get her home. Her attention is fixated on a run-down Victorian house with a big yellow neon blinking PSYCHIC sign in the window.

I grab her arm and try to pull her toward the car. "Are you crazy?" I laugh. "We're not going in there. It's late."

She tugs me back. "Come on, it'll be fun! I've always wanted to go, just to see what they say. The open sign is lit on the door."

"She's going to say 'ooh I see a man and lots of wine and naps in your future,' then charge you fifty bucks."

"So what? It'll be fun. I'll pay for both of us." Hooking my arm in hers, she leads me to the edge of the road and we wait for an opening in the traffic, then skip across the street.

"This place is scary," I say, peering up at the peeling paint of the house and the crooked green shutters. "They could be running a sex trafficking ring in there and the psychic sign is just a lure."

"I doubt it. I have a gun in my purse, if anything shifty happens, I'll pull it out, and you run for help."

"Great plan. I feel safer already."

We climb the worn stone stairs, press the glowing amber doorbell, and wait. A few seconds later, an older woman with huge gold hoop earrings, an entire palette of eye shadow, and about ten gold necklaces draped around her neck answers.

"You ladies must be here for a reading," she says.

I lean closer to Ditra and whisper in her ear. "Wow, she's got the gift! She knows why we're here!"

She elbows me in the gut and answers the woman. "Yes, we'd love to have a reading."

"Come on in." The woman swings the door open and we enter a dim parlor room. Pictures of tigers line the walls in mismatched frames. They're all crooked and I want to straighten them all *right now*. We follow her through a beaded curtain into an adjacent room.

"Please have a seat," she gestures to two old cloth chairs facing a wooden desk covered in candles, statues, tarot cards, and crystals. Cones of incense are burning on a bookshelf in the corner. Ditra and I sit while the woman lights a bundle of sage before settling into the ripped chair behind the desk. The room smells distinctly like the sweet scent that clings to almost every object in Headlines, one of my favorite local stores to buy silver jewelry and the faerie figurines that Lyric collects.

"My name is Loretta. Would you both like a reading tonight?"

"Yes," we respond at the same time, but inside I'm wondering, *shouldn't she know the answer to that already?*

"Would you like the readings in private, or together?"

Ditra and I glance at each other and then answer in unison. "Together."

"Very good. My fee is fifty dollars per reading."

Fifty dollars!

"Do you take credit cards?" Ditra asks, pulling out her wallet.

"I do."

Ditra hands her a credit card. "I'm going to pay for both of us."

"Thank you," I whisper as Loretta runs the card. The mix of burning incense and sage is filling the room with smoke that tickles my nose, putting me in that awkward I-think-I-have-to-sneeze-but-I'm-not-sure mode.

The psychic hands the card back and eyes me as Dee signs her name on the receipt. I'm sure I'm still making a strange sneeze face.

"You're interested, yet skeptical," Loretta says.

I nod. "Yes." Her comment doesn't mean she's reading my mind. I'm sure everyone who walks in here is interested and skeptical. Her talents still remain to be proven.

"Let's see if we can change that," she says. "Who wants to go first?"

"Me!" Ditra pipes up.

"Give me your hands, love." Loretta reaches across her cluttered desk to grasp Dee's hands in hers.

"Do you need my name and birthdate?" Ditra asks.

Loretta smiles. "No, that's not necessary for a reading."

We both watch quietly as Loretta rubs her thumbs against Ditra's palms. The psychic closes her eyes, exposing bright blue and purple-covered eyelids.

"You work with your hands," Loretta says.

Don't we all, really? We can't do much of anything without using our hands.

"I do," Dee confirms.

"You've recently settled down. I see love for the first time."

"True."

"I see many changes coming for you. A wedding."

"Mine?" Ditra practically yells.

Loretta smiles. "Yes. Yours. You will not wear white."

"There's a shocker," I tease, which gets me a quick glare from Loretta.

"Sorry," I whisper.

"A child will be coming into your life. Soon."

"Nope, not me, sistah," Ditra says. "We have no plans to have children."

"I didn't say it was yours," Loretta clarifies, and Ditra's mouth falls open.

"Well then, whose is it?" Ditra asks.

"I cannot say, love. But it will change your life."

"That's an understatement. What else do you see? I'm marrying Billy, right?"

"I cannot see names or faces. But if he is your true love, then yes."

"Good. He is."

"Someone is watching over you. An older man with dark glasses. He loves you very much."

"My grandfather!"

Loretta nods. "He says to be patient. Be open with your heart."

"Oh my God, that is so him!"

"Your sister will need your support soon. You will have to put your feelings aside to be there for her."

Aha! Fail! Ditra is an only child.

"I don't have a sister," Dee says.

Loretta opens her eyes. "She is sitting right next to you. Sisters come in many forms."

Shit. What the hell will I need support with?

"Wait," I say. "What's going to happen to me?"

Dee touches my arm. "We're sisters. I'll be there for you no matter what."

"We will get to you," Loretta says.

"Let's do her now! I'm happy with my reading. Thank you so much," Ditra says, pulling her hands from Loretta's.

"Give me your hands, love." Loretta reaches for me, but I'm not sure I want to do this now. My heart is pounding, my palms are clammy, and I still feel stuck in sneeze limbo.

"I don't know...." I stammer.

Ditra rubs my arm. "Piper, don't be scared. You'll be fine."

Reluctantly, I put my hands in Loretta's. Warm energy flows up my arms and into my chest.

"You have been waiting a long time," the psychic says. "For love and happiness."

"Ain't that the truth," Ditra exclaims.

"Shhh..." I hush her.

"You have a very warm heart."

"Thank you."

"You have been on a journey. Finding yourself. Finding that person you love."

I nod.

"You have found him, but he has not found himself."

"What does that mean?" I ask.

"He is shrouded, his thoughts are not always his own. You must be patient with him."

"I am. I always have been."

"I see a family. With you and him. But he will not be a father."

My heart sinks. "What does that mean?"

"There are many turns coming. Many decisions will have to be made. I see traveling, fun, and fortune. I see keys, and rings. There is a house of books and feathers."

My mind spins. "Keys? Like house keys?"

"Perhaps," she replies. "There will be illness. I see a dark cloud of death looming. It is not good."

I yank my hands from hers. "I don't want to hear anymore," I say, near tears. "This is ridiculous."

"*She's* not dying, right?" Ditra demands. "Tell her she's okay."

Loretta shakes her head somberly. "We all die in different ways. We are all okay in different ways."

I stand up, almost knocking my chair backwards into a bookcase full of more candles and statues of angels and devils. "This is bullshit. Let's go, Dee."

"I'm sorry," Dee apologizes. "Piper gets emotional."

Loretta nods, nonplussed. "Some things are hard to hear. I am not here to lie. I do have one more thing to tell you."

"Oh, great," I say sarcastically.

"There is a brown dog here with you. He is showing me a black and white toy, bringing it to your bed."

That sends me over the edge. Bursting into tears, I grab Ditra's hand and drag her out of the old house. The cold air hits like a wall and I breathe it in deeply, hoping it will cleanse me of all the bad things going through my mind.

"Oh my God, Dee. What the fuck was that?" I ask when we get to the sidewalk. "Do you think I'm dying? Do you think I'm sick?"

"Honey, no. She's just a crazy old lady. This is for entertainment. That's all. It's not real."

"Really? She mentioned Acorn! And his penguin!"

"She could have been guessing. Most people have had dogs at one point in their lives, or a relative or friend has one. It's not specific enough."

"I don't know..." I say swiping my fingers at the mascara burning my eyes and running down my cheeks. "That was creepy as hell. I'm shaking!"

"Piper, she said I was having a kid. How far-fetched is that? You know me. I will *never* have a baby."

I shake my head. "No, she didn't say that. She said a child was coming into your life. Maybe I die and you get custody of Lyric!"

"Oh my God, why would I get custody of Lyric? Wouldn't she go to her father, or your parents? Do you have a will set up naming me as her guardian?"

"No! You don't even like kids! Why would I leave her with you?"

She frowns. "But I like Lyric. I would take care of her for you because I love you."

"Holy shit. Do you think that's what's happening? Do you think I have a disease? Should I go to the doctor? Maybe I can stop it."

She grabs my arms and shakes me. "Piper! Calm down. You are *not* dying. You're totally healthy and gorgeous."

"She really freaked me out."

"That's her job."

"She didn't say those things to you!"

"No, I think that's part of the game. She tells one person good things and then tells the other bad things to create drama. See? She wants us to go tell our friends so they come here, too. So she can make more money."

"I can't believe you just paid someone fifty bucks to mess with my head!"

We cross the street and head for my car in the empty lot. "I didn't know. I thought it would be fun. I'm sorry, Piper."

I unlock the car doors from my key chain and we climb inside. Pulling a tissue out of my center console, I clean up my eyes and blow my nose.

"What did she say again?" I ask. "Shrouded? Keys and travel?"

"I don't even remember. That incense was making me high, I think. My head feels floaty."

"Mine too. Do you think she drugged us?"

"Don't be silly. I don't think you can drug someone with incense."

I rub my hands together. "She made my hands feel warm and vibratey. Maybe she had some kind of druggy stuff on her hands?"

Ditra rolls her eyes. "Stop it. Your imagination is running wild. Don't make me slap you," she teases. "I will slap the crazy right out of you if I have to."

"It's not funny, Dee. I could be dying right now."

"I'm just trying to make you laugh. And she never said *you* were dying."

"So it could be someone close to me. But not you, because apparently you're going to support me." I start the car and throw it in reverse, backing out of the parking space. "Do you think it's Lyric?" My heart seizes in my chest.

"No, I don't."

Blue. It must be Blue.

"If it's not me, then it's got to be Blue that she was talking about."

"Piper... if Blue was going to die he'd be dead by now. He was found in a desert a few years ago with no food or water or anything, remember? And he's been doing drugs like it's his job for years. He's fine."

"I don't know. I'm worried."

"Don't be. Things are going good with you right now. You've been so happy."

"What if she's right, though?"

"I want you to stop dwelling on this. No one is dying. She's a paid entertainer who knows exactly what to say to rile people up. I saw this on television with a famous psychic. They showed how he played with the audience and how he convinced those people to believe him. It's a mind screw, that's all."

"Do you really think so?"

"I *know* so."

"I feel like I should give you your fifty dollars back."

She waves her hand at me. "Stop it. You bought dinner. We're even."

"Do you think it's bad that I want to believe the Acorn part? I like the idea of him being close to me."

"You don't need some crazy psychic to tell you that, Piper. Just like I believe my grandfather is watching over me, I think Acorn is still with you."

My hands are still shaking from the psychic ordeal when I drop Ditra off and pick Lyric up.

"Thanks for watching her," I say to Billy, pulling my daughter into a hug. That nutty fortune teller better not have meant that something is going to happen to Lyric.

"Anytime. We played video games," he replies. Ditra kicks off her heels and settles onto the couch next to him, kissing his cheek.

"I'll call you tomorrow," Ditra calls after me as I head for the front door. "And remember what I said!"

"What did Aunt Dee say?" Lyric asks on the way to the car.

I put my hand lightly on her head. "Nothing, sweetheart. Just big people talk."

"Is it about me meeting my real dad next week?"

"No, but I'm very excited about that."

She beams up at me. "I am, too! I have a present for him, but it's a secret."

"I think he'll like that very much."

A week from now one of my long-time wishes will be coming true. My daughter will finally meet her father. I've spent the past two and a half months having short, fun conversations with Lyric every few days, slowly trying to explain to her that Blue and I met when we were very young, and that he had to move away, how I wasn't sure how to call him to let him know he had a beautiful little girl, and how we finally found each other again. It's hard to explain a very complicated relationship to a child, but she took it all extremely well, and has been nothing but curious and excited. The last thing I want is for Lyric to feel like Blue didn't want her or abandoned her.

Ditra is right, I have to forget the strange comments from the psychic and focus my thoughts on the positive things happening in my life with Lyric and Blue.

CHAPTER THIRTY-SIX

PIPER

Lyric and I are meeting Blue at the park. *Our* park. It was Blue's idea, and it feels right—to go back to the place we first met. The park is common ground, and a familiar place where Lyric feels safe and comfortable. Her school is nearby, and I bring her there sometimes because she loves the swings. There have been times, however, when I have avoided this park when I was especially upset or angry with Blue.

But those days are in the past, and hopefully will stay there where they belong.

Today is all about new beginnings.

Blue is already here waiting at our old favorite picnic table with his guitar case, and a Celtic harp. Lyric tugs on my hand as we get closer, and I can feel the excitement and nervousness emanating from her.

"Mommy, is that really him?"

I smile down at her. "Yes, that's him." She looks adorable today in blue jeans, tiny black combat boots, a white top, and a faded, distressed denim jacket. Her blond hair has been growing like a weed and is well past her shoulders now.

"He has a guitar... and a harp." Her voice is soft and whispery with awe.

"He certainly does."

Blue flew in on a private plane last night and insisted on bringing the harp he purchased for Lyric with him so he could give it to her himself. My first thought was to say no. I didn't want him trying to buy Lyric's acceptance, or spoiling her from day one. Then I realized this was about *music* for him. His passion. Giving his daughter her first musical instrument is much more than a gift. He's hoping they share a talent and it will help them bond.

I hope so, too.

He's smiling nervously as we approach, and stands to give me a quick, friendly hug which feels incredibly awkward considering this man has ravaged every inch of my body numerous times. Lyric hangs on to my hand tighter, and I squeeze hers back reassuringly.

"Lyric, this is your dad. His name is Blue."

"Like the color?" she asks.

Blue laughs. "Yup, like the color."

She cranes her neck to look up at him. "You're really tall."

Lyric has definitely inherited my petite genes. She's shorter than all her classmates and looks much younger than most of them.

Blue kneels down in front of her and winks affectionately.

"Is that better?" he asks.

She nods, smiling shyly. "Much."

"I'm really glad to finally meet you, Lyric. You have a beautiful name."

"Thank you."

"Why don't we sit down," I suggest, sensing a bit of shyness between them. Blue flashes me a grateful smile as we sit on the wooden bench. It warms my heart when Lyric chooses to sit between us.

"You have an earring," Lyric observes, pointing to the feather that still flutters against Blue's mane of hair. I can't believe it's lasted for so many years.

"It's the feather of a pet bird I used to have."

This, of course, fascinates her. "You had a pet bird? He didn't fly away?"

He nods. "Birds make great pets, and no, he didn't fly away."

"How come?"

"I don't think he knew he could."

She giggles. "That's silly. All birds fly." She turns to me. "Right, Mom?"

"Usually, but I think it's possible some don't. Or maybe they just don't want to."

"I heard you want to learn to play the harp," Blue says, bringing the harp closer. It's bigger than I pictured, a little over three feet tall, and made of a beautiful tiger maple wood. "I have a friend who plays the harp, and she told me this one would be perfect for you. It used to be hers when she was a teenager."

Lyric stares at the harp with wide eyes. "It's for me?"

"It is... and guess what?"

"What?" she asks excitedly.

"She taught me how to play 'Twinkle, Twinkle Little Star' on it, so now I can teach you."

The sheer look of amazement on Lyric's face almost makes my heart burst with happiness.

"Can you play it for me?" she asks.

Grinning, he pulls the harp closer to him. He places his large hands on the strings, and plays an absolutely beautiful, angelic version of the simple lullaby. Something about his tattooed fingers moving over the elegant instrument is incredibly sexy. I shouldn't be thinking such thoughts right now, but damn, I can't help it. He just oozes so much subtle sexiness. I want to kiss him in the worst way but we agreed not to be too kissy feely in front of Lyric until she feels comfortable around him.

"That was beautiful," I say when he finishes. "But I'm not at all surprised."

He lets out a low whistle. "*I'm* surprised. I'm not used to all these strings."

"Can you teach me now?" Lyric asks. "Just like you just played it?"

"Hell yeah, I can. I bet you'll play it even better than me."

I watch quietly as he shows her how to position the harp against her shoulder, how to place her hands on the strings and pluck them properly. It's an easy song, and she picks it up quickly and plays it surprisingly well. Seeing Blue and Lyric together is like a dream. It's clear she likes him and feels comfortable with him. She's not pulling away when he guides her fingers to the right strings, she's not looking to me for reassurance. I've never seen Blue interact with a child before, and to be honest, I worried he'd be awkward, quiet, and moody, but he's doing better than I could have hoped.

After the mini harp lesson, Blue plays a few songs on his guitar at Lyric's request, and she's totally enamored with him by the time he's done. A few people walking through the park stop to listen to him, but I don't think they recognize him as the lead singer of a popular rock band.

"I want to play just like you someday," Lyric wishes out loud. "Only on the harp with the strings up and down and not across like the guitar."

"I think you'll be an amazing harp player," Blue says. "You just have to practice a lot. Like every single day if you can. And soon? It'll become a part of you."

"Since Blue was nice enough to bring you the harp, I found a teacher for you. You can start taking lessons in about two weeks."

"This is like Christmas!" she exclaims. "A dad and a harp and lessons. I can't wait to tell Uncle Josh!"

Blue's smile falters and I cringe inside. Josh might still be a sore spot, but he's part of our lives and Blue's going to have to accept that whether he likes it or not.

Josh and I never did go on a date. Maybe we both realized it never would have worked between us.

Or maybe it was because Blue and I have spent almost every night on the phone together, slowly falling in love all over again.

Whatever the reason, it seems that all the pieces are finally falling into the places they're supposed to be in.

After putting the instruments in my car, we take a walk through the park and stop to let Lyric play on the swings. Blue puts his arm around me and kisses the top of my head as we watch her pump her legs up and down, soaring high toward the sky and smiling at us.

"She's awesome," he says. "Do you think she likes me?"

I wrap my arms around his waist and hug him. "I think she's crazy about you already, just like I am."

"I feel like the luckiest man alive right now. It's like fuckin' torture not being able to kiss you, though."

"I know. But tomorrow night we'll have some time alone together."

He pulls me closer, his hand tight with desire on my hip. "I can't wait. It's been a long-ass three months."

It has. We haven't seen each other since that night in the parking lot, but we've shared a lot of late-night phone conversations that ranged from deep to serious to sweet to sexy. I've been lucky enough to wake up to a few sensual and romantic emails that have been wicked forms of teasing foreplay, which I'm sure was his plan—to make me crazy for him.

We have dinner at a quiet local restaurant, then I drive Blue back to the Marriott hotel just a few blocks from the park.

"Did you have fun?" Blue asks, turning in the passenger seat to talk to Lyric in the back.

"I did. Will I see you tomorrow still?"

"Yup. I'm coming over to your house in the morning."

"Can I show you my room?"

He grins. "I'd love to see your room. You can show me where you're going to keep your new harp."

"What should I call you?" she asks.

Blue looks to me for guidance and I give him a subtle nod. I want him to be able to make his own decisions with her.

"That's up to you. You can call me Dad...or you can call me Blue." He reaches across the seat and holds on to my hand on my thigh as I turn in my seat to see them both better.

Lyric is deep in thought, her small mouth quirked to the side. "I think I want to call you Blue," she finally announces. "It's my favorite color."

"Mine too. I'll see you two beautiful ladies tomorrow." He leans across the car and gives me a quick kiss that leaves me wanting more. "I'll call you later?"

I nod, wishing he didn't have to stay in the hotel and could come home with us but I'm determined to set a good example for our daughter even if my body is not exactly on board with that plan.

"Will you call me later, too?" Lyric asks, which puts the biggest smile on Blue's face.

"What time do you go to bed, darlin'?"

"At nine usually."

"Then I'll call you before then to say goodnight."

"So?" I ask, glancing at Lyric in the rearview mirror on the drive home. "What are you thinking about, sweetheart?" She's been quiet since Blue got out of the car, which could be good or bad.

"I like him. He's not what I pictured as a dad. I think he might be better. He looks like someone on television."

"He likes you a lot. He told me."

"I like his hair and his earring. And all his tattoos. He's fun to look at."

I try to stifle a laugh. "I think he's fun to look at, too."

"I can't believe he got me a real harp, Mom. Can I really take lessons?"

"Of course. All I have to do is call and make the appointments."

"Is it okay if I don't call him Dad like other kids do? I like Blue better."

"Honey, you can call him Blue if you want to. We're not going to force you to call him Dad."

"Is he going to stay my dad now? From now on?"

Her words sting my heart. She shouldn't have to be worrying if he's going to leave her life. Little girls should be able to trust their fathers with all their heart and soul. Or at least I thought so until my own father ostracized me for an unplanned pregnancy and still refuses to get over it. I hope Blue can be better than that.

"He's always going to be your dad, and he's going to see you as much as he can. It won't be every day, because he lives in a different state and he travels, but he told me he'll see you as much as he can."

"Shouldn't we all live together? Now that you found him? Are you guys divorced like?"

God. Why couldn't she ask these questions while he was still in the car?

"Well, we've never been married so we can't be divorced. Remember, I told you he's in a band and he has to travel to play concerts? That's why we can't live together."

"But he'll come see me?"

"I'm sure he will."

Holy heck I'm glad she's never been the mega-questioning type, because trying to come up with answers on the fly is like being on the witness stand. I don't even know if I've given her the right answers. I want her to feel safe, but I don't want to paint an unrealistic picture for her, either. I *know* Blue. Even though he's been great the past few months, I'm still cautious when it comes to him because he could take a U-turn at any moment and disappear on one of his 'walks.'

At exactly 8:45 my house phone rings, and Lyric vaults off the couch, scaring the heck out of Archie, who runs for cover down the hall. Probably to get revenge by barfing on my carpet.

"I'll get it!" she yells, running to grab the phone from the kitchen. A few seconds later she's wandering through the living room on her way to her bedroom, chattering away. I give her a few minutes of privacy before I check on her. She's sitting on her bed telling Blue all about a TV show we were watching before he called.

"Do you want to talk to Mommy now?" she asks. "Okay. I'll see you tomorrow, too. Nighty night." She holds the phone out. "He wants to talk to you now."

Adorableness.

"Okay, you should get ready for bed now." I lean down to kiss her and take the phone from her.

"Night, Mom. I love you."

"I love you, too."

"Damn... this is so crazy surreal," Blue says on the other end of the phone as I walk down the hall to the master bedroom. I close the door a few inches behind me.

"You doin' okay?" I ask. "I know this is a lot to take in."

"Yeah. It's just crazy. Like *bam*. Now there's this little girl who wants to talk to me."

"Are you okay with that?"

"Hell yeah. She's so damn cute. She's like a tiny version of you," he sighs. "It just blows my mind that she's mine. It's gonna take a while for that to really sink in. Right now I kinda feel like I'm dreaming all this."

"Right after you got out of the car she started asking me questions. She wanted to know if you were going to be her dad from now on."

"Shit. I'm such an asshole, Piper." His voice deepens. "I fucked up so bad not being there for her."

"Blue, we can't change that. Be there from now on. That's all you can do."

"I will. I promise, babe. I'm not going to hurt her. I'd rather saw my own arm off."

"She asked about us living together, too. I think she wants us to be like the families she sees on TV. I told her you have to travel a lot."

"I'll figure it out somehow. Ways to fit you guys into my schedule. I promise. I can do this."

"We'll take it one day at a time. I don't want you to feel overwhelmed. I know you're not going to be instant family man."

"I know but after spending the day with both of you... fuck. It's like I stepped through a door into a whole new world all of a sudden. And it's scary as hell but I like it. Reece told me that once I actually saw her everything would change and damn, he was right."

I sit on the floor with my back leaning against the bed and Archie immediately crawls onto my lap. "I like hearing you so happy," I say softly. "And I'm so relieved you two got along so great."

"It's odd. I feel like I've always known her. Do you think that's a parent thing? Like an instinct?"

I let out a lighthearted laugh. "Yeah, I think it just might be that."

"I know I just spent the whole damn day with you but I miss you. I'm not gonna be good at not touching you. I'm not going to grope you in front of her or anything, but you know how I am with you, babe. I need to be able to touch you and kiss you or I'll go crazy."

"All right," I relent, smiling from ear to ear. "Tomorrow we can touch a little more in front of her if you keep it clean."

His sexy, deep laugh floats through the line. "I'm never gonna be clean, baby. But I'll do my best."

I don't think I'd have him any other way.

CHAPTER THIRTY-SEVEN

PIPER

Lyric has been leaning over the back of the couch next to Archie, staring out the front window for half an hour waiting for Blue to arrive.

"He's here!" she yells. "Can I let him in?"

"Of course." I'm amused with how she runs to the front door and throws it open. I'm compelled to do the same since it's been years since he's come to my home, only this time I'm not going to let him leave to run an errand. I might even tie him to the bed.

Blue's standing in the doorway with a bouquet of flowers in one hand, a big teddy bear tucked under his arm, a tray of coffees in his other hand, and a brown paper bag under his other arm.

"You look like a pack mule!" I say, running over to take the drinks and the brown bag from him as he steps inside.

"This is for you." He hands the bear to Lyric, then extends the flowers to me. "And these are for you."

"I love bears!" Lyric announces. "And Mom is always saying she never gets flowers like all the ladies at her office do."

Blue leans down to plant a kiss on my heated cheek. "I'm glad no one is sending you flowers," he whispers.

"They're beautiful," I reply. "Did you find the house okay?"

"Yeah, no problems at all." He sweeps his gaze across the living room. "This is nice. You always have the nicest colors. All my walls are white."

"We learned in art class that white is the absence of color," Lyric says, and Blue nods.

"I'd agree with that."

"I'm going to put my brightly colored flowers in a vase. You two want to come in the kitchen?"

"I actually showed up with the bagels this time," he jokes as he follows me.

I throw a mock glare at him as I retrieve a vase from the cabinet under the sink. "Very funny. I was actually just thinking that I may have to find a creative way to detain you so you can't disappear again."

A hint of wickedness glints in his eyes. "Lookin' forward to that," he says under his breath as he removes the drinks from the tray.

"I hope you like hot cocoa?" he asks, putting one of the cups in front of Lyric, who's already sitting at the table picking out a bagel.

"I do!"

"And I hope you still like vanilla soy latte with a dash of cinnamon?" His eyebrow tweaks up as he hands one of the cups to me.

"I can't believe you remembered."

He takes the empty seat at the table, the one no one has ever sat in before. "I remember everything about you."

"Will you remember everything about me?" Lyric asks, breaking through the silent conversation Blue and I were having with our eyes locked onto each other.

"I will from now on," Blue vows.

"I have a present for you. I made it myself. Can I go get it, Mom?"

"Sure."

Blue puts his hand on my thigh under the table as Lyric runs to her room and comes back with a photo album with a big black ribbon wrapped around it. I helped her put it together, but it was all her idea to give him an album full of pictures of her, me, Acorn, and Archie. She also added a few short poems she's written. She has a strong creative spirit that seems to be getting stronger as she grows up.

Lyric narrates each photo for Blue, and his hands shake as he turns the pages. I hope her squirming into his heart isn't too overwhelming for him. Other than myself, Reece, and Acorn, I've never heard him mention anyone else who's been in his life for any length of time. No ex-girlfriends, no other friends, not even family.

"This is awesome," he says with glistening eyes when he's reached the end of the photos. "And your poems are epic. Did you know I write poems and songs, too?"

"Mom told me. But she said I'm not old enough to listen to your music yet because you say bad words."

He laughs and gives me a playful side-eye. "She did, huh? Well, that's probably true. I could write you a poem and give it to you next time I see you."

"Really?"

"Really."

"Can I tell my friends I have a dad now?" she asks, touching the ends of his hair.

"Um, yeah."

"Are you going to tell your friends about me, too?"

"I already did. I told them you're the cutest, smartest, most badass kid in the world."

"Blue...." I nudge him under the table with my foot.

"What?" he says innocently. "She is."

Lyric giggles and I shake my head at them. I can already tell Blue's going to be the 'cool dad' who probably won't ever be much help in the child discipline department, but that's okay. He's here, he's making an effort, and we're all getting along great. I can't ask for anything else.

"I don't want to leave."

Five words.

That's all it took to sway me.

I'm weak. *Defenseless.* Craving his touch. Crazy in love.

Lyric went to bed a little over an hour ago, and we've been on the couch all tangled up in each other watching a movie since.

Kissing, mostly. There hasn't been much movie-watching at all.

He rolls on top of me and leans up on his elbows to study my face. "Let me stay..." His mouth covers mine, his tongue licking over my bottom lip, teasing me with what's to come.

"Blue...."

"Say yes."

I undo the remainder of the buttons of his shirt and push the material away, running my fingertips from his chest down to his narrow waist.

"Okay," I say between kisses. "But you have to be in the guest room when Lyric wakes up. *Not* in my bed."

"I can do that." His lips curve into a smile against mine. "Didn't you say you were going to do something so I couldn't leave?"

"Do I need to worry about you leaving when I'm not looking?"

I tilt my head to the side and my eyes fall closed at the nip of his teeth and the flick of his tongue on my neck.

"Not a chance, Ladybug," he whispers.

"You better not."

Lifting his head up, he touches my chin, coaxing me to meet his eyes.

"Trust me." He takes a deep breath. "Please?"

I nod, keeping my eyes on his. "I'm trying to," I say softly.

He stands and lifts me in his arms, and I wrap my legs around his waist. He carries me to my bedroom, gently putting me on my feet next to the bed.

"Leave it open a little," I say when he turns to close the door behind us. "I never close the door all the way."

He swaggers toward me with a panty-melting grin on his face, his hands unbuckling his leather belt. "Think you can be quiet, Ladybug?"

Nope.

"I'll have to be, won't I?" My pulse flutters with anticipation as he closes the space between us, jeans unzipped and hanging low on his hips. I skim my fingers over the tribal ink design that spans his abs and disappears beneath the band of his boxers.

"Yeah. You will." The low huskiness of his voice makes me

breathless for more. "I think I'll have to keep your pretty little mouth extra busy." He fingers a lock of my hair, winds it around his hand, and tugs me closer. "Just to be sure."

I've missed bedroom Blue.

My lips part to reply but his mouth crushes mine, his tongue diving deep, the metal bar sliding against the roof of my mouth. I clutch the fabric of his shirt, yanking it off his shoulders and down his arms. He shrugs it off and wraps his hands around my waist, lifting me off my feet. Our tongues clash and caress in a dance of love and desire.

He lowers me onto the bed and removes my clothes like he'd unwrap an unexpected gift. Slow. Quiet. Intent. His mouth and hands explore. Reclaiming what he never lost.

My body hums under his touch.

A soft moan slips from my lips when his hand travels up my thigh, fingers sliding into slickness.

"Shh..." he whispers, kicking off his boots and stepping out of his jeans.

His silhouette is stunning in the moonlight filtering through the window. Wide shoulders and chest taper down to that muscular v of his waist. He's a six-foot-four onyx, rock star statue.

"Lie down, beautiful."

I fall back long ways across the bed and watch him walk around to the other side of the bed. Grabbing my shoulders, he pulls me until my head is at the edge of the bed. Bending over me, he moves his hands over my body, caressing my breasts, dipping down to my waist. He kneels on the bed, legs spread above me. Grasping and spreading my thighs, he lowers his face between my legs.

Lips on lips. Wet on wet.

Bending my neck backward, I take his cock into my mouth. I grasp his hips, pushing and pulling him in sync with his thrusts. He spreads my thighs wider, fucks me with his tongue and two fingers. My legs vice around his head. His hair is like cool silk against my sensitive skin.

His erotic growls vibrate against my lips. He moves us until my head hangs off the bed, and his shaft sinks deeper; pushing against my throat. I gag on his width and he eases his thrusts, softens and slows his tongue, lets me do the same. I surrender to the lust and take more, sucking harder. His mouth is pure magic on my pussy, sending me into that frenzied euphoric place that feels like heaven. I try to hold back, not wanting the ecstasy to end. It's impossible. He plays my body like he plays his guitar. Expertly. Effortlessly.

My thighs tremble. I shudder against his mouth, whimper and moan around his throbbing cock. His moans soon echo mine. I swallow his hot spurts and rake my nails down his thighs.

He separates from me and turns his body around. Our mouths are wet and hot when he kisses me and moves between my thighs, filling me with his still-hard cock.

Leaning up, he stares down into my face, brushing stray hairs from my damp forehead. "I love you, Ladybug," he whispers. "This time is forever. I promise."

I slide the curve of my foot up and down his leg. "Blue... don't make promise—"

His lips linger on mine. "I promise. The only thing in my life that I've ever known for sure, the only thing that's always with me, even when I'm fucked up, is that *I* love you and *you* love me. I need you to believe in us."

"I do. I always have."

I've heard his promises before, but this time is different. This time, the emotion in his voice, the shimmer in his dark ocean eyes, prove that *he* believes his words.

I'm just not sure either of us can trust him.

CHAPTER THIRTY-EIGHT

PIPER

"Of course Lyric can stay with us for a week," my mother says, not looking up from the crossword puzzle she's doing. "Where did you say you were going? It's a business trip?"

"No, Mom, it's not for work. I told you I'm going to Seattle to spend time with Blue."

"Who?"

I press my finger against the dull throbbing in my temple.

"Blue. Lyric's father."

She lays the crossword book in her lap, takes her reading glasses off, and stares at me.

"Oh. Well. When did all this happen?"

"It's a little complicated. We started talking a few months ago and he's come to visit us a few times. Lyric loves him. He's great with her."

"Suddenly that loser decided he wants to be a father?"

I thought my dad was asleep in his recliner across the room, but apparently he's been just sitting there with his eyes closed listening to us.

I lean back into the squishy couch cushions and cross my arms. "He's not a loser, Dad."

"If he's such a great father now, why isn't your daughter going with you?"

"He wants her to. I thought it would be best if I visited him alone first, to see how things go, see where he lives. It's still very new so I'm being cautious."

"Honey, are you involved with him? We were under the impression all that ended years ago."

All that. Is that what we were?

"We're trying to figure it out, Mom. Right now we're taking things one day at a time."

My father scoffs. "Figuring what out? How he can use you?"

"Use me for what, exactly?" If he brings up the milking the cow scenario again I'm going to walk right the heck out of here.

"Who the hell knows? But you're going to just let him do it, whatever it is."

"There's nothing he could use me for. I don't have anything. His band has a double platinum album. He's got a ton of money now. He's very good-looking. He could probably have any woman he wants."

"Then what's he doing with you, Piper? If he's living the life of a celebrity what does he want with a single mother living in a small town in New Hampshire?

"He loves me. Is that so inconceivable?"

"Actually, it is. If he loves you so much he would have been in your life long before this. And he probably *is* getting any woman he wants. Why wouldn't he? Some men just like women they can treat like toys and throw away, Piper. Especially ones that fall at their feet and keep taking them back. That's not love."

My mother shakes her head. "Bill, for God's sake what's wrong with you? We don't even know him." She turns to me. "It's a bit of a shock, honey, that's all. We had no idea you still had feelings for him after all this time. Or that he was any part of your life."

I've mostly kept all things Blue hidden from my parents over the years, only mentioning him casually. My father has never forgiven me for getting pregnant by a disappearing homeless man. He's treated me as if I'm carrying a contagious disease since the night I told them I was pregnant. The chances of him ever accepting Blue as part of our lives are obviously slim.

That's a bridge I'm going to have to cross if things move forward with Blue.

"We've always loved each other. The timing has just never been right."

"And now it is? Just like that?" My father snaps his fingers.

"Yeah, Dad. Just like that."

"So you're just going to abandon Lyric for a week to run around with him?"

I slide my tongue over the edge of my teeth to keep myself from telling my father to fuck off.

"I'm hardly abandoning her. She's staying with her grandparents." *Grandmother* is more like it. "I haven't taken a vacation since she was born. I think I'm allowed."

"Of course you are, Piper. You work too much. You deserve to get away and have some fun. Lyric and I will have a great time. Just ignore your father."

"Don't tell her to ignore me. I don't want to see our daughter get hurt again by some hooligan who somehow managed to become famous by swindling people."

"How are you coming up with this crap? Swindling hooligan?" I snort. "He's famous because he's talented and that's the only reason. Honestly, Dad, it's ironic that you don't want me to get hurt, but your attitude toward me is what really hurts me."

"I don't have an attitude."

"You do. You have for years and I'm tired of it. You can stop punishing me."

"I'm not punishing you. I'm disgusted that you threw your life away."

His words are like a punch to my stomach. "And I'm disgusted you threw *me* away. So, we're even." I stand and zip up my pink hoodie. "I'm leaving. I'll bring Lyric by next Friday, Mom."

She stands and walks with me out to the kitchen, to the back door that leads to the driveway.

"Don't pay attention to your father. He's stressed at work and it makes him irrational and grumpy. I know he doesn't show it well, but he loves you and worries about you. More than he does your sisters. You've always been more fragile than they are." She pulls the zipper of my hoodie up higher. "I think because you were such a teeny tiny baby that we've always been overprotective of you. He's just... abrasive."

"He's like a cheese grater, Mom. Please don't let him be mean to Lyric while she's here. She's not used to condescending remarks being made at her. She's so happy right now to have her father in her life, I don't want Dad making her feel like Blue's a bad person or that she's some kind of mistake."

"I promise you, he won't. He's always nice to her. Do you really think I'd let my granddaughter be uncomfortable here or that I'd let him hurt her feelings? I love her just like I love you. I'll have a talk with him tomorrow about all of this. Don't worry."

"I wish he'd just let it go. It's been almost nine years, Mom. And you know what? Regardless of how I met Blue and how he was living at the time, I loved him and he loved me. We may not have had a conventional relationship, but Lyric was conceived out of love. We *still* love each other."

She nods. "I know that. And for what it's worth, I hope you can find happiness with him if that's what you want. It must count for something that you two have never forgotten each other."

I kiss her cheek, grateful that her and I have been getting along better recently. "I hope it does. Thanks, Mom. I'll see you next week with Lyric."

As I back out of the driveway she waves at me from the door. One of No Tomorrow's songs is playing on the radio.

So many nights, my heart bled for you
These veins begging to be slit
I'll hold the blade and you hold my hand
Together we'll end it all, and I'll take the fall
Ladybug, ladybug, fly far far away
Come back to me some other day

When the skies are blue and the darkness fades
Maybe we'll find some other way....

The accompanying bass is deep, thumping like a heartbeat, reverberating through the speakers and vibrating into my chest. Blue's voice wavers and drifts off at the last line, and it gives me chills.

What goes through your head, Blue?

CHAPTER THIRTY-NINE

PIPER

First class.

That was my first clue that I was entering Blue's new world—a world I know nothing about other than what I've seen online.

He insisted on making all my travel arrangements for me, including paying for everything. I fought him at first because I wanted to be a strong, independent woman.

I lost that battle. Right now as I'm sitting on the plane in a seat that four of me could fit into, I'm glad.

First class is amazing. No strangers squished up around me on all sides, coughing and talking. No bathroom line. No teeny tiny aisle.

The flight attendant brought me a hot fudge sundae. It's like she just magically knew I love ice cream.

I even took a nap, completely undisturbed, under a nice soft blanket.

Blue promised he would treat me like a princess and right now, I'm feeling like one.

My heart nearly stops when I see him waiting for me at the baggage claim area. He looks like a whole lot of sexy bad boy wearing faded jeans with ripped knees, untied combat boots, and a long-sleeved black shirt unbuttoned all the way down to the top pack of his six-pack abs.

His long hair hangs in tousled waves over his shoulders and down the middle of his back. Several leather corded necklaces with crosses, feathers, and stones hang from his neck.

He smiles when he sees me, and pushes his mirrored sunglasses up to the top of his head.

Last year I read an interview on the internet accusing him of wearing mirrored sunglasses to hide his blood-shot, stoned eyes. At the time he replied, "I wear them so people can see themselves and not me." I wonder why Blue wants to hide from people. Not let them in to meet the man behind the words and the music. Thankfully, he lets *me* in. Most of the time, anyway.

Capturing my face in both his hands, he backs me up against the wall near the luggage conveyer and kisses me like he's going to do me right in the middle of the baggage claim area. I'm breathless and frazzled when he pulls away.

"I missed you," he says, his head still bent close to mine.

I take a deep breath. "I missed you, too."

It's been two weeks since he last visited us in New Hampshire, but it's felt like an eternity.

"How was your flight?"

"Awesome. Thank you for getting me a first-class ticket. It was so comfortable and quiet."

He grins. "I'm going to like spoiling you, Ladybug."

"You don't have to spoil me."

"You waited forever for me to get my shit together, babe. You deserve to be spoiled."

I run my fingertip over the leather cord of one of his necklaces. "I only want you."

"I know." He winks at me and grabs my hand, lacing our fingers. "Let's go get your bags and get out of here."

I only have one large suitcase, which we find quickly, and then we maneuver our way through the busy terminal to the exit.

"Oh my God!" a girl suddenly shrieks, jumping right in front of us. "You're Blue from No Tomorrow! Holy shit!" Her friend has joined her, and they're now jumping up and down in front of us like Mexican jumping beans.

"We've been to almost all your concerts!" the second jumper says. "Can we get your autograph?"

"Sure." He gives my hand a squeeze before he lets go to take a marker that one of the girls has whipped out of her purse.

"Can you sign my shirt?" she squeals.

"I'll sign the back," he offers.

"Mine too!"

I watch with a smile as he signs their shirts and answers their questions about his next tour.

"Are you his actual girlfriend?" the first jumper asks.

I stammer for a few seconds, because I have no idea what I actually am or what he wants the public to know.

"She is," Blue answers, surprising me just as much as the two fans.

"Oh my God I am soooooooooooo jealous," she says. "Of course you're like twenty-one, right? I guess it's true rock stars only date young model chicks."

"Um, I'm thirty," I reply.

Both the girls' mouths fall open. "Get out! There's no way you're thirty!"

"I really am."

Blue puts his arm around me and kisses the top of my head. "She really is. We've been together for like almost ten years."

Their mouths gape wider. I think I'm gaping, too. "Shit, that's crazy. You are soooo lucky."

I try not to laugh. "Thanks."

"We really gotta roll. Thanks for saying hi to us," Blue says, steering us away from them.

"Wow," I say when we're a few feet away. "My first fan experience. Does that happen a lot?"

"Yeah. You handled it great."

"They were cute."

"They aren't always that nice."

"You told them we've been together for almost ten years. That's not exactly true." We've been apart more than we've been together.

He looks down at me with a crooked smile as we exit the airport. "Yeah it is, babe."

I guess he's right. There are different degrees of being together.

"I wish Lyric was here too. How's she doing?"

"She's great. Staying with my parents. She brought her harp with her so she can practice every day."

"She played for me over the phone the other night. She's playing music by ear. Did you know that?"

"Yeah. Her teacher is really impressed."

"Our kid is kickass." He lights up a cigarette and leads me across the parking garage to a souped-up, black muscle car with wide back tires and a spoiler in the hood. He unlocks the door and throws my suitcase in the back, then holds the passenger-side door open for me.

"This is your car?"

"Well, I ain't stealin' it. Hell yeah, it's mine. 1969 Mustang, babe. The hottest car on the fucking planet."

Damn. Blue traded in walking for a car as hot as he is.

"Do you like it?" he asks when we're both inside. I nod as he puts the key in the ignition and the engine roars to life.

"It's beautiful."

He runs his hand over the steering wheel. "It's the first car I've ever owned. I've wanted this exact car since I was twelve years old."

"And now you have it," I reply, smiling with pride.

"You wanna drive?"

I quickly shake my head. "God, no. I've never driven anything this nice or fast before."

"You're not gonna crash it. I trust you."

"I don't know how to drive a stick."

"I'll teach you."

"Right now?"

"Yeah."

I have visions of seizing up his transmission before I even make it out of the parking lot. "Maybe another time," I say. "I'd rather you drive."

"Okay. You're off the hook for now. Are you hungry? Do you want to grab a bite to eat?"

"I'm not really hungry yet. I ate something on the plane." Something meaning two ice cream sundaes.

"You mind going to my place? You can call Lyric, let her know you're here."

"That'd be great."

After some debate, I decided I'd stay at his place rather than at a hotel because I want to spend as much time as possible with him while I can. Now that I'm here, I feel a mix of excitement and nerves. We've never spent more than two nights in a row together, and now I'm going to be staying with him for a week. As much as I feel like I know him, it's like dating someone new. Our relationship has never progressed to the intimacy of sharing space and it could very well reveal things we might not like about each other.

"You okay?" he asks, turning the car onto the busy highway.

I glance over at him. "Yeah."

He lowers his sunglasses back over his eyes. "This is why I wanted you to come here. I'm not the guy in the shed or the voice on the other end of the phone anymore."

"I know. But you're still you. Right?"

"There's a lot of versions of me, Piper. Take your pick."

"Okay," I say skeptically.

He moves his hand from the leather shifter knob to my leg. "Hey. I've been fucked up for a long time. High, drunk, sober, poor, rich. You name it, I've fuckin' been it."

"I know. And I loved all those versions of you, but I *like* you the most when you're not all messed up."

"Don't worry, babe. I'm not falling off the wagon."

I hope not.

"Good."

"So I guess...." He moves the car into the fast lane. "Now we gotta figure out if you like me like this."

"Like this?"

"Yeah. With cars and money and autographs and traveling and stress and interviews and all that shit."

"That's not you, Blue. That's just what you do and what you have. You're still the same guy who makes me feel like I'm the only girl in the world."

"There are other girls out there?" he teases.

"Nope. None."

"You're the only one in *my* world, babe, and I'm gonna try like hell to make you want to stay in it."

Does he have any idea what it feels like—to be told I'm the only one? *Nope.* I think he's utterly clueless to the fact he gives me butterflies, makes me dizzy and breathless, makes my panties get wet. Without even trying.

"I don't want you to try. Just be you. That's all."

"That's what I'm trying to say, Piper. I've been up and down so many times, for so long, I don't know who the fuck I am anymore. I don't know what I'm doing. I just know I don't want to fuck this all up."

Why, oh why, is vulnerability so attractive?

"We'll be okay," I say softly. "It's new for both of us, right? We just take it one day at a time and see what comes natural. No trying, no stressing."

Nodding, he pulls his cigarettes out of his pocket and lights one up.

I see the shaking of his hand, the rise and fall of his chest as he takes deep breaths.

And then he flashes me his smile, and I see my own smile reflected in his sunglasses, and I forget everything else.

Blue told me a while back he and Reece moved out of their condo into a rented house because they wanted more privacy and garage space. I was expecting a basic two-story house with a three-car garage and a pile of dishes in the sink, laundry sitting in places it shouldn't be, guitars on the coffee table, and a huge drum set in the basement.

That's what the rock star bachelor pad looked like in my head.

In reality, it's a small mansion on approximately two acres of lush grass, right on the water. The state of the inside remains to be seen, but the outside is impeccable.

"Wow," I say when he parks the car in the driveway in front of a six-car garage. "You didn't tell me you live in such a—"

"House?" he interrupts. "Pretty fucked up, huh?"

"No, it's just—"

"Monolithic?"

I laugh. "Yeah." I peer up at the looming house.

We climb out of the car together and he retrieves my suitcase from the back seat, then comes around to stand next to me.

"Reece picked it out. He comes from money so he's gotta have the best of the best of the best. Me? I don't need all this. You know me..." He grins sheepishly.

I do. This guy used to sleep on the ground under a bridge with nothing but his duffel bag for a pillow and a solar lantern for light.

"How many cars do you have?"

"Just this one. And a Harley. I've only had time to ride it twice, though. Reece wanted all this garage space for his two cars and a hot rod he's restoring."

"Nice."

He nods off toward the edge of the property. "Later we'll go for a walk by the water. Every time I walk out there I wish you and Acorn were with me. The sunset over the water is incredible."

I follow him to the front door and he leads me into a foyer with a wrought-iron chandelier hanging high above. A wide staircase curves up to the second floor, and the main floor splits from the foyer. The walls are a very pale cream—not quite white as Blue described them— the tile floor just a few shades darker. The furnishings—at least what I can see—are a deep mahogany wood, the accents black metal. Strong and masculine, yet just enough softness to have its own elegance.

I like it.

"It's beautiful."

He smiles and puts my suitcase down. "You don't have to whisper, babe."

I'm not sure why I am.

"C'mon." He takes my hand and tugs me to the right archway, which opens up to a huge living room with a black leather u-shaped couch that looks like it could fit fifteen people. A matching, but much smaller, love seat sits in front of a wall of glass that overlooks a flower garden. Leather pub chairs in both black and white are placed strategically around the room along with dark accent tables, lamps, and statues. I feel like I've walked into one of those homes they showcase on houses of the rich and famous.

"Hey, you made it."

The decor has me so entranced I didn't even see Reece lying on one end of the couch. His long black hair blends almost perfectly with the leather. He stands and crosses the room to pull me into a hug.

"I made it," I say. "It's nice to see you again."

"I was just gonna say the same. Make yourself at home. You need anything? Just yell and we'll get it for ya."

"Thank you."

"I'll show you upstairs, babe. You can put your things away."

I give Reece a little wave and follow Blue upstairs, past large matted photos of the band, mingled with articles and awards hanging on the walls.

Everything is so neat and clean. Not a dirty sock or empty bottle in sight. I'm impressed.

Blue takes me to a bedroom down the right wing of the second level and places my suitcase just inside the door.

"Reece and I each have a master bedroom and a guest room. His rooms are to the left of the stairs, mine are down here. I thought you could keep your things in this room. The closets and dressers are empty, and it has its own bathroom so you can put all your makeup and stuff out."

I scan the huge room, wondering if any other women have ever stayed in here to visit him.

"Thank you."

He snakes his arms around me and pulls me tight against his body. "I really don't want you sleeping in here, though."

"No?"

He presses his lips to mine and slides his hands down to squeeze my ass through my jeans. "No. You always wanted me to have a bed. Now I've got one and your sweet little ass better be in it every night."

I go up on my tiptoes, wrap my arms around his neck, and smile up at him. "I can't wait to be in your bed. Maybe I can beg for your autograph," I tease.

"You want to role play, Ladybug?" His husky voice gets my pulse going. "I'll write my name on every inch of you and then make you scream it when I'm pounding into you."

"Ooh."

He picks me up in his arms like a new groom on his honeymoon and carries me down the hall to the last bedroom, kicking the door shut behind him.

"This one is mine. Now that you've teased me, I don't think I'm letting you out anytime soon."

I tighten my arms around his neck. "I never tease you."

He throws me onto the bed and falls on top of me, pushing my legs apart with his and pinning my hands above my head with one of his.

"Tell me about the tattoo," I ask as he moves his lips across the skin revealed in the V-neck of my T-shirt.

He lifts his head and shakes his hair out of his face. "Which one?"

"The ladybug on your hand."

A grin graces his lips. "When did you see that?"

"Years ago. At the hotel. I just never remembered to ask you about it."

Lifting his hand, he turns his wrist so I can see the tiny tattoo again. It's almost exactly like my own, only his is surrounded by the rest of his sleeve design. I'm not even sure how I noticed it that day.

"I got it a few months after I left. I wanted something to remind me of you. I told you the myth was true, didn't I?"

"You did."

"Do you believe it now?"

"I've always believed it."

He dips his head down again and presses his warm lips against my neck. "We should get married."

My breath catches in my throat, right beneath that sensitive spot his mouth is covering.

"Wh-what?"

"Me and you," he whispers, nudging the fabric of my shirt away with his face and dragging his lips to my collarbone.

I am utterly, without any doubt, shocked speechless. I raise my hand and touch his head, threading my fingers in his hair as he continues kissing me like he didn't just drop a huge bomb on me.

My brain fights through the tremors spreading through my body from his touch.

"Blue...do you have any idea what you just said?"

"Mmm," he hums, lifting my shirt and kissing my breast through the thin white lace of my bra.

"Evan?" This is a conversation that might require his real name.

Finally he looks up at me, his blue eyes smoldering. "I fucked this all up, didn't I?"

"I guess it depends on what *this* is."

"This is me trying to tell you I want to be with you forever."

I sift his hair through my fingers and search his face. "You used to be afraid of forever."

"You're right. I'm not anymore. Now I'm afraid of not having it."

"So am I. You kinda kept taking my hopes for a happily ever after away."

His jaw muscles twitch. "I'm trying to give it back."

"I know," I say softly. "And I love it so much. I just think we have to take things slow."

I hate saying those words. The last thing I want to do is take things slow. I want everything *now*—Him. Happiness. A wedding. My own family, together. I want it now before he changes his mind or something happens to take it all away.

He nods but says nothing. Just moves his fingers lightly up and down my ribcage and the curve of my waist.

"And I think you're not supposed to make any real big life decisions during your first year or so of being clean. Right?"

"Someone's been reading," he accuses, then moves his attention to the dip between my breasts. He slides his tongue over my goose-bump pebbled flesh.

"I have," I admit. "I want to understand, and help you, that's all."

"I know you do, babe. That's why I'm gonna be chasing you down with a ring in a few months." He leans up on his elbows, looking down at me with his notorious sexy smirk. "So you better take off running, or be prepared to get caught and have a diamond as big as an ice cube on your hand."

I laugh and he covers my mouth with his, capturing my laughter. Swallowing it. He grinds his hips into mine as he slowly pulls my clothes off. When I'm naked and lying in the middle of his bed on the slate gray comforter, he reaches into his nightstand and pulls out a pen. He twirls it in his fingers like an expert drummer.

"About that autograph..." he chides.

Staring up at him, I reach for his shirt, seductively undo the remaining buttons, then run my fingertips over his abs.

"I'm your biggest fan," I coo. "I know the words to all your songs."

He scrunches up his face, trying not to laugh. "I bet you do."

"Can I get your autograph?" I bat my eyelashes.

"Only if it's on your breasts."

This time it's me who tries not to burst into giggles.

"Oh my God. That would be soooo amazing."

He pulls the pen cap off with his mouth and spits it out onto the floor, then cups my breast in his hand, bending down to place a soft wet kiss on the tip before signing his name across my pale skin. I could've sworn I've always seen him write with his left hand, but he signs me with this right.

"I'll never wash it off," I say, twisting my body beneath his and rubbing myself against his thighs.

"You better not." He stands and tosses the pen onto his nightstand, then pulls his shirt off, throwing it onto the floor. My stomach still does a somersault every time I see him shirtless—or even better—when I see him totally undressed. While I appreciate a nice body, I've never really been the type to get all drooly over bodybuilders, movie stars, or hot naked men. But when it comes to Blue—there's just something so sensual about the confident way he moves and how his hair flows over his broad chest and shoulders like a Viking. The tattoos covering almost every inch of him are the icing on the cake and it all sets off sparks of desire in me.

"Do you bring a lot of women back here?" I ask, still using the sugary role-playing voice, but asking for myself.

He steps out of his boots and watches me watch him unbutton his jeans. They're my favorite on him. No zipper. Just five silver buttons. The jeans are worn and soft and fit him like he was born in them.

"Hundreds," he replies. "They're all buried in the backyard."

I laugh as he climbs onto the bed and between my legs.

"Do you like my room?" he asks. "And my house?"

"So far I've only mostly seen the ceiling of your room," I tease, leaning up to peer around. His room is like the others in the house I've seen so far. Neat. Clean. Four guitars stand in a row in front of the windows that overlook the front yard. Black and white paintings of birds hang on the walls. Several photos in silver frames sit atop one of his black dressers, and as I squint at them, I realize they're photos of me, Lyric, and Acorn.

"You have our pictures," I say softly.

"Yeah. I print all the ones you email me. When I feel like I might fuck up again, I look at the pictures. There've been nights when I've sat here for hours just staring at your picture, waiting for the demons to fuck off and leave me alone."

A vision of him flashes in my mind—sitting on the floor, taunted by drugs and alcohol and staring at photos of me, his daughter, and his dog while he sweats and struggles between all the things he loves and wants the most.

I swallow over the unexpected lump in my throat. "Does that work?"

"So far."

I don't know if it's good or bad that I've been both his muse and his therapy. I suppose some might say that's obsession and not real love. Some might say what we have is dependency and codependency. I wonder if it matters. Maybe all that really matters is that we make a difference in another's person life in the way they need it.

CHAPTER FORTY

PIPER

I smile at the note he left on his pillow for me. He's been incredibly sweet since I arrived yesterday. Dare I say romantic in many ways?

After I make his bed I find my clothes from last night and hold them against my body as I sprint down the hall to my room. I take the note with me and stash it in my purse so I can add it to all the others I have saved at home.

I shower and blow dry my hair, then pretty myself up with a little makeup. I'm not sure what Blue's got planned for us today, so I dress casually in skinny jeans, low black boots, and a purple gypsy top with wide butterfly sleeves.

The happy, carefree feeling I've had since I woke up takes a slight nose dive when I find him in the kitchen. I frown in confusion at the scene of disarray around me. The countertops are covered with glasses, mugs, bowls and dishes. All the cabinet doors are wide open, showing the bare shelves. Blue is standing at the center island, looking quite boyish and young in a band T-shirt with the sleeves cut off, black sweatpants, and black and white high-top sneakers with the laces untied.

I observe him quietly from the doorway. A niggle of worry burns my stomach. His eyes are darting from one piece of glassware to the next. He touches each one, lifts it up to the light to examine it, then places it with a different group of glasses or dishes.

"Hey, you." My voice comes out louder than I intended.

He looks up and smiles crookedly.

"Oh. Hey." He runs his hand through his hair.

I move to stand on the other side of the island. "I thought you were making breakfast?"

He nods quickly. "I am. I was. But when I took out the coffee mugs, they didn't match. And I hate that."

"They don't have to match, hon. I'm good with anything."

He moves a few salad bowls around, then stacks them within each other.

"No, they should match."

Reece appears in the doorway, and rolls his eyes. "Fuck me. Not this again," he says.

Blue holds up a glass. "One of these is missing. There's an odd number. There's five."

Reece blows out an exasperated breath. "You dropped it when you were wasted last year, remember? You stepped in the broken glass and bled all over the place. Guess who cleaned it up?"

"I don't remember that." Blue doesn't look away from the glass he's inspecting.

"Because you were drunk off your ass." Reece plucks a beige coffee mug from the assortment on the counter. "Stop sorting all our shit, Blue."

"Sorting?" I repeat.

Reece fills the coffee maker with water and adds coffee grinds from a marble canister on the counter before he answers.

"Welcome to my world." He gestures toward Blue with his hand. "His OCD gets in an uproar and he starts to sort everything by size or shape or color or who the hell knows what. A few weeks ago it was the towels."

"We had *one* white towel and sixteen gray ones," Blue explains, shaking his head as if it's absurdity.

"What's wrong with one white towel?" I'm almost afraid to hear the answer.

"It's just...unbalanced."

Reece and I exchange a glance. He leans against the counter and shakes his head as Blue continues explaining.

"Everything was a fucking mess in the cabinets. The glasses were mixed with the coffee mugs, the salad bowls were mixed up with the ice cream bowls. The tall glasses were in the front, the short ones in the back. Why can't you just put things back where they belong?"

His roommate shrugs. "Because it doesn't bother me, bro. I've got more important shit on my mind than to worry about stacking things by color and shape. We have a maid, tell her to do it."

"Does it really bother you that much, Blue?" I ask.

He looks at me with apology in his eyes. Like a little boy caught doing something he didn't want anyone to see. "Not *all* the time. But I wanted things to be nice for you. Mismatched mugs make us look fucked up. I'm not fucked up anymore."

"She knows we're not a resort, man. She doesn't give a shit about mugs." He turns to me. "Do you?"

"No... of course not. But I can understand why he wants things to be nice."

He's trying to impress me, that's all. He used to have nothing, now he has things and he wants it all nice. I don't see any harm in that. And I absolutely hate when I have a mismatched number of socks. Where do the missing socks go? And why do they never resurface? It's no big deal if Blue feels that way about other household items.

"I'll help you put all this away," I say. "Then we can have breakfast. I'm starving."

He chews the inside of his lip and glances at all the items spread out over the counter. A moment ago he seemed so determined to tackle this self-imposed task, but now he appears overwhelmed.

"I'm going to go have a smoke first," he says. "I'll be right back."

I nod and watch him go out into the backyard through the French doors in the adjoining dining room.

"Does he do this a lot?" I ask Reece.

"Not really. It's been worse since he stopped smoking weed. I think that used to calm him down."

"It's good that he quit, though. I'm proud of him."

"I am too. It's a bad scene when he uses and I've battled with him over it for years. I think he's just got some anxiety issues and without the drugs to calm it down, he gets a little batshit."

"He's okay, though, right?" I start to put the glasses back in the cabinet, hoping I'm putting them back the way Blue wants them.

Reece sips his coffee. "Seriously? He's brilliant. He's better than he's ever been. The new material he's been writing kicks ass. And he's actually living life now. He wants you and his daughter to be part of his life. That's a big thing for him, to let people get close. I think he just needs to find some balance and figure out how to deal with stress without using drugs and alcohol to fix all his problems."

"Maybe he should be on some meds for anxiety? I used to take Xanax when I was younger when my boss was a total bitch to me and stressing me out all day. It helped."

He looks skeptical. "I don't think he should take anything like that. He has addictive tendencies."

"Oh." I'm grateful his friend knows so much about him. Things I have no way of knowing. "I didn't think of that. I'm glad he's got you to look out for him. It means a lot."

"We look out for each other. He's not just my roomie and bandmate, he's family." He grabs a stack of bowls and places them in one of the cabinets. "That makes you family now, too, since it's pretty obvious he's keeping you around if you let him."

That's music to my ears. "I'm definitely sticking around no matter what."

Blue comes back into the room at that exact moment. "You two talking about my fucked-up obsessions?"

"No," I say with a smile. I touch his shoulder and crane my head up to kiss his cheek. "We're talking about how amazing you are." I hold up two matching black stoneware mugs. "Look. They match."

Coffee, bagels, and donuts have always been Blue's and my usual breakfast together. Not just because it's cheap, easy to get, and yummy. But also because we haven't spent many mornings together. And when we did, there were very few times we had a kitchen available to us.

Suffice to say, I didn't know Blue liked to cook, or that he's any good at it. But he is.

Sorting of dishes and glasses aside, he's a master in the kitchen. I watch him with a mix of pride and amusement from the table where Reece and I sit as Blue cracks eggs perfectly with one hand, whips up pancake batter from scratch, and fries sausage and ham. He puts a plate piled high in front of me that could easily rival what I'd get at a popular pancake house—complete with whipped butter and sliced strawberries.

I blink at it, wondering how on earth I can possibly eat all this.

"I had no idea you could cook."

"This is what happens when you're high all night, have nothing to do, and get the munchies," Reece says.

Blue puts a plate of food in front of Reece and laughs. "That's sad but true. I cooked, and Reece and whoever else was crashing at our place would eat everything I made. I'd watch those cooking shows on TV for hours." He sits next to me and winks at me. "You're finally seeing all my hidden talents."

Reece nods and swallows. "I'd rather not hear your hidden talents again tonight, man. I could hear you guys all the way from my wing."

My face heats with embarrassment. "I'm so sorry...."

Blue laughs. "Don't be sorry, he's just jealous. And payback's a bitch. How many times have I had to listen to your chicks yowling like cats all night?" He points his fork at Reece, who leans back in his chair and laughs.

"Yowling?" I repeat, cutting into my second pancake, which is surprisingly delicious and fluffy, flavored with a hint of vanilla. "Please tell me *I* don't yowl." I'll die of embarrassment if I'm considered a yowler in the bedroom.

"You are definitely not a yowler, babe."

When I first arrived, I thought hanging out with two rock stars would be uncomfortable and noisy—like staying with two teenagers. I envisioned Reece having various girlfriends in and out of the house and his bedroom. I expected the rest of the band and their friends and fans to be partying by the pool. I guess I watched too many music videos and let my imagination go wild, because Blue and Reece act just like two regular guys.

After breakfast we video chat with Lyric, and my mother stands in the background behind Lyric, trying to get a low-key glimpse of Blue. Lyric tells us she's been practicing her harp every day, and that my father told her he's never heard anything so beautiful in his life.

That gives me hope. Maybe my father will learn to accept Blue and me as a couple in time.

Later, Blue takes me for a drive to show me his favorite local attractions. We cruise with the windows open, rock music blasting, our hair blowing in the wind. He holds my hand and he kisses me into a frenzy at almost every red light. I feel like we're teenagers, enjoying young innocent love together for the first time, rather than two thirty-something-year-olds who've shared almost a decade of dysfunction and heartache with each other.

Maybe I'm crazy, but I think we're finally, *finally*, getting our new beginning.

After dinner we go for a walk along the water and sit on the rocks. We kiss with the sun setting and the sound of the water lapping the shore behind us.

"We should get a puppy together," he suggests, pulling me between his legs so my back rests against his chest. "We can go to the shelter and adopt the one with the saddest eyes and do whatever we can to make him the happiest."

My heart clenches at the sweetness and pure empathy of that idea.

"I've been thinking about a puppy. Lyric has been asking if we can get one."

"Then we should."

He puts his arms around me from behind and hugs me close. Hundreds of times I've read in romance books about feeling love pouring out of someone, and now, in his arms, I feel exactly that. It's even better than I fantasized it would be.

"I wish we could but that would be really hard with all the traveling you do, and me living back in New Hampshire...."

"Maybe we could sorta live together."

He says the word *sorta* like he's tap dancing around how I might react to the idea. Or maybe he's still getting used to such thoughts living in his own head, like new tenants who might either trash or cherish his space.

"Where?" I ask.

"I don't know...you could live here, or I could stay at your place sometimes. If you want me to."

In the past forty-eight hours he's brought up marriage, living together, and adopting a puppy.

I want all of that with him. It's everything I've always dreamed of and wished we could have together.

It's also everything he's always been scared of and avoided. Things I let go of, to give him the space and freedom he needed.

Now I don't know what to believe... or what feelings to trust.

Is he finally ready to move forward with our relationship? Has the absence of drugs and alcohol cleared his mind and made room for love and happiness with me?

Or is he mourning the loss of his other chemical loves and filling the void left by them?

I feel like we're walking a very fine line between what could be recovery and distraction for him, and I'm petrified of getting caught on the wrong side. My biggest fear is him making all these promises to me now, when he's at the very beginning of a sober life, only to realize later he doesn't really want those things.

That would completely crush and devastate me. My heart would be broken beyond repair.

He nudges his face behind my hair and touches his warm lips to my neck, inhaling deeply as he does so. "Think about it. That's all I'm asking," he says. "I love you, Piper. I promised you someday I'd make you the happiest woman alive. I'm not gonna give up until I make it happen."

I lean back against the comfort of his body, close my eyes, and try to believe in happiness.

CHAPTER FORTY-ONE

PIPER

"Stay another week."

He wraps his arm around me under the blanket, buries his face into the curve of my neck, and pulls me closer. Like magnets, our bodies are drawn together, his hard cock pressing against my ass.

"I wish I could." I close my eyes against the morning sun shining through his bedroom windows. I want to slip back into that sleepy dreamy place with him and avoid flying back home later today.

"You can." His voice is sleepy, his skin warm, his lips wet. Waking up to him is like waking up to Christmas morning every day. He's full of kisses, teasing touches, and sweet, sexy words.

"I have to go back to work. And I've never been away from Lyric for this long. I miss her, and she misses me."

He slides his hand slowly to my hip and grinds his cock harder against my ass. "You can work for me." He moves his lips to my shoulder, dragging the ball of his metal piercing across my skin. "Go get Lyric and Archie and bring them back here."

His kisses send shivers racing up my spine. "Mmmm...." I moan, arching into him, loving how his bare chest feels against my back, so warm and solid.

"I'm serious."

"I know you are, hon. I don't want to leave you. Ever."

Just the thought of not seeing him every day brings a lump into my throat. Everything has been so good between us. So perfect and even and normal.

Except for yesterday when he suddenly said he had to go out for a while and then disappeared for a few hours. After being practically glued at the hip all week, it upset me that he took off with zero explanation and didn't ask me to join him.

He took the car, so he wasn't doing one of his walks.

I worried he went out to get high, but he came back clear-eyed. He wasn't stumbling or slurring. He wasn't jumpy or moody. I wondered if he had just had enough of me and needed a break.

After Blue left, Reece watched me pace in front of the wall of glass in the living room, all while texting madly on his phone and telling me to chill out and not worry.

I wasn't chilled and I did worry.

It was hard to not interrogate him when he returned, but I kept all my questions inside. Not just because I didn't want to be a nosy, demanding, clingy girlfriend, but because I didn't want him to think he couldn't leave the house alone without me thinking he was going on a drug run.

My trust and faith in him is vital—not just for his recovery, but for our relationship and our future together.

And for me. I can't have an anxiety attack every time he leaves the house alone.

"Maybe I can convince you to stay…."

He rolls me onto my back , climbs on top of me, and kisses my mouth, deep and lazy. The kind of kiss that's made for mornings that don't have to end.

"What if I promise you amazing sex every day?" He moves his lips to my chin, then down to the hollow of my throat, pausing to suck my flesh between his lips. "Would that make you stay?"

I wrap my hands in his hair and arch my neck back. "That's very tempting."

He licks a trail down between my breasts, his hair tickling me as he descends. "And pancakes every day, too."

"Mmm…pancakes."

He looks up with a wicked grin on his face, his chin resting on my chest. "I think maybe pancakes turn you on more than I do."

Laughing, I pull his face up to mine, my hands still tangled in his thick hair, and plant a kiss on his lips.

"Your pancakes are amazing, but they don't come close to what you do to me."

"Show me."

It drives me wild how when we're intimate his voice changes to a tone used just for me. It's not the same voice he uses on stage—the voice millions have heard and love. This deep, husky, sensual version of his voice is mine only.

I reach down between us and slip his hard cock into my hand, palming the slippery tip. Groaning, he slides one hand under my body, cupping my ass and pulling my body up to his. My thighs are spread wide around him, and I guide him between my slick lips.

"Fuck me, baby. Take all of it."

I move my hands down to his hips and ride his cock from below, thrusting up to take him deep, then sliding myself down to the tip. He's completely still, eyes closed, his tongue at the edge of his parted lips, his hair hanging down over my breasts. He's breathtaking, so lost in us. The sight of him drives me wild, makes me even wetter with desire for him.

Sitting back on his heels, he pulls me up to straddle his lap and holds me up in his arms, rocking me back and forth on him. I hang onto his shoulders and kiss him hungrily. I love our size and strength difference; the way he can lift and move me with his arms like I'm a doll turns me on like mad.

He thrusts deep inside me and catches my whimper with his lips. Slowing, he gently grinds my body into his. My clit rubs against him in just the right place, my body clenches around him, and we explode together, our bodies slippery with sweat, our mouths never parting.

"That was definitely better than pancakes," I say breathlessly.

After a long shower together, we have breakfast on the back patio while hummingbirds flit around his flower garden. He excuses himself to take a call from his manager, and I go up to the guest room to pack my things. I'm leaving with more than I came with, because Blue took me out to dinner twice to fancy restaurants and insisted on taking me shopping beforehand for sexy dresses. One black, and one red—just like the one I wore that night years ago. He's also sending me home with some of his band apparel—a hoodie, a T-shirt, black thong panties, and my very favorite item—a T-shirt he wore yesterday that still smells like him. Weird? Yes. But comforting to have with me at home when I'm aching for him.

I've missed Lyric like crazy this week and I can't wait to see her, but I'm dreading leaving Blue. I feel like my heart is being torn in two, not being able to be with both of them. His schedule is going to be packed for the next few months, so we're going to have to rely on phone calls, emails, and the occasional weekend together until he settles down.

Rock star dating life, Reece said yesterday. *The true test of patience and trust.*

I'm the Queen of Patience. Perhaps the Jester of Trust. But I'm trying.

"You packed?" Blue's in the doorway, eyeing my suitcase on the bed.

"Yeah."

"But your flight isn't until tonight."

"I know, I just wanted to get it done."

He takes a deep breath. Clicks his piercing.

"I wanted more time."

"I do, too." I smile, but inside I'm crying. I'm already missing the groove of comfort we slipped into together. Breakfasts, walks, long talks in bed that stretched into the early morning. Romantic dinners, rocking out in his car. The mind-blowing sex. Him playing the guitar just for me.

He's my very own everything.

He crosses the room, leans his head against the window frame, and stares outside.

"We'll see each other soon. And Lyric, too," I say to his back.

"I know."

I go to him and put my hand on his arm. I touch my lips to his shoulder and let them linger against the warmth of his skin.

"Blue? You okay?"

He nods and turns to face me.

"Yeah. I just feel…off."

"Off?"

"The things that used to scare me? Now they're all I want. All I can think about. And I feel like I get a taste, and then it's gone."

A twitch of anxiety stirs in my chest. "Do you mean me? Us?"

"Yes. I love the band but it pulls me in so many different directions." He taps his head with his finger. "My mind spins all fucking around with everything."

I nod and push back the anxiety building in me. "First, I'm not gone. I'm here, with you, even when we're apart. And second, I know it's a lot of pressure but I think you just have to try to tackle one thing at a time." I feel helpless attempting to give advice. I know nothing about what goes on in his band and on tour and all the behind-the-scenes things that he must deal with.

"I guess I want to be in two places at once and I can't. And everyone else wants me to be in twenty places at once. I like you sleeping with me every night. I like the steadiness of the day with you. I feel content. At peace, like my aunt said the feather would bring. You're the only thing that's ever made me feel that way and I'm afraid without you I'm going to get jumbled up."

Jumbled up.

I want to be the parachute—the thing that will gently glide him safely through life. I could quit my job, homeschool Lyric, and travel with Blue to all the places the band takes him. It would be a different life for us but it might be exciting. Lyric and I could see the world. I could be there for him, night and day, to give him the peace he needs. I could keep him unjumbled and straight.

I swallow hard, ingesting the craziness that tried to fly out of my mouth and become a very unrealistic reality.

I can't uproot my daughter and my life right now. Someday... I would love to. When I know that Blue can promise us the same security and commitment we can give him.

I want nothing more than to support him and be his rock when he needs me. I always will be. But it has to be equal, or at least close to it. I need him to get there on his own.

"We can talk every day," I promise. "And video chat. Everything we have still remains even if we're not physically together, right? Hasn't it always?"

"Yes. Always."

"Then we'll be okay." I reach for his hand and I'm met with his— clammy and shaking.

His eyes are dark and intense, the smile I've gotten used to seeing this week is gone. "I don't want to lose you, Piper. I want to do everything right and I don't know how. I'm afraid I'm gonna screw everything up. Like I always do."

"You won't. You've been perfect. I've never been happier. You don't have to worry about anything." I squeeze his hand tighter.

"Do you think it'll last? With me being all over the place?"

I want it to. *More than anything.* But if we last depends on him.

I can't say that to him, though.

And I'm not sure if by *all over the place* he means as in traveling, or as in his *mind*.

"I hope so. That's all I want."

He looks uneasy. Worried. Lost in the forest of his thoughts again.

"I may have sorta fucked up," he finally says. He stares at the floor, avoiding me.

Please no. Not again.

My heart plummets then gallops rapidly like a horse trying to climb out of quicksand. I struggle to breathe calmly.

"Wh-what do you mean?"

He rubs his palm across his forehead. "Yesterday... I did something that maybe I shouldn't have done."

Shit.

"Did you go buy drugs? I had a bad feeling when you left. It was so abrupt, and you didn't tell me where you were going, you didn't invite me to come." I shake my head. "I just don't understand."

His face contorts with disbelief. "What? No." He pulls away and takes a few steps away from me. "Fuck, Piper. Is that what you thought?" he asks when he spins back around.

"I'm sorry, Blue, but yeah, it kinda crossed my mind. And now you're acting all weird."

"I didn't go buy drugs. I'm totally clean. And I'm not acting weird, I'm fucking nervous."

"What are you nervous about?"

He shoves his hand into his front pocket and comes out with a tiny royal blue velvet box. "This."

I stare at it in his hand as my heartbeats accelerate to warp speed.

"I don't know how to do this. I know I'm supposed to plan a big mind-blowing fucking moment. And I wanted to, babe. I really did. But the place I really wanted to do it is too far away. So now I just feel like I fucked this up and it's going to be another disappointment from me that you're gonna have to live with."

Oh my God. Is he asking me to....

He snaps open the box. "A long time ago I promised to give you all the tomorrows I could. I know I'm not supposed to make any life decisions, but fuck that shit, I'm making this one because nothing is going to change it. I know we can't get married until I'm cool and prove I won't slip up. But until then I want you to have this, so you know I'm dead serious. So you know you're the one, you're it, you're my home." He takes a deep breath. "I'm sorry if I fucked this all up and it's not mind-blowing."

It *is* mind-blowing.

It's raw and unplanned and painfully honest and just so *him*.

I stare at the big sparkly stone surrounded by little tiny sparkly stones in a band of white gold.

It's beautiful. Every woman's dream ring.

And it comes with the promise of him—my dream man— and all the tomorrows.

With him.

I catapult myself into him. I throw my arms around him and climb him like a tree, wrapping my legs around him and smothering him with kisses.

"I love you so much," I whisper between kisses. "And my mind *is* totally blown."

He cradles the back of my head in his hand and kisses me, smiling against my lips.

The sexiest, most awesome, special smile in the world.

CHAPTER FORTY-TWO

PIPER

Lyric and I are enjoying a lazy, rainy Sunday morning together on the couch. I'm immersed in a new book with Archie on my lap, and she's clicking away on her laptop. Blue flew in late last night to stay with us for a few days before he has to meet up with the band for their next show. He looked utterly exhausted when we picked him up the airport, and he was sucking down Red Bull like water in an attempt to keep himself awake to talk to Lyric and me.

By the time we got home from the airport he was suffering from one of his horrible headaches. He crashed on the bed, but tossed and turned from all the adrenaline and caffeine in his system, so I gave him one of the Valiums I have for the occasional neck spasms I get. That seemed to calm him, and he finally fell asleep. I snuggled up to him all night while he slept, stroking his face and his hair, whispering how much I love him. As he slept, a tiny worry nagged at me about the medicine. I tried to remember what Reece and I had talked about and I wondered if I did the wrong thing by giving him anything at all. Wouldn't Blue know to tell me he couldn't take it, like he did in the past, if he thought he shouldn't? I slowly rubbed his tense back and shoulders, praying that no ill comes of my well-intentioned action. He's sleeping soundly and that's what he needs. I don't even care if he sleeps the entire time he's visiting as long as he gets to rest and feels loved.

"I want to show you something," Lyric says, opening her laptop lid. "Look at him." She turns the laptop sideways to show me an adoption page from a nearby pet rescue. The page is filled with photos of an adorable little brown and white fuzzy dog with one floppy ear and one straight ear, and big sad eyes. "Look at his little face, Mom. He looks like Acorn only younger and kinda sad. His profile said he was thrown out of a car. How could someone do that?" Her voice cracks and her bottom lip quivers with emotion. "He must feel so unwanted. He's too lonely now. Someone has to love him."

She is so much her father sometimes that it's scary.

I put down my e-reader and look closer at the photos. I read the detailed bio about the adorable dog that I know will probably be frolicking in our backyard this time tomorrow.

I think I want the lonely little dog just as much as my daughter does. Maybe even more.

"Can we go see him today, Mom? See if he's the one?"

"We'll ask Blue when he wakes up, okay? This is a decision we should make as a family."

Her face lights up. "He'll love him. I know he will." She closes her laptop. "I'm going to go play my harp for him while he's sleeping. He likes that."

My heart swells with love for her as she goes off to play soft relaxing melodies on her harp for her father. She and Blue have developed a strong emotional bond, and she has taken on an almost protective role when it comes to him. He's amazingly patient and nurturing with her, always making her feel special and supported no matter what. Not once has he wavered in his commitment to her—or to me—since we became a family.

It's as if having love in his life has turned Blue inside out, and the man I always believed was inside him, is now on the outside.

"Thanks, baby," he says when I join him on my small back porch with a cup of tea for each of us. He's doing something he doesn't get to do much of anymore—watching the misty rain fall.

"You look much better today." I gently push his damp hair from his face. Twelve hours of sleep and a hot shower has done wonders for him.

"I always feel better when I'm home with you guys. I'm just pissed I lost a night with you by sleeping so much."

"We didn't lose anything. I got to have my way with you all night while you slept," I tease.

"Figures," he grins and sips his tea. "I miss all the good stuff."

I wrap my hands around my warm mug. "Has Lyric talked to you yet?"

He nods slowly, a smile spreading across his face. "Yup. Hope it's okay I told her we'd all go over there in about an hour?"

I smile. "Of course. I think a dog would be good for all of us. She's been waiting a long time, but since it looks like we'll be staying here for a while since you guys added more dates to your tour, then I think we should just go for it. There's really no reason to wait."

"I promise after all this tour shit we'll get a bigger house together so all our stuff is one place. So we're all not going back and forth from here to Seattle all the time. I hate it."

"We don't mind at all. As long as we're together, that's all I care about."

A muscle in his jaw twitches. "I've given you guys nothing. First Josh gave you a home, then you got one on your own. Aren't I supposed to take care of you? Lyric's not a little kid anymore, she must see what a fucking loser I am when it comes to taking care of my own family."

I have no idea where this sudden negativity is coming from.

"Blue, she adores you. Her mind doesn't think that way. She worships you. How many daughters can sit and talk to their fathers for hours about music and art and poetry? How many write songs together? Who sings her to sleep when she doesn't feel good, even if you're thousands of miles away in a different time zone? That's all you."

He stares into his tea but doesn't say a word.

"She also gets to see how you treat *me*. How you open doors for me, and leave me love notes. How you cook for us. She sees how you always make time for us, no matter how busy and crazy you are with the band. She sees how you treat me with love and respect. She sees how you're always so friendly to your fans and you never blow them off. *That's* taking care of your family, Blue, and trust me, our daughter sees that. She knows her father isn't just some rock star. She knows you're an amazing person."

A tear glistens in the corner of his eye and even though it's just a tiny drop I feel as if we could both drown in it.

"That's all I ever want her to see, Piper." His voice is strained, as if it hurts him to speak the words. "I don't ever want her to see the other side of me."

Going to the pet shelter is a harrowing experience that I wasn't expecting. All these dogs in rows of pens, barking, yelping, jumping. They stare at us with their pleading eyes as we walk up and down the rows. Lyric's smile deteriorates with every step and she's clinging to Blue's hand with both of hers.

"Here he is," the volunteer announces, stopping in front of one of the cages. The dog is huddled in the corner in a ball, trying to make himself disappear. "He's been here for six months. He's very quiet, never barks. Doesn't play. He goes days without eating sometimes. He was a bit of a mess when he got here, he had a broken leg and was scraped up pretty bad, but he's all healed now. We have some really adorable, playful puppies if you're looking for a nice pet for your daughter. I have to be honest, this dog is depressed and probably won't make a good pet." She narrows her eyes at Blue and her forehead creases. "Do you know you look like that guy from that band?"

"Unlock the pen," Blue says, his eyes riveted to the dog. "Now, please."

The girl obliges, and Blue immediately enters the pen and slowly approaches the dog, who's watching him with wide, terrified eyes. Blue kneels down, whispering softly to him, and gently strokes his head. The dog stills under Blue's petting, as if he's holding his breath.

"He's so scared," Lyric whispers beside me, and I wonder if maybe this is a bad idea. Bringing a dog home is supposed to be a happy experience, not a total downer.

While still petting the dog, Blue reaches into his pocket and pulls out a few small pieces of food and offers them to the dog one by one, first coaxing the dog to stand, and then slowly leading the dog right into his lap.

Sliced roast beef.

He must have taken it from the refrigerator before we left the house.

I laugh a little and shake my head as Blue picks the dog up and cradles him against his chest, then carries him out of the cage for us to gently pet. He's adorable, but does indeed have the saddest eyes of any animal I've ever seen. His tail is wagging ever so slightly, though, as Lyric kisses its forehead.

"We're gonna take this one," Blue tells the worker.

A half hour, and four pages of paperwork later, we're driving home with a sad-eyed little dog who has a rather shocked look on his furry face now.

"You're never going to get hurt again," Blue is whispering in the back seat next to Lyric, who's holding the dog in her lap. "And you're never going to be scared or lonely or hungry again. I promise."

"We have to pick a name for him," Lyric says.

"No, you have to wait. He'll tell you his name."

"How?"

"You just have to sit with him for a while, and talk to him, and look into his eyes. And suddenly, his name will pop into your head. It's like special dog telepathy."

I glance at them in the rearview mirror, and Lyric is smiling, totally buying Blue's theory.

"Did Acorn tell you his name?" she asks.

"Yup. Exactly like that."

"Is that how you got your name, Blue? Did it just pop into your head?"

He turns his head to look out the car window. "Yeah. One day I woke up with wings and I could sing, and suddenly my name was Blue."

His words sound poetic—like the words from his songs. And I can see that Lyric believes them as such.

But something deep in my gut is telling me they're not just words at all.

CHAPTER FORTY-THREE

2012 - PIPER

"When are you coming home?" I press the phone against my shoulder and finish rubbing the lavender moisturizer over my arms. This particular blend is supposed to enhance sleep, and if I had known he was going to call I wouldn't have climbed into bed and started putting it on.

"Um… next week? The week after, maybe? I don't really know, babe, it's like crazy o'clock here and I don't have a calendar in front of me. I don't even know what day *today* is."

Disappointment sets off a burn in my stomach and a heavy weight in my chest that's been growing heavier and heavier over the past few weeks. I'm afraid it will suffocate me soon.

I let out a breath that was intended to release the pressure in my body but instead takes on the sound of an irritated sigh.

"Piper…I know you're pissed, and I am too, but this shit is outta my control. Vic lined up some live radio interviews, and that late-night TV thing. I don't even fucking know anymore, I just go where I'm told."

"I know," I say. "I know it's not your fault. I'm not pissed." What I *am* is lonely and aching to have my fiancé home. I'm desperate to see his smile and feel his hands caressing me. I want to breathe him in and fill my lungs with his masculine, comforting scent. Nothing else has the power to get this weight off my chest.

"I miss you and Lyric. I fucking hate this. You have no idea."

Oh, I do have an idea, because I hate not seeing him just as much.

"I miss you, too. We both do."

"Do you? Or are you just finally getting sick of me and all this crap?"

"Of course I miss you. Lyric and I both miss you. And so do Archie and Mickey. It's just…" I choose my words carefully. "…hard to be without you for so long. We haven't seen you in what, a month?"

He groans. "Christ, has it been that long?"

"Yeah, it has. "

"Fuck, Ladybug. I'm sorry. I've got no sense of time anymore. All these different time zones fuck me up."

"I know. It's okay, hon. Really."

He coughs and I hear him taking a sip of something. "It's not okay."

I twirl the engagement ring on my finger, turning it so it's straight. The stone is so heavy it always tilts to one side of my small finger, but I refuse to have it resized and made tighter. I never take it off. It's this symbol of promises that keeps me going—our wedding. Our forever.

It's just taking way longer than I had hoped.

"Are you all right, Blue?"

"I'm tired, and my throat hurts, that's all. And I wish I was in our bed and not this hotel. I've got two places to live and I still feel homeless. The irony of my life is a scream."

"Don't say that."

"It's true. All I want is to be home with you. I wake up every night reaching for you, and when I realize you're not here, I lose my mind. I miss making you pancakes and I miss your giggles and your sexy little moans. Living like this is fucking painful and I don't even know why I'm doing this anymore."

"Because you were born to sing and bring music into the world. And that world loves you."

"Well I'm not loving the world. I love *you* and my daughter and those fuzzy creatures that get to sleep with my girl every night in *my* bed."

I'd give anything to have him in our bed right now. I need him to be here, in person, so I can look into his beautiful blue eyes and say all the things I've been waiting to say for weeks.

"Hopefully you'll be here soon and you can rest and recharge. I think you're just overtired." Every time the band travels overseas he gets agitated and depressed. I think the time difference and the erratic sleep patterns really mess with him and stress him out.

He coughs again, and the snap of his lighter follows. My heart sinks when I hear him inhale. Two months ago he quit smoking cigarettes. I'd bet anything the stress of this tour is what caused him to start up again.

"Ya know what, babe? I think I just want to be done."

My heart jolts. "What do you mean, done?"

"With the band. It's like a vampire, just bleeding me dry and I don't have anything left to give. I'm so fucking tired. I love to write and play but I'm not even doing that anymore. I'm like a robot half the time. The only time I love what I'm playing is when I play for you."

"Are you saying you want to quit the band?"

He inhales, pauses, exhales smoke.

"Yeah. I think I am."

"You're really going to have to think about that," I say. I can't deny I'd love having him home all the time and not being pulled in eighty directions all over the world, but he *is* No Tomorrow. There's no way they could replace him. His voice is too unique, his presence too charismatic. I don't think the fans would ever accept someone else in his place. It just wouldn't work.

But I also don't think the rest of the band is going to let him go without a huge fight. While Reece has expressed getting tired of it all as well, the other band members and their manager are loving the fame and fortune. They can't get enough of it.

"I've been thinking about it for a while. I'm just so fucking tired I *hurt*, Piper. I can't even explain it. I just want you in my arms every night, listening to the rain. That's it."

"I want that too," I say faintly. I'm almost afraid to verbalize the words for fear it'll jinx any chance of it ever happening.

"What are you doing now?" I ask, unsure if it's morning, noon, or night where he is.

"Just hanging out in my room. I wanted to take a nap before I have to head out but I can't get my brain to turn off. I miss you too much."

I reach for the sound machine next to the bed and pull it closer to me. I switch it to the rain setting and put the phone on speaker.

"I want you to get in bed, get all comfy, and listen to this. I'm going to be right here in bed with you. Just close your eyes, think about us, and the rain, and nothing else. Okay?"

The sound of sheets rustling and the creak of a mattress lets me know he's getting into his bed.

A deep sigh comes over the line. "You're amazing, Ladybug. You know that? I don't know what I'd do if you didn't love me."

I smile in the dark, and the pressure in my chest eases up just a little.

"You don't ever have to worry about that. My heart doesn't beat without yours."

I stay on the phone listening to his breathing, and after a few minutes I can tell he's fallen asleep. I keep the phone and the rain station on his pillow next to mine, and I drift off to sleep, too.

I dream that he's home, and he wraps me up in his arms and I'm finally able to tell him we're having a baby.

CHAPTER FORTY-FOUR

BLUE

I call her cell phone for what must be the fiftieth time.

Ring.

Ring.

Ring.

Ring.

"Hi, you've reached the voicemail of Piper Karel. Leave me a message and I'll call you back as soon as I can. Thanks!"

"Babe, it's me. Where are you? I've been calling you for hours. Not sure what's going on. Call me when you get this. I love you."

My hand shakes erratically as I end the call. Ashes spill off the cigarette I'm holding and sprinkle onto the hotel carpet.

I hold the butt to my lips and suck it like I'm syphoning for air. I hold the smoke in my lungs. Let it fill my hollow void, then let it out.

I pace the room. Exactly six steps to the balcony. Exactly six steps back to the edge of the bed.

Six.

Six.

Six.

Piper *always* answers my calls. She's a creature of extreme habit—

always at the same place at the same time of day every day. She's the one and only thing that doesn't fuck with me or confuse me.

It's five p.m. there.

It's ten p.m. here.

I woke at six a.m.

Didn't I? What day is it?

Does that even fucking matter?

Where is she?

Ladybug, have you finally flown away from me?

I light another cigarette. Now I've got one in each hand.

She's gone.

No more soft voices. No smiles. No love. No more hope.

No more peace. No more normal.

The silence is maddening, thrashing in my brain like a wild animal.

The emptiness is turning my blood to liquid ice.

I'm shivering from the cold.

She left you.

They all left you.

No.

Drink. It will melt the ice. You need the warmth and the heat in your veins.

No.

The drugs will cure you. You're sick. It will numb the pain. Silence the silence.

No.

No one will know. You're alone. You're always alone. You only have me. I won't tell.

No. They love me.

You disappoint them. They deserve better. They've run away. To hide from you.

They wouldn't do that.

Evan, you dumb fuck. They already have.

Go away. Please just go away.

Fly away from it all. You know you have wings. Use them. Come with me. Stand on the balcony. Just six steps. Fly with me. You'll never hurt again. You'll be free, just like me. Watch me fly. Do what I do.

No. I don't have wings.

Shhh. You can sing and fly just like me. I won't let you fall.

No. You're not real.

I snatch up the phone again and smash my finger on the speed-dial for Piper's house.

Ring.

Ring.

Ring.

Ring.

Ring.

"Hi, we're not home right now. Leave us a message. Thanks!"

Fuck.

What. The. Fuck.

I struggle to use my calm, sober, I've-got-it-together, nothing-to-worry-about-here voice.

I'd probably have an easier time singing the fucking National Anthem right now.

"Piper...I need you, baby. Where are you? I can't find you or Lyric. Please don't do this. I'm better now. I love you. Please come back."

I pace again.

I walk.

Out the door and down the stairs.

So many fucking stairs, I can't even count.

Every time I tell them don't give me stairs and yet, they still give me all the fucking stairs.

I'm walking.

Out into the night, into the cool, open air.

My heart is aching, my fingers are numb.

My vision is blurred at the edges like a burnt photograph. Everything is fading away.

I walk.

Step. Step. Step. Step.

One, two, three, four...

Every step grounding me. Clearing my mind. Moving me forward. Away, away, away from the voices.

Walking.
For as long as it takes, as far as it takes.
As long as I'm walking, I'm not able to fly.

CHAPTER FORTY-FIVE

PIPER

The doctor's words are still ricocheting around in my head, even though I'm sure a full five minutes has passed since she spoke them in her soothing voice.

"I'm so sorry, Miss Karel. There's no heartbeat. It appears the baby stopped growing at approximately nine weeks."

Three weeks ago, my tiny baby left me.

I didn't even know.

How could I not know?

And Blue, my love, never knew that a baby was waiting for him to come home. A baby that I wanted to surprise him with, in person, so we could do it right this time. Together.

A baby that he was never supposed to miss a moment of.

Gone.

Pain ripples through me and I shake my head as tears spill down my cheeks, and I hug myself, clutching my stomach.

My sobs are muffling the doctor's voice, drowning her words as she continues to say things no mother should ever hear.

"Are you sure?" I ask desperately as the nurse helps me sit up. "I've been fine. Totally fine, actually. I haven't been sick or had any cramps or bleeding or anything. I think it's a mistake. Or maybe the baby is tiny?

I'm very petite, and so is my daughter. She was just barely five pounds when she was born. At full term." I gulp and try to catch my breath. "Can you check again?"

Dr. Powell offers me a sympathetic shake of her head, snapping off her purple latex gloves.

"I'm sorry, Piper. There's no doubt. I know how devastating this is for you, and I'm so very sorry."

I'm wracked with waves of nausea, lightheadedness, and an overwhelming sense of detached reality.

At home, an itty-bitty black T-shirt with Blue's band logo on it waits for him next to the bed.

If I could just get this ridiculous paper robe off, get out of here, go home, and call Blue. I can tell him all about the baby, and none of this will be happening.

I can make it stop. I can bring him back.

It'll all stop. Our tiny one will be safe, nestled in my womb, waiting to come into our world and wear its little T-shirt.

Blue will be so happy. He'll tell me the baby will name itself—and I'll believe him.

Lyric will play lullabies on her harp next to my stomach.

It'll be a boy. I can feel that in my soul. Son of a rock legend who would follow in his daddy's footsteps.

Another kickass kid, Blue would say with that sexy, confident, proud grin of his that turns me to jelly.

I can see our baby so clearly, so vividly.

He's real. He can't be gone.

If only I had begged Blue to come home, if only I had flown out to London to see him when he asked weeks ago.

If I had not kept the baby a secret, if I had let Blue—or anyone else—know this tiny life existed, maybe this wouldn't have happened. Maybe he would have felt how loved and wanted he was by so many, and he would have stayed.

I'm admitted to the hospital for *a procedure* later this afternoon that will take my baby away forever.

I call Ditra, and we cry together like we've done many times since we were little girls, but this time is the hardest, the worst, the unimaginable.

Ditra takes control, arranging to stay at my house tonight to keep my daughter and my pets company. Tomorrow she'll take Lyric to school, then she and Billy will come get me and my car and take me home to *recover*.

Honestly I don't think I'll ever recover from this.

How does anyone?

I should call my mother, but I don't. I can't. I'm not ready to talk to anyone. I refuse to share my loss with anyone else until I can talk to Blue.

I have no idea how I'll find the words to tell him we lost our baby, and for a few moments I grasp at the idea of never telling him at all. I can protect him from this heartache, save him from more distress that will only add to everything else he's dealing with in his life right now.

Something awful like this could send him right over the edge again, back into the seductive arms of drugs and alcohol.

Do I dare risk all that?

Yes. I have to.

I stare at the ring on my finger. We promised to love each other for all the tomorrows. No matter what. Lies and secrets will haunt us and destroy us eventually. The truth always finds a way to take on a life of its own and come out.

Taking a deep breath, I decide I'll call him in the morning when it's all over. My cell phone is dead in my purse, anyway, and his hotel info is saved on it. If I call him tomorrow, he won't have to worry about me all night.

We can survive his addictions again if we have to, but I don't think we'd ever survive deceit. I'd lose him forever. And that, I cannot and will not risk.

CHAPTER FORTY-SIX

PIPER

As soon as I'm home I call Blue's cell phone, and it goes directly to his voicemail.

Shit. He always forgets to charge his phone, so it must be dead.

I leave him a message: "Hi hon, it's me. Give me a call when you can. I miss you, and I love you."

I dig my cell phone out of my purse and plug it in, waiting for it to have enough power to turn on. When the screen finally lights up, I'm shocked at the notifications I see on my screen.

One hundred and twenty-eight missed calls.

Twenty-five voice messages.

Ten text messages.

Holy hell.

All but four of the voice messages are him breathing, or the sound of the phone clicking with a disconnect.

The four actual messages range from sweet to what sounds like an all-out meltdown.

I'm better. Please come back.

Those familiar words he used to say so often when things were bad between us and he was fighting his demons. Somehow he got there without even knowing the truth yet, and now I'm petrified. What happened? Did he freak out when he couldn't reach me and just assumed I left him?

I hunt down the hotel information saved in my phone and call his room, but there's no answer. According to the email he sent me a few days ago, he should still be staying at this hotel. Immediately I call the front desk.

"Hello, can you tell me if Mr. Von Bleu in room 4032 has checked out? I've called his room and there's no answer. This is Piper Karel, his fiancée."

"One moment." I hear the receptionist clicking a keyboard on the other end. "I am showing that Mr. Von Bleu is still checked in. Would you like to leave us a message at the front desk to forward to him?"

My heart sinks even lower. "No, thank you."

I chew my fingernail with worry and sit on the chest at the end of my bed. I'm still bleeding and cramping, and feel groggy from the anesthesia yesterday and the painkillers I took this morning. I was given instruction by the doctor to rest and give myself time to heal mentally and physically. I've already spoken to Human Resources and requested a week of my vacation time.

Resting is simply not going to happen until I find Blue and get the chance to have a heart-to-heart talk with him about everything that's happened over the past twenty-four hours and to assure him that I most definitely have not left him.

I can't imagine why he would even think that when we've been so happy.

I pull up Reece's number on my phone, and he picks up on the second ring. Reece's phone is always charged.

"Hello?"

"Reece…hi…it's Piper."

"Hey…um…I was actually just about to call you—"

"Is Blue okay? I can't get in touch with him and I'm worried."

"Shit. That's why I was calling you. He's gone."

My heart jolts and my head spins with dizziness. How can he be gone? Blue doesn't do gone anymore.

"Wh-what are you talking about?"

"We can't find him. All his stuff is in his room except for his favorite guitar. His phone is going straight to voicemail so I guess as usual his battery is dead."

Everything just keeps getting worse. Blue could be traipsing around London right now with a dead cell phone and no way to charge it, which means there's no way for me to get in touch with him when I need him now more than I ever have.

As if that's not bad enough, while I was losing our baby he somehow jumped to the conclusion I had left him.

"Oh my God... I can't believe this... did he say anything to any of you? Yesterday?"

"No, it was a quiet day, we were all kinda hanging out in our rooms alone trying to catch up on sleep. Everything was great. We had an interview this morning and he didn't show. We told them he was sick and we had to do it without him. I have no fucking idea where he could be. I've looked everywhere. This is a big city, though, and he knows how to not be found."

That's an understatement.

"Reece." I gulp for air and exhale in shaky breaths. "We have to find him. I have to talk to him as soon as possible." Choking sobs start and I'm powerless to stop them.

"Whoa, Piper. Don't cry. I'm sure he's okay. I'll keep looking for him, I promise. You know how he gets...he always turns up."

"You don't understand...something *did* happen...I think he freaked out because he couldn't get in touch with me at all yesterday. I was in the hospital, and I wasn't able to call him right away."

"Wait—what? Are you okay? Please don't cry, I can't deal with it when women cry."

"I'm sorry," I sob, wiping at my face. "I'm just so scared."

"Where are you now? Are you still in the hospital?"

"No...I'm home now. My best friend drove me home earlier."

"So you're all right?"

Am I all right? I don't feel all right at all.

"I was twelve weeks pregnant," I say softly. "And I lost the baby."

He lets out a pained sound. "Ohh, sweetheart. I'm so sorry."

"Blue didn't even know I was pregnant. I was waiting for him to come home to tell him about the baby, but then you guys ended up staying out there longer and I just didn't want to tell him over the phone, I wanted to surprise him and...." Tears take over and my voice cracks and dies.

Reece breathes heavily into the phone. "Shit. I have to find him and get him home to you."

"Do you really think he took off again?" I ask weakly. "Do you think he's doing drugs again?"

"I don't know, Piper. Blue does weird things. I've been keeping an eye on him and haven't seen him do anything. Not a drop of alcohol, not even a joint. No bullshit, he was glad to be straight. He knows he can come to me about anything and I'll be there for him. He promised if he ever felt like using again he'd come to me and let me handcuff his ass to me so I could watch him. That's how bad he wanted to stay clean."

"I'm so worried about him... I can't even think straight. I'm sitting here shaking."

"Look, my sister went through this a few years ago. You should be resting and not getting all worked up."

Is he crazy?

"How can I rest when I don't know where he is or if he's okay or what's going on? I'm afraid he's going to disappear for months or years and I can't live through that."

"I get it, but you have to take care of you, too. He's a big boy, and he'll be okay. He's probably just walking around like he does and believe me, I know that's not helping you a fuckin' bit, but what I'm saying is that I'm sure he's fine, and I'm sure he won't be gone for long. Right now you need to do your best to stay calm and take care of yourself until I can find his ass and get him to you."

"I'm just so scared, Reece. I didn't think he'd ever do this again, especially now when I need him the most. He left me a bunch of messages and for some crazy reason he thinks I left him. Why would he think that? He knows I would never, ever do that to him."

"It's just how his mind works. It's not you. It's his way of coping, as fucked up as it is."

"I don't know what to think," I mutter, putting my face in my hand. "I just need him here."

"I'll find him, and I'll make him call you as soon as I do. I'm gonna shove the phone right in his hand. I promise."

"Okay." I feel utterly hopeless. "I guess all I can do is just wait, then."

"And rest. *Rest*, Piper."

"I'll try."

"I'm really sorry about the baby. And I know if he had any clue about this, he never would have done this. He loves you."

After we say goodbye, I change into my softest sweatpants and Blue's T-shirt before crawling into bed to rest. Ditra will be picking up Lyric at school and keeping her overnight so I can have some alone time to get my head together.

I try to focus on as many of the positives as I can so I don't get pulled under the wave of depression that's looming at the edges of my mind and heart. Blue loves Lyric and me. He wouldn't leave us. He probably just needed to think.

We're all going to be okay.

CHAPTER FORTY-SEVEN

PIPER

"Baby, are you sick?" He kisses my forehead and strokes his thumb across my cheek. "Tell me what's wrong."

I moan and turn my head to the side, begging sleep to take me away again.

"Piper, open your eyes for me."

I open my eyes and stare at the ceiling, my mind sluggish and groggy. The bedroom is dim, and a glance toward the windows reveals the sun is no longer shining.

When did it become night time?

"Hey…." His voice is soft and laced with worry.

"Blue?" Confused, I reach for him and my hand lands on his leg.

How can he be here if he's in London?

He lifts my hand to his lips and kisses it. "I'm here."

"How are you here? I couldn't find you…" I move to sit up and a wave of dizziness slams my head back down on the pillow.

"I couldn't find you either. I had a real bad feeling, so I jumped on a plane and here I am." He leans down and kisses me softly. "I was really fuckin' worried about you."

"I was worried about you, too. Reece is looking for you."

"Not anymore. I called him from a pay phone when I landed in

Boston because my cell phone battery died yesterday. He said I had to talk to you right away." He pushes his hair away from his face and looks at me intently. "What's going on, Ladybug?"

"I can't believe you're here." Tears leak from the corners of my eyes and drip down to my hairline.

"Where's Lyric? Is she okay?"

"Yes. Ditra and Billy are taking her to a movie and she's staying over at their house tonight."

His brow creases. "Why's she staying over there? They only live a few hundred feet away."

I try to sit up again, and have to close my eyes for a moment to stop the room from spinning. He grabs my arms, and the worry on his face is tearing my heart up because I know it's going to be a whole lot worse in a few moments.

"Piper, what's going on? You're scaring the shit out of me."

I reach for his hand and lace our fingers tightly together.

"I have to tell you something. When you couldn't get in touch with me yesterday I was actually in the hospital, and I—"

"You're sick?" he asks, and his beautiful voice is already cracking with emotion and panic.

"No," I say quickly. "No, I'm not sick. I really don't know how to say this, so I'm just going to say it, okay? Because I just don't have the words…" His eyes are wild when he nods. "I had a miscarriage. I'm so sorry… I love you so much and I wanted this baby with all my heart…" Saying the words, and seeing the expression of pure shock and heartbreak on his face, is more than I can handle. I can't hold back my tears for a second longer, and they stream down my cheeks like tiny rivers.

"There was a baby?" His dark blue eyes pool with tears and it's like staring into two oceans of pure desolation.

I swallow hard over the suffocating lump in my throat. "I was twelve weeks pregnant. I kept waiting for you to come home to tell you. So I could tell you in person. I was so excited to tell you, Blue. I just wanted it to be special and not over the phone. I'm so sorry."

"Baby, don't be sorry." He pulls me into his arms and hugs me so hard I lose my breath. "This is all my fault. I fucked up again."

I bury my face into his chest. "No. It's not your fault. The baby stopped growing weeks ago. Something must have just been...wrong."

He shakes his head violently. "I should've been here for you and the baby. You were upset when I got stuck in London longer. I should've just fucking left. Maybe this wouldn't have happened."

"Please..." I whisper. "Don't say that. *Please*. Just hug me."

We hold onto each other and cry for our little unborn baby. My heart aches so much I'm afraid it may never stop hurting, and I can't even imagine what he's feeling.

This wasn't supposed to happen this way.

"Are you okay?" His voice is raspy with pain. "Are you in pain? Tell me what I can do for you. Please. I don't want to lose you, too."

"I just need you to hug me, that's all. I promise you I'm okay and you're not going to lose me. Ever."

He takes a deep breath and his entire body shudders when he exhales.

"Does Lyric know?"

"No. I don't think we should tell her."

"Will there be a funeral? To say goodbye?"

Oh, my sweet Blue...

"No," I say softly, too brokenhearted to say any more.

"So that's it? The baby's just... gone?"

"I'm sorry."

I can actually *feel* the sadness engulf him like a black wave. His body goes entirely still. His breathing slows and quiets to a point of almost non-existent.

I'm terrified of what this could do to him, and to us. What happens when both people fall apart? Who picks up the pieces and holds us together?

He says nothing else, and neither do I. Our desperate hold on each other speaks volumes.

I carefully untangle myself from Blue's arms and climb out of bed. He's fallen into a deep sleep, exhausted from traveling and emotional overload.

Archie trails me to the kitchen, reminding me to fill his dishes which are inadequately filled. I make myself a cup of tea and call Lyric. She sounds happy—telling me about the movie Ditra and Billy took her to see and how she's been beating Billy at a video game. I decide I'll tell her tomorrow that her father is here. If she knows he's here now, she'll want to run home and I feel like we need a night alone together.

With Mickey following me closely, I take the phone out on the back porch and call Reece.

"Hey," he says. "I've been thinking about you two. Are you okay?"

"I think so. We're both upset. He's asleep right now, he's exhausted."

"How did he take it?"

"He's devastated. He's trying to blame himself. I told him it's not his fault. To be honest I feel like it's my fault. I've been stressed and upset..."

"Piper, stop. It's not your fault. Or his. It's just a horrible thing that happens in life."

I sigh and run my hand over my stomach. The pain is still lingering —physically *and* emotionally.

"You're going to have to keep an eye on him," Reece warns.

"I always do."

"More than usual. If he can't handle this, he could start using again to escape. So watch for him being in the bathroom too long, running the shower, or taking off randomly, look for track marks, sniffling, changes in his eating and sleeping, mood swings. If he's acting too calm, angry, or too happy. You hafta watch for all this shit. If you think something's up, call me, okay?"

Holy crap. All of that behavior could also just be normal. How am I supposed to know if something is a red flag?

"Okay," I agree, feeling overwhelmed.

"Blue's the kind of guy that will climb to the top of a fuckin' mountain to try to reach that baby's soul, Piper. I know him. And I know this is even harder for you. It's not fair you have to watch him like a hawk when you're grieving, but it is what it is."

"I'll be okay," I assure him with confidence I'm not actually feeling. "We both will."

"The rest of us are leaving here tomorrow. We're gonna take a break for two weeks and then we'll meet up in Seattle. I'll call Blue in a few days to see how he's doing. Are *you* okay? And Lyric?"

I pet Mickey's head, finding comfort in his soft fur and calm demeanor. This dog hardly ever leaves my side. He's a little ball of love and devotion, just like Acorn.

"We're okay. I'm taking some time off work. I think it will be good for us to spend some quiet time together."

Reece's warnings have scared the hell out of me. I don't want to have to treat Blue like an inmate. He's my partner and my equal. He's begged me to trust him and believe in him. If he senses I'm starting to doubt him, that'll add to the stress he's feeling over the band *and* the grief over losing our baby. I'm alarmed at how quickly he thought he lost me. At some point, I have to talk to him about that and figure out what was going through his head, and why he thought I would just leave him.

For now, I'm just going to do whatever I can to fill the next two weeks with as much love and calmness as I can.

CHAPTER FORTY-EIGHT

PIPER

Blue convinced me to tell Lyric about the baby, and once my head cleared, I realized he was right. She deserves to know that we lost a part of our family, no matter how young the baby was. We told her together the day after Blue arrived, and although she cried, she was amazingly understanding and sympathetic—showing mature concern for us that stretched well beyond her age.

Reece's words about Blue trying to reach the baby's soul have been haunting me, and I realize we all needed some kind of closure.

On Saturday morning, the three of us drive to a beautiful lookout point up in the mountains. Blue writes the baby's name on a turquoise-colored balloon, and Lyric plays *Somewhere Over the Rainbow* on her harp as we watch Nicholas Von Bleu's spirit gently float up to the sky and disappear. Blue stares at the sky with such an intense longing I fear he's going to leap right into the clouds and try to follow that balloon.

Later that night after Lyric has gone to bed, Blue takes me out on the back porch, lights a few candles, and makes ice cream sundaes for both of us, insisting I let him do everything while I wait on the porch for him with Mickey.

"You don't have to wait on me," I protest when he sits next to me on the wicker loveseat and hands me a dish of vanilla ice cream with whipped cream, rainbow sprinkles, and butterscotch syrup.

"I need you to think of me as someone who can take care of you."

"I do."

His tongue piercing clicks against his spoon as he licks hot fudge off it.

My thighs tingle in response. I want him—need him— desperately, but it's too soon for us to make love.

He shakes his head. "You feel like you have to take care of me. You're always afraid I'm gonna have a meltdown or show up with coke on my face."

I have never once imagined him doing coke.

"Blue, that's not true."

"It is. And ya know what? I don't blame you. It's my fault you have to worry about me. But I want to take care of *you*."

"You do take care of me."

"Not like I should be, and not like I want to. I don't mean just financially. I want you to be able to count on me for everything."

I wish he didn't feel this way because I do believe he takes care of me. I don't view him as weak or incapable. I just think sometimes he's way too trapped in his own head with his thoughts and fears and dreams.

"When two people love each other, sometimes one has to be stronger than the other. It's a tradeoff. There's not a score card. It's what love is about."

"I know that, babe. And I'm lucky as fuck that you feel that way or else you probably would have kicked my ass out of your life for good."

I lean closer to him and press my sticky sweet lips to his cheek.

"I could never do that. You're too irresistible."

A cocky grin crosses his face. "Yeah. Maybe I am," he teases.

There's no maybe. He definitely is.

"I've been doing some more thinking and I want to get out of the band," he blurts out.

I swallow the ice cream in my mouth. "Really?" I have a love-hate feeling for No Tomorrow. On one hand, I'm so incredibly proud of Blue and the band's raging success. He's amazing and talented and just a god on stage. But on the other hand, I can see it's slowly killing him. His heart is in songwriting and playing the guitar—not with fame and the rat race of being the front man of one of the most popular rock bands in the world. He told me a long time ago he wanted to be more heard and less seen and No Tomorrow flipped that on its ass. No matter how hard he tries, he can't find a balance.

He nods. "Yeah. Really. I talked to Reece about it and he feels the same. He doesn't want to do it anymore."

"Are you kidding?" I certainly didn't think Reece would be willing to walk.

"He's got a lot going on. His ex has relinquished custody of their kid."

"Relinquished custody?" I repeat. "What does that even mean? She's the mother."

He shrugs. "She doesn't want to be any more, I guess. Something's going on. I don't ask questions, ya know? But he's all fucked up over it and he doesn't want someone else raising his kid."

"I don't blame him." What kind of mother doesn't want her own child? My heart feels sick just thinking about it.

"When we all meet up in Seattle we're going to talk to our manager and the guys and figure something out. I don't want to talk about all that shit now or I'll get a fuckin' headache."

"Okay. We don't have to talk about it. I just want you to be happy. That's all I care about."

He looks at me like I'm a big shiny object that holds the secret to world peace.

"I know, Ladybug. I've always known that. And it fucking kills me that I hurt you so much, and I missed so much of Lyric's life, and I wasn't here when you found out you were pregnant or when you lost the baby, and you were here all the fuck alone and couldn't find me because I can't even be responsible enough to keep my fucking phone charged. How am I supposed to live with that?" His self-loathing is so strong he's literally shaking and grinding his teeth.

I take his ice cream out of his hands and put both our dishes on the small table next to us.

"Blue," I say softly. "None of this is your fault. You never hurt me on purpose. I know you're… different and complicated." He shakes his head and won't meet my eyes but I don't let that deter me from talking. "I love you more than anything in the world. I knew when we got back together that I would have to share you with millions of people. I knew right from the beginning, way back years ago, that we would never have a normal relationship. And you were always honest about that. But that never stopped me from loving you, or from wanting to spend my life with you. Even when things have been a mess, even when I'm scared, even when I don't know what the heck is going on with you, I still can't imagine my life without you."

He looks up toward the sky and screws his eye shut. He lets out a deep breath and clenches his fingers into fists.

"Tonight I wanted to take care of you. I wanted to feed you ice cream and see your smile. Then I wanted to take you to be bed and kiss every inch of you until you fell asleep and I wanted to hug you all night and make sure you knew how much I love you and care about you and appreciate you. I just wanted to give you some kind of happiness and security and instead you're worried about me. You're *always* worried about me."

"Because I love you."

"I don't want to be dead weight to you anymore. I want to be there for you like you've always been there for me. I don't want to be the fucked-up, lost mess anymore who lets you down every fucking time. I don't want you to wake up someday and wish you had someone better. That's what I thought when I couldn't find you. I was like finally, she came to her senses and left my fucked-up ass."

My chest clenches from his words and the negative way he sees himself. I rub my hand up his arm, gently squeezing his bicep.

"I can promise you that will never happen. You're not a fucked-up mess and there's no one better for me than you. Leaving you has never once even entered my mind. Nobody ever said love had to be easy and perfect, Blue. It just has to be real, and honest, and able to weather the storm. We have that. Anything else, we can work on together."

He kisses me, then picks me up and carries me to the bedroom, where he does everything he said he wanted to do. I'm smothered with kisses and soft caresses and lulled with whispers and promises. I wish he truly knew just how special and loved he has always made me feel.

CHAPTER FORTY-NINE

PIPER

I've never been faced with so many decisions at once in my life. I've made lists of pros and cons. I've talked to Ditra until her eyes glazed over and rolled back in her head.

Blue and Reece have already put the wheels in motion to leave the band. That discussion took almost two months of fighting, negotiating, and debating with the other band members, their manager, and their record label for them to finally come to an agreement. They agreed they would finish out the few tour dates they had left for the year, and then No Tomorrow would dissolve. Blue and Reece would not be replaced. The guys, however, are open to working together again sometime in the future for a reunion.

I suppose it was a bittersweet decision for all of them. Freedom from No Tomorrow would open the door for new opportunities, but also would leave the door slightly ajar for them to still work together.

Blue agonized over his decision to leave the band. I've never seen him struggle like that before. When he decided to leave me years ago, I only saw and felt my own pain and suffering from his decision. I often wondered if what he did bothered him. Or did he just walk off without a care in the world, with an out-of-sight, out-of-mind attitude? But now I can see how much he really does care about the things that go on in his life, and how he affects others. He barely slept during the entire negotiation period. For hours he talked to me about how he worried the guys in the band would hate him. He worried that he was ruining their lives and killing their dreams. He was afraid the fans would turn on him. All very valid issues.

Several times I thought he was going to throw in the towel and stay with the band. Especially after witnessing all his mental anguish over what leaving the band would entail. The change in lifestyle and finances. The effect it would have on the others. Giving up the spotlight and walking away from the high of thousands of fans waiting in a crowd just to see and hear them—whether he ever wanted that or not. It's a lot of change to take on, and years of work to walk away from.

But I've also seen the rare glimmer of hope and excitement in his eyes when he talks about the new life he wants to live. A quiet life as a family. He wants to write songs just for himself again—maybe produce an album of his own. I'm proud of him for wanting to chase his dreams and go back to the root of what he loves most about music. I admire the strength I see in him now and his unwillingness to make destructive choices as he used to in the past.

When he came to me with a smile and hug to tell me he'd made his final decision and would be letting the band go, I felt a mix of emotions. On one hand I was sad that he was letting go of a huge part of his life and success, but on the other hand I felt relief and happiness for our future together.

For the first time, we're both on the same page and can plan a future together.

But now it's my turn to make hard decisions.

Blue doesn't want me to work anymore. He wants us to enjoy life together, maybe travel and take Lyric to see fun and beautiful places. We talked about trying for another baby in the future, when we both feel ready, and how amazing it would be for us both to be home to raise the baby together. The mere idea of seeing Blue with an infant in his arms, and witnessing his reaction to his baby's first words and steps, makes me completely giddy.

Although my job can be stressful and not overly fulfilling, I've worked hard to climb the ladder at the office, so to speak. It's taken me a long time to reach a salary where I'm not living paycheck to paycheck. Money won't be an issue for us. His financial guy saved and invested his money for him, and he'll receive sizeable royalties probably for the rest of his life that will keep us beyond comfortable. I'd much rather be spending my days with Blue and Lyric than sitting behind a desk. It's hard to give up the independence I've worked so hard for, though. Giving up my job, my own income, and most likely my house, is a lot. Blue wants to support Lyric and me in every way possible, and that'll be an entirely new way of life for us. I've always paid for everything myself. All the checks Blue has sent me over the years I immediately deposited in a savings account for Lyric. I still feel strange using the gold card he gave me months ago for anything and everything Lyric and I—and even the pets—need or want.

We also have to decide where we want to live. Here in New Hampshire? In Seattle? Someplace entirely new? I've lived in this town my entire life. My best friend lives right behind my house. That kind of comfort is going to be hard to give up.

Then there are wedding plans to figure out once Blue's tour is over. Do I want a big fancy wedding? A destination wedding, maybe? Or something small and intimate?

My mind is boggled with all the option, questions, and decisions.

"Mom?"

I blink and stare at Lyric, who's giggling at me.

"The green candies go in the front."

I smile. "Oh. I see."

Blue winks at me from the other side of the kitchen table. We're building a gingerbread house—a huge one—completely from scratch. Blue and Lyric have been baking and gathering all the candies and other items for days. It's our first family project and it's had me silly with happiness. I've been slacking on my end of the project because I keep getting caught up in watching Blue and Lyric together. He's so incredibly good with her. Sweet, nurturing, funny. I've never seen him look happier. He's singing along with the Elvis Christmas album, and he looks hot as hell in a gray sweater that's perfectly tight around his chest and shoulders, old worn jeans, and black fuzzy socks.

He leans across the table with a handful of candy canes in his hand and kisses me.

"What are you daydreaming about, beautiful?"

I beam at him as I make a candy walkway leading to the door of our gingerbread house. "You."

"Mom!" Lyric teases. "Daydream about Blue later. We're right in the middle of our house."

Blue and I laugh at her. She loves to tease us about our public displays of affection and she pretends they bother her, but we both know that she actually thinks we're cute. She's at the cusp of starting to notice boys, so she notices anything romantic and lovey. Blue has set the bar high for any guy she might date when she's older. Every Friday he brings each of us a bouquet of flowers, and once a month he surprises us with a random, but extremely thoughtful and unique gift. Not only does he make quality time for me, but also for Lyric. He spends hours talking to her, writing poetry with her, and playing guitar with her while she plays the harp. He even makes sure to spend time with Archie and Mickey by brushing them and playing with them. At least once a week the three of us take Mickey for a walk together.

"How are we going to eat this?" Lyric asks, standing back to admire the half-finished, three-story structure. We're also decorating the inside so it looks more like an edible doll house than a gingerbread house. "It's just too cool to eat. I want to save it."

"Nah. It'll get gross. I promise we'll make one every year, okay?" Blue says. "There're tons of different ones we can make."

Excitement gleans in her eyes. We've never had a true Christmas tradition. I think Blue's idea is perfect and something Lyric can enjoy with us as she gets older. Maybe even share with a younger sibling someday.

"This is the best Christmas of my life," Blue murmurs into my neck.

"Mine too." I turn my head and meet his lips for a soft, lingering kiss. It's after midnight on Christmas Day and we're snuggling on the couch at my house under a thick fleece blanket with a goofy reindeer picture on it. This is the first Christmas we've ever spent together and it's been wonderful.

This morning we opened presents with Lyric, then Blue made us pancakes and waffles for breakfast, including a bone-shaped pancake for Mickey. Ditra and Billy joined us later to exchange gifts, and then we went to my parents' house for dinner, at my mother's insistence.

My mother has met Blue once before and admitted she liked him and thought he was beautiful and charming. Her words. I wasn't thrilled with subjecting Blue to my father's long-standing attitude on our first Christmas together, but Blue assured me he could handle my father acting like a jerk. Thankfully, my sisters and their husbands were super friendly over dinner. They fanned a little over Blue, which made me laugh, especially seeing my father's facial expressions when it dawned on him that Blue actually *is* famous. My father didn't talk much, but at least he wasn't rude, so all in all it was a nice dinner.

Now we're on the couch with the lights off, enjoying the twinkling lights on the Christmas tree in the corner and the fire flowing from the electric fireplace Blue installed last week. Blue gave me a special gift when we got home—a diamond tennis bracelet with a tiny red garnet ladybug charm. I told him I'm never going to take either of them—this one or the original he gave me years ago—off.

"This is what I've always wanted with you," he whispers, moving the scoop neck of my sweater off my shoulder and planting kisses on the exposed skin. "Memories that don't hurt."

"I have lots of memories of you that don't hurt." I thread my fingers through his soft hair. "And we're going to make lots more."

"Can we start right now?"

He lifts me in his arms, carries me across the room, and gently sets me on the floor in front of the fireplace. I love the way he smiles when I pull him on top of me, and the way the fireplace makes him look like he's radiating a halo.

He tugs off my sweater and reaches down to unbutton my jeans.

"What about Lyric?" I whisper. She's been in bed for hours, but we never fool around right in the middle of the house.

He touches his fingertips to my lips. "Shh...she won't wake up. We'll be quiet." With a crazy-sexy grin, he pulls my jeans and panties off. "At least *I'll* be quiet because my mouth is gonna be busy...." Kneeling between my legs, he slowly slides his hand from my breast all the way down over my hip to my outer thigh. He kneads his fingers there and then bends my leg up. "Not sure if *you* can be quiet, Ladybug." He kisses my inner thigh and sucks my flesh into his mouth. Teeth and metal send tingles through my limbs. "Especially with me licking your pussy." He drags his tongue over my lips and I let out a little moan and dig my fingernails into his shoulders.

"You gotta try harder than that, baby." His husky voice drips with raw sensuality and he descends on me, covering me with his warm mouth and slowly probing me with his tongue. He flicks the ball of his piercing over my clit, then plunges his tongue in deep, sucking my sensitive flesh between his lips and teeth. I spread myself open for him when he inches his hand up my thigh and slips one, then two fingers inside me. He works me into a frenzy with his mouth and hands and I writhe and wiggle beneath him, thrusting my hips toward his face. He tortures me—slowing and pulling back just when I'm almost over the edge, then mouth-fucking me back to that breathless, urgent place again. He drives me wild, tantalizing me with his tongue and hands, his hard body pressing against mine. I tangle my fingers in his long hair, imprisoning him so he can't pull away. When he finally lets me come, I can't stop from crying out with pleasure. He moves like lightning, capturing my mouth with his, kissing me so deeply that I can't breathe as he pistons his fingers in me. I'm a quivering, powerless ragdoll beneath him as he coaxes my body into another orgasm.

"You're so beautiful when you lose control," he whispers against my lips as I struggle to catch my breath. "And you can't be quiet for nothin'."

I giggle and snuggle into his arms. "It's impossible with you. You drive me wild."

He pulls the blanket from the couch and over our bodies, then leans up on his elbow to look at me. His hair is disheveled around his face. His eyes dark and intense, his lips full and cherry red from being ridden.

And that smile on his face is the best gift I could ever receive.

I remember our first Christmas together. How he decorated the shed with a tiny tree. I remember how badly I wanted him to climb over the wall he always kept between us and come home with me for the holiday.

Now there are no walls, he's home with me, and nothing could be more perfect.

"I don't want to ever stop having nights like this." He pulls me closer and wraps his leg over mine, locking us together. "You're the one high I'm never gonna quit, Piper. I don't care if we have five kids or we're married for twenty years, I'm always going to want to get lost in you."

"You can *always* get lost in me." I kiss the middle of his chest. "I promise."

As we lie in front of the flickering electric flames, I play with his hair —something he loves—and the words to his song, "Lost in You," echoes through my mind:

> *Take my hand baby and don't let go*
> *Anchor me here with your heart and thighs*
> *I'll swallow you down; intoxicate my dark soul*
> *Whisper my name, darlin', infect me with your sighs*
> *Please…drown out all the shit I've been told*
> *Keep me high, baby, and I'll never have to fly.*

CHAPTER FIFTY

PIPER

"I like this one. It's heavy." He holds his left hand out, fingers outstretched, and stares intently at the band on his ring finger. A shy grin spreads over his lips and he looks at me. "Do you like this one?"

I'd be happy with a string on his finger.

"I love it."

The saleswoman beams. "That one is platinum, and symbolizes pure and everlasting love. It's very durable, but can show some scratches and may patina eventually."

"I can dig that. I don't want it to look perfect and shiny forever. I kinda come with some scratches and dents. Right, babe?" He nudges his shoulder playfully into mine.

"I love your dents and scratches."

"I'll take this one," Blue says, taking the band off and handing it to the saleswoman.

"It's a wonderful choice, Mr. Von Bleu. And we're honored to have you as a client."

He thanks her and turns to me with a worried expression. "I think we should get Lyric a ring, too," he says softly. "So she feels like we're all in this kinda together. I don't want her to feel left out. What do you think?"

There is no way to describe the intense feeling of love that slams into me when Blue does amazingly sweet and romantic things like this. He's always so unsure and shy when he has these ideas, and that just makes them all the more special. I struggle to hold back tears and not smother him with kisses in the middle of the jewelry store.

"I think that's the sweetest idea ever. I know she'll love it."

He smiles and we start to hunt around the store for the perfect ring that will symbolize love, commitment, and family to a young teen girl. We find a dainty white gold ring shaped into the infinity symbol with a tiny diamond in the center.

He pulls me against his chest and kisses the top of my head as the woman puts our rings in a glossy black bag. My wedding band is just as beautiful—a platinum diamond eternity ring that fits against my engagement ring.

As we leave the store I'm feeling a bit in shock. We just bought wedding bands. Now we just have to pick a date and figure everything else out, but—rings!

"Are you happy?" he asks when we get in his car. "You're sure you like the rings?"

"Are you kidding?" I say excitedly. "I can't believe we just bought wedding rings. Oh my God!" I bounce up and down in the passenger seat. "I wish we could wear them right now."

"Me too. You're so fucking cute. Come here and kiss me."

I lean over to kiss him and he grabs my waist and pulls me onto his lap. We laugh and kiss, tapping our teeth into each other's but we just laugh and kiss until our giddy happiness morphs into hungry desire and we're pulling at each other's clothes.

"I want you right now," he whispers. He slides his hand under my shirt and squeezes my breasts, then moves his lips to the cleavage revealed at the front of my shirt.

"We're in a mall parking lot," I remind him, grinding myself against the rock-hard cock straining under his jeans. Even I'm tempted—but there are people walking by.

"We won't be for long."

Ten minutes later we're ripping each other's clothes off against the wall in a tiny room at a hotel across the street.

Later when we're driving home and he's holding my hand and singing love songs with his gorgeous, happy, heart-stopping smile, I'm wondering how I got so lucky. Wedding bands and spontaneous sex in a random hotel before noon on a Saturday afternoon. We've got plans for dinner and a movie later with our daughter. Then there will be late-night candlelit snuggles.

I seriously cannot wait to marry this man.

I'm pouting. I don't care. Watching Blue pack always gives me a hollow feeling in my chest and a lump in my throat. I don't think there will ever be a time that a little part of me won't worry that he might never come back. It's just one of those scars that may have faded, but will never truly disappear.

"How long will you be gone?" I ask, even though I've asked this at least three times already over the past few days. I keep hoping the answer might magically change.

"Two or three weeks," he answers, zipping his suitcase shut. Archie walks across the bed and plants himself on top of the suitcase, which he does every time Blue packs his clothes. I smile as Blue leans down and kisses the cat's head.

"I really don't want to go, babe. But the band agreed to it months ago, so I gotta honor contracts and agreements and all that other shit."

"I know. I'm just going to miss you. Everything's been so perfect."

He strokes his thumb across my cheek and gives me a sad smile. "I'm gonna miss you guys, too. But as soon as all this stuff is over, we can get married, go on an awesome honeymoon, and just…be together. Right?"

I turn my face into his hand and kiss his palm. "Right."

We could get married any time, technically. But we really want our wedding and honeymoon to be as stress-free as possible, with nothing hanging over us that we have to rush back for. Once Blue's commitments are complete, I plan on giving my notice at work.

"Are you going to watch me on TV?" he asks, grabbing his favorite guitar from its stand in the corner of our bedroom and putting it in its case with one of his old notebooks. It's the same guitar he played years ago in the park when I first met him. He takes it everywhere with him and I'm shocked he hasn't lost it with all the travelling and crazy rambling around he's done over the years.

"Of course. Lyric and I are going to make popcorn and watch you. I'm going to record it, too."

"When I smile at the camera, it's just for you. So you know I'm thinking about you."

No Tomorrow is playing at a live music awards show in two days. The next day they have an interview with a talk show, when they're going to announce that the band is going on a hiatus for an undetermined length of time. A few days later they have a guest appearance on another television show, then they have meetings with the lawyers, and the following week Blue has a guest appearance singing with another band. He'll be staying at his bass player's house in California while all this is going on since so many recording studios are near where Koler lives.

"I'll be watching for your smile," I say, already looking forward to seeing his special smile on our television screen. When he doesn't reply, I realize he's still kneeling on the floor with his guitar case, staring into it with a faraway expression.

"Blue?"

He stares blankly into the guitar case like it's a black hole.

I cross the room and lightly tap his shoulder. "You okay?" I ask softly.

He blinks, then suddenly looks up at me. "What?"

My forehead scrunches with worry. "You just spaced out. Are you all right?"

He shakes his head, pushes his hair out of his face, and closes the case.

"Yeah," he says, not looking at me. "I think I'm just tired."

I wonder if he's getting sick. It's eleven a.m. He slept until eight, and we got about nine hours of sleep last night, so he really shouldn't be feeling tired.

"Do you want to take a nap before I take you to the airport?"

He stands, still with a bit of a lost expression on his face, and forces a crooked smile.

"Will you lie down with me? And put the rain on?"

I wasn't expecting him to want to nap, but there's no way I'm going to turn down even a moment of cuddle time with him—especially when I'm not going to see him for weeks.

Wordlessly we remove each other's clothes, kissing softly in between, then we spoon under the blankets with the sound of the soft rainfall coming from the nightstand.

"I think I just needed more of this before I go," he whispers. "I just want to stay like this forever."

Me too.

CHAPTER FIFTY-ONE

PIPER

"I can't believe Blue is on TV, Mom," Lyric says, her eyes bright with excitement. Mickey is sitting between us on the couch, hoping we drop some of our popcorn. I may have *accidentally* dropped a few pieces already just to see his cute face munch on treats.

We've tried to keep Blue's band, his fame, and everything that comes with it out of Lyric's life so she can just be a normal young girl and not the daughter of rocker Evan Von Bleu. Blue and I decided since he's leaving the band, and because he promised the song they'd be playing would be a clean acoustic love ballad with no swearing, that we'd let Lyric watch him play live on television tonight.

And now she's absolutely entranced watching him sing and play his guitar. I'm surprised to see him playing his old beat-up guitar tonight, and a flash of pain hits my chest when I see he's got Acorn's worn black collar wrapped around his wrist. He sings with deep, haunting emotion, his voice raw and raspy like razors are slicing out the words.

> *If I could stay, I think I would*
> *If I could've saved you, I think I would*
> *If I could bring you with me, God knows I would*
> *But I'm on this road alone, doing nothing that I should.*

"Why is Blue so sad, Mom?" Lyric asks.

"He's not sad, sweetie. It's just the song."

She shakes her head, not taking her eyes off her father on the screen.

"No. He's sad. I can see it."

I wish I didn't love you
I wish you didn't love me, too
I wish I could change the things I do
I wish none of this was true.

Toward the end of the song he looks into the camera and his lips curve into a quick sexy smile before he turns away.

My heart swells. That smile was for me

"I didn't know he could sing like that," Lyric comments, with that same faraway expression Blue gets.

"Yeah. Your dad's pretty amazing."

She nods and tilts her head to the side as she watches him on the television screen.

"He really is," she agrees. "I wish he looked happier. When he plays for me here, he always looks happy."

I smile and pet Mickey. "He's happy. A lot of musicians have stage personalities where they look, dress, and act different than they do in their normal life."

"Kind of like acting?"

"Yes, exactly like acting."

She ponders that for a moment while Blue rises from his stool on stage and bows in thanks to the audience as they stand and clap. Even with his air of melancholy, he's magnetic and charismatic on stage.

"Someday if I play the harp for lots of people like Blue does, should I be different, too?"

"That's up to you. You'll have to see how you feel. It might be easier for you to play in front of people if you pretend to be a little different. Or you might just want to totally be yourself."

"I think I just want to be myself. It seems a lot easier."

I smile, knowing that would be my little girl's answer. She's always been authentic and true to herself and I love that about her.

"If Blue calls tonight, can I talk to him? I want to tell him how much I loved his voice and his song. And I want to make sure he's not sad."

If he does call, it will probably be after midnight, but she's so proud of him and excited to have seen him play live that I can't say no to her.

"I'm not sure if he's going to call since it's late, but tomorrow's Saturday so if you want to sit in bed and read or watch television for a while in case he calls really late, then you can."

She jumps off the couch to kiss me goodnight, then races to her room. She and Blue have an adorable bond and I hope it keeps getting stronger as she gets older. I know the teen years can be hard but I'm keeping my fingers crossed that she doesn't go through a rebellious or 'I hate my parents' phase.

While I wait up hoping Blue calls, I sit in bed reading a wedding magazine with four others piled next to me. These magazines are a rabbit hole of magical dreams. Pages upon pages of gorgeous flowing dresses, colorful bouquets, hair and makeup to die for. And cakes. Oh wow, the multi-tiered cakes that have intricate lace icing and candy pearls. I want everything. Blue said I could have anything and everything for our wedding. Honestly, I just want me and him and Lyric, in cool clothes, on a beach or in Vegas or in a gazebo in a park. That's all I need to be happy. This other stuff is fun to look at, but I don't need all this extravagance.

I'm starting to nod off and dropping the magazine every five minutes when he calls.

"Hi, handsome," I say into the phone. "You were incredible tonight. Was that a new song?"

"Yeah. It's the first time we've played it live."

"I loved it. And Lyric was just in awe watching you play on TV. She was glued to the screen."

"She really liked it?"

"Hon, I wish you could've seen her face. She really wanted to talk to you but I checked on her a few minutes ago and she's asleep. It's three a.m. here, so she's exhausted."

"Shit. I couldn't get away from everyone. I can never get away from everyone, Piper." Exhaustion weaves through his voice like a vine.

"Don't worry, she understands. It's okay."

"It's not. I want to talk to her again."

"You can try tomorrow. We'll be here."

He's silent on the other end of the line.

A few more seconds tick by.

And then a few more.

"Blue?"

Nothing.

Did he fall asleep?

"Are you there?"

"Hm?"

A familiar faint clink of metal vaults memories of Acorn to the forefront of my mind and heart. It's almost as if he's right here in the room, resting his head on my leg. But he's not. It's his name and rabies tags jingling together on his collar that must still be wound around Blue's wrist.

I swallow down the immense sadness that came with the unexpected memories.

"Are you all right? You just kinda stopped talking."

"I'm just tired."

"Is your head hurting again?"

"Yeah."

"Are you at Koler's house now?"

"Yeah. I'm in my room."

"You should try to get some sleep. Did you eat?" I'm turning into a level-ten mom but I don't care. I worry about him when he gets like this and I wish I could morph myself through the phone line and take care of him.

"I'm not hungry. I miss you."

"I miss you, too. Especially after seeing you on TV. You looked exceptionally hot tonight," I tease in a flirty voice, hoping to make him smile.

"Did you see me smile at you?"

"I did. Thank you for that. It made me all woozy inside."

"I'm gonna go lie down. Love you, Ladybug. So much."

His words seep right into my soul. Every time he tells me he loves me it feels like the first time. My heart still races, my insides still tingle with butterflies, he still takes my breath away.

"I love you, too."

CHAPTER FIFTY-TWO

PIPER

"I can't believe you made a raspberry danish." I take the plate from Ditra and set it in the middle of my kitchen table. "Were you really bored, or was this a dare of some sort? Did you lose a bet? I need a backstory for this danish before I eat it."

"We were at Billy's parents' house the other night and his mom was going on and on about how much he loves danish and how she used to make it for him when he was little and how we have to keep a man fed and give them babies to make them happy and I seriously just wanted to smack her but instead I went home and found a recipe for danish because this chick right here is never having a baby. I'll give that man all the danishes he wants, though."

"That seems fair to me." I pour boiling water into two cups with tea bags waiting in them and carry them over to the table where she's sitting.

"I thought so. I made two so I could give one to you and Lyric because that's the neighborly thing to do."

"I never bring you food."

"Because you're not a good neighbor, Piper," she says with a playful smirk. "But you *are* a great best friend. Didn't you take me on a shopping spree last week and clean my entire house when I had the flu?"

Archie enters the room and flops on a sliver of sunbeam shining on the floor.

"I can't believe that cat is still alive. How old is he?"

"I think around sixteen."

"Damn. How long do cats live for?"

I cut two pieces from her danish ring and put them on plates for us.

"At least sixteen years, apparently."

"He's almost old enough to drive. Think about that."

"His age doesn't matter since he wouldn't be able to see over the dashboard or reach the pedals." I take a bite of the danish and I'm pleasantly surprised. "Dee, this is delicious. Did Billy like it? Was it as good as his mom's?"

She nods. "He loved it. He even called his mom and told her it was better than hers. She probably hates me."

I cut another piece. "*I* definitely hate you right now. I'll eat this entire thing and gain ten pounds."

"You could eat twenty of these and not gain a pound."

I wish. Since I lost the baby I've had bouts of anxiousness and depression and I've been soothing myself by eating chocolate and ice cream.

My cell phone rings and I get up to grab it from the counter, licking raspberry puree off my fingers on the way.

"Hello?" I say, hoping it's Blue since I didn't get to talk to him yesterday. All I can hear is heavy breathing and gasping on the other end of the call.

"Hello?" I repeat.

"Piper."

"Reece?" His voice is barely recognizable. I can't tell if he's laughing, crying, or choking. "Are you okay?" My chest is already rising and falling fast with anxiety. It's five a.m. where the band is. Nothing could possibly be okay with a phone call this early in the morning.

Especially when it's Blue's best friend calling me.

Ditra flashes me a look of concern.

"Blue's fucked up...you need to get out here."

My stomach twists up into an immediate knot of fear. "Wh-what?"

"He's hurt really bad." He coughs and gasps again. "I don't know what the fuck he was doing...I don't fucking know...."

"What do you mean he's *hurt*?" A few seconds ago I was afraid he might be drunk or high again, but that one little word now has my body trembling with bone-chilling terror.

"He fell off the roof...."

"*What*?" My voice comes out in a shriek and Ditra jumps up to stand next to me. "What the hell are you talking about? What roof? How?" My head is spinning with a thousand questions and worries and insane gory visions and my gut is wrenching with nausea.

"I don't know, Piper. Everything is chaos here right now. Police and news and everyone's freaking the fuck out." He takes a deep breath. "I just know it's really bad and you should be here."

The dam of shock breaks and uncontrollable sobs rip through me. "Is he all right?" I ask with desperation. "He's going to be okay, right?"

Please say yes. Please say yes.

"It's bad." His voice pitches. "I'm sorry... but it's really fuckin' bad."

Crumbling to the floor, I drop the phone, and bury my face in my hands. This can't be happening. There must be some kind of mistake and Reece will take back everything he just said. Blue can't be hurt—it's just not possible. Blue's never been hurt before. And why would he be on a roof? It doesn't make any sense. Blue walks and sleeps—he doesn't climb up on things. I can't lose him. Lyric can't lose him. Not when we're so close to the happiness we all want and have been waiting so long to have.

Ditra's got my phone and she's nodding and writing on an envelope she pulled off my counter. I want to rip the pen and paper out of her hands.

No. Don't write things down. Don't make any of this real. I just want to go back to the table and eat danish and talk about the cat. Please...

Ditra kneels in front of me and forces me to look at her. "I know you're freaking out and you're scared, but you have to pull yourself together." I shudder and try to focus on her face. Tears are in her brown eyes, ruining her perfect eyeliner. "We need to get you on a plane, Piper."

"He has to be okay. I can't lose him, Dee. I can't... I love him so much."

She pulls me up, helping me stand. "I know you do; and he knows that, too. You have to be strong. I want you to go pack and I'm going to call your mom and Josh. We'll take care of Lyric and the pets. After I call them I'm going to get you a plane ticket and I'm taking you to the airport."

Everything becomes a whirlwind. I'm on autopilot, going through the motions that Ditra has set in place. Within hours I'm sitting on an airplane on my way to California and I can't even remember saying goodbye to Lyric. The only things I can are the awful things Reece said.

Fell off a roof.

It's really bad.

You should be here.

I'm suffocating in this plane with no way to escape the agony in my heart. I want to climb out the window, fall through the clouds, and find a hole in time so I can go back and undo this nightmare.

The confusion and uncertainty has every nerve in my body strung out. I can't sit still or relax my mind even for a moment. I fight the urge to get up and pace the aisle of the plane like a ranting lunatic.

Why didn't I call him last night when I didn't hear from him? Why did I go to bed assuming he was tired and had just gone to sleep? What if something was wrong and he needed me and I just went to bed—abandoning him?

What could he possibly have been doing on a roof? And what roof? Koler's house? Someplace else? And when—in the middle of the night? No matter how many times I turn it over and over in my head it makes no sense to me. Was my sweet Blue stargazing? Listening to the rain? Praying for our lost baby?

I need to see him. I need to hear his voice. I need to see his beautiful smile. I need to see him alive and breathing. I need someone to tell me he's going to be okay so this heavy weight in my chest will let me breathe and *think*. No matter what's wrong—no matter what's happened—I'll be there for him in every way. Without any doubt. I'll take care of him forever if that's what he needs. I can be nurse, wife, best friend, and lover. I can be everything he needs.

Anything. Anywhere. Anytime.

That's what love is.

I lift my hand and press my lips to my engagement ring, just like he does. I can see his intense blue eyes and hear his gravelly voice.

Love you, Ladybug.

I love you, Blue. Please hold on.

CHAPTER FIFTY-THREE

PIPER

I park my rental car practically sideways in visitor parking at the hospital but I don't care. All I care about is getting to Blue as fast as I can. I run inside, spin myself dizzy in the revolving doors, and stand breathlessly in the lobby, scanning the myriad of signs.

"Piper."

Reece comes toward me from a hallway to the right and I run to him.

"Where is he? Is he okay?"

Reece puts his arms around me and hugs me in that scary, desperate, apologetic way that screams all things awful. I'm already sobbing as I cling to his wide shoulders.

Closing my eyes, I take deep breaths against his chest, accepting the small comfort his embrace offers.

When I pull away I'm shocked at how terrible he looks. I've never seen Reece look even remotely tired but today he's got angry dark circles under his eyes, his dark skin is ghostly pale, and his black hair is a tangled mess.

"Can I see him?" I ask.

He shakes his head. "Not now. He's in surgery and—"

My heart lurches. "Is he going to be all right? What the *hell* happened, Reece? Please tell me something!" Anxiety and desperation are swirling like a cyclone inside me and I'm afraid I'm going to lose control and start screaming for answers.

"Piper, I know you're upset and this is fucking crazy scary for you and I'm still trying to wrap my head around it myself. I promised Blue a long time ago I'd always be here for you if something happened...."

I wrench my arms from his grip. I don't want him here for me. I only want Blue.

"Just tell me what's going on," I sob. "Before I lose my mind. How bad is it? How did he fall off a roof? Was he drunk? Just tell me. I won't even be mad. We'll help him..."

He grabs my arm again and pulls me to the side of the hallway. His dark eyes are pitch black and somber. The deep rise and fall of his chest hypnotizes me.

"He didn't fall, Piper. He *jumped*."

Reece's face blurs in front of my eyes. The corridor tilts and closes in, the walls crushing me with their whiteness. The floor rises up. I can't tell up or down. I can't breathe.

No. No. No. No....

"Piper, look at me."

I'm shaken like a doll. Rattled back to reality then held up by his big guitar-playing hands.

Hands just like Blue's.

"Look at me, Piper. Breathe." The puzzle of his face slowly pieces back together. I'm aware of people walking by us, eyeing me with concern as I sob in the arms of this bear of a man. They're taking all my air. I need to get out of here. I need to get to Blue. We just need to hug and listen to the rain and it will all be okay.

"Take some deep breaths. Don't pass out on me, kiddo."

"He didn't," I whisper. "He didn't do that."

"He did."

I shake my head. My bottom lip trembles and tears run down my cheeks as I stare up into his face, searching for truth amongst these lies.

"No...he wouldn't..." I can't even let the words come out of my mouth. It's too horrible; too unbelievable. Blue would never, ever try to take his own life.

We just bought wedding bands and he was happier than I've ever seen him. He was so excited about the wedding plans, and about finally living together permanently. Why... *why* would he want to end his own life?

It makes no sense.

Did he change his mind about getting married and didn't know how to tell me? Did I just not love him enough? Did he still feel alone, even with me and Lyric in his life? Did I want too much from him? Were his headaches getting worse and he couldn't deal with the pain? Oh my God... does he have a brain tumor? Was he afraid of dying a slow, painful death and just wanted to put his fate in his own hands? Was it all of it? What was going on that he wanted to *die*?

"I know it's hard, Piper. But you gotta believe me because this is going to get a whole lot harder before it gets any easier. He jumped off a three-story roof. Thank God for Koler's fucked-up huge bushes and trees, they kinda knocked him around and slowed him down, and the motion triggered the house alarm."

I shake my head violently, trying to thrash that image out of my head. "No..." I cry. "This is a mistake. It had to be an accident... he fell."

Reece's jawline clenches. "There was a note. And pills. It wasn't an accident."

My head reels and I cover my mouth with my hand so I don't scream my head off in the middle of this hospital hallway. Reece kneels down and puts his arms around me again, holding me like I'm a small child. I *feel* like a child. A little lost child that just found out everything they ever loved and believed in had vanished into thin air.

"Is he alive?" I force out.

"He was when they took him into surgery...but that's all I know."

I gasp and almost collapse into him. *He's alive.* He's still here. That's all that matters.

I'm completely numb and wobbly as Reece leads me to a small waiting room that has a PRIVATE sign on the door. He sits me in a chair and retrieves a paper cup of water from a bubbler in the corner. My hands are shaking so badly he has to hold it for me as I sip from it.

"Just sit and rest for a few minutes," Reece says softly from the chair next to me. "You're white as a ghost."

"How's she doing?" Koler's voice comes from across the room and I lift my gaze from the floor to stare at him, as if maybe some answers are going to be visible on him. Alex, the drummer, is sitting next to him and I realize the hospital must be keeping the band in this private waiting room to keep people away from them.

"I think she's kinda in shock like the rest of us," Reece answers.

"How'd he get on the roof?" I blurt out with my eyes still glued on Koler.

He shrugs and puts his hands up. "I don't know. I thought he was asleep. He told us he felt tired and he went to his room."

"Was he acting weird? Was he partying? Did he say anything to you?"

"No," Alex answers. "He was a little quiet but he wasn't doing anything."

"Do you think something else was going on in his life? Something none of us know about?"

"No," Reece answers. "I guess anything is possible but I don't think Blue had anything secret in his life."

"Then what was so horrible that he believed he had to *die*?"

They all look at each other and shrug.

I blink at them like they're speaking a foreign language. "I just don't understand any of this."

Reece squeezes my shoulder. "We have no idea what happened. We were all there and none of us noticed anything. We've been banging our heads against the wall for hours. He was acting normal. The interview earlier in the day went good. We were all bummed about going public about the band splitting up, but he seemed okay."

"He seemed fine," Koler adds.

"How does someone *seem fine* and then jump off a roof?"

They all shake their heads and I gape at them in disbelief. How could they have not noticed something? These are his best friends, his bandmates. They've been with him through everything—through all the good times and the bad.

Something must have happened or been said. People don't just attempt to take their own lives without acting strange or sad or depressed or giving off some kind of vibe.

"Did you guys fight about him wanting to leave the band and you just don't want me to know? He only wanted to be happy. That's all. He just wanted to get away from it and have some peace with me and his daughter. There's nothing wrong with that!" My voice starts to take on a hysterical shriek. They must be hiding something from me. Blue would never, ever, ever leave me and Lyric.

"Piper... there weren't any fights. Everything was cool with us. He was excited about a new start, the wedding, writing songs for other bands, maybe making a solo album. We're just as shocked as you are. Did he say anything to you that night? Did you guys maybe have a fight?"

I'm taken aback. "I didn't hear from him at all. I spoke to him the night before, after the live show, and everything was fine. We were happy."

"Blue's been fucked in the head for years. I think he just fucking snapped," Alex says, rubbing his hands over his face.

I glare at him with anger burning up inside me. "How dare you say that about him," I seethe. "He's exhausted from the tours and the stress and writing all the songs. That's all. I don't believe any of this." I stand and throw my water cup in the trash. "Blue would *never* try to take his own life. He loves me and he loves his daughter. You guys are all crazy and guilty because you pushed him too hard. You used him to do all the work. He probably just went to smoke a cigarette and he fell because he was so tired."

That's exactly what happened. Blue loves to look at the sky. He was probably exhausted and lost his balance. It was a horrible, terrible accident and he's going to be okay.

"Wake up, Piper," Koler says. "Blue's been a fucking mess forever. It's been a constant struggle for us keeping his shit together. Do you know how many times he almost ruined this band with his crazy shit?

Disappearing for days? Trying to sleep in strange places? His crazy-ass mood swings? His rambling? He's up, he's down. He's a goddamn ping pong ball. Yeah, he's a fucking god and the fans love him, and sure—he wrote all the songs. But *we* were the ones holding him up and picking up the pieces and doing constant damage control and babysitting. You never saw that side of him, you weren't on the road with us. You saw little slivers of him. He's always been on the edge of having a fucking meltdown and it finally happened." He takes a deep breath. "Ya know what? We shoulda quit this shit when he disappeared in the fucking desert. None of this was worth his life. We're all to blame for this."

"I can't listen to this," I spit out. "I'm going to find one of his doctors and I'm going to see him and he'll tell me the truth. *I know him.* He would never try to kill himself."

Reece grabs my arm and pulls me back down into the chair next to him.

"Give us a few minutes," he says to the guys, and I watch their feet as they stand and shuffle out of the room.

Good riddance.

"Piper," Reece says slowly. "We're not the enemy here. I know you're upset and scared, but you have to trust us."

I shake my head. "No. I don't. You guys don't know him like I do."

He pulls a folded piece of paper from his pocket, and I recognize the paper immediately because I have many notes just like this one at home.

"This was left for you. I'm sorry, but I read it when I found it in his room. So did the police. I asked them if I could give it to you since it's meant for you. If he doesn't live, it's considered evidence. The police photographed it and I wouldn't be surprised if this ends up online someday. Shit like this gets really ugly."

As I take the note from him, my heart races so fast and so hard it feels like it's going to pound right out of my chest.

"What do you mean *if he doesn't live*?" I ask weakly.

"He's got a lot of injuries. When I talked to the doctors earlier they were hopeful he'd pull through but there could still be complications. I think you should read the note." He stands. "I'm going to go sit over there but I'm not leaving you alone while you read this. Sorry, but I'm not doing it."

I nod and wait for him to walk away before I slowly unfold the note.

Ladybug,

I'm sorry for what I've done. I'm just so tired and my head hurts so much. I can't fight the voices anymore. I've tried so hard but I can't. I've failed everyone. The world is hating me. I've hurt everyone. Especially you. It's unforgiveable. I need you and Lyric to be happy. I can't let the voices and the monsters get you, too. They're getting louder and louder and closer and closer. So loud I can't hear my own thoughts anymore. I'm sure you've heard them in my head. I'm so confused all the time. It's hard to remember everything. The pain of it is killing me. I'm killing me. Please tell Lyric I love her. Thank you for bringing her into my life. Thank you for loving Acorn. I'm so sorry about the baby. I think he was sick like me and he heard the voices already. Thank you for always loving me and showing me what hope feels like. Thank you for giving me a chance, and for calming my soul. Thank you for letting me love you. I only made it this far because of you. You kept me going. You made me fight, but I'm not strong enough anymore. I wish I was.

I'll watch over you, I will. I'll always be with you. You're the only place I've ever felt quiet and loved and cared for. I'll spend eternity loving you. I'm never leaving you. I'm so sorry, baby. You deserve so much better. I loved everything we had, but I don't deserve any of it.

I'm going to fly now, I'm going to be free. Be happy for me. He says it will take all the bad away.

I love you like no tomorrow. Always. Always. Always.

~ *Blue*

My heart is broken—shattered—and all the pieces have fallen into the pit of my burning stomach.

I was wrong. I didn't know Blue. Not *this* Blue. As my tears fall onto the note and blur the words into tiny puddles, I'm not sure who I knew at all.

CHAPTER FIFTY-FOUR

PIPER

My broken heart is nothing compared to how broken Blue is. He's lying in a hospital bed with a broken ankle, a broken leg, four cracked ribs, a broken wrist, a dislocated shoulder, a fractured skull, and bruises and lacerations covering eighty percent of his body.

I only know all this because the doctor is telling us.

They found muscle relaxers, sleeping pills, anti-depressants, and painkillers in his system. Reece confirmed they also found those same pills in Blue's room—some of them in prescription bottles prescribed to Evan Von Bleu.

I've never seen Blue put a pill in his mouth and now I'm wondering if he hid them from me, or just never took them when we were together.

The doctor is also telling Reece and me that when Blue was awake, which wasn't for long, he was laughing one minute and crying the next.

Hearing that both devastates and petrifies me. What's happening to him?

"Can we see him?" I ask the doctor. I need to see him with my own eyes, touch my lips to his, hear his breathing. I need to see for myself that he's alive.

"No. It's still too soon."

Too soon? Is he crazy? It's been too long.

I step forward. "I'm his fiancée. Please let me see him. I'm sure he wants to see me... he's hurt, and probably scared... I can make him feel better, comfort him...."

The doctor shakes his head. "I apologize, but we cannot allow visitors until he has a psych eval. I understand your position, Miss Karel, and I know this is hard." He glances at Reece. "And I also understand we're dealing with a patient who is going to have a lot of people asking about him and wanting to see him, possibly attempting to sneak into his room and get information. We've moved him to a private room. Our priority is to do what's best for Mr. Von Bleu and get him well, physically and mentally. That being said, I think you all need to prepare yourself for a very long recovery. Not just for his physical injuries, but for his mental and emotional recovery as well."

Mental recovery? Blue is exhausted, and had a bout of depression compounded by stress. He needs to rest and get away from the crazy stress of the band and the fans. It's too much for him. Hell, it would probably be too much for anyone. He's not *mental*.

This doctor has to understand that I need to do *something* for the man I love. "Can I bring him some things and let the nurse give it to him then? Like his favorite dinner and breakfast? And his guitar? He always sleeps with his favorite guitar in his room."

"We can talk about diet tomorrow, but it will most likely be a few days before he'll have any interest in food. He can't have any objects in the room that he could use to harm himself. His room has been cleared and he has a round-the-clock guard in there to watch him."

A guard?

"I don't understand why I can't watch him, then. I'm more than happy to sit with him. I'll just read or watch television. He's not going to like a stranger in his room."

The doctor won't budge. "I'm sorry, but we can't allow you to do that. Once he does accept visitors, it will be with his approval only. You'll also have to remove any objects and clothing that could be used to harm himself or someone else. The nurse will go over all that with you."

"For God's sake, he's not a criminal." I look from the doctor to Reece. I don't understand any of this.

"We understand that, Miss Karel. I can assure you, this is all for his own safety. I suggest you folks go home and get some rest, and we'll see how he's doing tomorrow. I promise he's in good hands." He hands me a plastic bag he's been holding. "These are his belongings."

Reece walks me back to the main lobby. "You should go to your hotel, have some dinner, call your daughter. It's late and we're all exhausted. We can meet back here tomorrow morning. Maybe we can convince one of the doctors to let us see him. We're going to have to release a statement, too, since obviously the rest of our dates are cancelled now. I'll talk to Vic about it."

I don't want to leave. I want to park my ass right outside the door of Blue's room and be as close to him as I possibly can. I know as soon as he wakes up he's going to want me close to him and I don't want him to feel alone for a second. I don't even know if he knows I'm here.

"Reece, please make sure nothing bad is written about him. Nobody needs to know what happened, right? Can you just tell everyone it was an accident?"

Blue would never want the entire world to know that he attempted to take his own life. Especially after he's worked so hard to fix his reputation. And I don't ever want Lyric to read about this or hear about it. It would completely devastate her.

"We'll do what we can but it's really hard to keep things like this a secret, Piper. Blue is easily recognizable and I'm sure at least fifty hospital staff have seen him already. We can't make those people be quiet. They can run their mouths all they want."

"That's insane. Isn't it illegal and unethical for them to talk about patients? And to give out their names?"

"Fuck yeah it is, but it will be impossible for the hospital to figure out who leaked the info. All the news has to say is 'a source suggested' or 'possible suicide attempt.' Our lawyers can't stop rumors and that's all they need for a good story. There's no such thing as true privacy once you're anything close to famous."

"That's awful." I'm disgusted. "I don't understand why I can't see him. I'm not going to bother him, I just want to be there for him, so he's not alone."

"I know, but it's protocol. He attempted suicide. He heard voices, took a handful of pills, and jumped off a roof. They're not going to just let him waltz around and let people wander in and out of his room. Any one of us could be a trigger for him. He might try to do it again. They have to protect him. Even if it's from us."

I blink at him as everything slowly starts to truly sink in. Up until now, I think I've been in shock, operating on a sort of autopilot, just trying to get through it all without losing my mind and falling apart.

But Reece's words just whipped me out of the daze and into the scary, harsh reality.

Blue tried to kill himself.

He's been battling feelings inside that were so terrible, so scary, and so overwhelming that he wanted to end his own life to escape them—and I never even knew. I saw tiny glimpses of his struggles, but nothing like this. He said he heard *voices*. A chill creeps up my spine when I think about what that could mean. And how long has this all been going on? He never talked to me about it. He didn't give me, or anyone else, a chance to help him. He didn't even say goodbye.

He was going to leave me.

Again.

Forever.

CHAPTER FIFTY-FIVE

BLUE

The fucking bird lied.

I can't fly.

I didn't soar to the sky and find freedom and peace.

And where is he now, with his endless taunting and promises?

I haven't heard a peep out of him since I took a nosedive off the roof.

Freedom my ass, douchebird. You fucked me up even worse.

Look what you've done to me.

Look what you've done to *us*.

CHAPTER FIFTY-SIX

PIPER

I can't stand being in a hospital. Just the smell of it makes me feel queasy. And the germs that could be lurking in the air, and on any surface. The germaphobe in me is on high alert. I've washed my hands so many times my skin is dry and raw.

Worry and bursts of crying wouldn't let me rest or sleep and thankfully Ditra stayed on the phone with me almost all night long listening to my tearful tirade. I couldn't stop replaying my entire history with Blue in my head. I analyzed every memory, every word spoken, every action and reaction. I'm sure I must have missed some big clue that should've set a bell off in my head that something was wrong, but I didn't.

What I missed were hundreds of tiny clues. Some were cleverly hidden, and some were plain as day now that I'm looking for them, but not at all obvious at the time. The man I love with all my heart and soul was struggling in ways I can't even comprehend and I had absolutely no idea it was even going on.

A lump of sadness and regret sits in my throat that I can't swallow away. I let Blue down, I was blind and deaf to his pain, and I almost lost him.

How could I not know? What the hell was wrong with me?

Now I can't help but wonder—was he ever really happy, or was it all some kind of mirage he created?

"You never truly know a person," Ditra said last night. Maybe she's right.

Over the years Blue and I have spent hours upon hours talking. We've touched each other in every way imaginable, been as close as two people can possibly be. I've tasted him, swallowed him, slept with him, woken with him. I've laughed with him and cried with him.

So how did this side of him slip through the cracks? Was I always too distracted with our relationship to notice? Did he purposely distract me so I wouldn't see?

Reece and I meet up at the hospital at nine a.m., and the nurse can only tell us Blue is in stable condition because the doctor isn't available to speak to us. We wait in the waiting room until noon, when Reece convinces me to walk down to the hospital café to grab something to eat. He admits to me over lunch that he also was up all night asking himself the same questions and beating himself up.

As we're walking back to our designated waiting room, Reece stops short and stares at a woman standing in the main lobby of the hospital, who's leaning over the reception desk.

"Ho-ly shit," he mutters under his breath. "I can't believe she came."

I squint at the woman with the long, jet black hair who looks vaguely familiar to me. She appears to be in her early fifties, beautiful and very well dressed, with an air of class and control about her.

"I want to see him right now." I can hear her berating the nurse. "You get the doctor immediately. Do you know who I am? Who *he* is?"

"Who is that?" I ask Reece, glancing up at him. I know I've seen her before, but I cannot for the life of me place her face.

"It's Ellie Von Bleu, the opera singer."

I shake my head in confusion, not knowing who that is but of course I know that last name.

"Blue's sister," Reece adds, as if I should already know this.

My God. Suddenly it hits me. She's the woman from the park I saw years ago. The one who Blue said he stopped to chat with. She gave Acorn a tennis ball.

The room spins and I lean against Reece for balance. I had no idea Blue had a sister. He never mentioned her—other than that day in the park when he described her as just a girl he talked to sometimes.

"He's never mentioned her," I say. "How does she even know he's here?"

"I called her last night. I didn't say anything because I wasn't sure she would actually come."

I stare at him with mounting anger.

"You could've told me. Do I have to be kept in the dark about everything? I'm his fiancée and I have no idea what's going on. Now relatives are coming out of the woodwork and I feel like an idiot."

He blows out a breath of frustration. "I'm sorry, I just didn't want to add more confusion to the mix if I didn't have to. I told you, I didn't think she'd show up. They haven't seen each other in years."

"You still should have told me. What is she going to think of me? I'm engaged to her brother and I wasn't even the one who called her because I didn't even know she existed!"

Taking my arm, he leads me across the lobby toward Ellie, and I have no idea what I'm supposed to say to her. This is the most horrible way to meet a future sister-in-law. She's going to think I'm a total flake.

"Piper, trust me, she's not going to think bad of you."

She appears frustrated with the woman behind the reception desk, and turns in our direction as we near.

"Reece," she exclaims with relief in her voice. "There you are. Do you have any news? I can't get anywhere with these people."

They embrace, and she kisses one of his cheeks, then the other.

"We're waiting for the doctor. We just went to get something to eat."

I stand next to Reece awkwardly, feeling lost and small. Ellie is tall and gorgeous, and she has Blue's eyes, which are looking me up and down.

"You must be Piper," she states. A flash of fear zaps through me. What if she blames me? I'm Blue's fiancée—the one who should be making him happy. What if she thinks I've done something to Blue to make him miserable? People who are happily in love and planning a wedding don't try to commit suicide. What if everyone is secretly blaming me? What if they're right?

I swallow and nod, and she surprises me by pulling me into a hug and kissing my cheeks.

"How are you holding up? You look absolutely panicked." She holds my hands in hers and searches my face with kindness on her own. "I wasn't expecting you to be so young."

"I'm not," I reply. "I'm just really short."

She throws her head back and laughs. "You're adorable. I can see why Blue is drawn to you. Forgive my manners, I'm exhausted and stressed and I've been on a stuffy plane forever and this is all just so unexpected." She looks up at Reece. "Although I guess it's really not, is it? I mean, we all know Blue…"

Do we? Do any of us know Blue?

We go to the waiting room together to wait for the doctor. Koler and Vic, who were there earlier are now gone, so we have the room to ourselves.

"He's stable?" Ellie asks, removing her dark brown leather coat. "Do we at least know that much?"

Reece nods. "Yes. He's got a bunch of broken bones and he's beat up, but they told us he's in stable condition."

"Physically, at least?" she adds, raising her perfect eyebrows.

"Yeah."

She sits across from me at a small round table near the window, and I feel a bit cornered because I just want to be alone and sort through my thoughts. I'm still trying to pinpoint a moment of when Blue may have acted suicidal.

"I remember you," she says. "I saw you with Blue and his dog in the park. I was so hoping he would introduce us, but he just walked away…"

"I remember you, too. He told me you were just a girl he spoke to sometimes."

She shakes her head and purses her lips. "Of course he did. And I'm sure at the time, that's what he believed."

"Are you saying he had amnesia?"

"No, I'm saying that at times he wasn't exactly in touch with reality."

I wonder what's worse—not remembering things, or not knowing if your memories are real.

"So that day in the park, did he know you were his sister? Or not? I'm sorry, but this is all very confusing. He told me had a brother, but he never mentioned a sister."

"We don't have a brother," Ellie says simply.

I know for sure Blue mentioned an older brother.

I level my eyes on her. "He told me he had an older brother who got him started smoking weed when he was young."

"That's not true."

I stare at her and Reece, who don't seem fazed at all that Blue was talking about a brother he doesn't even have. "Why would he lie about that?" I ask.

"To him it's not a lie. It's like a child who has an imaginary friend. They believe the friend is real, until eventually, they realize they're not real. Blue has always battled with what's real and what's in his head."

My head and heart start to pound in unison. Could there have been times when he didn't think I was real?

"I honestly don't understand any of this," I say. "He acts a little strange sometimes, but I've never seen him talk to people that weren't there or hallucinate or do anything crazy. He has a very successful career, and he's a great father."

A sympathetic smile crosses Ellie's face. "I think he learned to hide it well, Piper. That's why he drank and did drugs, to try to stop all the craziness in his head. And it masked his confusion. He walked to keep his mind busy."

I lean back in my chair and cross my arms over my chest. "No. I don't believe any of this. I know he had a substance abuse problem, but Blue isn't crazy."

"Oh I wouldn't say he's *crazy*, but I think him jumping off that roof and landing himself in this hospital was probably the best thing to happen to him."

My jaw drops in shock and anger. "Are you serious right now? He almost died!"

"I know, and he's very lucky he didn't. But now he'll get the help he needs, and a real diagnosis. Something he's been running from his entire life."

I'm beginning to not trust or like this woman. Why is she even here? I can't tell if she cares about Blue or not.

She nods her elegant chin toward the engagement ring on my left hand.

"That's quite the ring," she says.

I pull my hand back, afraid she'll somehow take the ring's meaning away from me.

"Thank you. He surprised me with it. We were planning on getting married as soon as things settled down after he left the band. We have a little girl together. They adore each other."

"I know. Reece keeps me filled in. You're the only woman Blue has ever let in his life. He must love and trust you very much."

"Yes," I say, with tears threatening to start. "He does. And I love him. I've loved him for years."

Her blue eyes soften with understanding. Or pity? I can't tell. "I can see you do, and I don't have any doubt that he loves you. I'm not trying to upset you, Piper, but you need to know what you're dealing with, and I don't think you have any idea. Tell me, has Blue ever mentioned his childhood to you. Say, before he was a teenager?"

Has he? *Think, think, think...*

I answer her with reluctance. "No. He hasn't."

"I didn't think so. I was sixteen years old when Blue was born. Our mother had a lot of problems. She had bipolar disorder, schizophrenia, depression, and suffered episodes of mania. She never should have had any children, let alone two. And certainly not an infant later in life. When she was on her medication, she was somewhat functional, and fun, and loving. But when she went off her meds, she was mostly out of her mind."

I force myself to breathe and listen as Ellie tells me more. "Our father was a drinker, and quite frankly, an abusive asshole. He was not equipped to deal with a mentally ill wife and two children. I learned at a very young age to just stay away from them both and take care of myself. When I was old enough, I worked in town and saved all my money so I could get my own place and get as far away from them as possible. And then Evan was born, and suddenly there was a baby that nobody wanted to take care of. Luckily, he was an extremely quiet baby. Too quiet, if I recall. He never cried or made any noise. He'd just lay there, in his crib or on the floor, and stare at the ceiling or out the window. Our mother would forget to feed him, sometimes for days when she was having an episode, and he wouldn't make a sound. He'd just wait."

"That's horrible…" I almost scream. "That's child abuse."

"Yes," she agrees. "It was. I tried to take care of him. I know it sounds terrible, but I was just a teenager and didn't really understand the seriousness of it all. I was in denial, I guess, and didn't really know what to do."

I try to picture myself as a teen in the same situation. What would I have done?

"Our mother loved birds," she continues, and my heart plummets into my stomach because I already know where this is going. *I already know.* "She was obsessed with them and had all different kinds that she bought or rescued. And when she was good, she took wonderful care of them, and of Evan. He was too little to understand her massive mood swings, and the erratic behavior differences, and he believed that good mom and bad mom were two different people. And she let him believe that."

"An aunt? Did he think good mom was an aunt?" My voice shakes.

She nods with confirmation. "Yes. A wonderful, cool aunt. Evan was crazy about the birds. He was about four or five I think when he really started to spend time with the birds. He still wasn't talking, actually, I don't think Evan started to talk until he was almost six years old. He'd sit on the porch with the birds all day, listening to them chirp, and he'd chirp right along with them, and mimic their little songs, and he'd write in these old notebooks. One day I found him in one of the big cages with his favorite bird, chirping and writing away and I couldn't get his attention for anything. He thought the bird was talking to him, and I think he really believed he understood what it was saying, and he told me his name wasn't Evan, it was Blue. He was in his own world, and I knew right there, that he was screwed. Either he inherited what our mother had or she made him crazy or maybe it was both. I don't know. I eventually moved out, and I'd go back and check on him once a week and he seemed mostly okay. He was in school, and he was dragging an old guitar around with him, and even though he was still hanging out with the birds, he wasn't in the cage anymore. I thought he'd be okay. He was odd, and detached, but he seemed okay and not in any danger."

"You just left a little boy in a situation like that?"

"I did, and I've always regretted it, but I didn't know what to do. I was afraid of them."

"You should have gotten him help. The state would have taken him and put him in foster care, wouldn't they?"

"Yeah," Reece agrees. "They would have."

"I didn't *want* him to be taken away. I know that's selfish and I know now it was wrong, but I didn't want him taken away. I loved him. I thought he would be okay. I thought he'd be like me and just get through it and leave when he could."

I want to strangle this woman. I don't care if she was just a teenager, she knew right from wrong and she should have helped her little brother—not left him with parents who couldn't take care of him.

"Well obviously he wasn't okay!" I say. "You were older, you should have done something."

She nods, not breaking eye contact with me

"We can't go back in time and change it, Piper," Reece says softly. "Ellie's not a bad person. She was just a kid herself."

"I know that but—"

She cuts in. "Believe me, I've felt horrible about it my whole life. I tried to help him as he got older. By then, I knew he was messed up. Every time I tried to talk to him he either told me to fuck off or he acted like he didn't know who I was. Then he moved out of the house and into the shed, and then he lived with friends and again, I thought he would be okay. Later our father took off, never to be heard from again, and our mother passed away and she left him that house and he just let it go. I lived nearby, I'd see him in town walking around with the dog all the time, and playing that guitar for money, and I'd try so hard to help him, to get him to come home with me, but I couldn't get through to him. He would tell me he had a headache and that he had to walk from the voices and listen to the rain and the birds, and some days he seemed perfectly normal and we'd have a nice chat and play with the dog. I never knew if he was high, or sick like our mother, and I couldn't convince him to go to a doctor. I tried many, many times. I don't know why he chose to live on the streets like he did. He had a home, he had money, he had me. He just wanted to be alone."

"Wait," I interrupt. "Are you saying that house with the porch in Amherst—with the shed in the backyard—is his?"

She nods. "Yes. It's been his for years. It's just sitting there, falling apart. He had quite a bit of money left for him that our mother had from her own parents that she left for both of us, and as far as I know, he never touched it. I thought for sure once he got his life together, and made this amazing career for himself, that he'd either restore the house or sell it, but it's still sitting there."

The whole time he lived in that old dirty shed, Blue was home.

"I feel sick," I say, putting my hands up in surrender. "I really don't know if I can handle all this."

Reece stands and comes over to kneel next to my chair. He puts his arms around me and holds me as I cry, and I just want to disappear. My head is swimming with confusion and fear. Is Blue really crazy? Has he been crazy the entire time I've known him? I just can't believe that.

I pull away and wipe my face with a napkin Ellie hands me. "What about Lyric?" I ask, trembling. "Is this hereditary? Could she be sick?"

"No," Reece says quickly. "No. Lyric is fine."

He has to be right. Lyric has never acted strange. She's intelligent, and creative, and caring, social, and completely normal.

The door to the waiting room swings open and Blue's doctor enters. *Finally.*

CHAPTER FIFTY-SEVEN

PIPER

I'm fuming.

Fuming.

The doctor only allowed Ellie to go in to see Blue, because she's family. Not me—the woman who's loved him forever and has stood by him no matter what and who's been crying and going crazy with worry and who is the mother of his child.

"I can't believe this," I say to Reece as I pace the small room. "*We* should be in there with him. Not her. Does he even like her?"

"Maybe it's better if he doesn't like her."

I stop pacing to stare at him as if he's lost his mind. "What does that mean?"

"He's probably not ready to see us, because he cares about us and he knows we care about him. I'd guess we'd be pretty hard for him to face. Especially you."

God. He's right.

Ellie isn't gone for more than twenty minutes when she comes back to the waiting room. I practically jump on her like a starving wild animal.

"How is he? Is he all right? Is he in a lot of pain? What did he say?"

Reece touches my arm. "Piper, give her a sec."

I *am* giving her a sec.

She falls into one of the chairs and sighs. "He's a mess of casts and bandages and cuts and bruises. He looks like he went through a hurricane. It's dreadful."

"Oh my God…"

"But he's going to be fine." She grabs my hand. "He's going to heal, maybe get a little plastic surgery for that cut on his face, but he'll be good as new, Piper. It's going to take a while, of course, and he's going to need some physical therapy, but his body will heal."

"Good," Reece says with relief, but I'm still stuck on the plastic surgery comment. How deep did he get cut? "Did he talk at all?"

"Very little. He seemed surprised to see me, which I expected. His usual attitude is still there."

"But what did he *say*?" I ask impatiently.

"If you really want to know, he said he fucked this up just like he fucks everything else up."

Reece scoffs and shakes his head. "So typical," he says.

I'm crushed speechless. Blue actually thinks living is a failure? Does that mean he wishes he had died and still *wants* to die?

Why?

"He asked to see you," Ellie says to Reece, further annihilating my heart. "You have to see the nurse before you go in, she'll tell you what you have to take off. Like your shoelaces. And we're not supposed to ask him questions about why he did it, or say anything to guilt him or upset him in any way."

Confusion and heartache have me at a total loss for words as I watch Reece leave the room.

Blue must want to see me last. That's why he asked to see Reece before me.

"You don't want to see him like this, honey," Ellie says. "He's such a handsome man. You don't want to see him all bruised and swollen and cut up, trust me. It's not a pretty sight."

Does she really think I wouldn't want to see him? Has this woman ever loved a man before? "I want to see him no matter what, Ellie. I just want to tell him I love him and I'm here for him. I want to tell him we'll get through this together, so he knows he's not alone in this anymore."

CHAPTER FIFTY-EIGHT

BLUE

Oops.

I fucked that jump up hardcore.

At the time it seemed right.

Quick.

Easy.

Painless.

The perfect tragic and messy ending. The bird was talking to me again. He hadn't for a while, but then he showed up—when I was exhausted and strung out on uppers and downers and all-arounders. He sat on my shoulder and watched me read all the comments online about what a coward I am. How I've wrecked the band. How the fans hate me. How pathetic I am.

I was a fool to think life was going good. Was I really stupid enough to think I could just leave the band, marry my girl, escape everything, and live happily ever after?

I shoulda known I couldn't go quietly.

Then the bird started.

It's time to end the madness, Blue.

It's way overdue.

You can't escape. They won't let you.

You don't have to hurt anymore.

Nobody loves you. I do, though.

Everyone else hates you. You're a disappointment. A quitter. A freak.

Piper and Lyric will be embarrassed of you. You'll be a has-been.

Remember when it was just you and me? Remember how good it was?

Come up here. Near the trees. You can fly!

You can be free!

And here I am, all fucked up, numbed out on *approved medication*. Another failure to add to my list of many. I feel sick and cut open like someone put a window in me and they're all looking inside—seeing the river of disease in my veins. Everyone knows my secrets now.

I sorta feel relieved—for the same reason. Because everyone knows the real me now.

I don't have to hide anymore. It's been exhausting.

They'll take care of me now. They'll let me rest. Maybe they can make it all stop.

Is that even possible? To make it all stop?

Reece is standing near the door, the next in line after the sister I barely know. I laugh at how she calls herself family. Like that title gives her special privileges. I remember you, Ellie. I watched you leave.

I force myself to stop laughing, because judgmental eyes are everywhere.

"You look like shit." I tell Reece.

He smirks. "So do you."

"Turns out I can't fly."

"Did you think you could?" he asks, sitting in the chair next to the bed. He's not wearing shoes and his feet look strangely comforting here in soft white socks.

"The bird said I could. He said I could fly out of this world and get away from all the shit that hurts."

"We've talked about the bird before. You know he's not real."

"I know. But this time, he seemed really real."

He nods like this is normal and I'm not a level-ten lunatic. That's what best friends do.

"Why didn't you talk to me? Haven't I always helped you? You know you can talk to me."

"I don't know. I thought I was okay."

"You're going to get some help now, Ev."

I nod and a pain shoots up the back of my skull and radiates to my forehead. I blink away the stars that scatter in my vision.

"Piper wants to see you."

This time the pain knifes through my chest like a dagger straight to my heart.

"No."

"She's really upset. I think you should just let her see you for a minute, so she can see for herself that you're okay."

"No. I don't want her seeing me like this." I turn away from him and pain sears through my entire body. My brain hurts.

My heart hurts.

"C'mon, Blue. Don't do this to her."

The guard in the corner throws Reece a warning look.

Don't poke the crazy person. He might jump out the window.

I take a deep breath and my ribs scream in agony.

Every bit of pain well deserved.

"Will you give her a message for me? Since I'm not allowed to use a pen or pencil to write?"

"Yeah. Of course."

"Tell her I want her to go home."

"Blue..." He closes his eyes, but not before I catch the disappointment shadowing them, and he slowly shakes his head. "Don't do this."

"Tell her I love her and Lyric, but my head is way too fucked with fuckedupness."

He glares at me like I'm an unruly brat. "Do you think she doesn't already know that? She doesn't care if your head is fucked. She loves you. Plain and simple. You need her now more than ever. Don't fuckin' push her away."

"I don't want to see her."

No way can I see the pain in her eyes from what I've done to her.

The jump didn't kill me, but seeing what I've done to her will make me want to try it again, do it right this time, just to escape the unbearable guilt that's eating at me like maggots. I never thought I'd have to face the people I left behind and have to witness their pain and confusion up close and personal. The bird didn't tell me that, that little fuck. Like Reece with his dark analyzing eyes and his disappointed scowl. And Ellie with her *'I saw this coming'* face. I don't need to see Piper to know what I'll see in her. Heartache. Betrayal. Utter fear. Denial. Love's regret.

All because of me.

My little elf-like fiancée will spend days searching the internet and will transform herself into a nurse and psychotherapist in less than a week. She'll make it her life's goal to try to help me and I can't let her do that. I love her too much to put her through all that. I can't let her lose herself trying to find me.

All I've ever wanted since the day I met her is to be a real man to her. Someone who could take care of *her*. But that's never been the way it is.

She's already fixed me as much as she possibly can. More than I thought she ever could. She's the glue that held all my jagged cracks together, and I love her endlessly for it. Unfortunately, I've always known that eventually I'd break myself all over again and she'd be left with nothing but pieces.

CHAPTER FIFTY-NINE

PIPER

Ditra is waiting for me at the airport. As soon as she puts her arms around me in the baggage claim area, I start crying uncontrollably. Again.

I had a total breakdown when Reece told me Blue didn't want to see me. I jumped on the nearest elevator, ran down the hallway, and tried to get past the six-foot-three guard standing watch in front of Blue's private room. The guard literally picked me up with one hand and carried me, crying, screaming, and begging, to the nurses' station.

I could have easily been mistaken for an escaped patient myself. It was *that* bad. I trembled uncontrollably. My teeth chattered. My heart pounded and raced dangerously fast. My legs wobbled, my head became light, and I started to hyperventilate as Reece tried to gently guide me back to the elevator. Just as the doors opened, I collapsed, and I woke up some time later in a room of my own. I was diagnosed with a major panic attack episode, pumped full of sedatives for three days, had a visit with a psychiatrist, and was released with a prescription for anxiety meds.

After all that, I still wasn't allowed to see Blue. A part of me was hoping Reece would tell him that I'd become unhinged and he would want to comfort me. Of course the rational side of my brain understood Reece couldn't tell him, but it didn't change the fact that I was scared and heartbroken and just wanted the man I love to show me that he was still alive and still loved me. I desperately needed him to take all the anger, fear, and heartache away.

Instead I ended up like him, lying in a bed wishing I could escape it all and just go to sleep forever. Fortunately, I snapped out of it within seventy-two hours.

Blue didn't.

Reece made my flight arrangements. Ellie made Blue's transfer arrangements.

And here I am, back in New Hampshire, crying at the airport.

Once upon a time, I only cried watching *Titanic* and other sad movies. *What happened to that girl?*

"It's okay." Ditra soothes, stroking my hair. I wish I could believe her, but I don't think anything is okay and it might never be.

As much as I missed Lyric, I'm glad Ditra didn't bring her to the airport to pick me up. I'm sure she knew I'd be a mess and would need some time to pull myself together once I stepped off the plane.

"I'm so sorry, Piper," Ditra says when we get in the car. "I know this isn't how you wanted things to go."

"That's a massive understatement," I reply, digging a small pack of tissues out of her glove box.

"So he wouldn't even see you or talk to you? Nothing?"

"Nope. The only person he'll talk to is Reece."

She pulls out of the airport and cuts off a driver in a blue truck, who flips us off. Dee is totally oblivious, and just keeps talking.

"What are you going to do?"

"What can I do? My hands are tied. He doesn't want to talk to me, and now he's been transferred to a full-time psychiatric treatment facility for the rich and famous."

"I don't know...maybe it's time to just let this go," she says hesitatingly.

I turn to look at her, but her eyes are glued on the road. "Let go of what?"

"Him. The relationship. All of it."

"What?"

"Piper, you've been up and down with this guy for like fifteen years. Every time you think things are good, it all comes crashing down. But this? This is really just…beyond comprehension." I open my mouth to interrupt her but she just keeps on talking. "He threw himself off a freakin' roof. You said they found drugs in his bloodwork and in his room."

"Not *drug* drugs, Ditra. They were prescriptions. That's totally different!"

She gives me the wicked side-eye. "Okay, Piper, but he's not supposed to be mixing them all up into a cocktail. I know you love him, but this guy has got some *serious* issues that can't be ignored anymore. It's worse than we even thought. He's not just some random homeless guy turned rock star who has a drug and alcohol problem. Now we find out he's got a lifelong history of some kind of mental illness."

"Don't say it like that!" I sob. "I don't want to hear this."

"You have to hear it. This is the father of your child. You have to think about her."

"Of course I'm thinking about her!"

"Do you really want someone like that near your daughter? Or in your life? Is this honestly the type of guy you want to marry and have kids with? When the hell does it end with him? I'm not even involved with him and I'm exhausted and just done with it all. I can't even imagine what you must feel like. And now he won't even see you or talk to you? He just lays this epic bomb on you and then hides? Fuck that!"

I want to throttle her for her harsh comments but I know she loves me and is genuinely worried about me so I refrain from smacking her upside the head. Reece and I talked about this before I left. We knew most people wouldn't be supportive or understanding. I just wasn't expecting to have to deal with this kind of reaction so soon.

After I give myself a moment to calm down, I fix my runny eyeliner with a tissue and then attempt to talk to her without screaming and crying.

"First of all, he didn't do any of this on purpose, Dee. He's not trying to hurt me. I believe that with every part of myself. And he's not hiding, he's sick. Now he can be properly evaluated and diagnosed—for the first time in his life, I might add. The doctors are very optimistic that with the right medication and treatment, he'll get better and hopefully won't have these episodes anymore. I mean, even without treatment, he's led a pretty productive and functional life. So *with* treatment, he should be okay."

"Well, Jesus, I really hope so, but what if he's not?"

"Please try to understand how hard this is for me. You're right—I'm exhausted. I'm confused out of my mind. I feel betrayed; I feel like I failed him. I'm upset he won't see me but I also understand that he feels awful and he needs time to come to grips with what he's feeling before he can deal with what *I'm* feeling. This is about *him* right now. He's sick, and he needs to get better. I have to deal with *my* feelings about it separate from him."

"But how is that fair for you? Isn't this almost abusive? You get your heart broken and now what? What happens to your wedding plans? You're just in limbo now? Left to be an emotional mess all by yourself? I'm sorry, Piper, but I don't like this at all. I feel bad he's sick but damn, you do not need or deserve this at all, and neither does Lyric. What are you going to tell her now that he's going to be out of her life for who knows how long while he's at some glorified spa?"

That's another hurdle that I've sat up at night thinking about.

"I'm going to tell her he's touring with the band and it's taken longer than we thought. I'll have to take it one day at a time with her. The last thing I want to do is turn her against him in any way. Reece thinks that when Blue is feeling better that hopefully he'll call her and keep their communication and relationship going. She doesn't have to know where he really is."

"Hello? She's not a baby anymore. She reads. She goes online. She's going to find out what happened eventually. Some web sites are already speculating and spreading rumors."

My breath catches in my throat. "What? Already? Are you serious?"

She nods. "Yeah. Billy has been watching to see if anything popped up and a few of the rock music forums have some threads started. I think he said right now they're saying he's in rehab and had a meltdown after announcing the break-up of the band, but I wouldn't be surprised if they dig up the truth. They always do."

"Shit." I lean my head into my palm. "I can't believe this."

"This is what I'm saying. Is all this really worth it? Do you really want this to be your life? Don't you want nice and calm and...." She pauses and struggles for words. "*Normal*? No insanity? Like me and Billy have? You guys aren't married. You can still leave him and no one would blame you at all. You're allowed to walk away, Piper."

My blood is close to boiling from her hammering. She will *never* understand that leaving Blue is not even an option in my mind.

The buildings and trees outside blur by as we drive past, and I stare at them in a daze. That's how my life feels right now, like a dizzy blur, everything just fading into each other with no clear beginning or end. Ditra is right that I'm in a limbo. I hate it, and I wish I could change it, but I also have come to terms with it.

This *is* my life—the life I share with Blue.

"I love him, Ditra. That's all there is to it. I don't need to say the vows, they've been in my heart forever. Better or worse, sickness and in health—whatever life throws at us. I'm in it one thousand percent."

"I think you're totally crazy...." She shakes her head and glances over at me. "But I also respect the hell out of you, too. I just hope *you're* okay through all this. I kinda love you, ya know."

"Then just be here for me, Dee." I almost beg. "Don't bash Blue, or my feelings for him. Just be my friend, *please*. That's what I need."

She reaches across the car and grabs my hand, squeezing it hard in hers. She lets out a long sigh as she stares out at the road in front of us.

"Fine. If that's what you want, you got it. I don't want to lose you," she says softly. "But I have one request. I want you to see a therapist. I'll go with you if you want. I just think we have to take care of you, too, because it's not just about him. You matter just as much. He's not the only one messed up here, Piper. You are, too, and it's been building up for a long time. Lyric needs at least one of her parents to be mentally stable."

I nod in agreement, afraid to speak because a flood of tears is threatening to come pouring out.

CHAPTER SIXTY

PIPER

Every time my cell phone rings, I jump and grab it, hoping it's Blue. Today marks eight weeks since I left California, so when my phone rings I'm hoping all kinds of hope that it's him, but it's Reece's number on my screen.

"Hi," I say as my stomach twists into knots of anxiety.

"Hey. How are you guys doing?"

I get up from the couch and move to my bedroom so Lyric can't hear my conversation. "We're good. Nothing new, just doing our usual stuff." The usual being crying most of the night while hugging Blue's pillow, seeing a therapist twice per week, and eating my weight in ice cream and lattes.

"Good."

"How are *you* doing?"

"Eh. Feeling kinda overwhelmed and being pulled in a shit ton of directions. I'm okay, though."

Do I detect a hint of sadness in his voice? Or do I just analyze everyone now, afraid they might be having a mental break? I've searched the internet for signs of depression and suicidal thoughts in others, and this could very well be a red flag.

"Are you sure?" I ask.

I don't pry into Reece's life, even though a part of me wants to. He knows everything about Blue and me. We've talked for hours, but always about me and Blue. It's usually me rambling on and on. Most of the time I wonder why he even takes the time to call me because I'm sure he's tired of hearing my voice and having to pacify me. I know something is going on with him and the mother of his child, and I wish he would open up to me and tell me what's going on. Who does Reece talk to about his problems? Blue? Someone else? No one?

"I'm fine," he says. "I talked to Blue on the phone this morning."

My heart beats faster just at the mention of his name. "How is he?" My voice strains over the lump in my throat.

"He sounded really good. Before I say anything else, he said to tell you he loves you. And he said to tell you he loves Lyric, and Mickey, and Archie, too."

"Did he really?" A mix of happy and sad tears fall down my cheeks.

"No lie. You're the first thing he asked me about. I told him you're doing good. I'm supposed to keep the conversation upbeat for him."

I frown slightly with jealousy and frustration. Reece has been to several therapy sessions with Blue at the treatment facility. He gets to see him, and hear his thoughts. He gets to ask questions and be involved and *understand*.

I get a black hole of questions.

"Doesn't he want to talk to me himself?" I don't want to ask this question, but I can't stop myself either. I have little self-control lately.

"He says he's not ready yet."

The happiness I just felt is sucked out of me like a vacuum. "But why?"

He breathes into the phone. "It's really not for me to say to you, Piper. And believe me, I hate being in the middle like this, but I care about you both. I'm trying to keep a bridge between you two. He talks about you a lot—more than he talks about anything else. He's petrified. He's not ready to face you and how he's made you feel. He's afraid it's going to send him over the edge. He doesn't know what to say to you to make things better. He feels like nothing is enough and he can never make this up to you. He's afraid you might never feel the same way about him."

The ache in my chest grows heavier. "He doesn't have to say anything or make anything up to me. Please make him understand that. He doesn't have to apologize. We don't have to talk about any of it at all. I just want to hear his voice and tell him how much I love him and miss him. I want to tell him how Mickey learned how to sit up like a gopher and how Lyric is playing Pink Floyd songs on her harp and I want to hear if he's seen any rainbows lately and—" A sob catches in my throat and I can't say anymore.

"The doctor is working on all of that with him."

"I just miss him so much."

"I know you do. Don't give up, sweetheart, okay?"

"I'm not. And I won't. It's just really hard because I feel so alone in this."

"I get that you feel like *he's* given up, but he hasn't."

I collect those words and wrap them up in a nice pretty virtual bow so I can unwrap them and hear them again later when I need them.

"Thank you…for saying that. It means a lot…."

"There's something else I wanted to tell you," he states. "Blue wants to come clean."

"Clean?" I open one of the bedroom windows for fresh air and stand in front of it, looking out at the dragon statue Blue put in the rock garden. "About what?"

"About the suicide attempt, his mental illness, the drug use. Everything. He wants to let Vic release a new statement. He might do an exclusive interview when he feels up to it."

This is unexpected news, especially after the band's management and PR team went through so much to cover it all up.

"He really wants to do that?"

"It was his idea. He thinks people should be made aware of depression and mental illness, instead of hiding it like it's some big-ass taboo thing. There're other musicians in the facility, and they're thinking of starting like a non-profit to help others. I think he wants to try to get some sort of good out of this, Piper. He's got a massive fan base, he's in a good position to spread the word, so to speak. I think it'll get him a lot of respect. And if it makes him feel better, he should do it. I told him I'd do whatever I can to help him. The whole band's behind him on this."

I'm filled with pride for Blue—for wanting to face this and let the world know, and to try to help others. It shows he's getting stronger. I just wish he could also face *me*.

"I think that's great," I finally say. "He's right, it shouldn't just be hidden away and swept under the rug. Maybe if it was talked about more, people suffering wouldn't feel so alone. They'd be more open to talking about it, right?"

"Some might. That's what he's hoping."

"Do the doctors have any idea when he might go home?" As the words leave my mouth I wonder where Blue considers home now. In Seattle? Here in New Hampshire with me? In California where the fancy facility and doctors are?

"Not yet. He's not being kept there. Right now he wants to be there until he feels ready. It's a good place. You'd be surprised how many musicians, actors, and actresses are there."

I wish I could somehow get more answers. My therapist keeps telling me to just be patient and supportive with Blue, but to also live my life, and focus on what *I* need and what makes *me* happy. Much easier said than done, though. I've gone through so many stages of emotions—denial, anger, betrayal, abandonment, devastation. I've worked hard with my therapist to not let this all drag me under, but it's hard.

"Well, I should get going. Lyric is waiting for her lunch," I lie. "Thanks so much for calling, Reece. When you talk to Blue, please tell him I love him with all my heart." I swallow and wet my lips. "And please tell him I'm not going anywhere."

I end the call and stare out the window at the light drizzle falling, hoping a rainbow will appear to touch the sky with color. I'll never be able to see gray clouds and rain without thinking of Blue.

I've become one of those women who deals with her problems by doing insane amounts of housework. As soon as I hung up the phone, I cleaned all the bathrooms, vacuumed the entire house, cleaned the cat box, and came close to re-painting the front door. I decided to save it for another day when I'm feeling emotionally neurotic.

And then, just to make sure I obliterate the past two hours of keeping my mind busy and in a healthy place, I put on the recording of Blue's last performance—the live TV show he did. I haven't been able to watch it before today, but now I suddenly feel like I can't go another second without watching it. Maybe there was something I missed when I watched it live that night—like a sign that he was struggling. I sit on my bedroom floor with my face approximately two feet from the screen and watch the man I love come alive.

Seeing him so vivid, looking so confident and in control on the stage is a blow to my heart and only makes me miss him a hundred times more than I already do. Glued to the screen, I watch his every movement and look for a glint of sadness or mania in his eyes, but I don't see anything out of the norm for him. Blue always has a darkish, sort of sensual and brooding aura on stage and this night was no different.

His voice does what it always does to me—caresses me like a warm breeze, leaving tiny goosebumps over my skin. But this time I listen to the lyrics of the new song more closely....

> *If I could stay, I think I would*
> *If I could've saved you, I think I would*
> *If I could bring you with me, God knows I would*
> *But I'm on this road alone, doing nothing that I should*
> *I wish I didn't love you*
> *I wish you didn't love me, too*
> *I wish I could change the things I do*
> *I wish none of this was true.*

A chill slides up my spine. Blue always expels his feelings through his lyrics. Were these words a cry for help? A surrender? A goodbye? Or just the words to a mellow love song that was suitable for a television audience?

And then there's Acorn's collar. Why didn't I question him that night on the phone about the faded collar and tags that were wound around his wrist? I just assumed it was a tribute of some sort to his dog. Was he trying to say something?

I touch his image on the TV screen as the cameraman zooms to his face, and Blue gives a quick smile, then looks down, taking a deep, shuddering breath.

At the time, I thought his smile at the camera for me was sexy, but watching it with the knowledge I now have, his expression changes as the camera pans out. The smile fades, his eyes darken as they lower toward the floor, and he looks completely overcome with sorrow.

The camera moves to Reece, then Koler, and when it swings back to Blue, he looks normal again. But I saw it—that desperate, grief-stricken look.

I wish I had seen it that night, but would it have changed anything? What would I have done, other than ask him if he's okay? And if I did, what would his answer have been?

"I'm just tired," as he always says, or *"I'm thinking of hurling myself off the roof"*?

I'm sure the latter never would have come out of his mouth.

"Mom?"

I tear my eyes away from the screen to see Lyric standing in the bedroom doorway. "Hi, sweetheart. What's up?"

She steps inside and looks at the TV just before I turn it off.

"Were you watching Blue's concert?"

I nod. "Yeah, I miss him and just wanted to see him."

She sits on the floor next to me, in the same position I'm sitting.

"Blue's not okay, is he?" Her soft voice could have been a horrific scream and it would have had the same gut-wrenching effect on me.

"What makes you say that?" I ask, forcing a smile.

"I guess I kinda feel like something's wrong inside."

She knew he looked sad that night. She asked me why he looked so sad, but I didn't see it. Oh, how I wish I had.

I realize I can't lie to her anymore. She's too intuitive—too wise beyond her years—to have blinders pulled over her.

"Well… no. He's going through a rough time right now. He's been emotionally exhausted for a long time, and he's been…confused." She listens intently, nodding as if she understands, and I wouldn't be surprised if she does. "He had a very difficult childhood, and the memories of that still hurt him and make him feel sad and sick. Does that make sense?"

"Yes."

"So he's in a special hospital for a little while, and they're helping him rest, and they're going to give him medicine that will make his head stop hurting and make him not so sad." I can't bring myself to tell her he tried to harm himself. Not when she's looking at me with her huge, hopeful eyes.

"Will I see him again?"

"Yes, definitely. I promise you, he'll be back. Actually his friend Reece called me this morning, and he said that Blue said to tell you he loves you and he misses you very much."

"Can I call him and tell him I love and miss him, too?"

"Not yet, but I promise as soon as we can talk to him on the phone, we will."

Disappointment puts a frown on her face. "Okay. I sorta thought something was wrong when he was writing the bird prints in his book and asked me if I could read it. I hope he feels better soon, I really miss him. Are you still getting married?"

If I have anything to do with it, then hell yes, we're getting married.

"Of course we are, it's just postponed until he feels better. Don't worry, okay? Come here and give me a hug." Smiling, she crawls across the floor and hugs me, then tells me she's going to take Mickey in the backyard to teach him how to do new tricks.

It's not until I hear her outside with the dog that I remember what she said about the bird prints and Blue's book. Confused, I go to the closet where he keeps some of his things, and sure enough, one of his old journal books are in there. I pull it out and flip through a few pages of journal entries until I get to a page of the scribbles—only now I see they're not just random scribbles as I've always thought. They're actually bird tracks.

What the hell? Here's a huge red flag that's been right in front of me for *years* and I was completely clueless.

I wonder how many people with mental illness are walking around suffering in silence, smiling on the outside, and doing things like this that their friends and loved ones are just passing off as being weird, never realizing that they might need help.

Maybe I never did enough, or said enough. I always let Blue lead. I always waited for him. That couldn't have been good for me, or for him.

I grab my phone and send Reece a text:

> Can I write Blue a letter? Can you give it to him for me if I send it to you?

Reece
Yeah…as long as it's not harsh on him.

> OMG no, I'm not going to say anything bad. I just want to reassure him that I'm still here and I still love him.

Reece
His doctor might read it first, or with him. Just so you know.

> I understand. That's totally ok.

Reece
Send it to me and I'll bring it to him next time I see him. I plan on going there next week. I think he'd really like to get a letter from you.

I go to the kitchen and find a stationary set someone gave me as a gift at the office holiday party a long time ago, and I sit at the table and write a letter:

Dear Blue,

You've written me so many letters over the years, but I've never written any to you. Don't say I sent you emails, because those don't count. ;-)

Reece called me today. I'm sure you already know this, but he's been incredibly sweet and helpful. He gave me your message that you love me and I want you to know I love you, too. <u>Please</u> know that, and believe it. I love you with all my heart. Nothing has changed that. Nothing will <u>ever</u> change that. I miss your smile and your laugh and I am missing the hell out of your pancakes.

Lyric misses you, too. She's learning so many cool songs that she can't wait to play for you. We've taught Mickey new tricks. He's such a great dog and I'm so glad we adopted him.

I met your sister, Ellie. I like her. When she met me, I think she thought you were engaged to a teenager. LOL. I think your voice is better than hers. ;-)

She told me some things but I want you to know it doesn't change a thing from my end. You're still the man I love and the man I choose to spend my life with. That's not going to change. You have nothing to worry about when it comes to me, and us. The ladybugs put us together, remember? They knew what they were doing.

Reece told me you're going to go public and I stand behind you 100%. You have nothing to be ashamed of in any way. You're a strong, talented, amazing man. I'm proud of you.

I know you need time. I understand. I know a new Blue may come out of this, and I'm here to meet him. I love Evan, I love Blue. I love all the parts that make you YOU. If you're afraid to see me, or talk to me, please don't be. We can get through this together. Let me be here for you. I've loved you since I met you.

I've been yours since you screwed my brains out under the bridge. ;-) You're my one and only and my everything. I've loved you at your best and I've loved you at your worst and I'm going to continue to love you through anything and everything. Even if you decide you can't have me in your life anymore, I'll still love you, and Lyric will still be part of your life. I promise.

I'm still wearing your ring, and I'm still planning on spending my life with you, if you still want that, too.

I love you, always.

Piper xo

I carefully fold it, put it in its matching envelope, and address it to Reece. I can't just sit and wait for Blue to contact me while he's in a hospital worrying that I might hate him or that I don't want him anymore or that there's no chance for us anymore. *Screw that.* I'm making the first move, whether it's right or wrong—I feel like he needs to know I'm okay, and that I still love him no matter what.

CHAPTER SIXTY-ONE

EVAN

My hands shake so bad as I read Piper's letter I can hardly read the words.

Breathe, Evan.

All the words I needed to hear are right here on this light pink paper with the faint purple butterfly in the corner. This paper came from her kitchen drawer with the wiggly knob under the coffee maker. I know because it smells like the tiny vanilla candles she keeps in that drawer. Sometimes when we sit on the back porch late at night we light those candles for ambience. It's a hint of home, and a flood of memories of her naked on my lap with the glow of flickering flames dancing on her skin and holy fuck, her words and the scent practically suck me into a portal and transport me right back to her and her cozy little house.

This is what I needed to help pull me out of the lingering haze I've been fighting to get out of for the past few weeks.

Since I've been in therapy, I've tried to look at my jump—as I've appropriately nicknamed it—as a new start. *A reset.* I was at my lowest low, ever, when I was admitted. That's pretty low considering the shit I've done in my life. A deep, dark hole was holding me prisoner with no hope of ever finding a way out. Humiliation, regret, and shame consumed me for not only doing what I did, but for failing so horribly at it.

And the very worst part—for committing the ultimate betrayal to the woman I love. I promised her a future, and then I ripped it away from her in the worst way possible, along with her heart and her trust and her years of patience and unconditional love. I'm sure for the lover left behind, suicide is the most evil form of breaking up imaginable.

I didn't see that when I was standing on the edge of the roof.

The bird convinced me she was better off without me, and that I could take care of her better from somewhere above.

Even though I've known for a long time the bird doesn't exist, there have been moments of exception when he broke through the wall of reality and was real.

Now with the right meds tweaking my brain, the bird is gone. I thought I would miss him, but I don't. I miss the real bird—the tiny blue pet bird that kept me company when I was a little kid. The bird whose feather I wear. But I don't miss the bird that was in my mind that gave a voice to my illness.

I miss my ladybug. I miss her beautiful bluish-green eyes and the way her honey hair moves like silk over her thin shoulders. I miss her giggle and her smile and the way she purrs like a kitten when my hands and mouth are on her. Mostly I miss how she loves me the way I need to be loved.

Ladybug,

Your letter was like a light thrown to me in a dark tunnel. It helped me get through some of the hardest steps that I wasn't sure I could take.

There's so much I want to say to you. My mind is jumbled but not in the fucked-up way it used to be. I have bouts of clarity I've never felt before. Words and thoughts come at me now at lightning speed. It's overwhelming. Before, everything was always muddy and slow. I had to dig through it all to find and understand my own thoughts. Some days, I'm completely exhausted, but in a different way than I used to be. I feel clear and happy one day and sluggish and moody the next. The doctor says I'll level out and things won't always feel this way, but you're right, a new version of me could emerge from this and I can only hope that you'll still feel the same way about me. Right now I honestly don't know who's living in my head.

Before I keep rambling about all sorts of shit, I love you. I love you so damn hard and I'm so fucking sorry. I never meant to hurt you, or Lyric. Reece told me Lyric doesn't know what I did. I wish she would never have to know but I also think she needs to know. I'll leave it up to you on when and how you want to tell her. You can tell her, or I can tell her, or we can tell her together. I only want her to be okay and not be hurt or scared by what I've done. I hope she can forgive me. I'll spend the rest of my life showing you both how much I love you and appreciate you. I'll never hurt either of you again. That much I do know for sure.

I know I severed our trust. I don't expect you to let that go easily and I don't want you to. We have a long road in front of us, but we've been down long bumpy roads before and I hope we can get to the end of this one together. I can't do it without you. Please keep wearing my ring. I'm still hoping we can get our happy ending.

I never told you I went to a regular doctor on the road and got meds for anxiety and depression and insomnia. I thought it would chill me out so I could enjoy more of our wedding and not feel so distracted in my head. I didn't know the wrong meds could make me worse. Apparently neither did he. I could feel my head getting worse but I didn't know how to stop it. So, I took more pills. I guess Ellie was right and it's good this happened because I never knew what was wrong with me. I just thought I was different, confused, eccentric, depressed, and basically fucked up. I drank and did drugs because I didn't know how else to deal with how I felt inside or how to make it stop. Now I know what's wrong with me has a label. Several. Bipolar, depression, personality disorder, dissociative, hypomania. I forget the rest, but that's enough. My entire life I lived in this crazy abyss of emotions, voices, and confusion. I tried to exist in a world where others couldn't see or hear things the same way I did. Now I have to try to sort it all out and find who I am in this when the dust settles. Some days I worry my ass off. What if I'm too different? What if you don't like me? What if Lyric doesn't like me? What if all my creativity is gone? What if I can't write or play guitar anymore? What if I feel like a zombie all the time? What if the bird comes back?

I want you to know that all my feelings for you were always real. Everything we shared was real. I understand you might doubt that now. You were never a part of my delusions. You were my only anchor. I always knew with you what was real and what I could trust. You saw the real me. I felt my best when I was with you.

I'm sorry this is a rambling mess. I'm still learning and still getting better. I'll probably never be normal, but I'm sure I can be more normal than I was. The doctors are helping me and they'll keep helping me after I leave. I promise to stay in treatment and on the right meds.

Physically I'm starting to feel better. I'm in physical therapy and still have some lingering pain but I'm not taking any pills for pain.

Fuck, I just ramble a lot now. I hope that gets better or I'm going to be annoying as fucking hell. I was hoping to still write songs after I left the band but now I'll be writing songs with ten thousand words.

It's time for me to go to group and share my feelings. I'm not kidding. I'm going to tell them I finally got up the guts to write to you. Maybe I'll get a gold star.

I miss you, baby, so much I can't even put into words. I'm going to call you when I feel a little less rambly and jumbled.

Thank you for not giving up on me and for always being everything I need. I hope you believe that and I hope you can someday let me show you how much I love you. I hope you're okay and taking care of yourself. I don't want you worrying about me all the time. I want you to be happy and feel safe and loved. I still want to give you everything in the world, but for now, we're back where we once were and all I can give you is my love.

I love you like no tomorrow,

Evan

CHAPTER SIXTY-TWO

PIPER

Evan.

First a crystal vase of beautiful exotic flowers arrived, and then two days later a letter came. Both from *Evan*.

I wonder what it means that he's suddenly signing with his real name. Is the doctor forcing him to? Or is he doing it on his own?

Regardless, he's reaching out and slowly letting me back in. I wouldn't have minded if he rambled on in a letter of a hundred pages. All that matters is that he's alive, he's getting real help, and he sounds realistic and hopeful.

And he still loves me. He's not giving up on us.

I needed to hear his words just as much as he needed mine.

I'm filling the vase with fresh water from the kitchen sink when my phone rings. I don't recognize the number on the caller I.D. and almost don't answer it, but I give in and pick it up on the fourth ring.

"Hello?"

I'm met with silence on the other end, but my heart already knows who it is. I can actually feel his nervousness buzzing through the line.

"I was just giving the flowers fresh water," I say. "They're beautiful. Thank you for such a nice surprise. I was having a bad day when they came, and it totally cheered me up."

"Why were you having a bad day?"

God, his voice. It's been almost three months since I've heard his sexy, gravelly voice, and it brings me back to the times we'd go years without talking, and when he'd finally call, my insides would quiver and quake at the sound of his voice. Just like they're doing now.

I should keep the conversation casual.

No tears. No questions. No pressure.

"The usual stuff. I had to sit through five boring meetings at work and listen to people be assholes about unrealistic deadlines. Then my computer crashed and I lost what I was working on because it didn't auto-save. It was just a yucky day. Getting surprise flowers from you turned my entire day around."

"Oh yeah? Just like that?"

My fingers tighten around the phone when I catch a hint of his familiar teasing tone.

"Yup. Just like that," I reply. "I got your letter a few days ago, too."

"Did you need a decoder ring to decipher my non-stop rambling? Maybe an IV of Red Bull to keep yourself awake?"

"Nope. It was perfect, and it made me just as happy as the flowers did. Maybe even a little more."

"Piper..." His voice fades into unspoken words.

I swallow hard and take a breath. I have to be strong. I can*not* fall to pieces.

I keep talking so the silence doesn't eat us up. "Lyric taught Mickey a bunch of tricks. He can sit up on his hind legs, he gives paw, he can roll over, he'll walk backward, twirl, and dance."

"She really taught him all that?"

"She did. She spends hours with him every day. And when she's not training the dog to do something, she's on the harp. Practicing constantly just like you told her to. She learned some Pink Floyd songs."

"Holy shit. One of my fave bands."

I smile "I know. Mine too."

"Damn. I can't wait to hear her play. And see Mickey do tricks. Is she home?"

"No, she's at my mom's."

"Oh." He pauses. "Does she know? About me?"

"No. Not yet."

"Do you think I could talk to her next time I call?"

"Of course. You don't have to ask for permission, she's your daughter. Nothing's changed. She misses you and can't wait to talk to you and play songs for you."

"I really miss her, too."

"You can call any time. You can come here any time," I say softly.

His breathing deepens. "I'm so sorry, Piper."

I close my eyes for a few seconds and push back on the tears creeping up on me.

"Don't. You have nothing to be sorry for."

"No, I have *everything* to be sorry for."

I don't know what to say to him. I wanted to keep the conversation light and happy so he wouldn't feel pressured to talk about any of what happened. I wanted to show him that we're still okay, just like we've always been.

"I miss you, Ladybug."

"I miss you, too."

The click of his tongue piercing… a sound I've missed.

He coughs nervously. "Can I maybe see you sometime?"

My heart jumps so hard a tiny gasp comes out of my mouth in response.

"I'd love to see you. More than love, actually, but that's the only word that even comes close."

He lets out a short laugh. "I want to see you, too. Really fuckin' bad."

I'm so excited I start to shake. "Whenever is good for you. Just let me know. I can come there, or you can come here."

"Let me think about it and talk to my doctor about when and what's best."

"Okay."

"Piper…." Another long pause leaves me breathless with apprehension "I just wanted to say thank you. For dealing with all my shit. And for making this easier for me than it probably should be."

"I don't *deal with you*. I love you. In every way—I love you. And I know you love me. That's what makes it easy."

"Loving you is an understatement," he says. "I'll call you again... soon. I just need some more time."

I hold onto the phone for several minutes after he ends the call. A slush pile of feelings builds up inside me again. Hope, sadness, excitement, impatience, nervousness. I feel like a mental smoothie—everything thrown in and whipped up into gush. I wish there was a way we could fast forward and get to the part where we're happily married, enjoying our life together, with no more uncertainty or gray areas.

The front door opening and closing jolts me out of my daze and Lyric comes running in with Josh not far behind her.

"Mom! Uncle Josh took me to the mall on the way home from Grandma's and we had pretzels and then he bought me these awesome boots!" She throws a shopping bag on the kitchen table and pulls out a huge shoe box.

"Look at them! Aren't they cool?" She holds up a black boot with fringe hanging down the side.

"They are!" I exclaim. "I had a pair just like those when I was in high school."

"I remember," Josh says, leaning against the counter.

"I love them! I'm going to go put them away." She throws her arms around Josh. "Thanks, Uncle Josh. Love you."

"Love you too," he says as she skips off to her room.

I give him the side-eye as I pick the vase up out of the sink and put it back in the middle of the table.

"You're not supposed to spoil her," I remind him.

"I'm not spoiling her. They're just boots. They're not even real leather. Every time we walk by the shoe store she says she wants them. I thought they were cute, especially since you had a pair."

Josh has lived up to his word of continuing to spend time with Lyric. He always makes time for her, even if it's just to pick her up at my parents' house and take her to the mall for a quick snack before bringing her home.

"Thanks for picking her up and getting her the boots. She's getting more and more interested in clothes all of a sudden. She's going to outgrow her closet soon. I might need a bigger house."

"You can move back into my place. Remember? Where you both had huge walk-in closets…" He raises an eyebrow.

"Stop it."

He grins and shrugs. "I can't help it if I hate my empty house."

"Then sell it and buy one of those cool open concept expensive lofty apartments with the brick walls inside."

"That's not a bad idea. Did I tell you my ex and his partner adopted a baby?"

"No, you didn't."

"Yeah. When I wanted a baby, it was all *'Ooh I'm not ready yet'*."

"Well in his defense, that was years ago, Josh. Things change. People change."

"I guess you're right." He nods his chin toward the flowers. "Where'd the flowers come from?"

"Blue sent them."

His eyes widen. "Really? What's up with all that?"

"Nothing is *up*."

"So how is he?"

"He seems really good. He called me for the first time right before you and Lyric got here."

He crosses his arms. "Flowers and phone calls. Seems like apologies and groveling?"

I shoot him a warning glare. "Josh, we have to start somewhere."

"Or you could not start anywhere and just let it be over."

Ignoring him, I gently touch one of the flower petals and fall into one of the kitchen chairs.

"Piper… I'm worried about you. And Lyric."

"We're fine." I do not want to have this conversation again. Or ever.

He moves across the room and sits across the table from me, making it clear we are very much going to have this conversation.

"The guy put a ring on your finger and then attempted suicide, Piper. How could you possibly be fine?"

"Because he's getting help. He was sick and taking the wrong medication. He wasn't thinking straight. And I've been in therapy, too. I feel a lot better now."

"You shouldn't need therapy to be in a relationship."

"Don't be an asshole, Josh. I was depressed, confused, and really pissed off about what he did."

"As you should be."

"No, you're wrong. I really shouldn't be. That's like me being mad at you for being bi, and for you being confused about what or who you want. If you weren't, maybe we would have lasted. Maybe we'd be married with our own kids right now and be happy."

"That's really fucking low."

"Is it? Or is it the same thing? People can't change who they are inside, or how they feel, or how they're wired, Josh. That doesn't mean they should be dumped and forgotten."

He shakes his head at me. "It's not exactly the same."

"To me it is. I'm not going to split hairs with you. I accept you for who you are, no matter what. Just like I accept him for who he is."

"But you and I are friends. You want to *marry* this guy. What if he does this crazy shit again? Or acts all…fucky for the rest of this life?"

I cringe at his choice of words.

"I don't think he'll do it again. And if he does? Or if he acts *fucky* as you so nicely put it? Then we'll deal with it together, like couples are supposed to."

He blows out an irritated breath. "You don't deserve that. Don't you want a good relationship for once? Ditra and I talked about this a few weeks ago. For years we've watched you ride this rollercoaster with him. I'm not even saying you and I should try, Piper. I understand our ship sailed a long time ago. I'm saying you need an entirely new start with someone who can give you a hundred percent of themselves and not put you through an emotional grinder."

Did I miss the memo that the rest of the population was perfect? Maybe there're some couples out there who have never had a fight, never had any issues, and it's been smooth sailing for them, but it seems like most couples go through varying degrees of messy at some point, no matter how much they love each other.

"Honestly, Josh…I don't really think that exists with anyone. Nobody's perfect. Everyone has baggage. You know that just as well as I do. And why do I deserve better? There's nothing about me that deserves the Lamborghini of men. I'm just a boring average chick who only wants to be happy."

"I just don't know why you want to be with somebody so…high risk."

"Because I love him. People don't have to be perfect to be loved. They can be broken and sick and messed up and ugly. Everyone deserves love. And he makes me happy. When we're together and things are good, I can't imagine ever being happier than he makes me. I'm sorry if you don't understand it, or if you've never experienced it, but I don't have to justify our relationship to you, or anyone."

He leans back in his chair and locks his eyes onto mine. "You're sure? You're really sure you want to stick this out with him?"

"Yes," I answer without any hesitation. "I'm positive. And I want you to stop being so negative about it. Everyone has to throw in their two cents, and I'm sick of it, Josh. Ditra, my parents, people at work— everyone keeps telling me that Blue might lose his mind, or *I'm* the crazy one for wanting to be with someone with a mental illness. The only person who's supportive of me and Blue is Reece. I'd really like people in *my* life to be supportive and I shouldn't have to keep asking them to. If things work out, and I believe they will, he's going to be my husband. He's Lyric's father. I don't want him treated like some sort of criminal by my friends and family."

He stares intently at me for a few minutes, like he's trying to get into my head, or maybe see into the future to see what's in store for me. Or maybe for all of us.

"Okay," he finally says. "Ya know what? You're right. I'm being an asshole. I'm not going to say anything else. I'll do my best to be on your side, because I'm your friend. I'll even hang out with you guys when he comes back, and I'll make a sincere effort to get to know him and be his friend. I just hope this guy knows how lucky he is."

"Thank you," I say. "That would mean a lot to me. I just want peace and happiness and love. That's it."

I sound like a hippie chick from the seventies. This is what my life has come down to.

"I'm actually seeing a girl. So if Blue's going to be around, maybe we could all go for dinner?"

It may take a bit of convincing for Blue to want to hang out with Josh, since he's stayed a little pissy about us living together years ago, but if they at least tolerate each other and don't badmouth each other around me, I'll be happy.

I smile and fuss with my pretty flowers a little more. "I'd like that. What's she like? Any phobias or odd tendencies that will drive you mad before the fourth date?"

He laughs. "You'll be glad to hear that we've had more than four dates and I still like her."

I make an overly surprised, ridiculous impressed expression. "Wow. It sounds serious."

"It might be. Who knows. She's smart, she's wicked sexy, she's independent. I have no idea what she sees in me."

"You're smart and wicked sexy, too. Not very independent, sadly, as you seem to be afraid of the empty rooms in your house. But you guys could still be a great match."

"Very funny."

Lyric appears in the doorway, wearing her new fringy boots, with tears streaming down her cheeks.

"Honey the boots are beautiful, why are you crying?"

"Is it true?" she sobs. "About Blue?"

My heart sinks deep into my gut as Josh and I exchange a panicked look across the table.

"What do you mean?" I ask innocently, even though I know exactly what she means.

"On the internet... it said he tried to-to—" She bursts into tears, covering her face with her hands. Josh and I jump up. He knocks his chair onto the floor in the process as we rush to kneel in front of her to console her.

"Honey, he's fine," I say quickly. "I just talked to him this morning. And he sent me the flowers the other day."

Her eyes swim with tears. "He's not gone? Or dead?"

"No," Josh assures her. "Your dad is *not* dead."

Her bottom lip quivers. "But he *tried* to? Why?"

"It's very complicated, Lyric." God help me, I have no idea how to talk about this to a child.

She sniffles and rubs her eyes with her palms. "Why would he do that? Doesn't he love us anymore?"

"Of course he does. He just felt overwhelmed...and the doctor accidentally gave him the wrong medicine and it made him feel very confused. He would never leave you or hurt you."

"Then where is he? Why hasn't he called me in so long?" she demands. "You said he was playing concerts and then you said he was resting but he hasn't even called me. He *always* calls me. I learned all these songs for him, and he hasn't called me at all."

"Lyric, he really is at a hospital. He had some broken bones, so he's been in a lot of pain and sorta grumpy. And he had to talk to some special doctors about why he feels depressed and confused sometimes, but he's feeling much better, and his body is healing. He asked about you this morning and I told him all about your new songs and how you're teaching Mickey tricks. He's excited to talk to you and see you again."

She narrows her eyes at us. "Are you lying to me?"

"No," Josh insists, putting his hands on her shoulders and forcing her to look at him. "Your mom is telling you the truth. I promise you."

She stares at us both with the first look of severe distrust I've ever seen in her eyes and it cracks my heart in two. This is how children lose their magic and innocence—from the crap life deals.

"Why didn't you tell me? He's my dad..."

"It's very, very private. And he wanted to talk to you himself. When I talked to him this morning, we talked about him coming to visit. He loves you. It's hard for him to talk about all this and he's not ready yet.

You know how sometimes when you don't feel good and you just want to be alone, and lie in bed and nap and watch TV? That's how he's been feeling. He just needed some time alone to rest."

"You're sure?"

"I'm positive."

"When *can* I talk to him, then?"

"I'm not sure. But what I can do, is call his friend Reece and I can ask him to tell Blue that you'd like to talk to him, and I'm sure he'll call you soon. Okay?"

"I guess." Her face twists into a disappointed frown.

Josh smooths her hair and wipes her cheeks with his thumbs. "This is one of those things in life that adults understand but it's really hard for kids to understand. You have to try your best to just be patient and trust your mom, and trust Blue," he explains softly. "Why don't you write him a nice letter? I think it'll make you feel better, and I'm sure it will make him feel better, too. He must be missing you just as much as you miss him."

"Can I do that?" she asks. "And maybe make him a card with a poem and print it on the computer?"

I nod enthusiastically "I think that's a great idea. He'll like that a lot."

"Okay. I'm going to do it right now."

As we watch her walk back to her room with her head hanging down, the anger and frustration I felt weeks ago for Blue rises back to the surface and I clench my jaw in an attempt to suppress it and not start venting about it to Josh, which will only make things worse.

"He better fix that," Josh says when I glance up at him. "That's all I'm saying." He points down the hallway. "He needs to make this right somehow, because she doesn't deserve to feel like that. She's just a kid."

I nod. "You're right. And he will."

CHAPTER SIXTY-THREE

PIPER

I pack my clothes, throw my makeup bag in the suitcase, and kiss Lyric and Ditra goodbye at my front door. I tell them I'll see them when I get back from my business trip in two days. Lyric, as always, is excited about Ditra staying at our house with her because Dee is going to teach her how to bake a different cake each night. I have no idea when my best friend turned into Martha Stewart, but I hope there's some cake left over for me when I get back home.

I wave goodbye to them as I back my car out of the driveway, then I drive eight miles across town to the hotel near the park. My stomach burns with anxiety as I park my car in the parking garage and then make my way to the hotel lobby. I bypass the front desk and go directly to the elevator, getting off on the second floor.

Room 1205.

I hesitate in front of the door, fluffing my already-fluffed hair, straightening my already-straight shirt, taking extra breaths I don't need to take.

I knock lightly on the maple door and time seems to screech to a halt as I wait. My suitcase feels twice as heavy as it did a few seconds ago, the handle slippery in my damp palm.

I shouldn't be this nervous, and it's silly that I am, because it's only....

Blue.

Evan.

The door opens and I'm staring up into eyes the color of faded denim.

He steps to the side and I cross the threshold so he can close the door behind me. After placing my stuff on the floor I turn to face where he's still hovering near the door.

I expected him to look different after spending six months in a hospital recovering from various physical and mental issues.

But I didn't expect him to look so much *better*.

Not that he's ever really looked bad. He was born with the kind of good looks that can't look bad no matter what mess he made of himself. But holy shit, the man standing in front of me is like Blue version 2.0 with the extended elite upgrade package.

His wavy hair is a few inches shorter, just a bit past his collarbone instead of the mid-chest length it's been since I first met him. It makes him look mature and more handsome.

The feather still hangs from his ear, but he's explained it came from a *good* bird.

It's obvious he's not only put some weight on, but also muscle. The width of his arms and shoulders appears to be almost double what they were and I'm already fantasizing about what he must look like now with his shirt off. I'm surprised with how healthy and vibrant he looks —like one of those people who goes to the gym, gets eight hours of sleep every night, takes vitamins and drink lots of water. He no longer looks like a rock star who spent the majority of his life wasted and battling inner demons. He looks amazing and sexy and... *calm.* Nervous, yes, but also radiating an inner calmness.

A shy smile crosses his lips from where he's still rooted by the door, and it sends my pulse into a frenzy. Stuck between smiling back and crumbling to tears, I freeze under his gaze. I've missed him *so* much. For months I've loved and hated him and everything in between. That night, he instilled such a deep fear in me. He stripped me of my trust and left me abandoned with a filleted heart. I truly felt as if he was gone and I've been communicating with his ghost for all these months.

But he's here in the flesh and he's so incredibly vivid and real. His scent has already permeated the room, enveloping me, coaxing memories out of their hiding places. The warmth of his body is ebbing toward mine, luring me.

"Hi." My voice is a shy whisper when I'm brave enough to finally meet his eyes. The last time we saw each other was just before he left for California. Before it all went to hell. It's been six long life-changing months since we've touched or kissed. The sporadic letters, texts, and phone calls we shared during that time left many gray areas that we've been avoiding like sink holes. That is, up until a few days ago when he sent me a text asking me to meet him here for a weekend alone to *make things right* as he put it.

"Hey." He slowly steps closer to me, his smoldering eyes still locked onto mine. My heart flutters like a hummingbird as he backs me up against the wall, grabs my face in his hands, and lays a kiss on me that makes my legs buckle and steals my breath. He sweeps his tongue over my lips and into my mouth, seeking mine to dance with his. With a faint whimper, I reach up and wind my arms around his neck, pulling him into me. *Forgiving him.* Shaking slightly, he moves his hands to my waist and lifts me up like a doll, using his body to pin me against the wall as he kisses me with deeper desperation. I wrap my legs around him and pour all the emotion and passion that's been bottled up inside me for months into our kiss.

This wasn't what I was expecting, but it's without a doubt exactly what I want and need.

Him.

Us.

This.

He pulls back and we stare at each other breathlessly.

"I love you..." He strokes my cheek. "I miss you..." He moves his thumb across my lips. "Do you want me to stop?"

"No...never." I pull his lips back to mine and he plunges his tongue into my mouth, devouring me, sucking the air from my lungs. I grip his wide shoulders and tighten my thighs around him as he moves his lips to my neck, his teeth biting into my flesh, his tongue following. Hurting then soothing. Calloused fingertips dig into my waist; he grinds his hips into mine, igniting the desire between us.

So many questions; so many things I want to say perch at the tip of my tongue...but maybe the questions have already been answered, and nothing really needs to be said at all right now.

He unbuttons my shirt with one hand while he kisses me, and I follow his lead by pulling his T-shirt up and over his head. My eyes widen at the sight of his muscular shoulders and biceps, the glimpse of hard abs.

I trail my fingers over his tattooed chest, drawn to the solidity and hardness, the new aura of strength he exudes. Once again, I'm a moth to his flame.

He pulls down my bra and sucks my bare breast into his mouth as he unbuttons my jeans, pulls down the zipper and slides his hand beneath my panties. When his fingers glide over my clit and reach my wet lips he groans deep in his throat and flicks the warm slippery metal of his tongue piercing over my nipple. I arch my back against the wall, thrusting my body up into his mouth and hand, clutching his hair.

Reaching between us, he undoes his jeans, shoves them down, then tugs my jeans and panties down just enough to bare me to him.

I gasp and dig my nails into his back when he thrusts the full length of his cock into me, and his growling in response only makes me wetter and wilder for him. I've always been completely enamored with this feral sensual side of him that devoured me under the bridge years ago. Thank goodness the medication hasn't taken that part of him away.

I struggle to spread myself around him but I'm restrained by the jeans bunched around my thighs. Cupping my ass in his hands, he lifts me, then lowers me down, impaling me with his thick shaft.

"Fuck, I missed you, baby..." he rasps against my lips, kissing me ferociously, hammering harder and faster, chafing my back against the textured wallpaper.

"I missed you. So, *so* much."

Sighing, his eyes close and he stills, letting me take over. I ride his body slower, calming him, savoring every inch, every breath, every beat of our hearts. "Don't ever leave me again," I whisper.

"Never."

After our wallbang, he carries me to the bed, slowly removes the rest of my clothes, then his own. Wordlessly, he brings the white sheet and comforter up over us and pulls me to him, wrapping his arms around me. I snuggle my face into the warmth of his chest and hug him tight.

I promised myself I wouldn't cry today, but promises were made to be broken, right?

The moment I feel his heart beating against my cheek I start to sob; unable to stop no matter how hard I try to hold it all in. I was wrong to think I had resolved all the emotional turmoil during my months of therapy. I might have found strength, patience, and understanding, but those things can only reach so far. Parts of me are still broken, and I'm sure the same is true for him.

Stroking my back in slow circles, he presses his lips to the top of my head and whispers, *"I'm sorry,"* over and over again until I have no tears left. We cling to each other until my breathing calms and the hiccupping sobs have stopped.

"I'll be right back," he says softly, and I sit my sniffling mess of a self up and watch him disappear into the bathroom. He comes back with a handful of tissues and a washcloth dampened with warm water, which he uses to gently wipe my cheeks.

The sweet gesture almost renders me back to a sobbing mess. "I'm sorry, I didn't want to cry…I wanted to be strong."

"Shhh…" He touches his lips to my forehead. "*You* don't apologize, Piper. Not for any of this. You *are* strong. You're the strongest chick I've ever met. A weak woman would never be able to love me. You're a fuckin' warrior."

I smile weakly, not feeling like any sort of warrior at all. "I just want us to be happy. And together."

He climbs into the bed again and leans back against the headboard, holding his arm out for me to nestle into his side.

"We'll get there, Ladybug. I promise."

"That's all I want. For both of us."

I rest my head against his chest, slide my arm around his waist, and curl my leg around his, exactly how we used to sleep in the sleeping bag in the shed. How insane is it that those nights snuggling in the musty shed, listening to the rain fall on the tin roof with Acorn sleeping at our feet, were some of our very best times together? Life was simpler then, when I lived in a comfy bubble of naivety.

"I didn't want to die," he says in a low voice. "That's not what any of this was about."

Waves of sadness wash over me hearing those words. "Blue…you don't have to talk about this."

"I want to." He moves his hand to the curve of my waist and squeezes. "And I want you to go back to calling me Evan. Like when we first met. Blue's gotta go."

"Okay."

"Killing myself isn't what I wanted. There wasn't a plan. I didn't want to leave you. Or Lyric. Everyone just assumes I must have hated my life, and that's not true. I didn't hate my life at all. In fact, I was loving my life more than ever. There was finally a light at the end of the tunnel of getting out from under the band, I was looking forward to having a quiet life with you and Lyric." He takes a deep breath and rubs his bare foot against mine under the sheet. "But then shit kept popping up from the band, legal stuff, tons of decisions. A lot of the fans were pissed. I was getting hate mail every fuckin' day. The guys were getting it too and they didn't deserve it. It was my decision to end the band, not theirs. All this doubt seeped in. I was afraid you'd leave me. I didn't know which way to turn or what to do. My head started to fuckin' spin. I was going crazy from the agony and the noise and the voices and the fucking bird and I needed it to stop. I couldn't think beyond that. Everything else went black. I don't know how else to explain it, but I need you to believe that I never wanted to leave you."

It terrifies me to hear him talk about pain and voices and imaginary evil birds. What did that feel like, in his head? I can't even imagine.

"I believe you. I didn't at first, but now I do."

"I'm not going to hurt you again."

I rub my hand over his chest and weigh his words. I know it's very possible that while he might mean what he's saying one hundred percent right now in this very moment, that someday, he might unintentionally hurt me again. The part of him that he doesn't have full mental control over could come lurking out of its medicinal prison someday and wreak havoc on his life.

And mine. And our daughter's.

"What if it happens again?" I ask. It's the question Reece told me not to ask but it's also the question that continues to run rampant through my mind. How can I not ask such an important question?

His body stiffens, and he hesitates a beat before he lets out a deep breath and answers.

"I'm not gonna lie, Piper. It could happen again. But it shouldn't as long as I stay on my meds, try to keep my life as stress-free as possible, and stay in weekly therapy. Forever, basically. So if I start to get fucked up again, it'll get caught before it gets out of control. I feel great, though. Better than ever. A little tired and moody sometimes, but nothing crazy. No pun intended."

"Okay. That's good."

"If you see me acting weird, just say something, okay? I don't want you to be scared."

I chew my bottom lip. I *am* scared, but I don't want him to know that. He needs me to trust him, and have faith in him and his recovery. If I'm analyzing his every move and mood, waiting for him to have a meltdown, neither one of us will ever be happy.

"We're going to need some time, Piper," he says softly. "I thought a weekend alone together would be a good start. To see if you still want to be with me. I left you alone for a long time. Maybe I'm not what you want anymore. Maybe someone like Josh would be better for you, even though it fucking kills me to say that."

I lift my head to look at him. "No, he wouldn't be. I want to be with you and only you. That's not going to change. You should know that by now."

"Even if I have to take ten pills a day?"

"Even if you have to take twenty."

"Even if I'm not gonna be a rock star anymore?"

"I loved you before you were a rock star. That means nothing to me."

He grins playfully, and it's one of the most beautiful things I've ever seen. "Even if I want to ravish you every day?"

Smiling, I lean forward and kiss him. "You better."

"Even if I want to run away and marry you because I'm the luckiest guy in the world?"

It feels like I've been chasing the dream of spending my life with him since the beginning of time. It's been like trying to capture a butterfly—getting so close every time, only to watch him fly away out of reach again.

"And we have dreaded silence," he says.

I snap out of my worrying headspace. "No... I was just thinking."

His smile morphs into an embarrassed lopsided frown. "I shouldn't have said that. It's too soon for you to even think about that."

I shake my head and gently push his hair out of his face. "It's not. And you know what? That's what I want to do when the time's right. I don't want a wedding."

"What about all those wedding magazines with the color-coded Post-Its on your favorite stuff?"

"Eh. That just felt like what I *should* be doing. I'd much rather just elope with you and Lyric."

The silver specks in his eyes light up like tiny holiday lights. "Yeah?"

I nod. "Yeah."

He cups my chin in his palm and kisses me feather-soft, lingering near my lips.

"Thank you for always waiting for me," he whispers. "Want to know a secret?"

"Okay...." I say nervously.

"I knew I wanted to be with you forever right from the start. That's why I told you the ladybug myth. I wanted you to want me, too. And when you did, it scared the ever-lovin' shit out of me." He kisses me again. "Now that I know you're not going to abandon me like everyone else, I'm not scared anymore."

CHAPTER SIXTY-FOUR

EVAN

I like to watch Piper when she's completely unaware. Like now, when she's sleeping next to me, dwarfed under the beige comforter with just her head poking out with her blond hair loose and messy on the pillow. I stare at all the parts of her that captivate me. Her lashes—like tiny feathers resting on her cheeks. Her lips—the color of bubblegum. Her fingers—curled up in a fist under her chin like babies do. I was relieved to see the engagement ring still on her hand when she came into the room.

Watching her is an old favorite habit of mine. A guilty pleasure. I watched her for a long time before we ended up in that gazebo talking. She's the very reason I picked that park to play at every day—so I could watch her up close.

So I could *be* close.

She already knows about the time I saw her when Acorn and I were walking down the sidewalk past her office. She dropped her things on her way to her car and I turned to catch her kneeling on the pavement with her skirt riding up just enough to give me a tantalizing glimpse of her thighs. Her black sunglasses fell from the top of her head as she bent forward and I watched her wrestle to untangle them from her hair. Although she was dressed in office attire, the outfit contradicted the fact that she didn't look more than sixteen years old. She had tiny, faery-like features and was so short I doubted she could see over the steering wheel of her car. She cursed at herself under her breath and I thought she was the most awkwardly adorable chick I'd ever laid eyes on.

The second time I saw her she was in her car at a red light downtown. She was singing—horribly—along with the radio and looked so incredibly free and lost in her own world that I literally would have sold my soul to crawl into that world with her. To feel so unbound and oblivious. As I stared at her, lusting for her free spirit and wanting very badly to run my hands through her hair, she suddenly decided to turn on red and came close to running me over where I stood at the edge of the crosswalk.

She never saw me, but that only added to her appeal.

The next time was when I was scouting the park and stumbled upon her reading on a bench. It was a delightful surprise. By then, I didn't give a shit if I'd make a dollar or a thousand playing guitar there every day. I just wanted to be in the same space as her. My body ached looking at her—the way her legs were tucked under her, her small bare feet poking out. She was entirely engrossed in the book, her tongue sliding across her lips as she read, her eyes widening at the words on the page. I lit up a cigarette and watched her from my perch on the hill. Close enough to see her, but far enough where she didn't notice me. I squinted at her paperback, filled with curiosity over what my little magical faery would be reading. I grinned when I saw the embracing couple on the cover.

A romance.

She believed in love, or at least wanted to.

I didn't.

At least not yet.

She changed that. She made me believe in it, she made me want it, and she made it so I couldn't live without it. I fell hard and fast for her. She haunted me; lived in the fabric of my soul and inspired all the emotions and words that had always eluded me. Without ever even knowing it, she vaulted me to the top of my career.

I was going to leave that rainy night years ago. Once that fucking headache stopped, I was going to make myself gone. Get far away from her shy glances and childlike laugh and blushing cheeks. But I couldn't, because I couldn't let her go. I wanted her to be mine.

Does that make me fucked up? That her innocence made me hard as a fucking rock; made me want to corrupt her, ruin her for everyone else? To set the bar so high that anyone else would fail miserably?

But then she came, creeping through the fog on petite feet in high heels with a little bag of goodies and a smile that could knock me on my knees and a head of lemon-blond hair and big innocent eyes and those perfect pink lips and a sugary sweet voice. Then there was the skirt and the way the wind skimmed it across her pale thighs.

All that, I could have just ignored if I really wanted to. It was her breathing that did me in, the way her breath caught in her throat as I stepped closer to her, how she held me in her lungs and got high on me before exhaling over her quivering lips. She was scared, but not *of* me, of *wanting* me.

She was a rabbit hopping straight into the talons of a vulture.

I knew I was going to devour her. I couldn't stop myself. I wanted her too much, needed her too much... and when she didn't push me away, when she gave herself to me—that was it.

She made me want to stay, when all I ever wanted to do was run. She made me want more, and she made me want things I couldn't have. And worse, I knew she wanted things I couldn't give, and it created yet another battle inside me.

She wasn't made for flings, my little ladybug. She was the kind of girl you took home, if you had one. She was the kind of girl you kept. She was forever. *My* forever.

"You're awake early." Her soft voice pulls me from my trip down memory lane.

"Yeah. I'm supposed to wake up every day at the same time. For consistency and stability." The times of taking sleeping pills to force myself to sleep after taking speed to stay awake for days are over.

She kisses my shoulder, then rolls over onto her back, stretching her arms over her head. The comforter slips down her body, exposing her perfect naked breasts and I want to roll over on top of her and ravish every inch of her, sink myself deep into her until she whimpers and drags her nails down my back.

I don't.

I can't use sex with her to fill the vacancies of my addictions anymore. I wonder if she'll notice and I'm afraid she'll think I don't want her as much as I used to. The jump created fear and doubt where there wasn't before. My fault. Mine to fix.

Balance is a bitch.

"How about breakfast in bed?" I suggest, grabbing the room-service menu from the bedside table.

She sits up with a drowsy smile on her face. "That sounds amazing."

Half an hour later we've got two trays of waffles, bacon, fresh fruit, and toast spread out on the bed between us.

"This is good, but I really miss *your* breakfasts."

"I do, too. I haven't cooked in forever."

She tilts her head and sips her orange juice. "I just realized I haven't seen you smoke one cigarette since we got here."

"I don't smoke anymore."

Her lips part in surprise. "Wow! That's great."

"It's kind of fucked up, actually. When I woke up in the hospital, I had zero desire to smoke. It never came back. It wasn't even hard." I shrug. "I just...stopped."

"That *is* strange. Did you lose interest in anything else like that?"

"I no longer feel the need to walk to the ends of the earth."

Relief flashes in her eyes. "That's really good, too."

I nod. "It is. Different, but good."

I keep waiting for the urge to walk away from everything to come, like it always seemed to, but it hasn't. I hope it never does.

After breakfast she disappears into the shower and I join her five minutes later, unable to resist her wet and soapy body. The fiery desire in her eyes when she sees me naked under the water with her is exactly what I need. She likes the new me. At least physically, which is a start.

"You want to go for a walk in the park?" I ask her when we're both dry and dressed. My doctor keeps telling me I need to go outside in the fresh air. I think he forgets I spent most of my life outside.

"I was hoping you'd ask that." She glances over at my old guitar case in the corner. "Do you want to bring your guitar and play?"

She doesn't know that I haven't touched the guitar since I jumped because I'm afraid I won't be able to play anymore. Sometimes the new meds make me feel *blank*. It's an odd feeling I can't put into words, but I'm afraid I'm going to pick up that guitar and my fingers are going to be lost on the strings. I'm afraid I won't feel the lyrics and the melody in my veins anymore.

I had the same fears with Piper—that the intense love and wild attraction I've always felt for her would be killed by the meds. Thank fuck that isn't the case. If anything, my feelings for her are stronger.

I'm still worried about playing and writing songs, though. So, I'm avoiding it until I'm ready to find out.

"Nah," I reply, turning away from the guitar. "I just want to focus on you." I tie my hair back and put a black baseball hat backwards on my head to deter people from recognizing me, since I ran into two fans at the airport yesterday. Former fans, I should say, as they stopped me just to tell me how much I suck for breaking up their favorite band and ruining their lives.

Even though they're a trigger, I've read the ongoing shitty comments online, but having someone say them right to my face in public was like getting hit by a truck. People walking by stared at me with accusing eyes as the two girls went off on me. It made me want to never touch my guitar again. The thought of running to the airport bar and drinking their words away was temping. So was taking my rental car to the seedy edge of this town, a place I knew like the back of my hand, and buying tiny plastic bags of powder and pills and forgetting all this crap.

Yeah, I thought of all those things, but I didn't do any of them, and I didn't feel any regrets.

Instead I went to the hotel, drank a bottle of water, called Reece, took a long shower, and focused on what that really matters to me—

Piper, Lyric, and my future with them. All the other bullshit faded away.

Now that I'm walking through the park holding the hand of the most precious and beautiful woman in the world, I know without a doubt that I can do this.

I beat the monster.

CHAPTER SIXTY-FIVE

PIPER

Walking through the park holding hands with Evan feels strange, but not in a bad way. In a good way. It feels both familiar and new at the same time. I guess much like a first date would feel with someone you've known your entire life.

"Seeing you sitting there every day was the best part of my day," he says as we walk past my bench.

I smile up at him. "Really? Seeing you was the best part of mine, too." It seems like just yesterday I was watching the clock waiting for noon to come, and I'd walk to the park with the feeling of a thousand butterflies in my stomach.

Continuing down the path, we pass the picnic table we used to sit at, and go down the dirt path to the old stone bridge. He stops suddenly, and takes a few steps backwards until he meets the wall of the bridge. Leaning back against it, he smiles and pulls me against his chest, bending down to kiss me softly at first, then deeper as his hands circle my waist and slide down to cup my ass.

"There's no way I could walk by this spot without kissing you," he murmurs.

I clasp my hands behind his neck. "Oh! Is this where…." My voice trails off as I look around us, remembering.

"It is," he says, rubbing his nose along mine, awakening the butterflies again. "I still have your panties from that night. And the ones you were wearing the night before I left."

"I'm not sure if that's sexy or disturbing."

"Probably both."

Still holding my hand, he leads me down a short path through the woods until we come to a road, and I realize with surprise that we're at the end of the dead-end street where the house with the shed is.

His house.

We stand at the end of the driveway and stare up at it quietly together. I'm not sure if being here is good or bad for his recovery.

"Ellie told me you used to live here," I say softly. "How come you never told me?"

He shrugs after a few moments, with his gaze still on the old house. "I honestly don't know, Piper."

"That's okay."

He takes a deep breath and looks down at me. "Do you want to go inside?"

"Um…." His question is the last thing I expect. "Do *you* want to?"

"Yeah. I think I finally do."

"Then I'd love to go inside with you."

"It's probably going to be dirty and smelly," he warns as we walk up the driveway.

"That's all right."

We walk around the house and enter through the screen door of the porch. Everything is exactly as it was the last time I came here looking for him.

"When was the last time you were inside?" I ask.

"I think I was around twenty."

"You bought a lot of notebooks," I observe as we walk past the piles.

He stops in front of the door leading to the kitchen and looks back at the notebooks.

"Actually, I didn't buy them. My mother ordered them. Apparently, she thought she was buying a pack of twelve and she somehow ordered twelve hundred."

"Shit. That's a lot."

"Yup. At least I never run out."

I watch as he bends down to move a large ceramic planter near the door, and plucks a key out from under it.

"I lost my set of keys a long time ago," he says, unlocking the door.

Being inside the house is like stepping back in time. The refrigerator and sink are avocado green. There's still wood paneling on most of the walls. The kitchen chairs have plaid seat cushions. The air is stale and musty, but at least it doesn't smell like something died in here.

Evan sighs deeply and slowly walks farther into the room. "It's exactly like it was," he says with awe. "I'll bet there's still food in the fridge."

"Let's not look," I advise.

He grins. "Good idea."

Taking my hand again, we walk through the dining room, through the den, then to the living room. The rooms are huge, and everything looks as if his mother just ran out to get milk years ago and never came back. It's all untouched, still waiting. A teacup, a pair of reading glasses, and an old book, open but lying face down, are on the table at the end of the couch. I wonder what happened to her. Did she go crazy here alone? Did Ellie ever come back to visit her? Were there other relatives to look after her?

"Are you okay?" I ask. "I don't want this to—"

"Fuck my head up?" he asks.

"Well, yeah. I know you weren't exactly happy here."

"I'm fine. Living here was just like every other part of my life. Some days were good, some days sucked. But it wasn't all bad. Ellie made it seem all bad, didn't she?"

I nod.

"When my mother was good, she was fun to be around, and then my father wasn't such a dick. When she was having a rough time, it was hard to be around both of them. He drank and yelled and she cried and ranted. So I escaped into my own head, and into my music, and I talked to the birds. It became my normal."

"Evan...."

"What? I'm not going to hide it anymore. You already know I'm nuts."

I frown and cross my arms. "You're *not* nuts. I don't want you to hide anything, I just feel bad."

"Don't feel bad. C'mon, let's go upstairs and look at my room."

I follow him up the wide wood staircase, where there are four bedrooms and two bathrooms. The house must have been gorgeous in its time, before everyone left. Vaulted ceilings, crown molding, lots of windows, the wood trim and accents and angles known in the Tudor-style homes. I feel sorry for it, being abandoned for so long.

A bedroom door with a skull and crossbones painted on it is closed.

"Guess whose room this is?" he teases.

"I'm not surprised."

He swings open the door and it looks exactly as I pictured a teenage Evan's room would look. Rock posters cover almost every inch of the walls and ceiling. A small mattress is on the floor with an old black blanket thrown over it. There's only one dresser, and its drawers aren't closed all the way. Clothes stick out of them. An old radio and cassette player sits on top of the dresser, surrounded by candles dripping long-hardened wax. Empty cigarette cartons are thrown all over the place. Next to the bed is a stack of rock and guitar magazines and more notebooks.

Not surprising.

"No naked girl posters?" I tease, peering around.

He laughs and opens the closet door. "Nah. I was never into ogling women."

After digging around in the closet, he comes out with a guitar case.

"Look what's still here." He lays the old dusty case on the bed.

"What's that?"

"My first acoustic guitar."

"Oh. I thought the one you always have with you was your first."

"That was my second, actually."

I'm shocked, and confused, when he opens the case and the guitar inside is in absolutely pristine condition.

"It's pretty," I say. "It looks brand new."

Smiling ear to ear, he gently pulls it out of the case and turns it over in his hands.

"Do you know what this is?" he asks, clearly excited. "This is a 1934 Gibson Jumbo."

I blink at him. "Is that good?"

"Good? It's fuckin' amazing, Piper. They're wicked rare and worth a shit ton of money, not that I'd ever sell it. I just can't believe it's still here." He runs his fingers lightly over the strings before placing it back in the case. "I'm taking it back with us."

"Why did you leave it?" I ask.

"I only played it a few times. My mother bought it at a garage sale, she had no idea what it was, or what it was worth. Neither did the guy selling it. I knew, though. I was afraid to play it. It's just too…good. Ya know?" He snaps the case closed. "I bought my other one so I could save this one. Protect it from getting destroyed. I didn't get a chance to take it with me. I moved in the shed with Acorn, and then we just left. I never came back inside."

My heart still tugs at the mention of sweet Acorn.

"I'm glad it's still here. You should put it with your others. It deserves to be out, not shut in an old closet."

"You're right. I'm going to put new strings on it. I can't wait to show Lyric, I think she'll love it."

Lyric loves everything he shares with her.

We go back downstairs, and I'm relieved this visit isn't upsetting him. He looks happy, and excited about the guitar. I wait as he rummages through a kitchen drawer, then turns around and hands me an old photograph.

I take it from him gingerly, and when I hold it up under the light from the window, my heart jumps with joy.

It's a photo of Evan at about five years old, hair to his shoulders, and a tiny blue bird sitting on his shoulder. He's smiling like he's the happiest little boy in the whole world.

"Can I have this? Please?" I ask, meeting his gaze.

"Of course."

"You look so adorable. And happy."

He winks at me. "Told ya."

I step forward and wrap my arms around his waist, leaning my head against his chest.

"I love you," I say softly.

He holds me with his free arm. "I love you too, baby. Thank you for doing this with me. I wasn't planning on coming here, but I'm glad we did."

On our way back to the hotel we stop for ice cream cones in the park and sit at our usual table. Our little traditions mean the world to me and one of the things I love most about him is how he never forgets about them.

He's quiet for the rest of the afternoon, and I start to worry that visiting the house wasn't a good idea, after all. Perhaps it held too many bad memories that are now gnawing away at him. Later, over dinner in the hotel restaurant, we talk mostly about Lyric and things going on in my life, but he still seems a bit more distracted and subdued than he did earlier. I wonder if it's an effect of the medication.

"Are you okay?" I finally ask him when we're back in our room. "You seem quiet."

Sitting on the bed, he bends down and pulls off his work boots while I step out of my black heels.

"Yeah… I'm just thinking about something."

Worried, I move to stand in front of him and gently run my fingers through his hair.

"Do you want to talk about it?" I ask softly.

Wrapping his hands around my waist, he leans forward to kiss the spot between my breasts.

"I'm thinking about the house."

"Maybe we shouldn't have gone in there. Did it bother you?"

"I wasn't sure how I'd feel, but actually it didn't bother me. I just feel bad the place has gone to hell, just sitting like that. It belonged to my grandparents, did I tell you that?"

"No, I didn't know that."

"They died before I was born, but my mother told me she grew up there. My grandfather had it built for my grandmother as a wedding gift."

"Wow. That's quite a gift. It's a beautiful house."

"It could be," he says. "When I left the hospital, my doctor told me to 'go home and start your new life' and I realized I didn't even have a home." He pulls me down as he talks, until I'm sitting on his lap. "Reece moved out of the house in Seattle, and we were never there enough for it to feel like home, anyway. It was basically just a hub. And your place is nice but it's kind of a reminder that I was a fuckup for so long that you and my kid had to buy a house alone. It's weird. For the first time I want a real *home*."

It's funny that I wondered the very same thing about where he would want to go when he left the band, and then, where he would go when he left the facility. It's something we never talked about, even when we were discussing wedding plans.

"I think I want to completely remodel the house and live there," he says. "But I want you and Lyric and Mickey and Archie there, too. I don't want to live there alone. I think that house has had too much loneliness." When I don't say something right away, he continues to talk nervously. "It'll be like a brand-new house when it's done, not like it is now. We could pick out everything we wanted and make it ours."

My brain starts to twirl like a whirlwind with the unexpectedness of this conversation. I assumed he might want to keep some distance between us for a while to give himself time to think since he just got out of the hospital. I wasn't looking forward to that, but I was prepared for it.

I definitely wasn't prepared for him to be talking about moving in together.

"Evan…." I'm overwhelmed with all the things I want to say.

"Shit. It's too soon, right?" He plops me down on the bed next to him before he stands and crosses the room to stare out the window. "I fucked it all up again. Us. Our trust. Everyfuckingthing. You need time to figure it all out."

I walk over to him and hug him from behind, and he covers my hands with his over his chest.

"All those years you were waiting for me?" His voice is so low I can barely hear him. "I was waiting, too. I always wanted everything with you, I just kept tripping over myself and fucking it all up. But I want it all. I want to marry you and have another baby."

My heart wrenches at the thought that this sweet, vulnerable side of him has been buried under all his demons for years, trying to get out and be happy.

"You didn't fuck it all up. I think things happened the way they were supposed to happen. And in case you didn't notice…" I turn him around to face me. "I'm right here with you, and I still want all those things with you, too."

He palms the back of my neck and brings my mouth to his, kissing me fervently. "I don't deserve you, Piper."

"You do." I stand on my tiptoes so I can look into his eyes. "I don't need time, Evan. I've had more than enough of that. And I don't need to figure anything out. I love you. I want to be with you… right now, every day, and forever."

"What if—"

I quickly kiss him quiet. "What if you stumble? What if you need more help or different meds? What if you just need to eff my brains out sometimes? What if you just need a long hug and the sound of the rain? What if you start to feel bad again? It's okay. I don't need to think about it, I already know I'm going to go through anything and everything with you. There's nothing in the world that's going to make me walk out the door."

"You're sure? I could still have some bad days.…"

I've never been more sure about anything in my life. I love him and what we have—flaws and all. I always have.

"I'm positive. No matter what. I love the house, Evan. It was kind of our home for a while, wasn't it? I'd love to bring it back to life with you and move our little family in and turn it into a real home again. And we'll be so close to all our special places." I smile up at him. "I feel like we're supposed to be there."

He nods excitedly. "God, I love you. I want that, too. So fuckin' bad."

"Then let's do it. We don't have to wait anymore."

He lifts me up in his arms and we kiss the kind of kiss that's made of memories, hope, and new beginnings. We know we'll have good days and bad days and that's okay. That's the magic of love. It doesn't always have to be easy or perfect or normal. It can just be two people who believe in each other enough to be there for all the tomorrows.

EPILOGUE

2019 - SIX YEARS LATER - PIPER

Sometimes, certain sounds and scents can be like little time machines whisking us back to moments in our pasts that are so vivid, so powerful, that we can close our eyes and step into those memories again.

Those flashes through time can be beautiful, like visiting a lost love just one more time, for the briefest of seconds.

Or they can be devastating; resuscitating ghosts we'd rather never face again.

I experience both variations. Often.

Blue and I shared years of tomorrows that turned into yesterdays, and then one day he was gone. I can't explain how I knew, other than I watched him slowly drift away and disappear. Maybe it was the way his body relaxed and fell into a deep sleep. Or maybe the absence of the creases in his forehead. It may have been how his eyes remained the color of a summer sky—never shifting to that darker, nameless hue again. It could have been how his touch, once rough, demanding, and controlling, gave way to a sweet, patient gentleness.

I'll always miss Blue, but I welcomed Evan.

Evan said *I do*.

Evan placed our newborn baby in my arms.

Evan never walks away, sorts dishes, or believes he can fly.

He does, however, believe in the myth of little red bugs sealing the fate of soulmates.

I do, too.

The sounds of strings being strummed, arpeggios, and Evan's raspy, sexy vocals welcome me as I step out onto the sunny porch. Only now, our daughter has added her talents to the melody, and they play seamlessly together.

This particular song brings me right back to the park like it was yesterday. I remember the smiles. The rain. Blue's sexy wink. Clouds and rainbows. Naked flesh against flesh under the bridge. Ice cream and crazy heart flutters.

I remember the singe of fear and longing that would burn through me when I'd have to go back to work and life. As if my heart was telling me no, don't go too far. This is where you belong.

As soon as I put the tray of iced teas and lemon sugar cookies down on the wicker table in front of them, Evan and Lyric finish their duet and put their instruments off to the side to reach for their favorite cookies.

"I hope you made more, Mom," Lyric teases. "Dad will devour all of these himself."

Smiling, I sit on the cushioned loveseat next to Evan. The porch has become our favorite part of the house since we moved in. The house was gutted and rebuilt in record time. We left a lot of the original charm of the house—such as the hardwood floors and the crown molding, but we did some major restructuring to the overall layout. Many of the walls were removed or relocated to give the house an airy, open concept modern style. The bathrooms and kitchen have been completely updated. Our little shed in the backyard has been converted into a small studio—or mancave as Evan likes to call it. We insisted on keeping the original tin roof and have spent many a rainy night in that shed, snuggling on the futon with candles lit.

The house isn't lonely anymore, or a place Evan is afraid enter. It's now a home full of love, music, and happiness.

"There's lots more cookies inside," I assure them.

My husband puts his arm around me and pulls me closer. "Thank you for the cookies," he says, kissing my cheek. "They're good writing fuel."

He's been working on his first solo album, *Out of the Blue*, for several months. It's a compilation of new and old acoustic songs he's written that are much like the songs he used to play in the park with Acorn. Soft, dreamy, and a bit haunting.

"You're welcome." I smile, then shift my gaze to our five-year-old son, Noah. He's sitting on the floor with Mickey in the far corner of the porch, humming to himself. He stares out the windows up at the sky, watching the clouds go by.

Daydreaming.

He has no interest in cookies today. Or breakfast. He completely ignored my offer of fruit or cereal or pancakes earlier, only wanting to sit with the dog, listen to his father and sister play music, and look at the sky. Getting him to eat lately has been difficult.

Evan leans closer to me, nudges his face into my hair and whispers in my ear. "He's fine, baby. I promise."

I hope so.

I wonder. And I worry.

Noah could be like Blue. Lost. Confused. Struggling with thoughts and voices. Afraid to ask for help—or worse—not knowing he needs help.

Or, he could just be a thinker. A quiet daydreamer. Like Evan is now.

So I watch him closely—maybe too closely, I admit.

Evan gives my hand a squeeze, then grabs an iced tea and a handful of cookies. My gaze lingers on him as he walks to the corner of the porch. His old, button-down blue jeans still fit him in a way that makes my insides flutter with desire. A few strands of gray streak his long hair that's tied back today, accentuating his narrow jawline. He no longer tries to cover the faint, jagged scar on his cheek with his hair. I no longer think of that scar as a reminder he almost died. I think of it as a reminder he lived.

He sits crossed-legged next to our son, and Mickey immediately climbs into his lap. Noah nods at something Evan has said in a voice too soft for me to hear. He takes the glass of iced tea and sips it with an adorable grin that's a mirror image of his father's. My worry eases when Evan breaks a cookie in half and gives half to Mickey and half to Noah, who chews it and points up toward the sky. I'm sure he's explaining a cloud figure in great detail, and Evan listens intently, while gently pushing Noah's long hair out of his face.

He meets my gaze across the porch and winks at me, mouthing the words "I love you." Smiling, I blow him a kiss back, before turning my attention to Lyric, who's telling me about a guy she's been seeing.

She thinks he's the one. He's complicated, she says, but she doesn't care.

I understand. More than she knows.

I never wished for, or wanted perfect. I only wanted to love and be loved. I believe in the happy ending—for all of us.

ACKNOWLEDGMENTS

Thank you so much for reading this book! These characters and their story truly mean a lot to me, for many reasons. I hope you enjoyed their journey.

I don't like to publish names for privacy reasons. But I hope you amazing gals who are on my team know how grateful I am to have you at my side. Each of you mean the world to me and I wouldn't be able to write these books without you. Thank you for being there for me and putting up with me!

That being said, I have to say a massive thank you to Jeanne De Vita for taking me on, being so patient with me, and just being amazing and supportive in every way. I'm so glad I found you!

I have to extend my gratitude to photographer Regina Wamba for coordinating the original cover photo shoot and taking amazing pictures of Brandon Katz and Cherry Albrecht - you guys captured my characters perfectly! Thank you so much for all your hard work!

Thank you to all my readers and the groupies in my Facebook group! You all make me smile every day and you inspire me and push me to be a better writer. Thank you for being so patient while I wrote this book!

Huge thanks to all the bloggers who read my books, leave reviews, and promote. You guys are true rock stars!

Heartfelt thanks to all of you - whether you read my books, chatted with me, left a review, blogged, beta read, edited, proofed, pimped, commented, liked, attended a take-over, supported my models, posted hot pictures of guys or cute pets in my group, designed teasers and graphics, or just listened to me - thank you! I love you!!

And of course, thank you to my hubby, Eddie, for all your help and love, and for always talking about story plots with me. But mostly, for believing in me. I love you with all my heartbeats. ♥

ABOUT THE AUTHOR

Carian Cole has a passion for the bad boys, those covered in tattoos, sexy smirks, ripped jeans, fast cars, motorcycles and of course, the sweet girls who try to tame them and win their hearts.

Born and raised a Jersey girl, Carian now resides in beautiful New Hampshire with her husband and their multitude of furry pets. She spends most of her time writing, reading, and vacuuming.

Carian loves to hear from readers and interacts daily on her social media accounts.

Follow:
www.cariancolewrites.com